About the

Lauri Robinson lives in Minnesota where she and her husband spend every spare moment with their three grown sons and their families – spoiling the grandchildren. She's a member of Romance Writers of America and Northern Lights Writers. Along with volunteering for several organizations, she is a diehard Elvis and NASCAR fan. Her favourite getaway location is along the Canadian Border of Northern Minnesota on the land homesteaded by her great-grandfather.

The Historical Collection

The Historical Collection:

Falling for the Heiress

LAURI ROBINSON

MILLS & BOON

First Published in Great Britain 2023
by Mills & Boon, an imprint of HarperCollins*Publishers* Ltd,
1 London Bridge Street, London, SE1 9GF

www.harpercollins.co.uk

HarperCollins*Publishers*
Macken House, 39/40 Mayor Street Upper,
Dublin 1, D01 C9W8, Ireland

ISBN: 978-0-263-32043-5

MIX
Paper | Supporting
responsible forestry
FSC™ C007454
www.fsc.org

This book is produced from independently certified FSC™ paper to ensure responsible forest management.

For more information visit: www.harpercollins.co.uk/green

Printed and Bound in the UK using 100% Renewable Electricity at CPI Group (UK) Ltd, Croydon, CR0 4YY

MARRIAGE OR
RUIN FOR
THE HEIRESS

Dedicated to Ivadelle Salmon
for being such a wonderful fan.

Chapter One

Chicago, 1933

Disbelief rendered Jolie Cramer speechless. How could it not? She'd never expected her life would come to this. Being sold. Like she was a dress hanging in a store window. There was more to a dress than thread and material. There were hours of designing, sewing, pressing. And there was more to her. She had feelings, goals, dreams.

Staring out her bedroom window that overlooked the massive backyard of their prestigious downtown home, made with brick and mortar generations ago, she shook her head, trying to dispel the disbelief still holding her mind hostage like a mob victim. The bright sunshine of the warm summer day was out of place compared to the iciness filling her. "You can't be serious."

"He's a very wealthy and prominent young man. Not to mention handsome. You should be happy he agreed."

A peculiar burning sensation spread over Jolie as she spun around to face her mother. Disbelief was replaced with anger boiling hot enough to cook a three-minute egg in less than a minute. Everyone knew Randal Osterlund was wealthy and prominent, and every woman under the age of forty in all of Chicago knew he was handsome. His silver-blue eyes were so unique, in such contrast with his dark hair, that they caught and held attention. Like many others, she'd found him attractive, until the last time she'd seen Randal. She'd been mortified with embarrassment that day and hoped to never set eyes on him again. "Happy?"

"Yes. I myself was flattered." Mother stood and patted the short brown curls at the nape of her neck, and then ran a hand over the finger waves that flattened the hair on the crown of her head. She'd worn her hair that way for a decade, despite the fact the short hairstyles of the twenties were now in the past. With an exaggerated sigh, her mother said, "I would consider remarrying myself, but as you know, your father is the only man I will ever love. There's not another one out there like him. I will never get over his death. Never. I still cry myself to sleep each and every night."

Jolie rubbed her forehead at the woe-is-me tale she'd heard a thousand times over. It wasn't that she didn't sympathize with her mother. They'd all loved her father dearly—he had been a wonderful man—but her mother just didn't seem to realize there were other people in this family who were still alive. Who might need her to do her job as their mother.

"There's no reason to act so shocked. We discussed this, Jolie."

"Discussed is not the same as agreeing, Mother," Jolie insisted. She had in no way agreed to anything. In fact, when her mother had brought up the subject of marrying to *save* the family last week, Jolie had voiced that marriage was not the answer and that there were other ways to *save* the family.

Her mother smoothed the floral bedspread on the corner of the bed where she had been sitting. "The taxes are due by the end of the month. If they aren't paid, this house will be sold by the city. If that happens, we will have no choice but to move to Kansas and live with Uncle LeRoy. Is that what you want for your brother and sister? For me? For you?"

No, it wasn't what she wanted. Jolie closed her eyes at the overwhelming despair that overshadowed all of the other emotions running rampant inside her. Uncle LeRoy, her mother's brother and their only living relative, lived in Kansas, where they were not only experiencing the great depression blanketing the nation, they also had dust storms that were burying entire towns. She'd heard stories on the radio, read about them in the newspaper as well as the firsthand accounts Uncle LeRoy penned in his letters.

The dust storms that were plaguing the central plains is why people were calling it the *Dirty Thirties*.

Damn the stock market crash of 1929. That's what had started it all. It had wreaked havoc on the country and her family. Three months after that crash her father died of a heart attack, and for the four years since then, her family had barely survived on the small amounts of holdings and cash her father hadn't had invested in the markets. Hers wasn't the only family affected, but unlike others, who'd openly admitted their dire straits and did something, or at least attempted to do something constructive, her mother had kept their poverty hidden. And continued to. Very few people knew the

Cramers were surviving on bread crumbs bought with the pennies they'd managed to scrape out of the bottom of the washing machine and beneath the sofa cushions.

"We've sold everything worth selling," Mother said. "This house is all we have left. All we have left of your father. This is our only choice."

"No, it's not," Jolie argued. "We could get jobs. You and me and Silas. Even Chloe could—"

"I won't hear of such a thing! Your father must be rolling over in his grave to hear you say that! He did not believe in women working!" Mother spun around and marched to the door. "Silas has two more years of college. Once he graduates, he'll take over providing for this family. Until then, it's up to me. And you." She pulled open the bedroom door. "I suggest you change. Randal will be here in half an hour."

"Change into what?" Jolie threw her hands in the air as her mother shut the door as if she hadn't heard the question. "Everything I own has been made over so many times the material is worn out," she muttered and walked over to the bed, plopped onto the mattress.

She wasn't one to pitch a fit, but she was contemplating doing so on this occasion.

Randal Osterlund.

Huffing out a breath, she flipped onto her back and stared at the ceiling. Of all the men in Chicago, why him?

Jolie sat up as her heart began to beat like it had the wings of a hummingbird. Or is that exactly why? He knew how destitute her family had become. She'd hoped he'd forgotten about their encounter at the grocer, but obviously, he hadn't.

It had been so embarrassing. There had been money

in the bank to cover the check. She'd just made a deposit the day before, after getting paid for altering a dress for Mrs. Rivard—unknown to Mother, of course, because heaven forbid a female Cramer would work for a living. Jolie had done that often enough, altered clothing and sewn underclothes for Mrs. Rivard and her elderly friends, and put the money in the bank so when they needed groceries, anyone in her family could pick them up and pay with a check. No one in her family had ever written a bad check, and she was certain that Amy Casswell had put her name on *the list* on purpose—for no reason other than spite. Amy had hated her for years.

Why had she stopped at the Casswell store? Why? She knew better!

Randal had just so happened to be the next customer, and the cashier had just so happened to sweetly explain to him that the Cramer family's name was on *the list*—the list of people who couldn't pay with checks. The depression was felt by many, and no-credit lists, along with lists of people who were known to write bad checks, were commonplace. The Cramer name was not on any other list, just the one at Casswell's.

It had only been a few items, and Randal had offered to pay. Fully humiliated, she had refused his offer, told the clerk she'd never shop there again and left the store.

That had been two months ago, and Jolie had informed her entire family they were not allowed to shop at Casswell's. Amy had started a feud between the two of them in elementary school. One that had never ended. Last she'd heard, Amy had gone to Europe or Asia, or some such place, but that hadn't stopped her childhood enemy from embarrassing Jolie from afar. With her father owning the largest grocery store chain in the state, the stock market crash hadn't crushed the Casswells' business like it had others, and therefore had never affected Amy. Her clothes had always been the most stylish, and her attitude the haughtiest.

With all that circling in her mind, Jolie couldn't even begin to grasp at hairs as to why Randal Osterlund would consider marrying her instead of Amy, let alone agree to it.

It didn't make sense.

Amy Casswell was the type of woman a man like him would marry.

Jolie leaped to her feet. That was it! Amy had accused her of *eyeing* Randal last year at Marie Beyer's—now Marie Gains's—wedding. She hadn't been eyeing him, even though he had looked extremely handsome in his tuxedo. That had to be it. He and Amy must still be dating, corresponding while Amy was abroad—or had been abroad—and now Amy was attempting to humiliate her. Again.

That had to be it. He must be trying to embarrass her—for Amy. Get her family's hopes up and then expose their dire financial straits without marrying her.

That wasn't about to happen on Jolie's watch. Amy wouldn't win this time.

With all the determination of a bee finding the perfect flower, Jolie flew across the room, opened her closet door and homed in on the one and only dress she could wear for her meeting with Randal.

It was actually a skirt and blouse, but she'd used two old dresses to make the ensemble. The blouse, white with tiny blue polka dots, had gathered, flouncy sleeves that fell just short of her elbows, and the skirt, blue with tiny white polka dots, had a tight-fitting waist, with two tiny strips of the white material around the knee-length hem. It was one of her favorites, mainly because it was in the current popular style.

That would give her confidence in facing down Randal. Her family might be broke, but she wasn't broken.

Randal Osterlund stared at the door of the brick home in one of the older, downtown neighborhoods, where many shipping and railroad magnates had built homes during the previous century. Old money—and lots of it—had once filled these neighborhoods.

His family's home, just as big and just as expensive, was on the other side of town, where new money had created their own neighborhoods within the last couple of decades, as a way of distinguishing between the two.

Old and new money. He knew all about that, and the stories, trials and tribulations that went along with it. He also knew that there were empty houses in both old and new money neighborhoods due to the market crash.

It was his job to make sure his family home remained as is, and that his family maintained their status of being one of the wealthiest in Chicago. That had been driven into him since the day he'd been born.

His grandfather had arrived in America with little more than two coins to rub together in his pockets and had used them to create a family fortune. He'd struck oil in Pennsylvania and eventually sold his oil fields to Rockefeller and his Standard Oil company, before moving west, to Chicago. There, Randal's father had increased the family fortune in the stock market, and that's what Randal had inherited when his father had died seven years ago.

Stock market investments.

The crash had affected the family's finances, just as
it had nearly every other family in the nation, but he'd
taken steps before the crash had happened and diversified his holdings far more than other investors had. The
trouble was, that diversification wasn't enough to continue to bring in the money needed to hold their status,
and his grandfather was breathing fire down his neck
to do something about that, to make his own footprint
in the financial world.

One that would keep the Osterlunds on the top.

Money, that's what makes a man. That had been the
motto he'd grown up on.

Randal had discovered the way to make that happen—
airplanes—but he had one hurdle in his way.

Marriage.

He didn't like the idea. Marriage did little more than
make it harder for a man to focus on his plans and goals,
to be his own man. And love…that was dangerous.

He'd seen men go down that rabbit hole. Good men.
Men who'd thought they'd found love, the perfect wife,
only to have said perfect wife leave them for another
and take the contents of their bank account with her.

That wouldn't happen to him.

He might need a marriage, but he would never need
love. Never be broken by it.

At the click of the knob turning, Randal straightened
his stance and planted his best false smile on his face.
Never one to give in to nerves, he was surprised at his
own reaction to the idea of facing Jolie Cramer. He'd
seen her at a wedding last year and had been struck by
her beauty. That image had been the first one that had
come to him when he'd considered his need to marry.

"Mr. Randal, I'm sorry, I didn't hear your knock."

Amelia Cramer was middle-aged, with short brown hair, and appeared soft and small, but there was an undeniable shrewdness about her. He wondered if Jolie had that same shrewdness hidden beneath her quiet and meek exterior. Her family was about to lose their home and their only hope was for her to marry someone who could pay the taxes owed on it.

That was him.

The fact that Jolie was also very attractive was simply an added benefit.

"I do hope you haven't been waiting long," Amelia said.

"I just arrived and had yet to knock, Mrs. Cramer," Randal replied.

"Oh, please, call me Amelia." With a sly smile, she tugged on her earlobe. "After all, we will soon be family."

Randal lifted a brow. "Jolie agreed?"

"Yes, of course she agreed," Amelia responded with another coy smile. "Do come in. She will be down in a moment. Chloe, her sister, just went upstairs to tell her you've arrived."

Which told him that Amelia had been watching out the window for him. The woman was desperate. He had questioned Amy's tales that the Cramer family had lost all they'd had in the stock market crash and that the shock of it had caused the death of Joseph Cramer, because Amy talked like that about everyone. It wasn't until a couple of months ago, when he'd made a quick stop at the store and encountered Jolie, that he'd begun to wonder if Amy might have been telling the truth.

That unexpected encounter had planted Jolie on the

top of his list for possible partners. Quite unexpect-
edly, the opportunity to investigate if Jolie, and her
family, might be open to his plan, had appeared today,
when he'd bumped into Amelia Cramer at the courthouse this morning.

"Would you care for a drink?" Amelia asked as she
led him into the front room of the home.

He instantly noticed the empty spots on the walls
where paintings had obviously once hung, bare spots
on the floors where rugs had once lain, and the mini-
malist furniture and accessories in the room.

Amelia Cramer made no excuses for the missing
pieces as she stopped near a small wooden credenza.
"I have wine or brandy."

"No, thank you, I'm fine," Randal replied as his
attention was drawn toward the stairway that swept
upward along the elegant curve of the dark wooden ban-
ister until it disappeared beyond the ceiling of the front
room. A pair of white heels, gracefully stepping from
stair to stair, came into view, followed by a very stylish amount of stockinged legs. A white-and-blue dress
that highlighted her slender figure appeared next, and
then he got his first full look of Jolie.

Both at that wedding and the store that wouldn't take
her check, he'd acknowledged her beauty, but this evening, he was viewing it in a different light.

If he deemed that she was right for the position, and
if she agreed, they would marry. That was a sobering
thought. He'd sworn off marriage and love for years,
and had done so again, vehemently, a few months ago,
when Amy had laid down an ultimatum. Either he married her, or she would find someone else to marry.

He'd wished her well.

No woman would ever rule him.

Less than a week later, he'd questioned if he should have married her when he'd discovered that Carl Jansen was considering selling his airplane business—but only to a married man. Amy had been gone for months now, and though he'd fleetingly considered contacting her, he'd chosen alternatives instead. If he had to get married, he wanted it to be with someone he could live with. That wasn't Amy.

The only thing Amy was faithful to was money. He'd had people breathing down his neck to make more money his entire life, and didn't need a wife doing that to him.

What he wanted was someone quiet and kind, who would be happy simply running his household.

Watching Jolie stop shy of stepping off the final step of the stairs, he stepped forward. "Hello, Miss Cramer."

She gave a slight nod. "Mr. Osterlund."

He held out a hand, and when she took it, he lifted it to kiss the back of it while watching her closely. "You look very lovely this evening." Her light brown hair was parted in the middle, with both sides rolled and pinned back, exposing delicate ears with tiny pearl earrings dangling from each lobe, but it was her eyes that had snagged his full attention. They were dark brown, and full of hostility. In that moment, he questioned if she should be on his list. Let alone topping it.

She took the final step off the stairs and with the clear intent of letting him know he'd held her hand long enough, pulled it from his grasp.

"I've made reservations for us at the Congress Hotel Restaurant," he informed her, attempting to take the upper hand. As much as her mother may have suggested

Jolie was agreeable with his proposition, Jolie clearly
wasn't impressed with the idea.

"Oh, my, that is the finest dining site in the city,"
Amelia said. "The chef worked at the Waldorf Astoria
Hotel in New York before moving here."

Jolie provided no response to her mother, but the
hostility in her eyes gleamed a shade darker.

Taking full note of that, Randal said, "We can leave
whenever you're ready."

With her elegant chin lifted high, Jolie stepped toward the door. "I'm ready."

He wasn't thrilled with the idea of marriage any more
than she appeared to be, but he liked challenges, and
the idea of winning Jolie over was one he couldn't deny
thrilled him. He stepped around her, opened the door
and bid farewell to her mother as he followed Jolie outside.

His new, dark blue Cadillac was parked in the driveway, and he kept his hands to himself as she walked
directly to the passenger door. Though the sides of her
hair were rolled and pinned up, the back was left hanging loose, well past her shoulders, and shimmered in
the evening sunlight. The fit of her dress said it had
been tailor-made, which made him wonder if they were
as impoverished as he'd been led to believe. If not, his
plan may not work. Unless there was something else
that Jolie wanted out of the deal…

He opened the door, waited as she sat and swung in
her feet, then he closed the door and walked around the
hood of the car. As well-known as Jolie was amongst
the younger crowd, she'd never had a steady boyfriend,
and that intrigued him. Amy had declared that it was

because Jolie was as homely as a wet dog, which was another flat-out lie.

He'd barely started the car after climbing in when she said, "When did Amy return?"

It took a moment of thoughtful concentration for Randal to release the clutch and back out of the driveway, because he'd had to search his mind for the latest news that might have included Amy. He'd never paid any attention to rumors and had to wonder if he'd missed news of Amy's return. Although, it wouldn't have interested him anyway. "I wasn't aware that she had returned."

Jolie twisted and leveled those dark brown eyes, full of scorn, on him. "Don't the two of you correspond?"

"No."

"Why?"

He shrugged. "Why would I correspond with her? She left the country to find a rich husband, and I hope she does."

Her frown knit her brows together. "Weren't you rich enough for her?"

"Perhaps, but I had no interest in becoming her husband."

Her frown turned into a look of disbelief. "That's not what I heard."

"Perhaps you were listening to the wrong people."

She huffed out a tiny breath. "Perhaps, but I doubt it."

"I don't." He shrugged. "I have no idea where Amy is, nor do I care."

"But the two of you dated for some time."

"We attended events together, but that doesn't mean I was interested in marrying her." Sensing more than fully knowing, he asked, "Why didn't the two of you ever get along?"

"Who says we didn't?"

He glanced at her and grinned, letting her know that she wasn't hiding her dislike of Amy any more than Amy had hidden hers of Jolie.

She pinched her lips together as if hiding her own grin. "I'm assuming she told you about the ink episode."

"No, I don't know about any ink episode." But he was certainly curious now, given the tone in her voice.

She grew thoughtful for a moment, then asked, "She didn't tell you?"

"No."

After another moment of silence, she asked, "Is this about the episode at her father's store? Because I had money in the bank that day."

In his opinion, the store clerk should have been ashamed of her behavior. He'd wanted to catch up with Jolie after she'd left the store, and tell her so, but had figured she'd be too embarrassed to appreciate his thoughts.

"And," she continued, "I know, this…arrangement… between us has something to do with Amy."

He focused on steering the car along the curving road that led out of the neighborhood and into downtown. "This isn't about that day, and it doesn't have anything to do with Amy."

She waited until he pulled the car to a stop at an intersection, then leveled a steady, brown-eyed glare on him that he couldn't ignore. Turning, he waited, because she was clearly about to say something.

"Then, what is it about? And be aware, I can pick out a lie as easily as I can pick out a con man."

He withheld the want to grin and turned his gaze back on the traffic. There was more to Jolie Cramer than he'd imagined, and that didn't disappoint him. In fact, he appreciated her bluntness. "I thought you knew." He pulled the car onto the main road. "I need a wife, and it's my understanding that you need a husband."

Chapter Two

"I don't need a husband," Jolie insisted, irate that he wouldn't admit the truth behind his reasons. "I don't need anything."

"Except to have the taxes on your home paid. Or do you like the idea of moving to Kansas?"

That charged her ire even more. "Is there anything my mother didn't mention?" Because there was obviously plenty her mother hadn't mentioned to her.

"Such as?"

The list of things her mother could have said was longer than she was willing to discuss. Her mother was disillusioned and believed life could go back to what it had been before the market crash. Jolie knew that wasn't possible. "Why do you need a wife?" With his looks and status, nearly any woman in Illinois would fall at his feet, agreeing to marry him in a heartbeat. She wasn't one of them, and there was no reason for him to believe she might be such a woman.

"For the same reason you do." He glanced her way, flashing a smile. "Money."

Her insides shivered at the same time her heart skipped a beat. "You want money from me?"

He chuckled. "No."

"Good, because you'd be out of luck if that was your goal." She hadn't said that to make him laugh, but his chuckle didn't irritate her. It was the truth. A laughable one at that.

"I'm in need of a wife in order to complete a business deal that I'm interested in making," he said. "My plan is designed to benefit you, too. And your family."

Jolie held her opinion of that while he pulled the car into the hotel parking lot. She needed time to consider if there truly was any way she could benefit. Her family—possibly. Her—none that she could think of. That wasn't likely to change, either, no matter how long she thought about it.

"We can discuss it in more length over dinner." He turned off the car. "If you are still in agreement?"

She met him eyeball for eyeball. "I was never in agreement."

"I am beginning to understand that, although your mother led me to believe otherwise." He removed the key from the ignition without pulling his gaze off her. "But I have a sense that you might be interested."

A hint of her ire withdrew. She couldn't say why, other than he was right. Partially. She *might* be interested, only because the taxes did need to be paid, and because she was interested in what type of a business deal he was interested in making. She didn't want to become her mother, sitting at home crocheting doilies and being the perfect housewife, and then taking to bed, weeping and sobbing for months on end after her husband had died. Giving someone that type of power in the name of love was ridiculous.

It was 1933! Women had jobs, made their own money and didn't *need* husbands.

"Am I right?" He opened his door, but was looking at her, waiting for an answer.

"Possibly," she admitted. "I'll need to know more."

All she truly had left was her pride, and at times, it was a stubborn pride at that. Currently, it was telling her that nothing he could say would justify marrying him and giving up on what she wanted. However, her conscience was chiming in louder. More than just the taxes needed to be paid. Other bills, as well as Silas's tuition, were past due. There were no pennies left to be found in the washing machine or under the sofa cushions, and unless she was willing to move her entire family to Kansas—and have them all blame her for that the rest of her life—she needed to listen to what he had to say.

Agreeing would go against the grain, it would entail agreeing that she was willing to give over control of her life, and she wasn't willing to do that. Using the time it took him to walk around the car to open her door, she worked on convincing herself that she would listen to what he had to say only for the benefit of her family.

She stepped out of the car and walked beside him to the hotel. For all of her outer bravery, her insides were quaking as if she was about to face a judge and jury for a crime she hadn't committed.

Or maybe it was for one she was about to commit.

The murder of her hopes and dreams.

"We can go someplace else if you prefer," Randal said.

Swallowing some of her damnable pride that could be her downfall if she wasn't careful, she shook her head. "No. This is fine." There truly was no reason to pretend she wasn't nervous. About everything. She was; there was so much at stake. However, she could pretend that her last nerve was about to snap for other reasons. Lifting her chin, she said, "It's been a long time since I've eaten in a restaurant."

"I hope you will enjoy it."

She wouldn't, but to be fair, that wasn't his fault. In all reality, for reasons she couldn't understand, she was finding it difficult to dislike him.

Within minutes they were seated at table in a corner that allowed privacy, in the large and somewhat crowded dining room. The single flickering candle on each table was meant to add ambience, elegance to the already sophisticated atmosphere. So did the soft music being played by the quartet on a triangular stage near a small dance area where several couples were gracefully sashaying around the floor. It seemed prohibition had been all but forgotten. Dining clubs, such as this, were now as popular as speakeasies had once been. The one thing neither prohibition nor the depression could stop was people wanting to drink, dance and have fun, to go on living despite the obstacles. Maybe she could learn to do that, too.

"Would you care for a cocktail?" Randal asked.

"No, thank you." They were here, so might as well get down to business. "Exactly what will you get out of marrying me?"

He leaned back in his chair, and gave a slight shake of his head, as if he'd thought of something to say, but chose not to. "A wife."

Her teeth clenched every time the word was mentioned. She didn't want to be a wife. She wanted to be in charge of her own life. "Why do you need a wife?" She held up a hand for him to wait before answering. "And don't tell me it's for a business deal."

"That's the truth."

A great sense of frustration filled her. No one needed a wife in order to make a business deal. She withheld her response as the waiter arrived at their table and made small talk while filling their water glasses from a silver pitcher and providing them with two menus. When he took his leave, she idly opened the folded menu. "What is the rest of the truth?" Already frustrated, she added, "And please, don't make this more difficult by skirting the truth."

"I'm not skirting the truth, nor am I attempting to make it difficult." He set his menu aside. "My father, like yours, invested heavily in the stock market, and it was good to him. When he died seven years ago, I took over his investments and diversified them, which proved to work in my favor when the market crashed. I fared better than most and am now looking to increase my wealth by purchasing a business of my own, one where I'm in charge of the growth and success." He took a drink off his water glass. "The man who owns the business that I'm interested in purchasing will only sell to a married man."

Like the teeth on a zipper, things came together in her mind in one swift movement. As ridiculous as his reason sounded, Jolie believed him, because she knew the business and she knew the man. "You're interested in buying Dad Jansen's airplane company?"

Randal took another drink off his water. He couldn't deny he was impressed by her straightforwardness, and by her astuteness, but was a bit shocked by her knowledge and the fact she called Carl Jansen "Dad." Many people knew Carl, but only those very close to him called him Dad and, as far as he knew, Carl hadn't made it public that he was interested in selling his airplane business. Carl had two sons—married sons—that he'd turned his other businesses over to on their marriages years ago.

"That's why you chose me, isn't it?" she asked. "Because Dad's my godfather."

Through his research, Randal was aware that Carl Jansen and her father had been friends, but he had not known they'd been that close. However, that made her an even more perfect choice. He'd spent his life so far investing in other people's companies, and he was ready for that to change. He wanted to invest in his own company. Build it into something great rather than merely pushing numbers, and Carl's company had the potential of doing just that. "I did not know that he was your godfather."

She nodded her head slowly as the hint of a grin formed. "You didn't mention that you were interested in buying Dad's business to my mother, did you?"

"No. There was no reason."

She let out a huff. "If you had, we wouldn't be sitting here right now. She doesn't like Dad. Never has. If she did, she would have accepted his assistance after my father died, and my family wouldn't be in the situation we are now."

A plethora of questions filled his head, but Randal refrained from making any further comment as the waiter approached their table. Nodding toward her menu, he asked, "Do you have a preference of what to order or need more time? If not, I'll order the special for both of us."

Like him, she had barely glanced at the menu, and when she nodded while shrugging, he ordered the chef's evening special for both of them. The waiter explained the meal included braised pork chops and sweet potatoes, and after a few additional questions concerning options pertaining to the meal, left.

Randal took a moment before returning to their conversation about Carl Jansen. He wanted that company more than he'd wanted anything before, but if her mother hated Carl, that could be a real bump in the road.

Her mouth twitched slightly as she let out a loud sigh. "It'll never work."

"Why?"

"Because if Dad figures out you married me just to buy his company, he'll never sell it to you."

Randal had already considered that, and wasn't going to let it deter him. "He might, but I have to take that risk. I'm not looking for a loving wife, Jolie. I'm looking for a partner. One who will benefit from our union as much as I will, which is why I'm considering you."

A hint of something—he wasn't sure what—flashed in her eyes, but she remained silent, waiting for him to say more.

He chose his words carefully. "I'll pay the taxes on your family's home, pay your brother's tuition and other outstanding bills, as well as provide your family with a monthly allowance, and not demand anything from you, other than you perform the social duties of being my wife."

"Social duties?"

"Yes, attend functions, dinner dates, parties, those types of things, as needed."

"For how long?"

Interesting. He hadn't considered a timeline or end date. To him, marriage didn't have one. "I have no intention of going into this just for the short term and then seeking a divorce. No need to worry about that."

Brows lifted, she asked, "Do I look worried?"

"No, you don't, but I do recognize that your family would be back in the same position as they are now if that was to happen."

She opened her mouth as if she was going to speak, but then closed it and looked around the room.

"You don't have to decide tonight," he said, fully aware of just how life-changing this would be for both of them. "You can think about it for a few days."

"Is that what you are going to do?" She met his gaze squarely. "Think about it? Take the other women you are *considering* out for dinner?"

"If you were to say yes tonight, I would be ready to set the wedding date with you."

"And if I say no?"

"I would review my list of other potential wives."

She tried hard to not smile, but it eventually came through, along with an adorable dimple in one cheek. "I have to say, you do appear to be an honest man."

He gave her a nod. "And you appear to be an honest woman. Lying to each other right from the start wouldn't set a very good foundation for us."

"No, it wouldn't." She took a sip of water off her glass. "Will you tell me more about Dad's airplane company?"

"Yes." He leaned closer to the table. "Will you tell me about the ink episode?"

Her cheeks pinkened. "Why would you want to know about that?"

He shrugged. "Because it must be important to you, otherwise you wouldn't have brought it up." Watching the influx of emotions that crossed her face, he added, "And, for the record, I think that clerk at Casswell's should have been ashamed for the way she treated you that day. I was impressed by the way you handled it."

"By refusing your offer to pay for my items and walking out?"

"Yes. That took pride, dignity."

She shook her head. "I should have known better than to go in that store."

"Why?"

"Because Amy has hated me forever."

He'd never put much credence in what Amy said about others because she'd never had a good thing to say about anyone—man or woman. "Since the ink episode?"

"Before then. That just increased her hatred."

"What happened?"

"We were in elementary school and the teacher asked me to fill the ink pens for penmanship, and that made Amy mad. She always called me the teacher's pet. Anyway, she acted like she was going to the pencil sharpener and along the way, tried to knock over a bottle of ink, but I caught it." With what appeared to be a regretful expression, she sighed. "And then let it fall from my hand. It hit the edge of the desk, shattered and splattered her with ink. She had blue freckles for weeks."

It sounded simple, but he'd seen the wrath of Amy

come out when a waitress had accidentally spilled a glass of water on their table once. He'd been embarrassed by her behavior, and after insisting to the owner that the waitress did not need to be fired, had left a hefty tip for the young woman.

"It was mean of me to do," Jolie said. "But I had still been mad over her cutting my hair."

"Amy cut your hair?"

Jolie nodded, picked up her napkin and placed it on her lap due to the approaching waiter. "Yes. A year before that. My desk had been in front of hers, and she'd cut one of my braids off right at the back of my neck." She pointed to a spot on the nape of her neck and grimaced. "I'd thought she'd just been pulling my hair, and ignored her, until she handed me the braid."

He picked up his napkin, and as the waiter set their plates on the table, asked, "Handed you the braid?" It wasn't a laughing matter, but her expression was so adorable, he truly wanted to smile.

"Yes, she flopped it over my shoulder. The rest of my hair had to be cut short, it was awful. It took a year of growing out before I could braid it again, and it's never been that long again since."

He thanked the waiter, and assured him they didn't need anything else, before he cleared a chuckle from his throat and said, "How long had it been when she cut it?"

"Down to my waist. I'd never had it cut before then."

"That sounds awful for you."

"You ought to tell that to your face."

"Tell what?"

"How awful it was, because you look like you're trying extremely hard not to laugh."

He met her gaze, and as her smile broke through, so did his. "So are you."

"It was awful, but like a lot of things, I can laugh about it now." She scooped up a forkful of mashed sweet potatoes. "Including the ink episode."

"That's very mature of you," he said.

"Maybe. Or maybe I'm just imagining her with all those blue freckles."

Chuckling, he cut a slice off his pork chop. He couldn't remember a time when he'd found a woman more likable in a shorter amount of time.

"Your turn," she said. "Tell me about Dad's airplane business."

As Carl's goddaughter, she might know more about it than him. "Do you know when he's putting it on the market?" he asked.

"No, I wasn't aware that he was selling it, but I do know that neither of his sons want it. He bought it four years ago, and they'd thought he'd been crazy to buy it at his age. It's just when you said the company you wanted to buy would only be sold to a married man, I knew you were talking about Dad. He always said that he was successful because of Anna. His wife."

"I've heard that," Randal replied. "And that he believes a man without a woman behind him will never amount to anything. Which is why I'm interested in getting married. With the right man at the helm, his airplane company could become the largest in the world."

"And you want to be that man?"

"I do." He looked directly at her and asked, "But the real question is, do you want to be the woman behind that man?"

Chapter Three

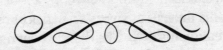

Jolie stared at the mail in her hand. Overdue bills. It had been four days since she had gone out for dinner with Randal and during that time, the turmoil inside her had grown. It had grown within the household, too. Her mother was barely speaking to her, and just this morning, before leaving for school, Chloe informed her that she'd run away before moving to Kansas.

Her sister was fifteen, and headstrong, making Jolie believe they could wake up one morning to discover Chloe had disappeared during the night. Chloe was also afraid. Afraid that if Jolie refused, she was next. Unfortunately, that was a real possibility.

Silas was the only one who appeared slightly understanding, stating—in private because Mother would have a fit if she heard him—that he'd quit college and get a job.

Jolie couldn't let that happen any more than she could let Chloe run away or marry some man their mother forced on her, and ultimately was leaning toward accepting Randal's proposition, despite how frustrating it was to think of giving up her own dreams. All she'd ever wanted was to design and sew clothes. She'd been doing that for her dolls and herself for years, and wanted to build a business out of it. Getting married could change all that.

In spite of her frustration, a grin formed at the memory of eating dinner with Randal. They hadn't left the restaurant for hours after finishing. They'd shared childhood stories, and he'd told her more about how he'd taken over his father's business activities but was dedicated to creating his own. She didn't know much about airplanes, but he certainly did, and it had been interesting hearing him talk about them.

She hadn't met someone that easy to talk to for a long time, and most certainly, never a man.

But none of that, the laughing and talking, made her ready to jump in and marry him. She'd loved her father, deeply, and missed him, but when he'd died, she hadn't wanted to die, too. Not like her mother. Her mother still had days when she didn't get out of bed, claiming she missed him too much to do anything. That was no way to live and not a fate Jolie wanted for herself.

Her mother had also been jealous. Embarrassingly jealous at times. Jolie wouldn't live like that.

Even now, four years later, her mother was fully dedicated to his memory—and in keeping everything just how father would have wanted it.

The house.

Silas's education.

Women not working.

Both of her parents had thought it was cute that she sewed clothes for her dolls, but as she got older, and sewed her own, they'd refused to let her wear them. They had considered home-sewn clothing a sign of poverty.

Her mother still did, and Jolie was concerned that Randal might feel the same way.

That, however, was only one issue.

The other one was her fear of not knowing exactly what Dad would expect from Randal's wife. If it was to merely be a housewife, she didn't think she could do it. She'd dreamed of doing more for too many years.

She wished Anna was still alive… Jolie paused as a thought formed and twisted about in her mind. Anna wasn't, but Dad was. She didn't want to jeopardize Randal's chances at buying Dad's business, but talking to Dad could be exactly what she needed. If she could find out exactly what he meant about a man having a woman behind him, she might be able to figure out if it would be worth it or not.

Before she had a chance to change her mind, she dropped the mail on the desk in the study and pulled open the drawer that held the keys to her father's automobile. The gasoline in the car was highly rationed for emergency use only. To her, this was an emergency.

She hurried upstairs, changed into a more fashionable dress—another makeover from old clothes—and collected her purse. Mother was nowhere in sight, and Jolie hoped she wouldn't hear the sound of the car starting and try to stop her.

Half an hour later, she pulled the older model Cadillac, which was not nearly as nice or elegant as Randal's, onto the long, tree-lined driveway leading up to Dad Jansen's stately home. Painted white, with black shutters and tall white pillars framing the double set of mahogany front doors, the house sat on a tree-filled, five-acre lot that she'd played on many times as a child, while her father had visited with Dad.

What had seemed like a simple enough act, as well as a smart one, at home, was now making her stomach burn. She hadn't seen Dad for a long time, too long, and hoped he wouldn't hold that against her.

She parked the car on the paved driveway that looped around the front of the house, and took a moment to appease the nerves flapping about in her stomach by drawing a deep breath before climbing out of the car.

The front door was opened by the same dark-haired and brushy-browed butler as years before.

"Miss Cramer," he said. "It's good to see you."

"Hello, Mr. Blocker, is Dad home?"

"Of course, miss, right this way."

She followed him through the entranceway of tall, dark wood-stained walls, and down a long hallway to a closed door.

Without a word, Mr. Blocker spun about, opened the door with one hand and gave her a slight bow.

"Jolie, Jolie." Smiling, Dad walked toward her, arms wide. "You gave my old heart a start just pulling in the driveway, but look at you! As beautiful as ever. More beautiful than ever!"

She didn't expect the emotions that struck at seeing his smiling, wrinkled face and shimmering bald head, and had to press a hand to her mouth to cover the sob that bubbled in the back of her throat.

"Now, now, none of that," Dad said, pulling her into an embrace. "I've thought of you so often, Joey-girl. So often."

He was the only one who had ever called her that. Resting her head against the front of his shoulder, she closed her eyes against the tears slipping out. "I'm sorry, Dad. Sorry I haven't been over sooner. Sorry I wasn't at the funeral." She truly felt awful about that, and had been very angry at her mother for months for not allowing her to go to Anna's funeral. She'd considered going anyway, but knew her mother would never have forgiven her if she had.

"That's all right, sweetheart." He kissed the top of her head, then gripped her shoulders and took a step back, smiling. "You're here now, and I'm very happy about that."

She wished she could say the only reason she was here was to see him, because she should have been here long before now for just that purpose, but couldn't lie to him. "I need some advice, Dad."

He gave her shoulders a squeeze. "I'm glad you thought of me. Come, let's sit down."

She walked beside him into the depths of the massive library and took a seat on the navy-blue velvet-covered sofa, setting her purse on the floor by her ankle.

Dad sat down next to her. "How is everyone doing? Your mother? Brother? Sister?"

"Everyone is fine. Silas is doing well in college, and Chloe is now in high school."

"How are the finances?"

Dad had never been one to beat around the bush. "We're managing," she replied.

"Managing?" He shook his head and huffed out a breath that was full of frustration. "I do wish your mother wasn't so stubborn. As you know, I've offered assistance."

"I know. She believes…" Jolie let out a long sigh and shook her head. "I don't know what she believes. Maybe that the few stocks we still own are going to miraculously make us wealthy again."

The tight grimace on his face said what he thought about that, but he was too kind to voice it. Instead, he asked, "Do you need money? Just tell me how much."

Her heart softened. She'd always known that she could ask him for money, but not only would that upset her mother beyond all else, it wouldn't solve anything. "Thank you for the offer, but I'm not here for money. Just advice."

"All right, about what?"

She was still feeling unsettled, and wasn't quite ready to broach that subject. "First tell me how you are doing. I was truly sorry to hear of Anna's passing."

His dark blue eyes shimmered with moisture. "She was tired, Joey-girl, ready to go be with the Lord, but I surely do miss her, every day." He patted her hand. "The card you sent meant a lot to me."

"I wanted to attend the funeral, but—" She stopped because of the way he was shaking his head at her.

Rather than pat her hand again, he picked it up and sandwiched it between both of his. "Your mother loved your father with all of her heart, and I'll never hold that against her. That's how it should be. A man should love his wife just as strongly, and your father did. He loved her, and his children, above all else." He glanced at the bookshelves lining the walls. "True love is a rare commodity, Jolie. When you find it, you have to hang on to it tighter than anything else, because it is the one thing that can both make and break a person."

His hands shook slightly, and she cupped her other one over his. Her heart ached for the pain she saw in his profile, but words escaped her.

He turned back to her, smiled. "Your mother just didn't like your father and I being such good friends. She was jealous, that's all it was. Joseph was as close to me as any brother would have ever been, and for some reason, that made her feel threatened."

He was right, but it hadn't been just him. Her mother had been jealous over all of her father's friends and business associates. "It never threatened me, Dad, and I've missed you."

"I've missed you, too, Joey-girl." He lifted their clasped hands, kissed the back of hers that was on top and then released his hold. "Now, tell me, what sort of advice is it that you need?"

She smoothed the material of her skirt covering her thighs, knowing she couldn't put it off any longer. "Fatherly advice." Drawing in a deep breath, she stared straight ahead at the bookshelves. "I'm thinking about getting married."

"Well, now, that is a big decision. Do I know the young man?"

Not daring to look his way, she said, "His name is Randal Osterlund."

"Do you love him?" Dad asked.

"Do you know him?" she asked in response, glancing his way.

"I know of him," Dad answered. "I knew his father, and I know his grandfather, although Ness Osterlund doesn't get out much these days. Arthritis, I hear."

She had no idea if Randal's grandfather had arthritis or not, but felt inclined to nod.

"From what I hear, Randal is an upstanding young man. Took over for his father at a young age, when his father passed away in an automobile accident, and did well when the collapse hit. I'd say he's someone your father would approve of." He paused for a length of time. "But, the important thing is, do you love him?"

Love Randal? She barely knew him, furthermore, she wasn't interested in loving him or any other man. Unable to come up with a response, she looked at Dad.

He was looking at Anna's portrait hanging over the fireplace. "Did you know that my first job was at a saddle shop?"

"No," she replied, thankful to be off the love subject.

"I was twelve, big for my age and strong. The man who owned the shop had hurt his hand and couldn't drive an awl in the leather for the stitching. He hired me to do that and there was a girl who sewed the leather together."

"Anna?" she asked.

He nodded. "She was two years older than me. Fourteen. And the most beautiful girl I'd ever seen. I still remember that first saddle, and I remember looking at it, thinking how we'd created it together. That neither one of us could have done it alone." He let out a long sigh. "We worked at that shop together for the next six years, until I was eighteen and she was twenty. Then we got married, bought the shop a year later, and, well, from there we went on to buy more businesses, build them up, sell them and buy others, all the while building a family, a couple of houses and a damn good life together, all because of true love."

Perplexed, she asked, "You and Anna found true love when you were twelve and fourteen?"

"It found us," he said.

Even more perplexed, she stared at him.

"Sit back, Joey-girl, and let me tell you about true love."

* * *

Jolie had been on Randal's mind nonstop. Sometimes he'd thought of her long and hard, and other times, just a fleeting thought would make him smile. But he hadn't expected to see her, not at his office. They'd left the restaurant the other night with the understanding that they would both think about the venture for a time, and that he'd call her in a few days. Dismissing the shock of seeing her with a mental head shake, he stood. "Come in," he said to Jolie and nodded at his secretary. "Thank you, Mrs. Adams."

He walked around his desk, held the back of the chair as Jolie practically sank into it, and then made sure the door was tightly closed before he walked around her chair. The desire to touch her shoulder in comfort was hard to withhold, but he wasn't sure she'd welcome his touch. "Is something the matter?"

Clutching onto the handle of the white purse on her lap with both hands, she looked up at him as if the world was about to end. "I'm sorry."

A good amount of hope that she would agree with his plan disappeared. He leaned back against the edge of his desk. "There's nothing to be sorry about. You agreed to think about it, and I appreciate that you took the time to do that."

She blinked and stared at him blankly for a brief moment. "No." Shaking her head, she said, "I mean, yes. My answer is yes to marrying you."

The hope didn't return. In fact, it sank even lower at the sadness that still filled her eyes. After their dinner the other night, he'd come to believe she was the perfect woman to marry. She'd agreed that she wasn't looking for love, either, and had suggested that a partnership that could benefit both of them was something she would seriously consider. "And you're sorry about that?"

"Yes. I mean, no." She stood up, set her purse on the chair and pressed both hands to her temples as she turned and walked across the room.

"Which is it?" he asked.

She was wearing a red-and-white-striped dress, with a fitted waistline, and puffed sleeves. A red scarf was wrapped around her head and tied at the nape of her neck, beneath the long hair flowing in waves across her shoulders and down her back.

She reached the wall before she turned to face him. "I honestly don't know."

He folded his arms across his chest. "You can take more time to think about it."

"No, I can't." Shaking her head, she walked toward him. "And that's what I'm sorry about. The date is set."

Shocked for the second time in about as many minutes, he took a moment to check his hearing before asking, "The date is set?"

Grabbing the back of her chair so hard the purse almost tittered off it, she sighed loudly. "Yes. The date of our wedding has been set. Two weeks from tomorrow."

He planted both hands on the desk behind him as a shiver zipped up his spine. Maybe he wasn't as prepared for this as he'd thought.

"I hope that date works for you."

"It'll have to," he answered, trying to get his head around what she'd said.

"It's a Saturday, so…"

"I realize it's a Saturday, so my office will be closed." He took another moment to absorb it all. "Two weeks?"

She nodded. "My mother will take care of most of the planning, if that, too, is all right with you?"

Although he'd paid for both of his sisters' weddings, he had no idea what went into planning for them. He'd steered clear of his sisters during that time, doing little more than writing checks. "That's fine." Things still weren't adding up in his head. "But you can still take time to think about it. We can change the date."

"No, we can't. I've agreed, and we need to go ahead as planned."

"Why?"

She threw her hands in the air. "Because if we don't, Dad will never sell you his airplane business."

"How do you know that?"

"Because he's paying for the wedding."

That struck and sank in instantly. "I see."

"Yes," she said heavily. "And that's why I'm sorry. I didn't expect—"

"Of course you didn't." He truly believed she was sorry. Her mother was the one who wanted the marriage and would have pulled any strings possible to make it happen. He'd wanted it, too, and despite the idea that it would be nice to have a fraction of time to get used to the idea, it was too late for that. Her mother must have contacted Carl. There was no backing out now. Not if he wanted the airplane company. Which he did.

However, there was one final stipulation he did need to let her know. "There will be no infidelity. On either of our parts."

She shook her head as if disgusted. "You don't have to worry about that. I promise."

Satisfied with her answer, he pushed off the desk and picked up her purse, handed it to her. "Shall we?"

Frowning, she took the purse. "Shall we what?"

He stepped around her chair. "Go buy you an engagement ring."

"I don't need—" She stopped upon noticing the look he gave her.

"We need to make this look as real as possible," he said.

She turned to walk to the door. "You can say that again."

"Don't worry. It's just while we are in public. In private, there will be no expectations whatsoever."

"Where will that be?" she asked. "Where will we live?"

He grasped ahold of the doorknob, but didn't open it, fully aware that Mrs. Adams would be able to hear once the door was opened. "At my house. My grandfather and sister Danielle, and her husband, James, live there as well, but the house is large enough to accommodate us all."

"How many siblings do you have?"

"Two sisters. Danielle and Willa. Willa, her husband, Dan, and their two children live in their own home a short distance from mine."

She nodded, but had yet to look up at him since they'd stopped near the door. Fully understanding her hesitancy, he offered, "We could live with your family, if you'd prefer." It wouldn't be ideal, or acceptable to his grandfather, but he'd do it for a time if it would ease her worries.

She shook her head. "No."

"Or we could look for an apartment if you'd prefer."

"It's fine, Randal. Your house is fine."

He didn't want to admit he was having second

thoughts, because this was his plan and it was all falling into place. He'd done his research, and Carl's company had the best potential of him making his own footprint.

Even while knowing all that, he couldn't help but feel guilty about pulling her into all of it. He might have thought he was made of stone, but he wasn't. She was proving that to him. "Do you want to call it off?"

She looked up at him, searched his face as if hesitant to say her true feelings. Then, a faint smile formed as she quietly said, "No, but thank you for asking."

That was her answer, and he had to abide by it. "All right then, let's go buy you a ring."

Chapter Four

Jittery, fraught with nerves, Jolie pressed a hand against her stomach and closed her eyes, blocking the image reflected in the floor-length mirror. She'd spent hours designing and sewing the dress, working into the wee hours of the morning, diligently making this her absolute best work.

That had greatly irritated her mother. Nearly every day for the past two weeks Mother had found errands they'd had to run or another wedding detail that had needed to be seen to immediately—all excuses to keep her from working on her dress. Despite Mother's refusal to accept financial help from him before, she had readily accepted the funds from Dad for the wedding, and continuously insisted that there was more than enough money to purchase a dress from one of the many department stores.

Jolie understood that purchasing ready-made clothing was the style and that many of the stores had some beautiful dresses. She'd even conceded and bought a few day dresses so she had a more stylish wardrobe for once she became Randal's wife. However, she'd also decided that if this was her fate, she was going to find a way to make it work for her.

She hadn't received the answers she'd sought from Dad, because she'd never got around to asking exactly what he felt a wife needed to do in order to propel her husband forward. Dad had talked about love, and assuming she wasn't sure what that was, he'd spent the better part of an hour explaining it to her. He'd said that love changes a person, makes them want different things, feel differently about things.

She'd seen what else love does last night, after the rehearsal, when her mother spent hours sobbing, wishing Jolie's father was here to walk her down the aisle.

But if her father was still alive, she wouldn't be walking down the aisle today.

Jolie huffed out a breath.

Randal was nice, and Dad was convinced that marrying Randal would be exactly what her father would have wanted.

She wasn't so sure. She had looked forward to hearing from Randal each day, and had enjoyed going out to dinner with him some evenings, but that could be because it had given her reprieve from her mother.

Last night hadn't been the only time her mother had shed tears over her father not being here.

Jolie sighed, wondering how she'd managed to add an entirely new dimension to this whole predicament.

Neither she or Randal expected love from their union, they'd discussed that, and it was a major reason that she'd agreed. She just wished she knew what was expected of her. She didn't like the unknown. Never had.

Slowly, she opened her eyes, and once again scanned her reflection in the mirror.

The gown she'd worked so hard on designing and sewing had turned out exceptionally well. It was made of snow-white silk and satin, with a fitted bodice, long, flowing skirt, a high neckline and long sleeves. It was the epitome of a high-fashion wedding dress, yet had been made on a depression budget. As was the long tulle veil attached to the pearl-encrusted tiara head-dress pinned into her hair.

It truly was her best work. She'd taken what was in style and added her own little twists and turns. The money from Dad had given her the ability to purchase the materials and notions needed to make her wedding dress become as much talk of the town as her wedding.

At least that was her hope. She hoped once her dress became the talk of the town, others would ask her to design clothes for them. The public outings she'd par-take in as Randal's wife could then continue to provide her the opportunities to show off her design work, and hopefully gain even more clients. That was a possibil-ity because Randal had a chef, a maid and a butler, so she wasn't expected to just be a housewife.

She truly was putting all of her eggs in one basket, but it was the only basket she had, and ultimately, she couldn't give up her dream of designing clothes.

Just couldn't.

When mother had pitched a fit over not buying a ready-made dress, Randal had put a stop to it by say-ing that if she wanted to sew her wedding dress, then she could sew it.

She had appreciated his support, because no one, not even her father, had ever supported her love of de-signing and sewing.

A sigh escaped her chest and she stared down at the

diamond engagement ring on her finger. It was a beautiful art deco, white gold, ring, with engraved foliate and orange blossom detail. There was a matching wedding band that he would slide on her finger during the service. He'd seemed to know how much she'd liked the ring the moment the clerk at the store had set it on the counter. The ring was extremely lovely, but she'd liked it so much because although intricate, it was also simple enough to be unpretentious.

That's what she wanted. Things to be simple.

But none of this was simple. She couldn't even pretend that Randal had roped her into this marriage. It was the other way around. She'd thought going to Dad would give her insight. Instead, it had been the catalyst that catapulted her into marrying Randal today.

Today.

Her heart beat so hard she had to part her lips to suck in air.

Dad, with his assumption that she'd fallen in love—that they, she and Randal, had fallen in love—had insisted the wedding take place as soon as possible. That true love shouldn't have to wait, and had set the date himself.

She hadn't been able to say no, and she still hadn't told Randal that she'd gone to see Dad. For a reason that wasn't crystal clear, but sat heavy inside her, she didn't want him to know.

But he was sure to find out today, and Dad was sure to question him about his love for her.

A knock on her bedroom door shattered her thoughts and increased the dancing of her nerves.

"The car is here." Wearing a pale blue, floor-length

dress, a store-bought one, Chloe entered into the room. "Oh, Jolie, you look beautiful!"

Jolie drew in another deep breath. "Thank you. So do you."

"I mean really, really beautiful." Chloe hurried across the room and circled Jolie. "Your dress! I saw it while you were sewing, but it's gorgeous!"

"Thank you, but let me look at you." Jolie took ahold of her sister's hands. "Do you like your dress?" Like her, Chloe hadn't had new clothes for ages, and her younger sister looked adorable with her hair pinned up beneath the tiny veiled pill hat the same shade of blue as her dress.

"I love it, and like you said, I'll be able to shorten the hem and wear it over and over." Chloe stepped closer and hugged Jolie. "Actually, I'll have you hem it." Her sister's hug became tighter. "Oh, Jolie, I'm going to miss you."

"I'm going to miss you, too." Although Randal's money would help financially, she didn't believe that would secure a future for her family. That took more than money, and she was sincerely worried about leaving Chloe and Silas.

"And I'm so grateful for what you are doing for all of us." Stepping back, Chloe shook her head. "I'm truly sorry for saying that I'd run away, but I just couldn't imagine moving and living with Uncle LeRoy."

"I couldn't, either," Jolie admitted.

"You saved our entire family," Chloe said.

Jolie couldn't help but question if she was saving anyone. She gave her sister's hands a final squeeze and then released them. "Well, we don't want to keep the car waiting." A car had been arranged to take her to the church. Her mother and brother had already left in the family car.

"Do you need me to carry anything?" Chloe asked.

Jolie looked around the room. Most all of her belongings had been sent over to Randal's house yesterday. It was surreal that this was the last time she'd be in this room. Once again, she pressed a hand to the somersaults in her stomach. "No. All I have to carry is my purse."

Chloe lifted the white purse off the edge of the bed. "I'll carry it for you."

In less than an hour from the time she'd left her bedroom, Jolie was walking down the aisle of the church, on Dad Jansen's arm, toward the altar where Randal stood.

Though sheer, the veil still hindered her sight, but not enough that her heart didn't skip a beat at how handsome Randal looked in his tuxedo. He was watching her, and smiling, and his silver-blue eyes were shimmering brightly.

She was glad the veil hid her face, because her lips trembled.

Her entire being trembled.

Right up to the point where Randal took hold of her hand. The warmth of his touch raced up her arm and spread through her body, chasing aside her shivers. There was something about him that grounded her. Perhaps because they were in this together. She wasn't the only one that was having to pretend. Neither one of them wanted love, just a partnership.

"Your exceptional beauty takes my breath away," he whispered.

The huskiness of his voice took her breath away, leaving her unable to do more than nod slightly. She truly could find no fault in him. He'd not only been patient and understanding throughout the past three weeks, he'd been supportive and kind.

That thought played over and over again in her mind throughout the service, as they repeated vows and slid rings on each other's fingers, but when Randal lifted her veil, her thoughts shifted. She'd known this moment would happen. That he would have to kiss her during the service. Her heart stopped at the shimmer in his eyes, the smile on his lips, as his face drew closer to hers.

She'd thought of this moment, more than once, with curiosity. She had no intention of falling in love with him or any other man, but that had made her wonder if their partnership included other wifely duties. She assumed it would. People slept together without being in love all the time.

At the first touch of his lips against hers, her eyes fluttered shut and a great wave of warmth washed over her, all the way to her toes, making them curl inside her shoes.

The sensation, the feel of his warm lips pressing against hers was so appealing, she cupped his face and stretched to keep their lips connected. His hands, on her waist, slid around her back and pulled her closer, sending another thrill through her system.

She'd been curious about kissing him, but hadn't expected this overwhelming feeling of complete surrender. She had never surrendered to anything in her life, but there wasn't a single part of her that wanted any of this to end.

Feeling, more than hearing, Randal's slight chuckle, she forced her mind to search for what he found humorous. Until she heard someone clear their throat.

Randal pulled his lips from hers at the same time her eyes snapped open. Winking at her, he glanced toward the minister.

Heat filled her cheeks, as she fully understood the minister had been the one clearing his throat as a sign to stop their kissing.

Randal caught her hands as they slipped off his face and then kissed her forehead before he turned his attention to the minister.

She closed her eyes in hopes of gathering her wits, which really wasn't possible with the way her lips were still tingling, her heart still thudding. She opened her eyes when the minster instructed her and Randal to face the guests.

Another wave of heat filled her cheeks, knowing well over a hundred people had just witnessed her and Randal kissing. He released one of her hands, but held on to the other and gave it a squeeze as they both turned toward the rows upon rows of people.

"Allow me to present Mr. and Mrs. Randal Osterlund," the minister said.

Looking out over the sea of people who stood up, clapping and smiling, Jolie's embarrassment grew, once again remembering the deceit she and Randal were committing.

As if he'd read her mind, he whispered, "It's going to be fine, get your bouquet."

It was a moment before she realized that Chloe was handing her the bouquet of red roses that she'd carried up the aisle earlier. She took the flowers and held on tighter to Randal's hand as they began to walk past the guests. Holding a smile on her face, she accepted congratulations from both people she knew and those she didn't. The guest lists had grown large, which had thrilled her mother.

Between her mother and Dad, keeping things simple, as Jolie had wanted, hadn't been in the cards.

At least it would soon all be over.

Randal turned to her. "Ready to get pelted with rice?"

The kiss they'd shared a few moments ago still had Randal's blood pounding through his veins. Never had a kiss nearly knocked his socks off, but that one certainly had. She'd melded against him as if their bodies had been made to fit together. He hadn't been prepared for that, nor for how gorgeous she'd looked walking down the aisle. The dress she'd sewn was spectacular, but her wearing it was the reason. He wasn't a guy that had read fairy tales, but he had two sisters, and if he'd had to describe how Jolie looked, it would be like a princess.

"I guess we don't have a choice," she said with a grimace.

Needing the space to breathe, he loosened his tie, and flashed her a smile. "No, we don't, but if we hurry, we can beat them to the hotel and have some quiet time before the reception starts."

"I'm game for that."

Her smile didn't say as much as the gleam in her eyes. He laid a hand on the small of her back and guided her toward the front door, where people were already lined up down the steps and along the sidewalk.

He needed more than some quiet time. It was going to take a whole lot more than quiet for him to come to grips with the fact that he'd married a woman who once again had proven he wasn't made of stone.

Furthermore, they needed to do more than hurry. As soon as the rice was thrown, they needed to run for his car and drive like bootleggers outrunning a posse of bulls in order to make it to the hotel without getting caught.

The moment the doors opened, he wrapped an arm around her, pulled her close and ducked his head over her, trying to take the brunt of the rice being tossed at them. Luckily, his car was parked at the curb, covered with crepe paper, with strings of empty cans tied to the back bumper and *Just Married* painted on the back window with white shoe polish. He'd expected all that. He'd helped others do the same to some of his buddies' cars when they'd gotten married, and he expected what would happen next.

Once they reached the end of the sidewalk, people shouted for her to toss her bouquet. He stepped aside as she whipped her flowers over her head. With little more than a backward glance, she said, "Let's go!"

"You've got that right!" Glad she understood the urgency, he grabbed her hand and they ran to the car.

"Look what they did to your car!"

"Doesn't matter! Jump in!"

She jumped in as soon as he'd opened her door. Closing it, he ran around the car and noted his friends making mad dashes to their cars.

He wasn't about to lose his bride to any of them. "Hold on!" he told Jolie as he started the car.

"Hold on? Why?"

He put the car in gear and laid his foot on the gas, squealing his tires as he pulled away from the curb. "Because we have to beat them to our hotel room."

"Beat who?"

The cans tied to his bumper clinked and clanged against the street, and bounced high enough he could see them in the rearview mirror, along with several cars pulling away from the curbs and blowing their horns. "Everyone who follows us."

"Why?"

"Haven't you ever been in a wedding chase before?"

"No."

"But you've seen them? Heard about them?"

"Yes, I've seen them. Heard the horns honking. Isn't it just for fun?"

"Yes, but there is a goal, too."

"What's the goal?"

He took the corner so fast the car felt as if it was on two wheels instead of four. "To steal the bride!"

"What? Steal me? What for?"

He wasn't going to let that happen. "Whatever they have planned to do!"

"Like what?"

"Whatever they decide. Joyriding, cocktails." He took another corner, then another fast right into an alley. "Jerry Hansen's bride was put on a bus for Springfield."

"What! Why?"

"It's all for fun, but Jerry had to get the police to pull the bus over to get his bride back." In hindsight, Jerry would have been better off if he'd let her stay on that bus.

"Jerry was one of your groomsmen!"

"Yes, he was!"

"Were you part of the group that put his bride on the bus?"

He took a moment to flash her a grin. "It was all in good fun."

"It's all fun and games until someone loses an eye!"

He glanced at her again, and laughed at the merriment on her face.

"I'm not going to lose an eye! I'm not going to lose you, either! Hang on!"

She twisted in her seat to look out the back window. "Drive faster! I don't see anyone, but I can hear horns honking!"

There was an excited urgency in her voice, and it was zipping through him. "So do I!" He took a left at the end of the alley and had to do some quick steering, weaving around cars to keep from hitting any of them. "But I know a shortcut to the hotel. And I anticipated this."

"Did you anticipate the cans hanging from the bumper? We're leaving a trail that even a blind man could follow!"

"Keep an eye out for Jerry's red-and-black Buick," he told her while weaving through more cars and running a stop sign. Used to seeing such antics, people on the sidewalks and in cars were cheering, clapping, honking and pulling over for him to pass. "That Buick of his has more horsepower under that hood than a Kentucky horse track!"

"I don't see a red-and-black car, but there's a green one coming up fast behind us."

"Leslie Graham. We have to lose him!" He shot around a bread truck and then hit the brakes and turned into another alleyway.

She let out a squeal at how bumpy the ride became, even as she shouted, "Don't slow down!"

"Hold on!"

"I am!" A second later, she shouted, "Red and black! It just flew past the end of the alley!"

He slammed on the brakes again to make a fast turn into a parking lot off the alley and then sped past the parked cars. "The hotel is only two blocks. Hold on, we are going to jump the curb!"

"I told you, I am holding on!" She laughed. "It's like we are bootleggers or something! Oh, no! Look! It's the red-and-black car again! He's coming up behind us!"

"I see him in the mirror!" He wrenched the wheel, making the car turn a complete U-turn, and then laid on the horn as they drove past Jerry, who was grinning and waving a fist out his window.

"He's flipping a U-turn, too!" she shouted.

He'd seen that in the mirror and shot between two cars in the other lane to enter another parking lot. "That's the back of the hotel. Right up there. Get ready to run for the back door. They're expecting us!"

"Expecting us? You had this all planned?"

"I had to. I'm not about to let them put you on a bus to Springfield, or anywhere else, but it's not over until we reach our room."

He kept his foot on the gas all the way to the back door of the hotel, then hit the brakes and killed the engine while wrenching open his door. Jolie leaped out of her side of the car and they met near the door, which a hotel worker opened and then slammed shut behind them.

"The service elevator is right over there!" the man said.

Holding hands, they ran for the elevator. An attendant quickly closed the metal gate and pulled the cord to send the elevator upward.

Laughing, Jolie said, "We made it! We won!"

Envisioning his buddies catching the elevator in the hotel's lobby, or running up the six flights of stairs, he warned, "Don't count your chickens before they're hatched. We still have to get to our room."

"It's unlocked, Mr. Osterlund," the elevator attendant said. "Like you requested."

Keeping his eye on the little level ticking past the floor numbers, he nodded. "Thanks, I appreciate it."

"You really thought this out." A slight frown formed between her eyes. "How many brides have you been a part of stealing?"

"Several," he admitted, and their grooms were all now working in tandem for payback.

The elevator came to a stop and he tugged Jolie closer to the door. "Our room is straight ahead, but the lobby elevator is on the other end of the hallway. We have to run."

As soon as the door opened, he pulled her forward, but was stopped by her screech.

"My heel! It's caught!"

Before he had time to react, she pulled her foot out of her shoe, and took off running. "Which room is it?"

She was running, but it was off kilter because she only had one shoe. He caught her around the waist, lifted her into his arms and ran toward their room just as the lobby elevator clanged to a stop at the other end of the hallway. Several of his groomsmen shot out of the gate, gleefully shouting.

"Room 612!" he shouted. "Get ready to grab the door-knob!"

As soon as he found the door, she grabbed the knob with one hand and pushed it open. He shot inside, kicked the door shut and leaned back against it. Within a millisecond, pounding and laughter from the hallway penetrated the wood.

Jolie's laughter echoed in the room. His did, too.

"We did it!" she exclaimed. "We won!"

"I never had any doubt," he said, still breathing hard from the mad dash down the hall.

The desire that struck as he looked at the excitement on her face drowned out the noise in the hallway. One of her arms was still around his neck, and her face was so close, he'd barely have to move in order to capture her lips. He couldn't do that, though, because he'd told her that he wouldn't expect anything from her in private. He'd never explained exactly what he'd meant by that, but he'd known. At the time, he'd thought it would be simple, that he'd never have desires for her, or if and when he did, it would be sometime in the future. Not on their wedding day.

If he scared her away by going back on his word this soon, it would all have been for naught.

Gathering his senses, he started to lower her, but stopped when she let out a little yelp and grabbed the tiara on her head.

"My veil is caught in the door," she said.

Laughter, shouts and knocking still emitted through the door, and he wasn't sure what to do. Knowing his buddies, this wasn't over.

She reached up, plucked two pins from her hair and removed the tiara.

"I promise you'll get it back," he said.

She frowned.

He slowly released her, lowering her until she stood beside him. The veil was stuck in the door and he took the tiara from her hands. "If we give them this as a consolation prize, they'll go away."

She laughed. "Then by all means, give it to them."

He nodded at the table. "Get the key and lock the door as soon I shut it again."

She grabbed the key and held it ready as he kept as much weight on the door as possible while cracking it open enough to toss the tiara into the hallway. Cheers echoed into the room as he slammed the door shut and she locked it.

Holding up the key, she said, "Now we've won."

He laughed. "Yes, we have!"

She dropped the key on the table and held on to her stomach. "Oh, my, I haven't had that much fun in ages and ages."

Although he was glad that she'd enjoyed the wedding chase, a part of him was sad for her. She had friends— several of them had been a part of the wedding—but he'd witnessed how controlling her mother had been over every part of the occasion, of her life.

His thoughts turned into concern as she turned about to walk farther into the room. "You're limping. What's wrong?"

"I only have one shoe."

The grimace on her face told him it was more than

that. "I'll get your shoe back, but did you hurt your foot?"

"I just twisted my ankle when my heel caught on the edge of the elevator track. It's fine."

He stepped forward and once again swept her up into his arms.

Chapter Five

The pain that had shot up her ankle a moment ago was completely forgotten as Jolie once again wrapped an arm around his neck as he carried her toward the cream-colored sofa in the center of the room.

"How bad does it hurt?" he asked.

She heard him, but at the moment, was remembering how he'd kissed her at the altar. A large part of her was hoping he would do that again. Until her senses returned. That kiss had been for show. Pretend.

"It—it doesn't hurt at all," she said.

"I don't believe you."

He really was a handsome man, and always smelled so good, fresh and a little bit spicy. She was feeling light-headed being so close to him. "Put me down. I'm fine."

"I will, and I will look at your ankle."

When he'd picked her up in the hallway, she'd thought the racing in her heart had been because of being chased, the fun and wild, crazy drive to the hotel, but her heart was racing all over again now. No one was chasing them. His shoulders and chest were firm, muscular, and being in his arms affected more than her heart. Every part of her was tingling, like when he'd kissed her. It was all a bit overwhelming.

He set her down on the sofa, knelt before her and planted her shoeless foot on his thigh, and for the life of her, the only thing she could think of was Cinderella and Prince Charming. She hadn't read that story for years and years, and it was a foolish comparison, but it was there, front and center in her mind.

"It doesn't appear to be swollen," he said.

He was softly caressing her ankle, and that was sending heat waves up her leg, as if the entire leg was on fire. Not a painful fire, rather an unusually exciting one. If there had been any lingering pain in her ankle, it was long gone, and she attempted to pull her foot off his thigh. "I just twisted it. It's fine now."

His fingers tightened around her ankle, keeping it put. "You're sure?"

"Yes, I'm sure."

A knock sounded on the door and Jolie tried harder to pull her foot off his thigh, but he still didn't release it. Instead, with a grin, he lifted her foot and gingerly set it down on the floor before he rose and walked to the door.

"Who is it?" he asked.

"The elevator attendant, sir. I have your wife's shoe. I waited until the hallway emptied to deliver it."

As Randal picked the key off the table, Jolie leaned back and pushed out the air that had been locked in her lungs. What had she gotten herself into? She'd already determined that she thought Randal was nice, and handsome, but this—the way her body had reacted, now and at the church—was ridiculous. From today forward, she'd be living with him, and couldn't go breathless every time he was near like some senseless ninny.

With her shoe in hand, he closed the door and walked back toward her.

Sure as the sun would rise tomorrow, her heart skipped a beat, stealing her ability to breathe all over again when he knelt down in front of her.

He lifted her foot off the floor and slipped her shoe back on. "Perfect fit."

Struggling to breathe as something inside her, deep and somewhat hidden, grew soft and warm in the most unusual manner, she managed to nod.

He set her foot back down on the floor. "Are you sure it's okay?"

Her foot, yes, the rest of her, no. Knowing she couldn't say that, she forced herself to stand. "Yes. See. It doesn't hurt at all." To prove that, she took a few steps away from the sofa.

"All right." He stood. "But if it starts hurting later, let me know and we'll leave the reception."

The reception. Dear Lord, would today ever end?

And what would happen after the reception? The thought hit her like a bucket of ice water. He'd said she wouldn't be expected to do anything in private, yet he'd rented the bridal suite for them. She knew this was the bridal suite because she'd seen the sign next to the door as she'd opened it. They were married. And married people sleep together. Why did she have to keep reminding herself of that?

"I'm sorry about the wedding chase. I knew my friends would do that, and I should have warned you."

"I have seen chases following wedding ceremonies, but never participated in one before. It was fun." That was somewhat of an understatement. Her heart had been racing as fast as he'd been driving. Mostly from excitement, with a touch of fear at being stolen mingled in. "Thank you for not letting them steal me."

"I couldn't let that happen." He stood near a round table and was holding a bottle in one hand and a glass in the other, which he held out toward her.

Recognizing the bottle was champagne, she crossed the room and took the glass.

The bottle made a popping sound when he uncorked it and fizzed as he poured it first into her glass, and then into the second glass on the table. "Can you imagine what your mother would have done if they'd caught you and put you on a bus to somewhere?"

She nearly dropped the glass, and held on tighter to the short stem. Her mother would have thrown a fit, but oddly, she found she wanted him to have saved her from being stolen because he hadn't wanted that to happen for himself, not her mother. "She would have had a heart attack," she said.

He held up his glass. "To us?"

"To us." She clinked the edge of her glass against his and took a sip. It was sweet, bubbly and smooth. She took another drink.

Carrying his glass in one hand, he took her elbow with the other and guided her back toward the sofa. Once they'd both sat, he said, "Your mother wasn't the only reason I didn't want you to be stolen."

"Oh?" She took another sip, acting as if another reason had never crossed her mind.

He nodded. "I wanted today to be everything you'd ever dreamed of your wedding day being, and highly doubted being stolen was part of that dream."

She couldn't remember a single time when she'd dreamed of her wedding. Marriage hadn't been something she'd spent a lot of time thinking about. Not until her mother had brought it up barely three weeks ago. That truly hadn't been enough time to get used to anything. Let alone dream about it.

"Did you want to be stolen?" he asked.

"No." She leaned back and looked at him. "I can't remember a time when I dreamed of what I wanted my wedding to be like."

"You can't?"

"No."

"My sisters did. That's all I heard about when they got married, that everything had to be just like they'd dreamed about when they were little."

She'd met his family, both sisters and his grandfather, a few times the past couple of weeks. They were nice and friendly, happy that he was getting married. She also knew that he'd paid for Willa's and Danielle's weddings, and that he continued to financially support their families. And now hers.

"Did your mother plan everything about today?" he asked.

"Yes. I told her whatever she suggested was fine with me." That wasn't completely true, she'd wanted it to be smaller, simpler. Shifting her thoughts to him, she said, "You said that was fine with you, too. Was it? Did you dream of something different?"

He laughed. "No, men, as far as I know, don't dream about weddings."

Truly curious, she asked, "What did you dream about when you were little?"

Without so much as a pause, he replied, "Being a pirate."

"A pirate?" His answer made her laugh, and question if he was teasing. "Really?"

"Yes." He flashed her another one of his signature grins. "But a good one. I didn't dream of stealing loot, only of finding all of the loot that the bad pirates had stolen."

She giggled. "An honorable pirate, that's a new one."

"Somewhat honorable. I was going to keep any loot that I found."

She laughed aloud, and realized that was something she'd done more since meeting him than she had the past few years. She'd forgotten how good it felt. After taking a sip of her champagne, she asked, "What were you going to do with all that loot?"

He winked at her. "I don't know, I only ever dreamed of finding it."

A new train of thought formed. "And now you're dreaming of acquiring Dad's airplane company."

"I can't say I'm dreaming about that, but I'm definitely working on it."

"What if he decides not to sell it?"

"He'll sell it." Randal stood, collected the bottle of champagne from the table and carried it back to the sofa.

"How can you be so sure?" she asked as he refilled her glass.

"Because in this world, everything is for sale. Carl's a businessman, he'll recognize a good offer when it comes from the right man." He filled his glass and set the bottle on the table next to the sofa before sitting next to her again.

"A married man," she said.

"Having second thoughts?"

It was too late for that. "No, I just wish I knew what Dad expected."

"What do you mean?"

She shrugged. "He believes a man needs a woman behind him, but what does he expect that woman to do?"

Randal refused to respond to the shiver that tickled his spine. Did Carl expect something specific? That wasn't what he'd assumed. "I think his belief is based more on the man. Marrying shows an ability to commit."

She frowned, but then nodded. "Perhaps."

He'd embarked upon this union with the best of intentions, and would remain true to that, despite the desire to kiss her that was still living large inside him. The one at the altar had been a sampling of something sweet and delectable, making him want more. But he wouldn't act upon that desire, not unless she demonstrated she wanted him to act upon it. "No matter what Carl may expect, you'll never be expected to do anything that will go against your will."

She nodded, but the light that had been in her dark brown eyes earlier was now completely gone. He didn't like that. Over the past two weeks, he'd come to see how heavily her family relied on her, on this plan. He'd also seen how controlling her mother was over everything, and that made him understand why Jolie would want to know what was expected of her. He believed that she'd had to walk a delicate line her entire life, one that hadn't left her a lot of freedom.

He took ahold of her hand. "I think it's time you start dreaming about being a pirate."

An enchanting smile slowly grew on her face. "A pirate?"

"Yes, a pirate."

"Why?"

Just looking at her made his lungs lock up. He had looked forward to seeing her, to spending time with her, the past couple of weeks, and hadn't been able to get her out of his mind when they weren't together. In fact, he'd looked forward to today, and wanted this marriage to benefit her as much as it would benefit him. "So you can figure out the treasure you want to find, and then start working on finding it."

Her smile remained as she nodded. "Is that all it will take?"

Attempting to sound like a pirate, he said, "Aye, mate."

She laughed aloud. "Did you dream of talking like a pirate, too?"

"Maybe."

"As long as you don't make me walk the plank."

Clinking his glass against hers, he said, "I have to get a ship first."

He loved the sound of her laugh, the gleam it put in her eyes and the shine it put on her cheeks. If he had searched for months, years, he wouldn't have found a more beautiful bride. Right up until the moment he'd seen her walking up the aisle toward him, he'd wondered if she might change her mind.

Relieved that hadn't happened, he relaxed deeper into the sofa and rested an ankle on his opposite knee.

"I don't understand why your mother was so set against you sewing your dress. It's beautiful. You're beautiful."

She bowed her head somewhat bashfully. "Thank you." With a shrug, she added, "Mother was afraid of what people might think."

"Think? That you're gorgeous? What's wrong with that?"

She took another sip off her glass. "Homemade isn't fashionable, isn't in style."

He didn't know a lot about women's fashion, but knew a beautiful gown and woman when he saw one. Something else clicked in his mind, too. All of her dresses were fitted, as if tailored just for her. "Do you sew all your clothes?"

"No. My mother would never allow that, but the past few years, she hasn't complained much about me re-making my old clothes to be more in style with what's being sold at the stores."

He was about to tell her how talented she was when the phone rang. He sighed. "I think people are wondering where we are."

She nodded as it rang again. "It's probably my mother."

"Do you want to answer it?"

She shook her head.

He reached over to pick up the receiver, but she grasped his other arm. "Don't answer it."

Dropping his hand away from the phone, he asked, "Do you want to skip the entire reception?" He wouldn't object.

"Yes." She emptied her glass and then stood. "But we can't."

He stood and took her glass. "You're right." Lifting a brow, he asked, "How is your ankle?"

"It's fine."

"You're sure?"

She made a point of testing it so he could see. "Yes. It doesn't hurt at all."

"That's too bad."

She laughed. "It might start hurting later."

He set both of their glasses on the table, and took ahold of her elbow to escort her to the door. "Just tell me when, cutting out early sounds good to me."

She eyed him somewhat critically, then nodded. "I like the way you think."

"I think we are more alike than we'd imagined." He paused before opening the door. "I envision you and I will make a good team."

"We have to, there's no other choice."

He heard her words, but it was the unfaltering smile on her face that made his heart thud a bit faster. Opening the door, he gave her a slight bow, "After you, Mrs. Osterlund."

She lifted her chin in a haughty, yet saucy way. "Why, thank you, Mr. Osterlund."

They took the main elevator this time, which was more opulent than the service one. The attendant greeted them by congratulating them on their marriage and swiftly delivered them to the main floor.

The lobby was full of people, of which many clapped and shouted with glee as the caged door of the elevator slid open. He draped an arm around her shoulders, to protect her as he had when they'd left the church.

A man carrying a camera hurried forward, meeting them as they stepped out of the elevator. "You left the church so quickly I didn't get any still shots. Can we do them now?"

Jolie looked up at him hesitantly. "He's the photographer Mother hired."

Randal nodded, already having figured that out at the church when the flashbulbs had gone off nonstop.

"Right over here will work," the man said. "Near this wall."

They moved to the spot the man directed, and posed for several pictures before the man asked, "Where's your veil? We should have you wearing it in some of the pictures."

"We don't need the veil," Jolie said. "And I think that's enough pictures."

"Your mother—"

"Is not the bride," Randal said, cutting the man off. "My wife is, and she said that's enough pictures." As far as he was concerned, Jolie being controlled by others was over as of today.

The somewhat surprised, yet happy, expression on her face was all the encouragement he needed. "Shall we, Mrs. Osterlund?"

Laughing, she nodded. "Yes, Mr. Osterlund."

They had barely made it ten feet down the hallway when her mother entered the hall from the ballroom.

"Jolie!" Eyes glaring, her mother stomped toward them. "Where have you been? I had the desk call your room! What were you thinking? Leaving the church like that!"

If necessary, he'd apologize tomorrow, because he didn't want to disrespect his mother-in-law, especially this early on, or cause undue issues, but Jolie had already had enough chastising over the wedding. "We were having fun," he said while steering Jolie around Amelia and toward the ballroom. "And will continue to."

"Well!" Amelia huffed. "Her veil is—"

Randal saw the veil as soon as they arrived at the entrance of the ballroom, hanging from one of the chandeliers. "We see it," he said over his shoulder to Amelia. Whispering to Jolie, he asked, "Should I tell her to be glad it's only your veil?"

"Dear heavens, no," Jolie whispered.

"I'll find someone to get it down," he offered.

"No. Leave it," she answered. "Your friends must be proud that they managed to steal something."

He appreciated her sense of humor about his friends and their shenanigans. It could have been far worse. Leading her toward their table, he said, "I'm sure they are."

"I'm happy it was only my veil."

"Me, too," he replied, glancing at where a number of his friends were gathered, laughing. Perhaps, within time, he'd miss being a part of the rowdier, single crowd. Only time would tell.

Chapter Six

The moment Jolie realized which table was theirs amongst the dozens upon dozens of tables draped with white tablecloths and hosting bouquets of flowers, she questioned twisting her ankle on purpose so she and Randal could leave. Both of their families, including Dad, were sitting with them, and she worried Dad would bring up her visit.

It had been an innocent meeting, but still filled her with guilt that she hadn't yet told Randal about it. She could tell him—put it in proper context he'd surely understand—but she didn't want him to know that she'd been wondering about love. Love had nothing to do with their marriage. Neither of them wanted that. It was about dreams and making them come true. But she didn't want to talk about that, either. Her dream had been squashed too many times in the past. If it got squashed again, if she'd have to give it up, she wouldn't have anything.

"Do you want to use the powder room before sitting down?" Randal asked. "I should have asked while we were upstairs, but didn't think of it."

"Yes," she said almost before he'd finished asking. Any excuse for a bit more time was welcomed. Even more welcome was Chloe walking toward them, carrying Jolie's purse. "I'll be back in a moment."

Jolie hurried forward, took the purse her sister held out. "I'm going to powder my nose."

"I'll join you," Chloe said. "Mother's been in a snit since the church."

"I saw her in the hallway," Jolie replied as they crossed the room toward another open door.

"You did? You looked really happy when you and Randal walked into the ballroom."

She couldn't stop a smile from forming. "We were laughing about my veil."

"You should have seen Mother's face when she saw that!"

"I'm glad I didn't."

"She was about as mad as she'd been at the church when you left. That had to have been the most exciting wedding chase ever! Tires squealing, horns honking. Did they chase you all the way to the hotel?"

"Yes. It was crazy, and exciting, and fun. Very fun."

"How did your veil end up hanging from the chandelier?"

They'd reached the doorway and Jolie glanced over her shoulder. Randal was near their table, but surrounded by his friends, and laughing. "Randal's friends. My veil got caught in the door of our hotel room when he carried me in and they wouldn't stop pounding on the door until he opened it and threw the veil in the hallway as a consolation prize."

"He carried you over the threshold?" Chloe asked gleefully. "Just like a fairy tale."

As the fairy-tale image of Randal slipping her shoe back on her foot formed, Jolie pressed a hand against her breast and the skipping of her heart.

"You're blushing," Chloe said.

"Because I was embarrassed. Randal had to carry me down the hallway and into our room because I'd lost my shoe when it got caught in the elevator track. We were racing his friends to get to our room so they couldn't steal me."

"That all sounds like so much fun."

It had been fun, and so had talking with him in the room. Jolie pulled her gaze off Randal and stepped into the hallway. "It was. Thank you for remembering my purse."

"You're welcome." Chloe slipped an arm around Jolie's elbow. "I'm sure you need to touch up your lipstick after all your kissing."

Jolie's cheeks warmed all over again at the thought of the entire church watching them kiss.

"You're blushing again." Chloe was still giggling as they entered the ladies' room.

Rooms actually. The first one was the waiting area, with flocked blue-and-cream floral wallpaper and a fainting couch covered in dark blue velvet, along with a floral-printed divider screen that gave privacy for those needing to reapply makeup or check their appearance in the mirror behind the screen. The door that led into the facilities room was beside the divider.

Finding her lipstick in her purse, Jolie stepped closer to the mirror as the door to the hallway opened.

"I'm telling you, it's homemade," a woman's voice said. "Katherine DeWitt sold Jolie the material just two weeks ago."

"Her new husband must not be as wealthy as he portrays," another woman said. "Or as wealthy as Amelia is claiming."

Jolie's hand trembled as her heart sank deep into her stomach.

"The whole wedding seemed fishy to me. So quick. And now a homemade wedding gown," the first one said. "Disgraceful. That's what it is."

"Deceiving, that's what it is. But I expected no less. We all know Amelia's been putting on airs for years, pretending as if her husband left them well off when he clearly hadn't. This just proves it," the other said.

"Yes, it does. And her veil hanging from a chandelier? I've never seen anything so distasteful. It's probably homemade, too."

The door to the toilet area opened and Jolie spun around. Chloe's lips were pursed and anger shone in her eyes. Catching her sister's attention, Jolie shook her head, knowing Chloe had heard everything and was about to respond—Chloe style. Her sister often spoke without thinking.

Hoping for the impossible, Jolie pressed a finger to her lips, but Chloe's eyes had already narrowed. A sure sign she wouldn't stay quiet.

Jolie's stomach sank deeper. Her dress certainly hadn't received the attention she'd hoped for, and her sister was about to make things worse.

"Well, if it isn't Mrs. Emmerson," Chloe said, with a tone Jolie knew well. "And Mrs. Goode. Clucking as usual."

Needing to act fast, Jolie shot out from behind the screen and grabbed her sister's arm. "Shush."

The eyes of both of the matronly women were wide and their jaws were dropped, leaving their mouths open.

"My sister—" Chloe started.

"Has her groom waiting," Jolie said, tugging Chloe forward, past the women.

"Sewed her dress because she wanted to, and Randal is far wealthier than either of you!" Chloe managed to get out before Jolie pulled her out of the door and into the hallway.

Jolie closed the door firmly behind them.

"You aren't going to let them—"

"Stop, Chloe. Don't say anything. Not to anyone." She pulled her sister down the hallway toward the ballroom.

"But, Jolie—"

"Please." Jolie's stomach was curdling. Her mother had been right. She should have bought a dress.

"Those old biddies don't know a beautiful dress when they see one. Did you see what they were wearing? Their dresses had to have been hanging in their closets since before I was born."

"Talking about others doesn't hurt them, it only makes you look bad," Jolie reminded, trying to get her own anger under control. She'd never imagined that sewing her dress would have made people question Randal's worth.

"They started it, and what they said did hurt you. I could see that on your face."

"No, it didn't hurt me," Jolie lied. "So don't worry about it." They turned to step into the ballroom, and as if she didn't already feel rotten enough, her stomach hit the floor. Randal was sitting at their table, talking with Dad. "Oh, no. No," she muttered.

"What?" Chloe asked.

Searching for an excuse, Jolie nodded at a nearby waiter. "The meal is about to be served."

"This wedding sure is a wingding," Chloe said. "Everything Mother wanted."

"Yes, everything Mother wanted," Jolie replied, huffing out yet another breath and wishing it was all over.

Randal stood as she arrived at the table and held her chair as she sat between him and Dad.

She pulled up a smile as a thank-you, but noted the way his brows were knit together.

"Is your ankle hurting?" he asked next to her ear as he took his seat again.

She shook her head.

"Then what does?" he whispered. "You're as white as your dress."

As if Chloe had heard him, she asked, "Randal, don't you think Jolie did an amazing job sewing her dress?"

Jolie shot a glare at her sister.

His arm was across the back of her chair and he cupped her shoulder, rubbed it as he looked at her. "Yes, I do," he answered. "Her dress is beautiful. *She* is beautiful."

The soft glimmer in his eyes made her cheeks grow warm.

"I think so, too," Chloe said. "Others—"

Jolie flinched, and twisted to respond to her sister, but her mother was quicker.

"Chloe," her mother interrupted with warning. With a smile that looked painted on—because it was, with bright red lipstick—her mother turned her attention on her. "Everyone agrees that Jolie's dress is pretty. Some of us were just concerned that she already had enough to do planning the wedding in such a short time, but as you all see, it turned out lovely, so we aren't going to worry about it."

"I wasn't worried, Mother," Chloe said. "Just like I'm not worried about her veil hanging from a chandelier."

Jolie balled her hand in a fist to keep from pressing it to her forehead, where a headache was starting to form.

Randal leaned next to her ear. "Who—?"

She stopped him by shaking her head.

"I think that the bride is exceptionally beautiful," Dad said. "And I like where the veil is hanging." Chuckling, he added, "That was quite the chase. I'm glad they didn't catch you."

"So am I," Jolie responded. "Thank you, Dad, thank you for everything." Remembering what Randal had said earlier, she continued, "I couldn't have dreamed of a more perfect wedding."

"It was an honor, Joey-girl." He leaned over and kissed her cheek. "I wish you all the happiness in the world."

Randal watched Jolie closely throughout the meal, noting how her smile never reached her eyes. He'd always been protective of his sisters as they'd grown up, and felt the need to protect Jolie ten times over. He wanted to put himself between her and everyone else at the table. He also wanted to know who had said something about her dress. That really got his ire up.

It seemed like hours before he and Jolie were able to make their way through the ballroom, taking the time to thank people while heading toward the exit into the hallway. Color had returned to her face, and if he didn't know better, he'd believe the happiness she portrayed was real. His, too. They were both happy to be leaving the room.

This entire plan, of marrying to advance his financial goals, had made sense when he'd created it, but now he was questioning the consequences. Somehow, he'd expected his life to go on as usual, but that wasn't about to happen. Not with the way his mind was full of her.

The day had a lot to do with that. Perhaps once it was all in the past, things would return to normal.

A new normal. One that included her.

Laughter pulled his thoughts back to the present, and his heart skipped a beat as Jolie pressed a hand against his chest, right over his heart. Her eyes were gleaming as she laughed, looking up at him.

Leslie Graham was laughing, too. Randal figured his friend had said something, a good-humored joke, that he was the brunt of, no doubt. Although he had no idea what had been said, he laughed and steered Jolie around the table that Leslie was seated at along with several other friends.

"You've been subjected enough to these geniuses," he told her.

The table erupted with more laughter at his teasing insult. Face aglow, she asked, "How long have you been friends with them?"

A part of him wished he'd heard what Leslie had said, only because of how happy she looked at this moment. "Too long." He'd been friends with some of them since grammar school, and right now, wanted to leave them in the dust as much as he had during the car chase. There were about half a dozen tables between them and the door. "How fast do you think we can make it to the door?"

Her forehead creased slightly, but she was still smiling. "I don't know, how fast can you run?"

Without a word, he grasped her hand and took off. He didn't run, but they both jogged at a good pace, side-stepping around chairs in their pathway and waving at the table occupants that they sped past.

The entire room started clapping and cheering, and once they reached the door, he paused and pulled her close with the intention of turning around to give a final wave. That changed the moment he looked down at her. The jubilance on her face struck him, and whether it was because people might have expected it, or because he thought it might be his last chance to do so, he cupped her face and kissed her.

Increased cheering from the crowd gave him a reason to continue the kiss. Or perhaps that came from within, too, because of her response. Her hands were on his chest, her fingers curled into the lapels of his suit jacket, and she was on her tiptoes, stretching upward as if she too wanted to prolong the kiss.

Few things in life had been difficult for him, and stopping the kiss was definitely one of them. Pulling his lips off hers was like losing a treasure, one he'd never expected to find, but he stopped the kiss, and winked at her before turning to wave at the crowd.

Jubilance followed in their wake, spilling into the hallway as they hurried to the elevator, past more people clapping and shouting congratulations.

Once in the elevator, their eyes met, and he joined her in a laugh that echoed in the shaft as the attendant closed the door and pulled the cord to take them upward.

Moments later, with the weight of the day behind him, Randal twisted his shoulders as he and Jolie entered their room. His back had been itching for hours, but with everything else on his mind, he'd ignored it. That was no longer possible, and as soon as the door was closed, he leaned against the corner of the door-jamb to scratch his back.

"What's wrong?"

"It must be the starch in my shirt. My back has been itching for hours."

"Take off your jacket and I'll scratch it for you."

Grateful for the assistance, he stepped away from the wall and shrugged out of his tux jacket.

"And your vest," she said.

He removed the vest, tossed it on the chair along with his tailed coat. The touch of her nails against the burning itch was like heaven, making him involuntarily arch into her scratching.

"I think I see the problem," she said.

Her hand was rubbing up and down his back, which felt nearly as wonderful as her scratching. Twisting his neck to look at her, he frowned. "Problem?"

Leaning around his shoulder, she nodded. "Yes. Problem. You have rice stuck between your dress shirt and undershirt."

He let out a growl and started unbuttoning his shirt.

"Careful." She grasped both of his shoulders. "Don't just pull it off, we'll have rice flying everywhere."

"What do you suggest I do?"

"Undo your cuff links and slowly remove your shirt. I'll try to keep as much as I can from falling on the floor."

Removing his cuff links, he asked, "There's that much?"

She rubbed his back again. "From what I can feel, there's enough to make rice pudding."

He could feel the grains of rice sliding down his back as her touch loosened it. "No wonder I've been itching for hours."

Grasping his shirt by the shoulders, she slowly lifted the material and pulled it back so he could slide his arms out. The action sent grains of rice into the waistband of his pants.

"Now it's running down my legs, into my shoes."

She giggled. "I'm trying to catch as much as I can in your shirt."

He pulled the tail of his shirt out of his waistband. "It sounds like you're enjoying this."

Her short silence as she completely removed his shirt was followed by soft laughter. "I can't believe you spent the entire evening with this much rice in your shirt."

He turned, stared at the amount of rice she held cupped inside his shirt. "I can't believe I didn't feel all that."

She set the shirt on the table. "Turn around, let me see if we got it all."

The touch of her hand on his back ignited the itching of his skin. Somehow sensing that, she gave his back a good overall scratching. "Thanks, that feels so much better."

Giving his back a final pat, she peeked around his shoulder. "I'm glad I could help."

"How about you? Do you have rice stuck inside your dress?"

"No. Between you and my veil, I barely got hit with any." Grinning, she walked farther into the room. "Thank you for that."

"You're very welcome." He crossed the room and sat

down on the sofa, kicked off his shoes and put his feet up on the coffee table.

She sat in the adjacent chair and did the same.

Grinning at her actions, he asked, "Tired?"

"More like worn out." She sighed. "It's been a crazy couple of weeks."

"It has." He couldn't take his eyes off her, and knew why. The kiss they'd shared at the altar was still alive and well inside him, and repeating it in the ballroom doorway a few moments ago had only reinforced how perfectly her lips fit against his. He had to be careful of his thoughts, and actions. Although he was comfortable around her, things were delicate between them. They barely knew each other.

Her hands were clasped together across her stomach, and her thumbs were slowly circling each other. Nerves? Probably.

He threaded his fingers and put them behind his head, leaning deeper into the sofa. "I think we should take it slow from here. Just let things play out as they may."

"What things?"

"Our marriage." Her frown had him explaining further. "As in us truly becoming man and wife."

Her gaze went past him, to the door that led to the bedroom. "So we won't…"

"Not tonight. That will happen when we are both ready." He could be ready in less than a heartbeat, but had come into this with his eyes open. However, the way the brows above her eyes knit together, he wondered if he'd spoken too soon. If he should have let the marriage become real tonight.

She glanced around the room, twiddled her thumbs

some more. "Your friend, Jerry, the one you said his wife was put on the bus?"

He nodded.

"Couldn't his wife attend the wedding?"

"They're divorced." He could elaborate, tell her how Jerry's wife found another man within months of their marriage, but he held his tongue.

"Oh. That's too bad."

He held his opinion. Jerry was doing better now, but would never be the same man. Learning his wife had been unfaithful and was carrying another man's child had devastated his friend. Randal had never seen a good man go bad so fast. All because of love.

"So what do we do now?" she asked. "It's too early to go to sleep."

He left the couch, walked to his suit coat and dug in the pocket. Holding up a deck of cards, he asked, "Cards?"

Her frown increased. "Do you always carry a deck of cards in your pocket?"

"No. Leslie gave them to me earlier today." His body jolted slightly, one specific part at the reason his buddy had given him the cards. The gift had been a joke, that all of his friends had laughed about, but it was early, and they did need some way to pass the time.

"Why?"

"To play poker."

"Poker?"

Strip poker had been the reason Leslie had given him the deck. "Do you know how to play poker?"

"Yes, my father taught me, but I don't have any cash."

He had a few bills in his billfold, but not enough different denominations to make the game worth playing.

Glancing at his shirt, he scooped out a handful of rice and walked back to the sofa. "We'll play for rice."

"Rice?"

Slowly releasing his pinky finger, he let a pile of rice funnel onto the table in front of her, and then a second pile on his side of the table. "Yes. We might as well put it to good use."

Eyes sparkling, she scooted off her chair and sat down on the floor near the table. Rubbing her palms together, she said, "All right. We'll split for the first deal."

Chapter Seven

Jolie picked the small, tightly corked bottle off the corner of the desk. The contents made her grin. No one would ever believe that she'd spent her wedding night playing poker, with grains of rice, and had won. Won Randal's entire pile. They'd played until late into the night, and the following morning, she'd collected her winnings in a handkerchief, telling him that had been the most she'd ever won in a game of poker.

Randal had found her the bottle that evening after they'd arrived home and every day since, the sight of it made her smile.

She stood and, holding the small bottle, wandered around the large room that she shared with Randal. The area with the large four-poster bed and matching dressers comprised of the size of her old bedroom, and that was a mere corner of this room. There was a large sitting area, complete with two armchairs and a long sofa, upholstered in a rich brown brocade that matched the draperies hanging on the long windows, and the bed covering. The walls were painted a pale green, except for the one that housed a large bookcase that went from floor to ceiling.

In another corner was the desk she'd been using all week, writing out thank-you cards for the many wedding gifts they'd received. Near it sat her sewing machine, having been delivered from her mother's house. She hadn't lifted the top, opened the machine, since it had arrived. There was no reason. Even the newspaper had specifically pointed out that *"the bride hand made her dress"* in their wedding announcement on the social page.

Hand made.

Not designed.

Not created.

Hand made.

That must be the polite way to say homemade. When would people understand that every woman's body was different? For a dress to fit properly, it had to suit a woman's unique figure. So did the undergarments. For some dresses, the undergarments were even more important.

She pushed the air out of her lungs and leaned against the back of the sofa. No one, it appeared, understood that.

At home there had always been something to do. A floor that had needed to be scrubbed, clothes to wash, meals to cook, but here, at Randal's house, the cook, maid and butler took care of everything. She did clean this room, because she was perfectly capable, but also because she didn't want anyone to discover that Randal slept on the sofa every night.

It was his house, his bed. If anyone should be sleeping on the sofa, it should be her. He wouldn't hear of that, though, even though she suggested it each night.

As she glanced down at the bottle in her hand, her

heart thudded. She knew why, and it wasn't only because of the poker game. The grains of rice reminded her of the two times Randal had kissed her.

With little else to do, she'd thought about those kisses a lot the past few days. People don't have to love each other to kiss. She'd kissed boys before, and certainly hadn't loved them.

People don't need to love each other to sleep in the same bed, either. She'd never done that, but knew it happened all the time.

She liked Randal, and wouldn't mind kissing him again. What she would never do was like him so much that she fell in love with him, or become jealous of everyone he spoke to, or live her life for him alone.

She'd spoken to Chloe and Silas, and her mother, and so far, they were doing fine without her.

She was the one not doing so fine.

Her plan to become a clothing designer had failed. With that, and with no one needing her, she had no idea what she would do now that she'd finished the last of the thank-you notes. All that was left was to carry the stack downstairs. The butler, Peter, would see that they were mailed.

Huffing out a breath, she pushed off the sofa to cross the room back to the desk. She shouldn't be so despondent. Her family's bills had all been paid, there were groceries in the cupboards, fuel in the car and money to buy more.

She'd just sat down at the desk when the bedroom door opened.

"Are you still writing thank-you notes?"

She stood, surprised to see Randal. "What are you doing home? It's not even noon yet." There were times, like right now, when her fingers would tingle, remembering the feel of his back. The hard muscles. The ripples of his rib cage. The firmness of his waist.

He entered the room and closed the door. "I took the rest of the day off."

"Why? Is something wrong?"

"No. I thought I'd take you out for lunch, and then we'd go for a drive or something." Stopping next to her, he continued, "Unless you are too busy with the thank-you notes."

"No. I finished the last few. They just need to be mailed."

His hand touched her elbow, then ran down her arm until his fingers wrapped around hers. The action stole her ability to breathe for a moment, and when her lungs did release the air locked inside them, a long sigh escaped.

He reached around her and picked up the stack of envelopes with his free hand. "We'll mail them on our way to the restaurant."

She gave her head a clearing shake because it was thinking about kissing him. "I need to get my purse."

His thumb ran over the inside of her wrist. "You won't need it for anything."

"How do you know that?"

He lifted an eyebrow. "Because you'll have me."

She bit back a smile. "And that's all I'll need?"

"Yes."

He could make her smile with nothing more than a look. "And if I need a comb or lipstick?"

"Your hair looks perfect." His gaze slowly moved from her hair to her mouth. "So do your lips."

Dear Lord, but the desire that struck right then weakened her knees. Why was she wishing that he would kiss her? Randal had married her in order to buy Dad's company, and she'd married him in order to have her family's bills paid.

"What are you thinking so hard about?" he asked.

She forced her thinking to clear. "Nothing. Just wondering if I'll need my purse or not."

"Not." He tugged her toward the door.

By the time they walked out the front of the house, his excitement had become so evident, it was seeping into her. "Where are we going?"

"I told you, out to lunch and then for a drive."

"I know what you told me, but something tells me you have more in mind."

He opened her car door and, once she was sitting on the seat, handed her the envelopes. "We'll mail these first."

He jogged around the front of the car, climbed in, and they were off, driving toward downtown. They made a quick stop at the post office, and then he parked near a cute little café where they sat outside, in the shade of an awning over the tables lining the sidewalk. She wondered if this had been his secret, because she sensed he had one.

"This is lovely," she said, after they'd placed their lunch order, referring to the flower boxes on the widows of the café as well as the vases of flowers on the table.

"I thought you might enjoy getting out," he said.

"I do, thank you." She hadn't been out of the house since their wedding. The next day, the house had been full for the gift-opening party and starting Monday morning, he'd left for work early each morning. Upon returning home, they'd spent the evenings downstairs, with his grandfather listening to radio programs or hearing Ness share many of his stories of years gone by. It was enjoyable learning more about Randal's family.

"I couldn't get away for a honeymoon, still can't, not until I know when Carl will put his company up for sale."

"I never expected a honeymoon."

"I know you didn't." He put his elbows on the table and leaned toward her. "You've been very unselfish about our arrangement from the beginning. The only thing you asked for was to sew your dress."

The newspaper announcement flashed across her mind and she had to look away. "I shouldn't have done that. I'm sorry."

"Sorry? Your dress was lovely and admired by many."

That article had been festering inside her since she'd read it, and the frustration of that was screaming to get out. "No, it wasn't admired. It was labeled homemade, and that made people question..." She swallowed the lump in her throat.

"Question what?"

Maybe that's what this was all about, her dream and how it had not only crumbled, it had affected him. "Your wealth," she admitted. "I never thought of the consequences of that."

"The consequences of my wealth?"

The weariness inside her grew. "Not necessarily the consequences of your wealth, but the consequences of them not believing you *are* wealthy."

"Them?" He shook his head and leaned back. "Did I miss a portion of our conversation? Because I don't understand how your dress could make people question my wealth."

She folded her arms across her midsection and leaned closer to make sure no one walking past or sitting near could hear their conversation. "The nation is in the middle of a depression, and anything homemade suggests that the depression is affecting your family, too."

"The depression is affecting every family in one way or another."

"Yes, but by sewing my dress, I gave people cause to believe that you may not be as wealthy as they'd once thought."

His frown increased, but he didn't comment as the waitress brought them the food they'd ordered and set it on the table. After the waitress had walked away, Randal said, "Did you enjoy sewing your dress?"

She unfolded her napkin and laid it on her lap. "Yes. I've always enjoyed designing clothes."

He lifted his knife and fork. "Good. Then that's all I care about."

"You have to care what people are thinking. It was printed in the newspaper."

His fork paused near his mouth. "What was printed in the newspaper?"

"That my dress was homemade."

He chewed and swallowed before gesturing at her plate with his fork. "Aren't you going to at least taste your food?"

She scooted a green bean around on her plate with her fork. "You don't seem to understand the implications—"

"Yes, I am understanding," he interrupted. "And I'm annoyed at what the newspaper printed, because I can see that it upset you. I also understand that we haven't had the chance to learn that much about each other, so

I should let you know that I'm rarely interested in what the newspaper says, or what other people think. Other than those I care about."

Although she attempted not to, Jolie looked up from her plate.

He'd set his fork down and was looking directly at her. "I care about what you think, and I hope you're interested in what I think."

She nodded.

"Good, because I think you shouldn't put much stock into what the newspaper or anyone else has to say. If you want to sew, to design clothes, then that is what you should do. Just like you did with your wedding dress. Your mother wasn't pleased about that, but you didn't let that stop you."

She shook her head. "It's not that easy."

"Why isn't it?"

Flustered that he truly wasn't understanding, she said, "Because what I do affects you, now that we are married."

"I'm aware of that." He reached across the table and ran a finger over the back of her hand. "And as your husband, I will support you in whatever you want to do." He grinned. "As long as it's legal."

He was still rubbing the back of her hand with the tip of one finger and the warmth spreading up her arm was affecting her ability to think. "Legal?"

A smile spread across his face as he removed his hand and picked up his silverware again. "Yes. I'm assuming there is nothing illegal about creating clothing."

"Well, no."

"Then I encourage you to continue doing so." He

lifted his fork to his mouth. "And I encourage you to eat your lunch, so we can go on our drive."

"You really don't care what other people think?"

"No."

"Yet, that is why you married me, because Dad thinks whoever buys his company needs a wife."

Once again, he waved his fork. "That is different. I'm simply abiding by his rules."

She considered that, but for only a moment because it didn't make sense. "I think you are talking out of both sides of your mouth."

"Perhaps, or maybe in this instance, I found a degree of agreement with his logic."

He sounded serious, but his eyes held too much of a twinkle to make her believe he truly was serious. "Logic?"

"Yes, logic."

That merely led her to have more questions, but his plate was almost empty, so she spent the next few minutes eating. During that time, her questions compounded, and she concluded that she didn't know much about the man she'd married at all. She also concluded that she liked him. Appreciated his honesty, even if she didn't understand his logic.

Upon leaving the café, he drove north out of downtown and then westward. Her mind was still in a quandary. She wasn't upset that she'd married him, wasn't even all that upset over the newspaper article or what others believed. Nor was she sure what any of that meant. Was there still a chance her dream could come true? She wasn't sure of that, either, but knew if there was a chance, she had to take it, but only if it wouldn't cause trouble for him. He might not put much stock into what the newspapers or others say, but that wouldn't stop others from putting stock in it.

When he pulled off the highway, onto a gravel road, she said, "This is the road to the airport."

"It is. I thought we'd drive out here, take a look at a few planes as one day, hopefully soon, we might own an airplane company."

He was driving with one hand. The elbow of his other arm was resting on the base of the rolled-down window and his fingers were curled around the top of the car. "We?" she asked, trying to decipher if she'd heard correctly.

"Yes, we. We're in this together. It'll be your company as much as mine."

She let that sink in for a moment. "If—if I wanted to be involved in the business, you wouldn't mind?"

"Why would I mind?"

"Some people don't think women should work, shouldn't have an interest outside of the house, their family."

"I'm not saying you have to."

"And I'm not saying that I want to, or don't want to," she said, confusing herself, but not wanting him to think she might not be interested.

"There's plenty of time for you to decide. Carl hasn't put it up for sale yet."

"But you're sure he will."

"Yes."

She already knew that. He wouldn't have married her if he wasn't sure. Drawing in a deep breath, she turned and looked out the window. There was truly something wrong with her. Nothing was making sense. She wanted to sew, and couldn't decipher why she also had a desire to help him with his airplane business. She couldn't do both…could she?

Randal saw the way she stared out the passenger window out of the corner of his eye and wondered what about her had gotten under his skin. And not in a way he was used to. He couldn't seem to get her out of his mind.

He wasn't impressed with the newspaper calling her dress homemade, that was for damn sure, and now he knew why she'd seemed so solemn all week.

Though she'd greeted him each evening with a smile, and had been content to sit downstairs, listening to a radio show or Grandpa telling one of his stories that everyone, less Jolie, had heard a million times over, when they'd go upstairs afterward she turned somber, quiet.

That's why he'd set this up today. Hoping if she saw the airplanes, rode in one, that she might understand why he was so interested in Carl's company. He'd known airplanes would be the wave of the future the first time he'd flown in one several years ago, and had started to invest in them. Now he was ready to have a company that others could invest in, and hoped that she'd see it that way, too, because it was a sure bet to be successful.

He pulled the car up near the hangar. A small silver plane with a red tail and wings was parked outside the big doors.

"Is that one of the planes that Dad's business builds?"

"No, though it is similar in size. Carl's business builds mail-carrying planes, but when we buy it, I plan on expanding beyond that, focus on passenger planes.

Right now, there are planes that carry up to twenty people. Someday, they'll carry a hundred."

"One hundred?" she asked, yet was smiling. "That would have to be as large as a bus."

"An airbus. I like the sound of that." He opened his door. "Ready to take a closer look at it?"

"I knew you had more in mind than just a drive," she said as he took her hand to help her out of the car.

"How did you know that?"

"The sparkle in your eyes."

His gaze lingered on her, because he couldn't look away. Nor did he want to. Her dark brown eyes were mesmerizing. They were twinkling like stars in the dark of night. Sharing a room with her each night had become an agony he hadn't expected. He had to keep reminding himself that they were taking it slow, getting to know each other, but he was ready for more. A man has needs and he'd planned on their marriage providing that. Love wasn't needed for that to happen. Love wasn't needed for anything other than heartache and misery. He wouldn't open himself to that.

"Randal!" Roger Wayne shouted from near the hangar. "I have her gassed up and ready to fly!"

"Are we going to watch it fly?" Jolie asked.

Randal took ahold of her hand and led her toward the plane. "No, we aren't going to watch, we are going for a ride."

She stopped walking and grasped his arm with her free hand. "In the airplane?"

"Yes, in the airplane."

Chapter Eight

Half an hour later, they were soaring over the countryside, but Randal was hardly aware of specific sights Roger and his co-pilot, Allen, pointed out to Jolie. He and she sat in the two back seats, and though their chairs weren't touching, she hadn't released his hand. Not because she was scared, but because she was excited, squeezing his hand every time there was something she wanted him to see out one of the windows.

The plane was noisy, stuffy, and smelled of hot oil, fuel and metal, but none of that deterred her enjoyment. He'd never have believed she could look more beautiful, but happiness did that to her. The way she went from looking out her window, to leaning across him to look out his, and peering between the front seats to look out the windshield, was captivating.

Roger had warned her about turbulence and airsickness, but she didn't appear to be bothered by either. Shortly after takeoff, she'd squealed softly at some of the rougher jolts the plane had made, but quickly had laughed at herself and assured him she was fine, and now acted as if she was a seasoned flyer.

It was hard to hear, so they had to yell almost directly into each other's ears, which didn't seem to faze her, either. All in all, the want to kiss her again was back with a vengeance. He'd dated, kissed women often, but had never once wanted to kiss anyone the way he did her. He was trying hard to not put much significance on it, but that didn't lessen the want.

She was far more attractive than any woman he'd known. He'd realized that from the start. She also fit into his plan better than anyone else ever would have. Neither of those facts should instill the kinds of desire that smoldered and leaped to flames out of the blue at numerous times. Such as now, and in the mornings when he'd catch her walking out of the bathroom, all fresh and clean and wearing one of her fitted dresses. And at night, when he'd see her climb into bed, wearing a modest, loose-fitting nightgown that somehow, on her, looked completely tantalizing.

He had read the article about their wedding in the society page of the newspaper, but hadn't picked up on the line that stated her dress had been homemade. The fact that she had, and had been disturbed over it, bothered him. Her dress had been beautiful, and she was talented. Anyone who noticed the way her clothes fit would have to admit that, if they were being honest. But some people were never honest. They'd rather be snobbish and rude, putting the blame on social standards or some other excuse, because they were jealous.

Her handmade dress showed talent, not poverty. If she wanted to design and sew her own clothes, then that is what she should do. He'd see to it.

In fact, her reaction to that newspaper article wasn't all that different to what he'd been dealing with his entire life.

The mention of her dress being homemade had instilled doubt in her. Something his family had done to him since day one. Both his father and his grandfather had created a competition within their family that had pitted them against each other, and him against both of them. The wealth his grandfather had amassed had become something that his father had been expected to double, and then it was down to him to double what his father had amassed.

That competition had been instilled in other things, too. If another boy had mowed one yard, he'd been expected to mow two. If they'd split one cord of wood, he'd had to split two, and so on and so forth. He'd worked hard to meet every expectation put upon him and had learned early on that there were no excuses. Rain shouldn't stop him from mowing lawns and blizzards shouldn't stop him from splitting wood.

There had never been encouragement that he could do whatever the challenge had been. Only doubt, because in the end, there was no way he could be better than his father, than his grandfather.

The stock market crash hadn't changed the expectations on him. Hadn't wiped out the tally sheet that had been held over his head for years.

Jolie squeezed his hand, and understanding the signal, he leaned closer so she could shout in his ear. "Look, there's another airplane!"

He leaned across her to look out the window beside her. "It's a passenger plane!"

"Look at how big it is! It looks too big to fly!"

He tried to focus on the plane, but he could feel her breath on his cheek as she spoke into his ear. Unable not to, he turned, faced her and placed a soft, quick kiss on the tip of her nose. "I'm glad you are enjoying this!"

"I didn't know what to expect in the beginning, but this is amazing! So amazing!" She looked at him for a long moment, smiling, eyes sparkling, and then leaned forward and kissed his cheek. "Thank you."

Holding back his desire to kiss her lips, deeply kiss her, nearly killed him. "You're welcome."

Her gaze went back to the window, and he leaned back into his seat, knowing what he was watching— her excitement—was more amazing, more captivating, than what she was seeing out the window.

The flight lasted for over an hour, and she was still excited, still enchanting, when the plane touched down and rolled to a stop. Upon climbing out the door, Randal turned around and grasped her waist. She laid her hands on his shoulders for him to lift her down. He lifted her out of the plane, but didn't set her down until he'd carried her out from beneath the long wing of the aircraft.

There he lowered her, and to his surprise, as her toes touched the ground, she didn't release him, but slid her arms around his neck and pressed herself against him in a tight hug. "That was wonderful. So wonderful!"

He folded his arms around her, keeping her against him. He'd felt a unique bond with her from the beginning, but at this moment it was so strong, so real, he felt it deeper, as if his soul felt it, needed it.

That was impossible and he released his hold.

She lifted her head, but rather than release him, she kissed him.

Soft and warm, her lips met his, tentatively at first. The idea of not returning her kiss crossed his mind, but only for a second. She knew where things stood between them, and wasn't expecting love any more than he was willing to give it.

Within a flash, her lips became as demanding as his, unabashed and holding nothing back. He didn't, either, thrilled to know he had chosen the ideal wife.

Jolie's heart was still pounding when they drove away from the airport. The airplane ride had been beyond exciting, beyond anything she'd ever imagined, but her heart was pounding because of what she'd done. She'd kissed him. The impulse had struck so fast and hard she hadn't been able to stop it. The moment their lips had touched, she had realized what she'd been doing, but then he'd responded and that had ignited some kind of flame inside her that just sort of took over.

There had to be a reason for that. Perhaps because inside, a part of her realized that she was no longer alone.

It could also have been because they were here, at the airport, a place her father had brought her to not long before he'd died.

He had been the backbone of their family, and that role had fallen to her upon his death. A role she hadn't wanted and one that had left her feeling completely alone in so many ways. While in Randal's arms, she'd realized that was no longer true. She and Randal were in this together. Their wedding hadn't brought them together because of love, but they were married and she admired him, liked him, and that was enough. There were probably many marriages that had less than that.

If the last few years had taught her anything, it was to appreciate what you did have, every day.

She appreciated him, and had more to be thankful for than she'd had in a long time. He'd said she could work if she wanted to, and she did want that.

"Why didn't we see any larger, passenger airplanes at the airport?" she asked as he turned onto the highway.

"Because that was just a small privately owned airfield where Roger and Allen store their plane," he said.

Before they'd boarded the plane, he'd explained to her that Roger and Allen worked for the utility companies and used their plane to plot out new electrical and telephone line routes. At that point she hadn't known what to expect, but hadn't been afraid because he'd been beside her and had held her hand the entire time.

"The passenger planes fly out of the main airport," he said. "It's owned by David Albright and his brother. They also own the A and R Railroad, but David saw that airplanes were the wave of the future a few years ago."

"Like you," she said.

"Yes, I've been intrigued with planes for years, but after Lindbergh made his transatlantic flight, I knew they were going to be the next era of transportation. The airmail planes that Carl's company makes fly out of the main airport, too," he said.

"Where is that airport?"

"Southeast of downtown. Haven't you seen it?"

"No. I've seen the planes overhead, and knew about the small airport we were just at because my father used to drive out here for exhibition shows. I assumed it was the only airport around here."

"There are actually several small ones. Carl's company has an airstrip, but it's only for testing their planes," he replied. "You haven't seen the main one? Or Carl's company?"

"No, Dad bought it shortly before my father died." Guilt struck again, at still not telling him about her visit to Dad. She needed to, but still didn't want him to know what she and Dad had talked about. Love. She didn't want him to think that was what she expected from their marriage. "I've only seen Dad a couple of times since my father's funeral."

He took ahold of her hand, held it firmly. "Losing a parent is hard, painful. That pain never really goes away, but it does get easier to carry over time."

She knew he was talking from experience, and wanted to offer him some of the support he'd been showing her. She laid her hand over the top of his. "Yes, it does."

"Would you like to see the main airport and Carl's company?"

"Yes, if you don't mind, I would."

They discussed airplanes while driving. He told her that there were several books and magazines in the bookcase in the bedroom that she could read to learn more. Finding enough money to keep her mother's household going the past few years had been all she'd been able to focus on, and it felt good to know that she now had more time to read, to learn about other things.

The Albright airport had several large passenger planes, some solid gray with the numbers on their tails painted in black, and others brightly painted, including their aviation numbers. Randal explained how those numbers identified and also confirmed the registration of the airplanes like a car license plate. She liked how he would present things in a way that she could easily understand.

All the planes had long rows of windows for the passengers to look out once they'd boarded the planes via the tall ladder that was rolled up next to the door.

"Have you ridden in one of those?" she asked as they watched one of the planes take off.

"Yes." They were leaning against the front of his car, side by side, and he leaned over, bumped her shoulder with his. "We'll take a trip so you can fly in one of them."

"A trip to where?"

"Wherever you want."

His arms were folded across his chest as he stared ahead, at the airplane that was flying higher and higher. His profile made her smile. She could see how much the planes meant to him, feel how badly he dreamed of owning them. Folding her arms, she bumped him in the arm like he had her. "Where would you like to fly to?"

"South Dakota."

"Why?"

"To see the building of Mount Rushmore. They've been working on it for over five years, and although I've seen pictures, I'd like to see it in person."

She'd read about that, too, how the carving of George Washington was expected to be completed by next year. "That would be very interesting to see. I read recently that President Roosevelt had signed an executive order to place Mount Rushmore under the jurisdiction of the National Parks Service."

He glanced at her. "I read that, too, and that the pictures don't do it justice."

"They say it's truly massive. I'd like to see it, too."

"All right then, that's what we'll do. Fly to South Dakota and see Mount Rushmore."

The idea was exciting, but having been broke, searching for pennies to buy eggs and bread for so many years, she had to ask, "Is it expensive to fly?"

"Some think it is, but we can afford it."

"I wasn't implying that you couldn't, I just…" She let

her voice trail off, not sure how to explain the knot that formed in her stomach when she thought about money, about spending it.

He touched her shoulder. "Those worries are over for you."

Involuntarily, she leaned toward him, as if her body ached for a form of support because her mind knew it wasn't that easy. After not having money for so long, no longer worrying about it couldn't happen overnight. Even while writing out the thank-you cards, she had calculated the cost of each card, each stamp. Every time she sat down at the table to eat at his house, she couldn't stop from adding up how much had to have been spent on the food. That had all become a part of her, and she wasn't sure she wanted it to go away because it made a person think before they spent.

Randal's arm slid around her shoulders. "Shall we drive past Carl's company now?"

"Yes."

He kept his arm around her as they walked to the passenger door, and she missed the weight and the comfort when he removed it for her to climb in the car.

The airport was on the outskirts of town, and they headed farther into the countryside. As they drove, he told her more about Dad's business, how he made the mail-carrying planes because it was a government contract, and how that was enough to make the company fruitful, but how that was also holding him back from making it as successful as it could be because the contract kept them compliant, and not branching out into other models and ventures.

His motivation and determination had her commenting, "You must have been encouraged to never give up as a child."

"I can't say *encouraged* is the right word," he replied.

His tone was light, but it was laced with something heavier. "Why?"

"I was told not to fail. I was given goals that I had to meet, then surpass, double, triple. There was no other option."

"What sort of goals?"

"I started mowing yards for the neighbors when I was seven. By the time I was ten, I was mowing ten yards a day, but that still wasn't enough. I was expected to find more customers. I started on the first yard at six in the morning and didn't get home until dark, but that was an excuse."

"An excuse? You were expected to mow yards in the dark?"

"That was one option, but I found another option."

"What?"

He stopped at a stop sign and waited for a car to pass before crossing the road. "Hire someone to help me."

She grinned because she would not have thought of that. "That certainly was another option."

"When I turned fifteen I sold my lawn mowing business to a competing company, and used a portion of the money to buy my first trades."

"And saved the rest?"

"No, I bought my first car. Brand-new."

"You had to have been proud of that. And your father had to have been proud, too."

"I was, but my father was furious."

The idea of anyone being upset at him after he'd worked so hard irritated her, and filled her with sympathy for him. Reaching over, she laid a hand on his arm. "Why?"

"Because I'd failed."

"Failed? How?"

"I hadn't diversified enough." He glanced at her. "I'd put my eggs in one basket, instead of five, or ten. It was a lesson learned, and one I've remembered."

"That's why the stock market crash didn't hurt you as badly as it did others, because you were more diversified in your investments?"

"Yes, it worked in my favor."

"Is that why you want to buy Dad's company? To be even more diverse?"

"Yes, and no. I'm willing to invest far more in buying the company than I have in any other investment. It's a chance I'm willing to take because I've researched it thoroughly. I know what I'm getting into. The past few months I've been working on balancing incoming funds with the outgoing funds so that we'll be fine until the investment starts to pay off."

She knew all about incoming and outgoing funds, and guilt struck hard. "I'm sorry. I know my family—"

"It's all part of the investment," he said. "And doesn't affect the bottom line any more than my family does."

She flinched slightly at being referred to as an investment. She also wondered about his family. Danielle and James lived in the same house as them. Willa and Don didn't, but visited regularly. Don worked at his father's drugstore as a pharmacist and James was a photographer. Did he consider them all investments?

"This is Carl's company," Randal said, gesturing toward an area that had several large buildings and a few airplanes in a field behind the buildings.

The yellow-and-red planes were much smaller than the passenger ones. "Those planes do look like the one we flew in."

"On the outside. Inside there's only room for one pilot, the rest is cargo space." He continued to explain more about the planes and the company as they drove around the buildings, past the planes, and then back out to the road.

She found it all interesting, but had so many other things on her mind, she was having to compartmentalize things: the number of people he was financially supporting, within her family and his, the airplanes and Dad's business, and how badly he wanted his dream to come true.

"I have one more place I'd like to stop," he said as they entered the city again. "If that's all right with you?"

"Of course."

The smile on his face was like earlier today, at the house. A secretive one. Like a pirate would have. She glanced out the side window and bit her lips as her smile formed.

"What are you smiling about?"

"You," she admitted, looking at him. "And your pirate smile."

"Pirate smile? What's a pirate smile?"

She twisted in her seat so her back was toward her door and it was easier to look at him. "The one on your face. It was there earlier, too, when we left the house."

He glanced her way. "Was it?"

She slapped his arm playfully. "Yes, and you know it. It's a smile that says you have a secret. So what is it this time?"

"You'll see."

Chapter Nine

It had been a long time since he'd enjoyed a day this much, and Randal wasn't ready for it to end. This had been the most significant amount of time they'd spent together since their wedding day, and it had given him a deeper understanding of Jolie. He sensed he'd barely scratched the surface, but liked what he had discovered and had no doubt the trend of that would continue.

"Here we are," he said pulling up next to the curb.

She glanced out the window, at the department store, and then back to him. "What do we need here?"

He flashed her a grin and pulled open his door.

A quizzical frown still tugged on her brows when he opened her door and took her hand to assist her out of the car and into the store.

He didn't know much about sewing, but had seen bolts of cloth and other sewing notions near the back of the store, and that's the direction they walked.

She quickly caught on, and as her steps slowed she shook her head. "Randal—"

He pressed a finger to her lips. "If my wife wants to design clothing, then that's what she's going to do."

"But—"

He pressed the finger more firmly against her lips. "I want you to pick out whatever you need. However much you need."

Shaking her head again, she closed her eyes.

Sliding both hands over her shoulders and down her arms, he wrapped his fingers around her wrists. "I like the clothes you design." He held her arms out at her sides. "I like how they fit you." She was wearing the same blue-and-white polka-dot dress as their first date. Then, he'd noticed the fitted waist, but now, like her wedding dress, it was the way it fit around her breasts that really caught his attention. It wasn't tight or revealing, just fit her in a way that emphasized the perfection of her figure.

He brought his eyes back up to her face, and the redness of her cheeks said she'd known exactly where his gaze had been moments ago.

"May I help you?"

Keeping his eyes on Jolie, he told the clerk, "Yes, my wife needs material for several new outfits. She designs and sews clothes, and I admire that very much."

Jolie shook her head again, but this time, she was biting back a smile.

He liked that, but liked how dark her eyes had grown even more. "It's just one of the many things I admire about her," he said.

The clerk made a mewing sound along with a long sigh.

Jolie's smile broke free as she whispered under her breath, "Stop it. You're going to make her swoon."

"I don't see why. Everything I've said is the truth." It was either kiss her, or release her, so he released one of her wrists and waved a hand at the bolts of cloth lining the wall. "I'll help you pick out some material."

"Do you know anything about material?" she asked.

"No, but I like how the blue of your dress makes your eyes that much darker."

The clerk, a short woman with curly blond hair and a double chin, met them at the fabric wall. "We have some lovely blue eyelet embroidered batiste that just arrived the other day."

He had no idea what eyelet embroidered batiste was, and looked at Jolie for help. She shook her head, but then shrugged and nodded.

"Let's take a look at that," he told the clerk.

"Randal," she whispered. "This isn't necessary."

"Yes, it is." He winked at her. "I want to witness the start-to-finish process."

Her cheeks pinkened again, and she rolled her eyes, but stepped forward to examine the bolt of material the clerk held.

It was pretty, and he encouraged Jolie to tell the woman how many yards she'd need, but other materials caught his attention, especially a deep blue silk. He laid the bolt on the counter for the clerk to cut next. From there, he pointed out others that caught his eye, and watching her expressions, knew when he'd found one that she too liked. Those all went on the counter with the others. Every so often, he'd purposefully picked out some he knew she wouldn't like, just to make her laugh.

She would pay him back by finding an equally ugly one and hold it up against his chest, threatening to make a shirt for him out of it.

When they'd reached the end of the bolts, he pointed out the lace and ribbon section. "You'll need some of this stuff, too, won't you?" A spool of thick braided cording caught his attention and he lifted it off the shelf. "Especially this."

She frowned. "What would I need that for?"

He unwound a large section off the spool. It was white, with specks of gold in it, and as soft as spun silk. Holding the spool in one hand and the loose end in his other hand, he looped it over her head and let it fall down her back. Once it landed near her waist, he wrapped the lose end around his palm, increasing the tension it to pull her close. "I can think of several things I'd use it for."

She planted her hands on his chest to keep from colliding against him. "I don't believe it's intended to be a lasso."

"It works as one."

Glancing over her shoulder, at the clerk who was indeed watching them, Jolie whispered, "Put that back."

"Why?" he asked innocently.

"Because you're causing a spectacle," she whispered. "Am I?"

"You know you are."

He wound the rope tighter around his palm, bringing her even closer. "So you want me to let you go?"

"Yes."

She was looking up and he was looking down, making them almost nose to nose, but it was lips to lips that he wanted to be. "What will you give me?"

"Give you?"

"Yes." He lifted a brow. "To let you go?"

Her giggle was soft, almost silent. "Am I being held for ransom?" She lifted a brow. "By a pirate?"

"Aye, mate," he hoarsely whispered.

Laughing, she wiggled against his hold. "Will you stop? And let me go before you turn us into a real spectacle."

"Kiss me," he said. "That's your payment. One kiss."

Her lips parted as she gasped. "You can't be serious. We're in a store."

"I know where we are. What I don't know is how long you're willing to stand here, caught in my pirate rope." Shrugging, he added, "I could stand here all day."

She searched his face for a moment. "You're serious, aren't you?"

He nodded. "I'm not moving until you kiss me."

She glanced around, but he kept his eyes directly on her. He was indulging himself, fully aware that he hadn't had this much fun, felt this young and carefree in...well, forever. He'd dreamed about being a pirate while mowing lawns, wished he could just find a treasure chest of gold big enough to satisfy his father and grandfather so he could go have fun like the other kids he knew.

"Oh, good grief," she whispered, then stretched onto her toes.

Her plan was a quick peck, he knew that, but he had his own plan. As soon as her lips touched his, he parted his and caught her bottom lip between his, not letting her pull back. He felt the moment the tension left her body and she gave in to the kiss. He took full advantage of that and teased, tasted her lips with his for several sweet moments. The kissing didn't last nearly as long as he'd have liked, but he, too, was aware that they were being watched and didn't want to embarrass her.

When he finally released her lips, she was fully up

against him, with her finger curled within the lapels of his suit jacket.

"You're incorrigible," she whispered.

He understood she was trying to blame him for how much she'd enjoyed the kiss, and was more than willing to take the blame. "And you're beautiful." He kissed her forehead before unwinding the cording from his hand and lifting it back over her head.

Her breasts rose as she drew in a breath of air while stepping back. "Now put that away."

"This?" He held up the spool.

"Yes."

"No." He wound the cording back onto its spool. "I'm buying this. I've always wanted a pirate rope."

Jolie was so overwhelmed she could barely think. Not from all the material and sewing notions, but from kissing him in the middle of a department store, in full view of clerks and customers alike. She tried to calm herself by picking out thread, buttons, trimmings and such, but by the time they carried everything out to the car, she had no idea what all he'd purchased. Other than the entire spool of white cording with gold specks. And a couple yards of pearl-gray linen with enough tint of blue in it that it matched the color of Randal's eyes to perfection. The prospect of making him a shirt out of that material elated her. She couldn't wait to get home and open up her sewing machine.

He took the last package from her and set it in the trunk of the car. Now that they were outside, away from being overheard, she said, "Thank you, but this really wasn't necessary." He'd just spent an extravagant amount on sewing supplies.

"I felt it was." He closed the trunk and stepped in front of her, trapping her between the car and him. "I admire your clothes and look forward to seeing the new ones you create."

No one had ever supported her dream, and she appreciated that he did, but couldn't get over the fact that it would affect the way society looked at him.

He brushed her hair from one temple. "You worry too much."

There was no use pretending that she wasn't, he'd see through it. "I'm just afraid of what people might think."

"I don't care what people think, and I wish you didn't."

She shrugged. "It's embedded in me."

"It's funny how that happens, isn't it? How things end up living inside us, driving us, even though it's not how we really feel."

He was clearly referring to something embedded inside him, leaving her unsure how to respond. She wished that wasn't so, and wondered how she could help him. Lifting her chin, she smiled. "Maybe that's something we can work on together."

"I like that idea." He placed a tiny, soft kiss on her forehead and slid his arm around her shoulders to walk her to the passenger door.

She truly didn't know what to think about the way he made her feel. Every touch filled her with a warm excitement. Perhaps because she'd never had a boyfriend. She had dated a small amount while in school, but then the stock market crashed and her father died, and life had completely changed.

"You're worrying again." He pulled open the car

door. "I can tell because right here." He touched her forehead. "Between your brows, a little wrinkle forms."

No one had ever teased her the way he did. Like everything else when it came to him, it made her happy. "And you think that's funny."

"I didn't say that."

She pressed a finger into the tip of his chin. "You didn't need to. I can see it in your eyes. They're twinkling."

"Twinkling?"

"Yes." She stretched up on her toes and whispered next to his ear. "Just like a pirate."

He poked her in the ribs with one finger, the absolute most ticklish spot on her body. That was her downfall. The one thing she couldn't control at all. Being tickled.

The way his eyes sparked, she knew he knew, and jumped in the car before he could tickle her again.

He laughed, closed the door and was still laughing when he climbed in the driver's door.

She pinched her lips together and stared straight ahead.

"You're that ticklish?"

"I'm not ticklish."

"Yes, you are."

"No, I'm not."

"Yes, you are."

She huffed out a breath, fighting both laughter and looking at him. "Just drive." Was there no rhyme or reason to her? One second she was worried, the next second she was breathless from his simplest touch— or more specifically, kisses, which truly did more than take her breath away—and the next second, she was laughing, happy.

"Where else are you ticklish?" he asked.

Continuing to refuse to look at him, she replied, "No-where."

"Just the ribs, then."

"No. I'm not ticklish at all."

"Liar."

She saw his hand move from the steering wheel out of the corner of her eye and reacted swiftly, grabbing his wrist in hopes of stopping him from touching her in the ribs.

He laughed as his hand settled on the gear shifter and he shifted gears.

Not trusting that he'd only shifted to prove that he hadn't been going to touch her, she kept her hand wrapped around his wrist, and he kept his hand on the shifter.

Their hands remained like that until he pulled into the driveway at his house. Their house now, as it was where she lived, too. She'd accepted that readily enough, it was the obligations that went along with it that she was still uncomfortable about because she wasn't sure what those obligations included.

"Time to unload the trunk," he said.

Nodding, she released his hand. He turned off the engine and then wrapped his fingers around hers while opening his car door with his opposite hand. He tugged her to follow him. She scooted across the seat, passed the gear shifter and steering wheel to climb out his side of the car. Cautious, because her body was still sensitive at the idea of being tickled, she scanned his face as she swung her legs out of the door.

"I'm not going to tickle you," he said.

Not certain she could completely believe him, due to his broad smile, she asked, "Promise?"

He released her hand and stepped back, holding both hands up, palms out.

"That's not a promise," she said.

Laughing, he walked to the back of the car.

She climbed out, shut the door and kept her distance as he opened the trunk. It might be foolish. Many people found tickling funny. She didn't. She hated the way it left her with no control over her body.

"You're worrying again, Jolie."

Today had been fun. More fun than she'd had in a long time, and here she was, worrying about a silly thing like being tickled. She walked to the trunk to assist him in collecting packages.

With their arms full, they entered the house, through a door that the ever-somber-looking Peter held open.

"Would you like me to take those for you, ma'am?" he asked.

"No, thank you, I have it," she replied.

"We're good, Peter," Randal said. "Thanks. We just picked up a few things that my wife needed."

Peter closed the door and gave a genteel nod. "Very well, sir."

Jolie waited until they were out of earshot before she said, "I didn't need anything. This was all you."

"Yes, it was," he answered as they crossed the foyer.

"Then why did you say I needed a few things?"

"Peter would never believe that I needed yards of material."

She glanced at him as she started up the stairway to the second floor. "Or pirate rope?"

"He's probably never seen pirate rope. I hadn't until

today." He leaned closer. "Nor had I met someone so worried about being tickled."

A shiver rippled over her. "You promised."

He lifted a brow. "No, I don't think I did."

She shot up the steps so quickly a bag slipped from her hands. There wasn't time to stop and retrieve it. He was right behind her. Even though she didn't want to be tickled, she couldn't help but laugh at the excitement that raced through her as she ran up the stairs.

He landed at the top of the steps at the same time she did, and with a laughter-filled squeal, she ran down the hall toward the bedroom. His laughter echoed off the walls, and though she wondered what others in the house might think, she didn't let it slow her down.

At the bedroom door, she grasped the doorknob, twisted it and shot inside, but Randal was too close for her to get it shut in time to keep him out. She dropped the two bags she was still carrying and ran toward the bathroom door, seeking sanctuary there. Barely a step later, Randal caught her around the waist and lifted her feet off the floor.

"No! Please don't tickle me," she pleaded. "Please!"

He set her feet on the floor, pivoted her around to look at him. "Give me one good reason not to."

"Because I don't like it."

Excitement was racing through his veins. Not only had he not chased someone up a flight of stairs in years, he'd never enjoyed doing so more than today. He slipped his hands around her waist, to the small of her back, and pulled her closer. "Why don't you like it?"

She planted her hands on his biceps. "Because there's nothing I can do about it."

The way she was looking at him, full of sincerity and honesty that penetrated clear to his bones, he felt rotten about teasing her. She was so prim and proper, so sweet and innocent, he'd enjoyed seeing her blush, but he sincerely didn't want to hurt her. Not now or ever. He also knew how hopeless a person could feel.

"I won't tickle you. I promise." He touched his forehead to hers. "Cross my heart."

She sighed softly. "Thank you. I know it's silly, but—"

"It's not silly. We all have things we don't like."

"What is something you don't like?"

Failure, but he wanted to keep things light, so he said, "Beets."

She leaned back and looked up at him. "Beets?"

"Yes. I've never liked beets."

She smiled. "Well, if I have the opportunity, I'll make sure you don't have to eat any."

"Thank you. I appreciate that."

Halfway through her nod, she gasped. "Oh!"

He twisted, glanced over his shoulder to see what she saw. Bags and packages were spewed across the floor, as well as their contents.

"Look at the mess we made!"

"I'll help clean it up."

"Yes, you will," she said, laughing. "You helped make it."

Chapter Ten

Once everything was put away, to her specifications, which meant stacked neatly on the small table that was sitting near the desk, he crossed the room and removed his suit jacket, tossing it over the back of the sofa in the sitting area.

"As long as you are taking things off, remove your shirt, too, please."

He spun, stared at her. "Excuse me?"

Her back was to him as she dug in a basket. "Take off your shirt, please."

"Why?" he asked, as he began unbuttoning his shirt. A dozen things raced through his mind. She'd been open to kissing today, but he wasn't completely sure she was ready for things to advance that quickly.

Turning, she held a tailor's measuring tape in one hand and a pencil and paper in the other. "Because I need to take your measurements."

"What for?"

"The first thing I'm sewing out of the material you just purchased is a shirt for you," she said, crossing the room.

Removing his shirt, he tossed it on the sofa with his jacket. "I didn't buy material for me, I bought it for you."

She twirled a finger in the air, indicating he should turn around. "I know, but I picked out material so I could sew you a shirt." She set the pencil and paper on the table beside him. "Now turn around and hold still."

He spun about. She stretched the tape measure across his shoulders, and down his back, pausing to write numbers on her paper between each action. Then told him to hold his arms out at his sides.

Many tailors had measured him over the years, and she had the lightest touch he'd ever felt. The simple brush of her fingers made his breath stick in the back of his throat.

"Turn around," she said. "I need to get your chest and waist measurements."

Keeping his arms out at his sides, he shuffled in a half circle to face her. "Like this?"

"Yes." Her cheeks flushed as she used both arms to stretch the tape measure around his back and then pull it taut over his chest.

By the time she finally wrote a number on her piece of paper, Randal figured it would take a good ten minutes for his heart to slow down to a normal beat again. Then she wrapped the tape measure around him again, this time his waist. The back of her knuckles brushing over his lower stomach sent more than his heart throbbing. He tried to make light of that. "It's like my pirate rope."

She pinched her lips together. "No, it's not. It's a tape measure and I'm not holding you captive."

He trailed a finger along the side of her face. "You could."

"Both arms out and hold still."

"Why do I have to put both arms out?" He touched her earlobe.

She tried to brush his hand away with her shoulder. "So I can get an accurate measurement."

"My arms aren't attached to my waist."

"I know your arms aren't attached to your waist, but I need both arms held out at your sides."

He exaggerated a sigh, and held both arms straight out long enough for her to get a measurement, but before she could reach for the pencil, he caught hold of both of her elbows. "Aren't you going to ask for ransom before you let me go?"

"No."

"Why not?"

"I already said that I wasn't holding you captive."

"Why aren't you?"

"Arms out again. I need to measure the circumference of your upper arm."

He'd never been vain, but as he held his arms out again, he considered flexing his biceps, in hopes of impressing her. His entire body was reacting to her closeness, and the blush on her face said she wasn't unaffected, either.

She measured both arms, wrote them down and then looped the tape measure around his neck. "One last measurement."

"Then I have to kiss you?" he asked, hopeful.

"No."

Using a knuckle, he lifted her chin so she was looking at him instead of the tape measure at the base of his neck. "But I want to."

She nibbled on her bottom lip and glanced away. "I

thought we were taking it slow, getting to know each other."

He cupped the back of her neck. "We have been. We've been married a week."

"Tomorrow will be a week."

"I know."

When she looked at him, with her eyes sparkling, he could barely remember his name.

"Fine." She tilted her face, brought it closer to his.

Not dipping his head and capturing the lips she was freely offering was the hardest thing he'd ever done, but he wanted her to know she was in charge. It was her choice. The seconds that ticked by were some of the longest in his life.

And worth the wait. Her hands cupped his neck and pulled his head down to meet her lips.

It wasn't just one kiss, nor was it one-sided. As soon as their lips parted, they came back together in mutual agreement that more was needed.

When he'd come up with this plan, when she'd agreed, he'd known their lives would become entwined, and had expected they'd form a friendship, a mutual agreement of fulfilling obligations, and grow accustomed to each other, but he'd never expected the overwhelming desires that filled him.

At first, he thought the sound was merely his pulse, echoing in his ears, but when she broke the kiss and bowed her head, preventing him from capturing her lips again, he heard the knocking on the door.

Damping down his frustration, he responded to the knocking by saying, "Yes?"

"Forgive me for the intrusion, sir." Peter's voice came through the door. "You have a telephone call."

Peter had been with them for years, and wouldn't have disturbed him if the caller had been willing to leave a message. "I'll be right there." Regretting having to leave, he rubbed her shoulders. "I have to take the call."

"Of course." She stepped back and scooped the pencil and paper off the table.

He picked the tape measure off the floor and handed it to her. "I'll be right back."

Not bothering with his shirt, he crossed the room and pulled open the door. The bag Jolie had dropped during their run up the stairway was sitting on the floor. Smiling at the memory, he picked up the bag, set it inside the room and hurried down the hallway. He'd never spent enough time in his bedroom to merit having a telephone line extension installed in that room, but he would have Peter order one as soon as possible.

The caller surprised him. Carl Jansen, inviting him and Jolie to a dinner party the following night. Randal accepted the invitation and encountered his grandfather on his way back toward the staircase.

"I was wondering," Grandpa said, leaning on his gold-knobbed cane.

"About what?" Randal asked.

"This marriage of yours, to a girl you'd never mentioned until you announced your engagement."

He'd been expecting this conversation, had been surprised it hadn't happened before now, and at this moment, didn't want to take the time to have it. "You should be happy. You've been telling me to get married for years."

"You insisted you didn't want to get married," Grandpa pointed out.

"I didn't, until I met Jolie."

Grandpa grinned. "Then why have you been sitting down here every evening? Listening to the radio when you should have been up in your bedroom? The reason you needed to get married was to carry on the Osterlund lineage. You're the last male."

That had been shoved down his throat for years. "Because we didn't want to be rude." He stepped around his grandfather. What was between him and Jolie was no one's business but theirs, yet he couldn't stop from saying, "It's good to know we no longer have to worry about that."

"Dinner will be served soon."

"Same time as always," he replied, already leaping up the stairway.

A unique sense of excitement was still singing through Jolie's body, so strongly it was hard to concentrate on the people or food. Randal was sitting at the head of the table, next to her, and all she could think about was kissing him. She tried hard to not think about it, but it was impossible. Nearly as impossible as remembering the sight of him without his shirt on.

Why did she find him so attractive? Would that make things more complicated? Or would it make things easier? It certainly made kissing him easy. Or was it because he'd bought enough material that she could sew to her heart's content?

Dear Lord, was she already turning into her mother? Rather than sitting home crocheting doilies, she'd sit home sewing clothes? Or was he trying to turn her into her mother? He'd said he didn't care what others thought, that she should sew if she wanted to, but he would when the gossip started, and spread, about them having *handmade* clothes. That couldn't happen. She wouldn't let it. She would show him how well she could sew. Men and women's clothing, and then show him how she would never depend on him for everything. That she could and would contribute to their partnership.

She was glad when the meal ended and when Randal explained she had some sewing she wanted to complete. Before dinner, she'd had time to create a pattern from tissue paper and had told him she wanted to get it cut out yet tonight.

She would do more than that.

Randal escorted her upstairs, and when he entered the room behind her, she said, "You can go listen to the radio show."

"No, I'll stay up here with you."

She glanced toward the table where she had the material laid out.

"I won't bother you." He walked to the sofa. "I'll just keep you company." Removing the suit coat he'd put on for dinner, he asked, "Or will that bother you?"

"It won't bother me." Chloe had often sat in her bedroom, talking while she'd sewed at home. She could have his shirt done in time for him to wear it to Dad's dinner party tomorrow night. The dinner party invitation made her nervous, but they had to go.

"I'll just sit over here, as quiet as a mouse, and read," he said. "Unless there's something I can do to help?"

"Actually, do you know if you have an ironing board and an iron?"

"Yes, I know we do. I'll go get them."

"Thank you, and a bowl that I can use for water?"

His frown had her quickly adding, "I need to sprinkle it on the seams when I press them open."

"Okay. I'll get a bowl, too."

She was in the midst of cutting out the pattern pieces when he returned, along with Peter. The two of them set up the ironing board near the sofa, where there was an electrical outlet handy, and she bit her lips together to keep from smiling at the size of the bowl he'd brought her. It had to be the biggest mixing bowl in the kitchen. One a tenth of that size would have been more than sufficient.

Assuring that all was exactly as she needed it, she thanked Peter and then sat down at her machine to stitch the first pieces together. Once done, she carried it to the ironing board. Randal had filled the bowl with water for her use and had set it on the table in front of the sofa, where he sat reading a magazine.

"I wasn't sure how much you needed," he said.

She grinned at how the bowl was filled to the rim. "This is perfect." Carefully, she dipped her fingers in the bowl and sprinkled the water over the seams.

"Why do you do that?"

"Pressing the seams open prevents any tiny puckers when I'm sewing on the adjoining piece, and the water creates steam, so they hold their shape and stay in place," she explained, while ironing. "What are you reading?"

"An airplane magazine."

"Tell me about the article." She collected the material and walked back to the sewing table to pin on the sleeves.

"It won't bother you?"

"Not at all."

* * *

The hours that passed were truly enjoyable, with her sewing and him reading the articles in the magazine aloud and then the two of them discussing what he'd read. It was about passenger planes and the airlines that owned them, how they'd hired young nurses to be stewardesses to take care of the passengers and their frequent airsickness. They had hired young men at first, but the article explained that nurses were better equipped to know how to care for the passengers who frequently threw up.

"When you buy Dad's company, who will you sell your planes to?" she asked, walking to the ironing board again. The shirt was complete, except for attaching the collar and cuffs, buttons and buttonholes.

"No one."

She sprinkled the pocket she'd just sewn on with water. "No one?"

"No, I not only plan on building planes, I plan on creating an airline." He set the magazine on the coffee table next to her bowl of water. "I figure it will take about five years before we see a return on our investment."

Setting aside the iron, she picked up the shirt. "Five years? It'll take that long to build the planes?"

"Not the first few, but it'll take at least that long to build up the company. Once the first plane is built, staff will need to be hired to fly and maintain it while more are being built. Within five years, I hope to have enough planes in the air, filled with enough passengers, to make back my investment as well as ongoing operating costs."

"That seems like a long time." And costly. Everything was costly, and she couldn't help but think about the money he'd spent on all the material today.

"Don't worry. I have plenty to get us through."

She couldn't help but worry, and waved a hand for him to stand up. "I need you to try this on so I know if I need to make any adjustments before putting on the collar and cuffs."

He stood and she told herself to look away as he unbuttoned his shirt, but for the life of her, she couldn't. In an attempt to not focus on his chest being revealed, she spun around and turned off the iron, then unplugged it from the outlet.

"You don't need to iron anymore?" he asked.

Still keeping her focus off him, she coiled the cord around the handle, being careful of the still-hot metal. "Not tonight. I'll mark any adjustments and finish it in the morning."

"Say, this fits really well."

She set the iron on the board before looking up. Not gasping was hard. The pearl blue-gray material did match his eyes perfectly.

"It's not tight across the shoulders at all," he said, testing the fit by pumping his arms in front of his chest. "And the length is perfect."

"Let me see." She twirled a finger for him to turn around so she could examine the back first. Pride filled her as she smoothed the shoulder yoke. The material tapered exactly as his body did, framing him perfectly. "Put your arms out," she said, watching as he lifted both arms to make sure the material didn't pucker or constrict movement.

"It feels good," he said.

"Turn around." Once again, she smoothed the material, this time along his arms, down his sides and across his chest. Then she held the two front sides together in the center, to check for fit once the buttons were attached. Once again, she was proud of how perfectly it fit.

"I like it," he said.

"So do I," she admitted. "There's still plenty of length on the sleeves to add the cuffs. Do you like one or two buttons on your cuffs?"

"One. I rarely use the second one."

"All right then. You can take it off. I'll finish it in the morning."

"I can't believe you sewed a shirt in one evening."

Even though she'd been examining the shirt, it had been the body underneath that she'd felt. The muscles that rippled his arms, chest and shoulders, and that had her hands trembling. Once again, she turned about in order to not stare as he removed the shirt. "It's not done, and it's after ten." Seeing the water bowl, she picked it up to carry it into the bathroom.

"Where should I put this?" he asked.

"You can just leave it…" Words escaped as she looked up, saw nothing but his bare chest, splattered with dark hair, and immediately her hands began to tremble again.

"I'll get a hanger so it doesn't wrinkle," he said.

She closed her eyes to block the view. "Okay." Drawing a deep breath to collect her bearings, she took a step. A very stupid thing to do with her eyes shut, and made worse because her knees were oddly weak, and didn't want to work. A yelp escaped her throat as the water sloshed and the bowl slipped from her fingers, landing upside down on the sofa. "Oh, no! I'm sorry! So sorry!"

* * *

An hour later, she was not only sorry, she was mortified. The water-soaked cushions meant that Randal was in the bed beside her. Right beside her. She could hear him breathing, feel the covers move up and down with each breath. Feel the heat radiating off his body. Feel the slope of the mattress because of his weight next to her.

The mortifying part was what all that did to her body. Her heart was pounding, her palms sweating, and a tingling sensation zipped up and down every inch of her.

"What do you think of Air America?" A second later, he said, "Sorry. Didn't mean to wake you."

"You didn't."

"Then I didn't mean to startle you. I felt you jolt."

She swallowed and licked her lips, knowing nothing would settle her heightened nerves. "What is Air America? I've never heard of it."

"I'm thinking that's what we could call our airline."

"Oh." She silently repeated the name several times. "That sounds like a good name."

"Our planes will fly to every airport in America," he said. "Someday, every airport in the world."

"Will it really take five years to earn back your investment?"

The bed shifted as he rolled onto his side. Her eyes had adjusted to the muted darkness some time ago, and she could see him looking at her, with one elbow in the pillow and his head propped on his hand. "If we're lucky, it'll only be five years."

She rolled onto her side to face him and tucked both hands beneath the pillow under her cheek. "Won't that be a long time with no money coming in?" The past few years had taught her that money going out and none coming in didn't make for an easy life.

"That's where other investments will come in. Keep us fluid."

So many people expected him to keep them fluid.

He touched the spot between her eyebrows. "There you go, worrying again."

"I can't help it."

"Just like you can't help caring what people think?"

"Yes, because I do care what others think, and you will, too, when they are gossiping about your wife and her homemade clothes. How you can't afford for her to buy new things."

"I can and will always be able to afford to buy you whatever you need, but you like designing clothes, and you're good at it. Your wedding dress, the shirt you made me, are amazing, and show how talented you are." He rubbed her upper arm. "Designing clothes makes you happy, so that's what you should do, despite what anyone says."

There was so much more to it. More than she could explain. "I don't want you to be embarrassed because you married me."

"Do I look embarrassed?"

Hardly. He looked wonderful. Even in the dark, she knew exactly what his bare chest looked like, how beautiful his eyes were, how his face was perfect in every way. And the rest of him. The parts she hadn't seen unclothed. Embarrassing herself with her own thoughts, she closed her eyes. "I don't mean right now. But it will happen."

He rolled onto his back and put both hands beneath

his head. "Why do you care so much about what others think?"

The memory that struck was painful, so dark and ugly, a tear slid out of her eye. She'd kept it hidden, refused to think about it for so long, that it gave her a chill. Grasping the blanket, she rolled over and pulled the blanket up over her shoulder, tucked it beneath her chin.

He laid a hand on her shoulder. "I'm sorry. I didn't mean to upset you."

"You didn't." She sucked in a breath. "I've never told anyone."

"Maybe it will help if you do." He tugged on her shoulder, until she rolled onto her back again. "I won't tell anyone."

His gaze was thoughtful, sincere. Uncurling her hand from the blanket, she drew in a deep breath. "When I was in grammar school, some kids held me down on the playground and tickled me until I wet my pants," she said quickly, before she lost her nerve. As soon as the words were out, she added, "I can't believe I just told you that. I've never told anyone. My mother doesn't even know about it."

"The school never told her?"

"No. Thank goodness. Mother would have been mortified that I'd done something like that. The nurse gave me dry panties and an ugly brown skirt, that she had to pin to make it small enough to fit around my waist. I had to wear that skirt all day, until I got home and threw it away." Even with the pin, she'd had to hold on to the waistband of the skirt to keep it from falling off, and everyone had noticed.

"Didn't the other kids get in trouble?"

"For what? Making someone laugh?"

His fingers wrapped around hers. "For holding you down."

"All the teacher saw was them tickling me, and didn't think there was anything wrong with that."

His other hand slid beneath her neck and pulled her up against him. "I was born peeing my pants. Did it for two, three years, straight."

Her mortification disappeared as she fought smiling. She snuggled her head deeper onto his shoulder. "That's not the same."

Randal tightened his hold around her and kissed the top of her head. He hadn't thought of Amy since his first date with Jolie, but was now, because a sixth sense told him Amy was one of the kids who had held Jolie down, tickling her until she wet herself. Amy was not only mean, she was sly, would have known they wouldn't get in trouble for tickling. That was part of the reason he'd dated her, because she wasn't likable, and therefore, no one, not even his grandfather, would have expected or encouraged him to marry her. That had kept him safe, because he would never enter something that was sure to fail. That was also why he chose to marry Jolie. Their marriage wouldn't fail, as long as they both got what they wanted out of it.

All thoughts shifted back to her. "I know it's not the same, I was just trying to make you feel better. Some memories stick with us. Affect us more than we realize."

"Your lawn mowing business?" Jolie asked quietly.

That was one that had stuck with him over the years. "Yes, I should have learned what was expected when I was told that one lawn should be two, two should be four, four should be eight, and so on."

"Learned what? You built a business that you sold when you were only fifteen."

He grinned at the mixture of pride and indignation in her voice. "I learned that failure's not an option."

"You didn't fail!"

He rubbed her arm, tightened his hold on her. In his father's eyes he had failed and had vowed it would never happen again. Not in any aspect of his life.

She snuggled closer to his side. "I'm proud of you for being so young and successful."

She'd would never know how much her words meant to him. "Thank you." He rested his chin on her head. Whoever those kids had been that held her down, he'd like to find each and every one of them. More than that, he wished he'd been there that day, to make them stop before they'd hurt her, embarrassed her. "Is that when you started sewing? Because of that ugly brown skirt?" He'd heard loathing in her voice when she'd mentioned it, more than when she'd mentioned the kids that had held her down.

She lifted her head, looked at him. "How did you guess that?"

He'd wanted her all day, and the way she was looking at him with those shimmering brown eyes, increased those desires. Pressing her head back onto his shoulder, he replied, "Because you always look perfect. Your hair, your clothes." Her body and face and everything else. "I can believe that wearing an ugly brown skirt, pinned to fit, would have been traumatic for you."

"It was. I ran all the way home and upstairs to my bedroom before anyone could see me, but it was actually Dad's wife, Anna, who introduced me into sewing a few weeks later. I'd gone over to their house with my father, which I did a lot, and she was sewing. She let me help, and when I went home that day, she put together a small sewing kit for me. Material, thread, straight pins, the measuring tape I used on you today, everything I needed. I sewed clothes for my dolls and my cat and—"

"Your cat?" He couldn't help but interrupt.

"Yes, Thomas, my cat."

He loved how happy she sounded. "Was he fond of that?"

Her soft laughter made her entire body jiggle against his. "Well, I still have a scar on my thigh from one particular dress that he really didn't like."

He wanted to see that scar. "Because he was a boy, wearing a dress?"

"No, he never minded that. It was the pin I'd accidentally left in the dress that poked him right under his little kitty arm."

"Ouch."

She giggled again. "You might want to remember that when you're trying on clothes for me."

"I will."

There was a short length of silence. A nice, comfortable silence.

"My father bought me my sewing machine for my birthday a couple of years before he died, and I sewed some clothes for myself, but Mother would never let me wear them in public."

"Because it wasn't fashionable?"

"Back then it could have been because they weren't very good. But she never knew about the dresses I fixed. Ones she bought me that didn't fit right. I'd put in darts or pleats to make them fit better. She never noticed. Not until after my father died, and to keep our wardrobes in style, I had to make things over. Or make two old dresses into one new one. I did that for all of us. Even my brother. I remade most of my father's clothes to fit him as he grew."

Another silence ensued, and he wasn't sure if he should break it.

"I did some sewing for neighbor ladies, but it wasn't until my wedding dress that I totally designed and sewed a dress completely from brand-new material."

At that moment he'd never been happier about a purchase than he was the material he'd bought today. "I would have never guessed that."

"Thank you for all the material you bought today."

"You are very, very welcome."

The silence that followed was so long, he wondered if she'd fallen asleep.

"Randal?" she asked, in barely a whisper.

"Yes?"

"I...I like you."

The warmth that rushed through his system was like nothing he'd ever known. He pressed his lips against the top of her hair and held them there for a long time. Feeling the warmth. Inhaling her sweet, flowery scent. "I like you, too." Very much, and that was something he could live with, because they would be living together for the rest of their lives.

Chapter Eleven

"My Anna never cared for cigar smoke," Carl said, lighting the end of a stogie. "I try to not expose other women to that, but I do enjoy one after a fine meal."

"The meal was delicious." Randal sat back in the solid leather chair in Carl's den. "Thank you for the invitation."

"I'm glad the two of you could make it." Carl took another puff off the cigar, blew out smoke. "I also wanted a moment of your time to mention something."

Randal gave him a nod.

"I have this little airplane business," Carl said, "that not a lot of people know about."

Randal picked his drink off the table, trying to hide the excitement that zipped through him.

"And I thought you should know," Carl continued. "That it's in my will to go to Jolie."

Randal's excitement froze. He lowered his glass, swallowed the bourbon in his mouth, let the burning sensation in the back of his throat, down into his chest, overtake his senses for a moment, giving him time to form a response.

When the burning eased, he asked, "Is Jolie aware of that?"

"No." Carl tapped the ashes off the cigar in an ashtray on the table between their chairs. "We didn't discuss that when she came to see me about marrying you."

For the second time in a matter of minutes, Randal was taken aback. He'd assumed Jolie's mother had contacted Carl about paying for the wedding. Not Jolie. She'd never mentioned talking to Carl about their marriage. "I was more than willing to pay for the wedding," Randal said.

"I'm sure you were," Carl said. "That's not why she came to see me. She needed some fatherly advice on love."

Love? Randal's insides churned.

"I was happy that she'd sought me out, and offered—actually, insisted—that she let me pay for everything." Carl drew on his cigar again as he glanced at an oil painting hanging over the fireplace. "Anna and I never had a daughter. Just our two sons, they were our blessings and I'm proud of them. But Joey-girl, she stole our hearts. I'm her godfather, you know."

"She mentioned that," Randal answered. Jolie had mentioned that, but hadn't mentioned that she'd gone to see Carl for fatherly advice about love. What kind of trick was she trying to play?

His stomach somersaulted. Had she known about Carl's will, but figured he wouldn't give her the company if she wasn't married? And needed to know if love had to be a part of that marriage?

He didn't want to believe there was a conniving bone in her body, but there certainly was in her mother's, and the apple doesn't fall far from the tree. His jaw tightened.

It would be a major failure for a man to make a fortune on a company that had been given to his wife. Doubly so for him. That certainly wasn't the Osterlund way of doing things. His father would roll over in his grave and his grandfather would probably fall right into his if the family fortune was expanded that way.

"Her father, Joseph, and I were best friends," Carl said. "Had been for years, long before he married Amelia. She never liked me, Amelia that is. Anna used to say that Amelia was a young bride and jealous of the time Joseph spent with me because that meant he wasn't with her. We did a lot of business together, Joseph and I. I tried to get him to invest in things outside of the market, but that's where he was making the bulk of his money and he just wasn't willing to take the risk. I didn't blame him for that, nor did I blame Amelia. No one should come between a husband and wife, and I tried hard to make sure that I never did that."

Randal nodded, but was only half listening. His mind was still reeling that Carl was willing to give away the very company he wanted to buy to increase his fortune, his status in the business world. If he did that with a company given to his wife, people would think that was the only reason he'd married her—for her money.

"Because we made money together," Carl continued, "Amelia never stopped Joseph from coming over, and she never stopped him from bringing Joey-girl with him. Anna and I treasured those visits." He stubbed his cigar out in the ashtray. "Joseph is the one who came to me with the idea of the airplane business. He was intrigued with them. Went out to watch exhibitions at the airfield west of town regularly. If the stock market hadn't crashed, we would have been partners in the company. I went ahead and bought it and I told Joseph the company was half his. He wouldn't hear of it, and..."

Carl shook his head, sighed heavily. "A month later, he was dead. The day of his funeral, I changed my will. Told my boys that the airplane company goes to Jolie when I die."

That explained why Carl had refused offers to sell the company. Randal had known about offers, and had been using those numbers as a base for the one he'd been preparing. "How did your sons respond to that?"

"They have other businesses, other interests, and are fine with my decision, because it was my decision to make. They are quite a bit older than Jolie, but knew how much Anna and I loved her. She's called me Dad from the time she could talk, because that's what Anna called me and Jolie just assumed that was my name, or maybe she just assumed all men were called Dad. I loved having her call me that, and still do."

Randal was having a hard time swallowing all this. On one hand he was happy for Jolie, that she'd had Carl and his wife's devotion for so many years, but on the other hand, his dream had just been destroyed. He'd have to find another business to buy. Which wouldn't be easy.

Worse yet, this would mean his marriage was a failure, too. Jolie wouldn't need him, or his money, once she inherited the company.

His guts knotted together. "When do you plan on telling Jolie all this?"

"Well, that's why I'm mentioning it to you first. She's a good girl. Good woman. Strong, dedicated and stubborn. I wish she would have come to me when they were in need, but that would have been going against her mother, and she wouldn't do that." He shrugged. "I considered contacting her, giving her the company more than once over the past few years, but I was afraid of what might happen. Of men coming out of the wood-work to marry her, just for the company. Unsavory men. Jolie deserves to be loved. Deeply and wholly. If she hadn't come here, needing advice, I may have questioned if she was marrying you just to save her family. I know you paid the taxes on their home."

"I did," Randal replied, but withheld the fact that he and Jolie didn't love each other. Never would. They'd agreed to that.

Carl winked at him. "And let me say, I agree with you giving Amelia a monthly allotment. She was another reason I couldn't give the company to Jolie earlier. Amelia has never been good with money. What little Joseph left them only lasted as long as it did because of Jolie."

Randal nodded, having already figured out all of that, and asked again, "When do you plan on telling Jolie of what she will inherit?"

"That depends on you," Carl answered. "I want you to have time to get all your affairs in line."

"My affairs?"

"It's my understanding that you are quite diversified in your investments, and that you were able to manage losses due to the market crash far better than most. That takes considerable time and effort. I have an excellent manager at the company. Duane Mills. He's trustwor-thy and handles the day-to-day affairs with no issues, but there is room for growth within the company. I'm too old to put in that time and effort. You aren't. Jolie may not want anything to do with the company but it will be hers, so she can sell it, keep it as is, or look to expand. Personally, I hope she keeps it, and that as her husband, you will dedicate your time and expertise in helping her succeed."

"I don't mean to sound…" Randal searched for the right word. "Indelicate, but it's difficult to plan when someone might inherit something."

Carl laughed. "I did forget that piece, didn't I? I'm not waiting until I die to give it to her. I want to do it soon, within the next few months. Can you arrange things so you'll have the time to assist her by then?"

His affairs were already completely in order to dedicate all of his attention to the airplane company, but he'd need more than months to find another company to buy and put another plan in place. Even longer to make it be worth more than the company Carl was giving his wife.

He didn't like the idea that Jolie was not the woman he should have married, but it sure appeared that way.

"You can review the time you'll need, and we'll talk again in a few weeks." Carl stood. "Right now, we better get back to the rest of the guests. I invited David Albright and his wife tonight because I'd like you two to get to know them. David owns the main airport in town and will be a real asset when you and Jolie take over the company."

Randal knew what an asset David Albright would be, and he hated the conflict battling inside him right now. Sleeping with Jolie in his arms last night had been heaven on earth, and now he felt like he'd been plunged into hell. A man who became rich off his wife was no real man. He didn't want a failed marriage, either. Right now, it was one or the other.

"Oh, and one final thing," Carl said. "Let's keep this between the two of us. I want it to be a surprise to Jolie when I give her the company."

Jolie had been making small talk for what felt like hours, with people she barely knew, and some she'd only met tonight. Dad, wanting to enjoy one of his cigars without exposing anyone else to the smoke, had asked Randal to join him in his den some time ago, and they still hadn't returned to the room.

"Sit here. There's plenty of room."

The invitation, including the patting of the cushion beside her, had come from Jane Albright, a beautiful blonde woman, who was very pregnant. They had been introduced earlier this evening, before the meal had been served.

"My feet couldn't take standing any longer and I'd love to have someone to talk to," Jane said.

"Thank you." Jolie sat, glad that the doorway was within eyesight. Her nerves were a jumbled mess, wondering if Dad had told Randal about her coming to see him for fatherly advice. Waking up snuggled up against him this morning had been the most wonderful thing. She'd never felt so safe, so content. She should have told him about visiting Dad last night, while they'd been lying in bed talking. But she hadn't.

"I heard about your wedding dress," Jane said quietly. "I wish I could have seen it."

Jolie's spine stiffened. Jane Albright had seemed so nice and kind earlier.

"Oh, horse feathers!" Jane said. "I should have said that I heard your gown was absolutely stunning. That's what I meant. Forgive me, please? I'm usually not such a simpleton. I swear this baby just steals my mind at times." She rubbed her stomach. "Which is fine, but I truly didn't mean to insult you. I used to sew all my clothes. When I lived in California. My sisters did, too. But from the sounds of it, we never created anything as lovely as your gown. And don't worry about what the newspaper printed. They wrote unflattering things about me when I first arrived in town, and my family in California even heard about it." She laid her hand on Jolie's arm. "And now I'm rambling. Just tell me to shut up. I won't mind. Just, please forgive me, and my baby."

Jolie grinned at the woman's honesty. "There's nothing to forgive. Is this your first baby?"

Jane's face glowed as she laid both hands on her stomach. "Yes. If it's a boy, his name will be Gus. Augustus David Albright. Named after the two most wonderful men on earth. Gus is David's grandfather and he's absolutely delightful."

Jolie heart skipped a beat, wondering if she'd ever know the happiness that exuded off Jane. "And if it's a girl?" she asked.

"Mary Jane. Mary after David's grandmother—Gus's wife—and Jane because David insists." She sighed. "He's so wonderful, but so is your husband. I've never met him before, but I've sent him a thank-you note every month for years."

"You have?"

"Yes, from the soup kitchen. I chair the fundraising committee. Randal is one of the few that when the need increased and donations decreased, he doubled his contribution, and has continued to be one of our largest donors every month. Many people have benefited from his generosity."

Jolie didn't know what to say. "Randal is a generous man."

"Yes, more than many others." Jane let out a huff. "I was so glad when his past affiliation ended. The only person Mr. Casswell has donated to is his daughter, making her an even bigger spoiled brat." Jane slapped a hand over her mouth. "I'm sorry. I did it again, and believe me, I know that no wife wants to talk about her husband's former girlfriends."

Jolie was liking Jane more and more. "That's all right. Amy is a spoiled brat."

"Such a brat her father had to send her overseas to find a husband." Jane twisted her shoulders and leaned back against the sofa, as if trying to get comfortable. "Just blame it on the boobs."

"Excuse me?" Jolie asked.

Jane laughed. "See, there went the brain again. I was talking about mine, not Amy's." Leaning closer, she whispered, "They've gotten so big and uncomfortable. I swear, half the weight I've gained has gone straight to my boobs. David says they're beautiful, but he doesn't have to carry them around. And they don't fit into any bra."

Glancing around to make sure no one was within listening distance, Jolie wasn't sure if she should laugh or be embarrassed over talking about such personal topics.

"If I find one big enough for my boobs to fit in, I have to tie knots in the straps to keep them from falling off my shoulders, and then it doesn't fit around the middle so it's always riding up. Like right now." Jane fidgeted with the sides of her dress. "But the alternate, one with straps that don't fall down, is worse. So tight

I can't even breathe once I manage to get it on. And the way they squash my boobs is painful."

Jolie could relate to that. She'd had issues with bras since she'd started wearing them. Not because her *boobs* were overly large. At any size it was difficult to find a fit that was comfortable because women were all made differently. "I could help you with that," she whispered.

"Pulling it down?" Jane asked, still tugging at her sides, although discreetly.

Jolie giggled. "Well, if you need, I could do that, too, but I've sewn my own bras for years and they are much more comfortable than anything you can buy. I sew them for my sister, too, and for a couple of elderly women that used to be my neighbors."

"Sew them? I never thought of that." Jane slapped the cushion between them. "If you could sew me one that's comfortable, I'd empty my husband's bank account to pay you." Jane's expression was serious. "And he wouldn't mind because ever since I became pregnant, I've been complaining about my boobs."

With another glance to make sure they were still not being overheard, Jolie said, "I would have to measure you, or tell you how to measure yourself." Lowering her voice even more, she added, "With no clothes on. I need exact measurements to get the exact fit."

"I have two sisters," Jane said. "We measured each other all the time, you just tell me when and where. I'd do it right now if we had a tape measure."

"Well," Jolie said, glancing around, not sure if she should take advantage of what she knew.

"Well, what?" Jane asked excitedly. "Do you have a tape measure?"

"No, but Dad's—Carl's—wife, Anna, her sewing

room is just down the hall. I knew her very well, and her sewing items might still be there."

"Seriously? Can we go check?" Jane shook her head. "Please don't think badly of me. I love being pregnant, knowing David and I created a life, and that it's inside me, safe and warm, and growing until it's ready to come out, but I'm so frustrated by being so uncomfortable."

"I don't think badly of you," Jolie assured. "Let's go see if Anna's supplies are still there."

Hurrying beside her across the room, Jane whispered, "Thank you! I've even tried going without, but that wasn't any better."

"I'm positive I can make one that will work for you." Jolie led the way down the hall, past the closed door of Dad's den and into Anna's sewing room. Memories flooded, making her eyes sting as she noticed everything was in the exact same place as when she'd been here years ago.

"Oh," Jane said softly. "You must have really loved Carl's wife."

"I did. She was like a grandma to me. She gave me my first sewing kit." Jolie shook her head in order to focus on the task at hand. Opening a drawer of the cabinet that held Anna's sewing machine, she took out the tape measure. She also retrieved a pencil and paper.

Jane was already removing the stylish, short black jacket that was over her cream-colored dress. "I'll have to ask you to unbutton the back of my dress."

"Of course." Jolie stepped around and quickly unbuttoned the dress.

"You'll see where I tried to take in the sides, but it didn't help."

Jolie did see the stitches on the sides of the bra, and

how the bunched-up material was leaving red marks on Jane's skin. "Your bra is made of tightly woven cotton and that doesn't give, nor does it move with the body. Also, the elastic is stitched on, which makes it lose its ability to stretch." Anna had been the only person she'd been able to talk to about sewing, and being in her sewing room, Jolie just couldn't seem to stop. "And the whole seamless bra that they are touting is ridiculous. Without seams, it won't fit any woman's body, furthermore, if your underclothes don't fit your shape, your outer clothes won't, either. I use darts, four of them, so the material conforms, but I also use two layers of material, back-to-back, so there are no seams to irritate the skin or distort the outer clothing."

"Do you have one on right now?" Jane asked as she stepped out of her dress. "Could I see it? I know that sounds crazy, but I'm usually not a complainer and I really want to be comfortable and enjoy every part of my pregnancy. I'm so excited that you could make that happen."

"Sure," Jolie agreed. Randal was wearing the new shirt that she'd completed this morning, but she was wearing a red-and-white dress that she'd remade before their wedding, which buttoned down the front. She unbuttoned it and let it fall off her shoulder.

"Oh, my goodness! That is so pretty! Is it silk?" Jane asked.

"Yes, but cut on the bias so there is some elasticity to it, and the elastic is inserted through a hemmed fold, so it doesn't bind."

Jane laughed. "I never thought I could be this excited over a bra, but I am!"

"Me, either," Jolie admitted. "I'm excited, because I know I can help you."

The two of them laughed and talked and laughed some more. Once Jolie had all the measurements she needed, and they were both fully dressed again, they left the room. The door to Dad's den was open and the room empty, causing Jolie's heart to skip a beat. It skipped another one as soon as she entered the front room and saw Randal. His smile filled her with a delightful warmth as their gazes met.

"Oh, good, our guys are together," Jane said, her arm looped through Jolie's. "Let's go tell them that you and Randal are coming to dinner on Monday night." Giggling, she added, "I'm so excited, I'm giddy."

Jolie had promised to have a bra for Jane by Monday at the latest. It wouldn't take her long to make one—after her shopping trip with Randal, she had all the materials needed—but she didn't feel comfortable saying she'd sew it tomorrow. A bra was not something she'd want Randal to see her sewing. It seemed too personal.

"Hey, there, big guy," Jane said to her husband as she slid her arm around his back. "Did you miss me?"

"You know I did, doll face." David wrapped his arm around her shoulders and kissed his wife's upturned face, before he said, "We were wondering where you two were off to."

Randal rested a hand on her lower back and Jolie, longing for what she saw between Jane and David, had to stop herself from snuggling up to his side. She and Randal didn't love each other the way Jane and David did. Nor would they. Ever. She didn't want that and neither did he. She was just caught up in the excitement of helping Jane.

"Someone said the two of you disappeared together," Randal said to her.

She would have replied, but the smile he'd flashed moments ago was gone and the dullness in his eyes stole any reply that might have formed.

"Outfit mishap," Jane said. "And Jolie was kind enough to help me. The two of you are also invited to our house for dinner on Monday night."

"Splendid idea," David said. "Randal and I have a lot to discuss."

Randal nodded, but his stiffness, his aloofness, made Jolie's stomach sink.

"Seven o'clock?" David asked.

"That sounds fine," Randal replied.

"Oh, good! I can't wait!" Jane wrapped her other arm around her husband's waist.

David pulled Jane even closer as he laughed, and Jolie felt a longing that she couldn't describe. And regretted.

They visited for a few more minutes, before the couple took their leave, and a short time later, she and Randal thanked Dad and bade him good-night.

"Come see me again, soon," Dad said as he kissed her cheek.

"I will." Her emotions were all mixed up because she knew Dad had to have mentioned her visit to Randal.

Shortly after he'd driven out of Dad's driveway, Jolie squared her shoulders, knowing she had to get it over with. "Dad told you I'd come to see him before our engagement, didn't he?"

He never took his eyes off the road. "Yes, he mentioned that."

"I was going to mention it to you."

All he did was nod. It was dark outside, and in the car, but she saw his head move, slightly, and she waited for him to say something. But he didn't.

"I didn't mention it," she said, "because I didn't want you to think I was attempting to undermine your chances of buying his business."

"Why would you think that I would think that?"

She'd never heard him sound so distant. Berating herself for not telling him, she looked out the side window. "I don't know. I didn't know you at the time, so I didn't know what you would think."

"Did you talk about his airplane company?"

"No. It never came up. I went to see him because I wanted to know what he expected. What would be expected of me if I did marry you. You'd said that he'd only sell to a married man, and I wanted to know why. What a wife had to do with a business deal."

"What did he say?"

"He didn't. He assumed I was there for a different reason."

"Assumed?"

"Yes."

"What did he assume?"

She huffed out a breath. "That I didn't know what love was."

"And that's what you expected?"

"No." She bit down hard on her bottom lip, forcing her emotions to not get involved. There was no reason to be upset about any of this. "That's what Dad expected, and I couldn't tell him otherwise, or he would have..."

He waited for a long time before asking, "Have what?"

"I don't know, maybe tried to stop me, or maybe

figured out that you only wanted to marry me so you could buy his business." That was the only reason he'd married her, and she knew it, so why did it bother her now? "I acted like he was right, and agreed when he set the date."

"Carl set the date? Not you? Not your mother?"

"Yes, he set the date. He said true love shouldn't have to wait."

Chapter Twelve

Randal stayed downstairs after they'd returned home, nursing a drink and staring at a newspaper that he had no intention of reading, sitting in the room that had been his father's office, waiting until he was certain that Jolie would be in bed, and hopefully asleep.

As if it wasn't bad enough that he'd never be able to buy the company he'd set his goals on owning, he'd seen something in Jolie's face tonight that made him feel like a total heel. That's what he was, as much of a blackguard as any pirate ever had been. It was disgusting. He'd pulled her into this because he'd wanted to outdo all of his past accomplishments. Turn a company from earning hundreds to making millions. Like his grandfather had. Like his father had. Like what was expected of him.

He'd put everything in place, so nothing could fail.

But it was. His perfect plan was quickly becoming a plan of shambles.

Not just because of Carl giving the company to Jolie, but because of him.

When he'd seen Jolie walk into the room while he'd

been talking to David Albright, his body had reacted. Had remembered waking up next to her, with her head on his shoulder, the sweet scent of her filling the air. For a brief moment, all Carl had said, hadn't mattered. What his grandfather expected hadn't mattered. What anyone else might think or expect hadn't mattered. In that brief moment, when he'd seen her, he'd remembered how she'd said that she liked him last night, and how he'd admitted he liked her.

He'd thought that was fine, for them to like each other, but now...

He took a sip off his drink.

Now, he knew that Jolie wanted more.

Anyone around Jane and David Albright saw the love between the two of them. Jolie had seen it, and she wanted it. He'd seen the longing in her face as she'd looked at Jane and David.

Carl was right. She deserved to be loved.

Randal squeezed the glass in his hand harder. He couldn't give it to her.

This very house had once been filled with love, but he'd seen his father brought to his knees when his mother had died. It had changed his father into someone who'd hated everything and everyone around him. Love had done that.

Randal shook his head. There was no way he'd ever give a woman that kind of power over him. Cause him to fail.

Not even Jolie.

Another thought washed over him.

Carl would give her the airplane company before long and Jolie wouldn't need him for money when that happened. That had been all he'd had to offer her, and she would no longer need it.

Randal's throat burned at the reality of that.

He stood, crossed the room and stared out the window into the dark night. He had a choice to make. Continue being a heel, a blackguard by forcing her to stay married to him, or call the entire sham off, have their marriage annulled so she could someday find the love that she wanted.

There truly was no reason to continue it. His dream of buying Carl's business no longer existed, and he could never give Jolie what she wanted.

He'd had every intention of sharing the company with her if he bought it, but having it given to her, he couldn't claim it as his. Couldn't take advantage of something that belonged to her to further himself and the Osterlund name. It wouldn't be right.

No man could be proud of that.

He hated the idea of failure, but there was nothing he could do.

"What are you still doing up?"

He turned, saw his sister Danielle in the doorway. "Just thinking."

"About what?"

"Nothing in particular," he lied. "What are you still doing up?"

"Hoping to talk to you." She walked into the room. "James is going to talk to you tomorrow, but I saw the light on and saw you, and…" She closed the door. "Oh, Randal, I hope you will understand."

"Understand what?"

She sat down on a chair, looked up at him with a frown. "When I got married, I said that I'd stay here and run the house as long as you needed me to, and I'm—we—are hoping that now that you're married, I can turn those duties over to Jolie."

He leaned against the windowsill and crossed his legs at the ankles. "I would need to speak to Jolie about that." Requiring anything from Jolie was not something he was open to committing.

"She already knows everything I do. We've talked about it."

"About her taking over your duties?"

"No, not taking over, just what I do. You know, approve the menus and shopping lists, check that everything was cleaned to Grandpa's standards." She sighed and threw her arms out at her sides. "Make sure the help doesn't steal the silver."

Caught off guard by that, he stared at her.

"Of course, no one is going to steal the silver. It's just a saying, I was joking. Criminy, Peter's been here longer than I've been alive. Mrs. Hoover almost as long, and I've never made a change to her menus, and as for Darla, she needs this cleaning job to feed her children. She wouldn't chance losing it for anything."

"Darla?"

"She cleans, three times a week, you've never met her, but Jolie has, and all of the staff like Jolie, everyone is glad that you married her. Even Grandpa. Haven't you noticed that he's not as grumpy these days? He was worried that you might marry Amy. We all were."

Randal was not willing to comment on any of that.

His silence gave Danielle the opening to continue. "Grandpa really likes Jolie. He likes how she listens to his stories. Did you know that after you leave for work in the morning, she stays at the breakfast table, talking to him? She does the same at lunch. Tonight, at dinner, he asked me why you are making her sew in your bedroom, when the bedroom next to yours is empty. She could turn the entire room into one just for sewing. He's going to tell you that tomorrow."

"Why do you need to give up your duties?" he asked, needing for his own sanity to change the subject.

"Please don't tell James that I told you."

He was growing tired of secrets. Very tired. "You haven't told me anything."

"Like I said, James is planning on talking to you tomorrow morning, to tell you, that…well, he and I would like to move out."

"Move to where?" Without waiting for her to answer, he continued, "I said I'd buy you a house—"

"We don't want you to buy us a house."

He wouldn't insult her or James, but without his help, they couldn't afford to buy a house.

"We want to rent an apartment."

"Why?"

Her face lit up like it used to when she was little and he'd come home from school. "James and I are going to have a baby."

That didn't surprise him, he'd expected it sooner than later. "Wouldn't you want to stay here, so you have family to help?"

She stood up and walked to the desk, ran her hand over the top of it. "You're my big brother, Randal, and were more of a father to me than our father ever was. Even though you worked as long, as hard, as much as he did, you still had time for tea parties, bedtime stories and to teach me how to ride a bike, amongst many other things. I've always appreciated all that you've done for me. I love you, will always love you, and I know that no matter what, or where, or when, that if I need something, I can come to you. But James is my husband. I love him and he loves me. He and I are a family now, and he wants to take care of his family. Provide for his family. I want that, too. We, James and I, want to build something, just like Grandpa did when he came to America."

Love. His jaw grew tight. It's not the wonderful thing people think it is, but Danielle didn't want to hear that. She thought it was, and she thought she knew what she wanted.

"James has his pride, Randal, and so do I, please understand that."

He did understand that, and he also knew Danielle wouldn't listen to reason. He'd tried that when she'd announced that she and James were in love and getting married.

Jolie couldn't lie in bed any longer. If she'd been going to fall asleep, that would already have happened. She climbed out of bed, picked up the robe she'd left lying across the foot of the bed, and shrugged it on while crossing the room to turn on the light.

Randal must still be downstairs, where he'd stayed upon their arrival home. Should she go make sure he was all right? Or just leave him be? She hadn't expected him to be this upset over her meeting with Dad that he… She shook her head, stopping the thought because it would only make her eyes sting all over again.

She reached the light switch and clicked it on, just as the door opened.

Silent, she and Randal stood still, staring at each

other for a long moment. She was relieved to see him, but he didn't look relieved.

Breaking eye contact, he walked into the room and closed the door. "I thought you would be asleep."

She considered not responding, but only for the briefest of moments. "I said I was sorry."

He loosened his tie, pulled it off and tossed it on the back of the sofa, all the while toeing off his shoes. "No, I don't believe you did."

Unable to recall their conversation word for word, she accepted that he might be right. "Well, I am. I'm sorry that I didn't tell you about meeting with Dad."

His suit coat landed on the back of the sofa, atop his tie.

"What more do you want me to say?" She should have told him, wished that she had, but there wasn't anything she could do about that now. Other than feel bad, which she did. She felt awful.

"Nothing. You met with Carl because you wanted fatherly advice. End of story."

"If it's the end of the story, why are you still mad at me?"

The shirt she'd made for him landed on his coat. "I didn't say I was mad at you."

Flustered, she crossed the room, collected the shirt, coat and tie, and carried them to the closet. "You don't have to say it. Your face shows it."

"Whatever my face is showing isn't anger at you. I'm not mad at you."

She took down a hanger and hooked the coat over it. "Then who are you mad at?"

"Myself."

Hanging up the coat, she took down another hanger

for the shirt. "Why?" She couldn't fathom a reason for him to be mad at himself.

"For believing in a plan that will never work."

A shiver rippled her spine as she hung up the shirt and hooked the tie over a hanger holding several others. "Yes, it will." It had to work. There was no other option.

He opened the wicker trunk beside the sofa, took out the pillow and blanket.

A lump formed in her throat, reading what that meant. "Why do you think it won't?"

Tossing the pillow and blanket onto the sofa, he walked back to the door.

"Where are you going?"

"To shut off the light. Do you want to climb into bed before I do?"

"No. I want to know what's happened. Why are you mad? Why are you saying this won't work?"

He pivoted, looked at her. "Why do you think it will?"

"Because you are good at what you do. You'll be able to create an airline from Dad's business, just like you planned."

"So, I'm good at making money?"

"Yes. And providing for your family. And…" The things coming to her were all personal. Too personal to say out loud. Like how he made her feel happy, safe, secure, and how she wanted to help him make their agreement work.

He turned, walked toward the door. "You're right. That's what I'm good at. Making money." He clicked off the light. "Go to bed, Jolie."

"If you tell me what happened—"

"The only thing that happened was that I started something I shouldn't have." He reached the sofa, sat down.

She could see the outline of his body, how he had his head bowed. "Something must have happened."

"When we discussed this plan, I told you I wasn't looking for love."

Another shiver zipped up her spine. "I know." She had to swallow before continuing, "And I agreed. I was—I'm not looking for love, either."

"I don't believe you fully understand the consequences of what that means."

"Yes, I do." She knew the consequences better than most, and would not turn into her mother. Loving a man to the point that nothing else in life mattered. Not even her own children.

"Do you really want to live the rest of your life with a man who doesn't love you?"

It felt as if a knife had struck her right in the heart, which made no sense, because she hadn't changed her mind. "Yes. That's what we agreed to." She kept her chin up, even as it began to shake. "We like each other, Randal." At least they had... Right now, she wasn't so sure. "I'm sure some marriages don't even have that." She didn't want love, so there was no reason for his statement to hurt her, yet it had. Walking to the bed, she said, "Good night."

Randal squeezed his temples with one hand, wanting to inflict pain on himself. He'd just gone from a heel to a complete bastard. He had to give her the option to get out of their agreement, but he didn't have to hurt her, be a complete ass in the process. He didn't want to fail, especially not at this magnitude, but he couldn't hold her to something that should never have happened in the first place.

He left the couch, crossed the room and sat down on the bed. "I'm sorry. I shouldn't have taken my frustration out on you."

She rolled onto her back, looked at him. "Why are you so frustrated?"

Her voice sounded shaky, sad. The strong, deep ache inside him kept growing. He couldn't tell her why he was frustrated. Not tonight. Tomorrow, he'd call Carl and tell him that this was a secret he couldn't keep. Jolie needed to know, now, so she could decide what she wanted. He would abide by whatever she chose. Couldn't hold her in a marriage that she no longer needed. "Nothing you need to worry about."

"I can't help it. Just…just because we don't love each other doesn't mean we can't care about each other, and I care that you are frustrated."

This was a mistake. He should have stayed on the couch, let the guilt eat him alive. He put a hand on the bed to push off.

She grasped his wrist. "I won't stop caring just because you're on the sofa."

He wanted this day to end, but why? All of his issues would still be there in the morning. Not only with her, but with Danielle. Maybe that is something she could help him with. Talk some sense into his sister.

Sinking back down into the mattress, he said, "Danielle asked to speak to me downstairs."

Releasing his wrist, she sat up, pulled the blanket up and tucked it under her arms. "Why? Is something wrong?"

"She and James want to move out. Into an apartment."

"You don't want them to?"

"No."

"Why?"

"There's no need. There's plenty of room for them to live here."

"And?"

Of course she wouldn't simply agree with him. "They can't afford it," he said. "James is a good photographer, excellent at it, but he doesn't make much money. It will be years before he can afford to take care of his family. I should have seen this coming. Right from the start he wouldn't take any financial backing from me. That's why they've lived here, so he could invest profits back into his company, build it up, and why they need to continue to live here. Baby or no baby."

"Baby? Danielle is pregnant?"

"Yes, she just told me that downstairs."

"They are starting their own family, Randal, and want to do it on their own."

"That's what Danielle said, but she's my responsibility, has been since she was born."

"You were only seven when she was born."

"Old enough to know she needed to be taken care of. She was only a few months old when our mother died from pneumonia, and our father was so mad. Mad at Mother for dying." He clenched his back teeth at the memory of how he'd been mad, too. Because that's what had been expected. "We went through a slew of nannies. Grandpa has mellowed over the years, but back then, he and my father were tyrants, and nannies didn't last long. Some no more than a day. It was up to Willa, who was only five, and me, to take care of Danielle." She'd been so afraid of their father, of his shouting, anger at everything. Randal closed his eyes at remembering how he'd tried to shield both of his sisters from that, and how he'd worried about Danielle while he'd been at school or mowing lawns.

"Did Willa live here after she got married?"

"No. Don's family owns a drugstore and have other investments that have done well for them. James doesn't have any of that. His father died when he was little and his mother was one of our nannies. He and Danielle have known each other since grammar school. He and his mother had moved out of town for several years, and when he returned, he and Danielle dated, and then got married."

"Can I ask you a question?"

"Yes."

"Would you want to live with my family? In their house, have them provide everything we needed?"

"It's a man's duty to provide for his family."

"James is a man."

That's why she'd asked. It was a trick question. "Danielle is my sister. My family. My responsibility. I can't fail her now."

"You aren't failing her. James is her husband, and they love each other."

There it was again. Love. Nothing but trouble is what it should be called.

"They are going to have a baby together," she continued. "And James wants to be the one to provide for both his wife and child. He wants the privilege of providing for his family. Can't you give him that?" She touched his hand. "Very few people want to be dependent upon someone else, because there's no pride in that, but there is pride in taking care of your family. And there are many ways to do that. Can't you let them try? You can always help if they need it."

Randal wasn't sure if it was her well-meaning pleading, or the warmth of her hand, that was softening everything inside him. Or the fact that she was right on a few points.

There was a gentle, serene smile on her face as she scooted back down, beneath the covers. "It's late. We should get some sleep."

After last night, he didn't want to sleep on the sofa and wondered what she would do if he lay down beside her. He huffed out a breath. The sofa was lumpy and short, but it was where he should sleep.

"Lie down and go to sleep, Randal."

Chapter Thirteen

Rolling over and finding the space next to her empty, didn't stop a smile from forming on Jolie's face. Randal had slept there. She'd lain awake until she'd been sure he'd fallen asleep.

Love had not been a part of the deal, and still wasn't. But she'd been honest when she'd said she cared about him, and right now, was worried. She knew the pressure of taking care of siblings, and could relate to his concern about not failing Danielle.

She sat up and scanned the sofa. The back of it was all she could see, but when Randal slept on it, his feet always stuck over one arm. There were no feet there, and the bathroom door was open, the room empty.

After climbing out of bed, she made it, then collected a dress from the closet and entered the bathroom. Before going to Dad's dinner party last night, she'd bathed and her hair had still been damp when she'd pinned it into stylish rolls on both sides. A quick brushing left it hanging in waves around her face.

On her way to the door, she noticed the pillow and blanket were still on the sofa, in the same places they'd landed when Randal had tossed them there. She smiled the entire time she returned them to the wicker chest. He had already provided her and her family with so much. Knowing she'd helped him with his troubles last night made her feel as if she'd given him a little bit in return, even if it was just understanding.

Danielle and Grandpa, which is what he insisted she called him, were sitting at the table when she walked into the dining room. "I'm sorry, I hope you didn't wait on me this morning."

"We just sat down," Danielle said, while pouring coffee for the three of them. "James and Randal ate before they left."

Jolie nodded as if she knew that as she took her regular chair.

"Randal told Peter to get that other room set up for you today. 'Bout time if you ask me," Grandpa said.

Jolie's fingers shook so hard her cup clattered against its saucer. She placed her hands in her lap without picking up the cup.

"Grandpa." Danielle shook her head and handed him the bowl of scrambled eggs. "I think Randal wanted that to be a surprise."

"Well, she'll see Peter carrying everything out of the bedroom," Grandpa replied.

Jolie's heart was sinking deeper and deeper. Was he still intent upon things not working between them?

Danielle rolled her eyes. "Randal is having Peter create a sewing room for you in the room next to yours, the room that had been Willa's. She took all of her furniture when she moved out, and it's never been replaced, but there are a few things in the attic that will work for a sewing room, including a big table and a chest of drawers for all your material."

Squeezing her hands together to ease their trembles as relief flooded her, Jolie nodded. "Oh, that sounds wonderful."

"It's no sense using up all the space in your bedroom when there are other rooms just sitting empty." Grandpa passed her the platter of bacon that he'd nearly emptied onto his plate. "My wife, Virginia, used to sew. She made me a smoking jacket. A green velvet one. I loved that jacket. Wonder whatever happened to it." He was looking at Danielle.

"I don't know, Grandpa, I've never seen it," she answered.

"Would you be interested in having me sew one for you?" Jolie asked.

Grandpa took a bite of bacon. "I think I would."

"I don't have any green velvet, but I do have some blue," she told him. Randal had picked out a dark, royal blue velvet from the store the other day.

"I look good in blue," Grandpa said.

She also had several yards of blue silk that she could use for lining for the jacket. Jolie gave him a nod. "Then I will make you a blue one."

"I used to wear that jacket when Randal was little," Grandpa said. "I remember bouncing him on my knee while wearing it." He continued, carrying his memories into a long story that lasted until they'd eaten and the table had been cleared.

"I'll show you the room and the items in the attic," Danielle offered during a brief moment when Grandpa had paused to remember what he'd been talking about.

"Yes, do that," Grandpa said. "And tell Peter to scrounge up anything else she needs."

"I'm sorry he ruined Randal's surprise for you," Danielle said as they walked side by side out of the dining room.

"It's fine," Jolie said. "I hear congratulations are in order."

"Yes! We are so excited." Danielle pressed a hand to her throat. "I just hope Randal gives us his blessing to move into our own place. Between you and me, we are going to do it either way, but I don't want to upset Randal. He's... I know he's my brother, but he's more to me than that. He raised me. I know he's worried about us financially, but James wants the chance to prove he can provide for us. It's very important to him."

"I'm sure it is, and he deserves the opportunity. You both do."

"I don't think Randal thinks that."

"Maybe you just need to give him a little time to get used to it," Jolie said. She wasn't sure that would happen, but wanted to provide Danielle with hope.

"Did he discuss it with you?"

"We talked about it last night."

"I'm sorry I kept him down here so late."

"It was fine," Jolie replied. The conversation changed to her new sewing room as they continued along the upstairs hallway, to the stairs that led to the attic, where Jolie felt as if she'd just entered a treasure vault. There was a large, framed, freestanding mirror, stools, a dressmaker's mannequin and so many other things, she was speechless at times.

"I don't remember ever seeing any of this," Danielle said as she uncovered another treasure, a trunk full of material, lace, ribbon and a large roll of tissue paper. "It must have belonged to my grandmother."

"Do you think Grandpa will mind if I use it?"

"Of course not. He said to scrounge up whatever else you needed." Danielle stepped over a crate of books to gain access to another trunk. "And we're scrounging."

"Yes, we are," Jolie agreed, lifting a chair off an old dresser to see behind it. She then pushed aside a wardrobe screen. "Danielle, there's a baby cradle back here."

Climbing over more crates, Danielle made her way over to take a look. "Really? I have to see."

"There's also a crib and high chair," Jolie pointed out.

Danielle pulled open a dresser drawer and used it as a step to reach over the dresser and push the screen completely away. "And the table and chair set I had in my bedroom when I was little." She leaned over the top of the dresser and giggled. "Randal used to have tea parties with me at that table."

"He did?"

"Yes, he did." Danielle let out a long sigh. "Oh, I hope everything is going good between Randal and James."

Jolie rested her elbows on top of the dresser and stared at the baby furniture. "I'm sure it's going fine." She had far more thoughts about Randal than just his talk with James. Plenty of her thoughts included her. Although she tried not to judge people, she did consider herself a decent judge of character. Randal was a man of excellent character. She wholly believed that. She also believed that Danielle and James were not the only things that had been bothering him last night. She couldn't help but wonder if he'd been thinking about children, after seeing Jane so pregnant. Did he want that? Was that why he'd brought up living with a man who didn't love her?

"This means so much to me and James." Danielle turned around. "It's not that we aren't grateful, but no one wants their brother to pay for everything, forever. We know the depression has hit everyone hard and that photography isn't something that everyone needs or can afford, but James is very good at it."

"I'm sorry that we didn't hire him for our wedding," Jolie said. That hadn't been something she thought of before. She hadn't questioned anything her mother had suggested, other than her dress. Perhaps she should have.

"The apartment that is for rent is only a block away from James's photo shop. I could help him every day, wait on customers while he's developing photos or out taking photos. I know our leaving means work for you, and I'm sorry about that, but…"

Jolie frowned, not sure what Danielle meant, but remained silent.

"You already know what I do running the household," Danielle continued. "It's not hard. Peter takes care of most of Grandpa's needs and I could come back and help you whenever you need."

"I would prefer that you simply come back to visit, regularly," Jolie said. Contributing was something she wanted to do, too, and running the household would be a good place to start. It wasn't as if her few sewing projects would keep her busy. They'd be completed in no time. However, she had to wonder if Randal would object to her taking over for Danielle. Yesterday morning, she would have thought not. So much had changed in a very few hours.

"Oh, I will, I promise." Danielle stepped out of the dresser drawer. "Let's get this stuff hauled down to your new sewing room."

Between the two of them, they carried a large portion of the items they'd found to the empty bedroom, only needing Peter's help for the larger and heavier items, including a long table perfect for cutting out material.

An organizing of the room came next, along with a detailed cleaning of the items. She and Danielle were putting the dressmaker's form back together when Jolie spotted someone in the doorway. For a moment, she was annoyed at herself for being disappointed that it was James. Only James. Randal was nowhere in sight.

"And?" Danielle asked James.

Tall and slender, with short, wavy blond hair, James nodded and his face lit up as he said, "Yes. He agreed."

Danielle squealed and ran into her husband's open arms.

Jolie attempted to focus on the mannequin, giving the couple privacy, but she was smiling, very happy for Danielle and James. At the same time, she couldn't help but sympathize for Randal at how difficult that decision had been for him. There was also a part of her that wondered if rather than trying to put things in perspective last night, she should have agreed with him. She, of all people, knew what it was like to live with next to nothing, and it wasn't easy. It had been a considerable strain on her entire family.

"Thank you, Jolie," Danielle said. "Thank you."

"I didn't do anything," Jolie insisted.

"Yes, you did. If you hadn't married Randal, we wouldn't have this opportunity." Danielle then asked James, "Where is Randal?"

"He had someone he had to go see," James said. "He asked me to let you know he'll be back later, Jolie."

She smiled her thanks, damping down more disappointment. "Well, you two must have some planning to do."

"I thought we'd go see when we could move into the apartment," James said to Danielle.

"Oh, yes, but just let me finish helping Jolie—"

"Nonsense," Jolie interrupted. "I have this all under control." She waved her hands in a shooing motion. "You two go on, go see your apartment."

Danielle clasped her hands together. "I'll help you as soon as we get back."

Jolie appreciated the offer, but more than that, she loved the happiness shining on both James's and Danielle's faces. "Go. Now."

Laughter of happiness echoed in the hallway, and Jolie stood there for a moment, wondering if things were starting to make sense, or if she was just looking at them differently.

Randal shoved his hands in his pockets and rocked back on his heels in order to hide the frustration that was reaching a whole new breaking point. "Do you know when he will return?" he asked the butler who had answered Carl Jansen's door.

"Approximately two weeks, closer to three," the man responded.

"Weeks?" Randal took a moment to grasp his options. Waiting weeks was not one. He needed resolution now. "Is there a telephone number where I could contact him? I'd really like to speak with him."

"I'm sorry, Mr. Osterlund, there is not. Mr. Jansen and his sons are taking their annual fishing trip at their cabin near Springfield. He left for the airport a short time ago, and I don't expect to see or hear from him until he returns." The butler appeared concerned. "Is Miss—forgive me, Mrs. Osterlund all right?"

"Yes, yes, she's fine." More than fine. She's beautiful, kind, caring. He hadn't been able to leave her bed until the sun was coming up because lying next to her had been amazing, and had made him think about certain things differently than he'd ever have expected.

"If I do hear from him, sir, I will forward the message you wish to speak to him."

"Thank you." Randal held in a pent-up sigh. "Thank you, very much. Good day."

The butler stepped back to close the door. "Good day to you, sir."

The air seeped out of his lungs as Randal walked toward his car. The last thing he wanted was for Jolie to believe she'd been made a fool. That she'd married him when she truly hadn't needed to. At the same time, he couldn't defy Carl's request to not tell Jolie about her upcoming inheritance. There had to be a way he could talk to Carl now. Get it out in the open, let her choose if she wanted their marriage to continue, or to end.

That was a conflict inside him. He knew what he wanted, and what he should want. They weren't the same thing.

Maybe Carl's flight hadn't left yet. There was a chance of that.

He jogged the last few yards to his car and drove

straight to the airport. A large plane was coming in for a landing as he arrived in the parking lot; it was an amazing sight to see, and thrilling. The entire industry was thrilling, especially the potential that was there for the right investor. He'd dreamed of being that investor and had been so close, but Jolie had upheld her end of their bargain without a single complaint. Before he could decide what his next step should be, Jolie needed to know Carl's plan.

He left the car and entered the small building where passengers purchased their tickets.

The young woman behind the counter told him the plane for Springfield had left a short time ago, but that there would be another flight to Springfield in three days.

Randal thanked her, said he didn't need a ticket to Springfield and stepped away from the counter. Three weeks of holding a secret of this magnitude, of this importance, was not going to work. Maybe he should buy a ticket to Springfield. It couldn't be that hard to find Carl's fishing cabin. He could buy two tickets. Jolie wanted to fly in a passenger plane, after all.

The shine in her eyes, the glow of her face, when they'd talked about seeing Mount Rushmore flashed in his memory, and like some kind of magician's trick, made his heart tick faster. There were times when she looked at him that he became incapable of doing anything except staring back. In those moments, he couldn't even remember his own name—however, when she kissed him, when she was in his arms, he knew who he was and that he didn't want their marriage to fail.

"Randal? How did you know I was flying home today?"

His spine stiffened as he turned. Passengers from the plane that had landed were entering the building, and near the door, blocking the way so others had to skirt around her, stood Amy.

Her short, black hair was covered with a white pill hat and her lips were coated with bright red lipstick, and he wondered how he had ever been remotely attracted to her. Right now, he couldn't fathom it because there was nothing friendly, kind or even pretty about her. "I didn't know you were coming home." Nor did he care.

Her smile was much more of a sneer. "Then why are you here?"

"To buy tickets." He pivoted to approach the counter again.

The hand she laid on his arm made his skin crawl. A flash of anger filled him at the idea of her holding Jolie down, of humiliating a little girl who would never have hurt anyone.

He pulled his arm away and walked to the counter. The next flight to South Dakota was over four weeks away, but he still bought two tickets.

Amy stood in his pathway to the door, held out a hand. "Here are the tickets for my luggage. You can give me a ride home so I don't have to wait for a taxi. I have been traveling for well over a week and the flight out of New York was at a god-awful hour this morning."

Ignoring the ticket stubs in her hands, he stepped around her. "No, I won't give you a ride."

"Randal!"

He kept walking, wondering all over again why he'd aligned himself with her for so long. However, he wouldn't be in the situation he was now if...

His stomach fell. Amy obviously hadn't heard he'd

married Jolie, and was not going to respond well to the news. He wasn't going to respond well to her reaction, either, because he wouldn't tolerate a single moment of her hatred projected toward Jolie.

He wouldn't accept anything hurting Jolie, not from anyone. She was his wife, and that meant she had his full protection.

It wasn't love, but it was something he could give her. He contemplated that on the drive home.

Lunch was being served when he walked into the house, and the laughter coming from the dining room made him pause near the doorway. Jolie's laugh was a form of music all on its own. Light and lyrical, it had the ability to not only instill happiness, but evoke it.

"Are you just going to stand there, or are you going to join us?" Grandpa asked.

Randal stepped around the corner. "I was waiting to hear what you two found so funny."

Grandpa laughed harder. "You."

Randal lifted a brow at Jolie's blush. "Really?"

Covering her mouth with one hand, she nodded.

No one had ever made him desire something so badly, and he highly doubted anyone ever would. She was unique. Special. In so many ways.

"I was telling her about when you were little, not in school yet, and your mother told you to hurry and put on a pair of shoes if you wanted to go to the store with her."

"Ah, yes." He knew the story well and sat down next to Jolie. "Mother had told me to put on shoes. She hadn't specified that they had to be my shoes."

"So you put on your father's shoes and wore them

to the store?" Jolie's eyes were still shimmering, her cheeks still flushed.

"Yes. Peter had just polished Father's shoes, so they were in the kitchen. Mine were upstairs in my room, and she'd said to hurry."

"How could you even walk in them?" she asked.

"I don't remember, but I'm sure it wasn't easy." What he did remember was his mother laughing about it while telling his father, and how she'd looked almost as pretty as Jolie was right now. That was rare. Him remembering things about his mother. Specific things, but right now, he could almost hear her laugh. His father's, too. That was a rare memory. After his mother died, he never heard his father laugh.

"Jolie is sewing me a smoking jacket," Grandpa said. "A blue one. She got that sewing room of hers all ready to go and measured me so it'll fit just right."

Pausing as he spooned food onto his plate, Randal looked at Jolie.

She poured coffee into his cup. "Grandpa said he looks good in blue."

"Did he?"

"Yes, I did," Grandpa said. "I do look good in blue. So do you."

"So does Jolie." Randal hadn't seen her not look good. She was wearing a simple white blouse today, along with a black skirt, and looked as lovely as she had on their wedding day. As enticing as she had last night when he'd opened the bedroom door and saw her standing there, with her robe open, exposing a nearly translucent nightgown. It had nearly gutted him, to think of giving her up, and still did.

"She'll show you the room after lunch," Grandpa

said. "She found all sorts of things up in the attic. It's good to know they'll be used rather than sitting up there gathering dust."

"Yes, it is," Randal agreed.

Half an hour later, he was impressed by the transformation that had taken place in the once empty room, and was instantly drawn to the table, where dark blue material was laid out with tissue paper in odd shapes pinned to it. "Is this the smoking jacket?"

"Yes." She pointed to more material draped over the back of a chair. "I'll line it with this."

Twisting, leaning a hip against the table, he couldn't stop from voicing his disappointment. "I thought you'd make a dress for yourself from this material."

"I will. There's more than enough for both."

"When?" Regret rose up in him at the way she glanced down at her attire. "You look beautiful in everything you wear. I just thought that's what you wanted to do, sew clothes for yourself."

"I enjoy designing things for others, too." She walked around the other end of the table, touching the material. "Things that they want. Like a smoking jacket."

He believed that. She liked helping others. "All right then. Anything I can do to help?" He walked over to a shelf where material was stacked along with some notepads. "Need a bowl of water?"

Her laugh was soft as she picked up a pair of scissors. "No, but thank you."

He lifted a notepad off the shelf and flipped through the pages of drawings. Dresses and blouses, shirts and pants. All drawn in pencil. A page caused him to stop flipping. They were drawings of underclothes. Specifically, women's underclothes. With his blood flowing a bit faster, and hotter, he glanced across the room. She was bent over the table, cutting the material along the edges of the tissue paper pinned to it. He wished her blouse was transparent because he wanted to know if she was wearing a brassiere like the one in the drawing.

Really, most definitely, wanted to know.

Chapter Fourteen

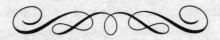

"Oh, my word, Jolie! It's not only comfortable, it's so pretty! I can't wait for David to see it. He's going to love it!" Jane Albright twisted, looking at her image in the mirror; one of several mirrors in the very large dressing room that held four mirrors, two freestanding closets, racks of shoes and a lovely dressing table amongst other things. Jolie had barely walked into the house on Randal's arm when Jane had asked for the men to excuse them and brought her up here, where Jolie had taken the bra, wrapped in tissue paper, out of her purse. She'd sewn it this morning, and had worried all day if it would fit or not.

"I bet Randal can't wait to watch you undress every night," Jane said.

Jolie's face burned and she had to turn away. Randal had never watched her undress, but the idea of him doing so certainly made her body react. Holding her breath at the rapid increase of her heart, she counted to ten, then breathed. It didn't help much, the idea was still there, but she turned about. "I'm glad it fits and I hope you find it more comfortable than your others."

"It already is more comfortable. I love it." Jane stuck her arm in a sleeve of the sleek, gold silk dress she'd unbuttoned to her waist to put on her new bra. "I'm burning those other ones. They are torture traps compared to this."

"Here, let me help you." Jolie held up the back of the dress for Jane to slip in her other arm.

Once the dress was buttoned again, Jane twisted, glancing at her image in the mirror. "Look at that. It makes my dress fit better. Look better. How can that be?"

"It's the way I sew the cups together in the front," Jolie explained. "I sew material between them to separate your boobs instead of bunching them together."

Jane examined her reflection again. "That's exactly what it does. And being so silky smooth, the material of my dress doesn't catch on anything." Wiggling and lifting her arms, she added, "No matter how I move." She then spun around and planted her hands on her hips. "You are a genius."

"Not hardly." Bras had been the one thing she had been able to design and sew that her mother never complained about. Mainly because she never knew about them.

"I think you are." Jane hooked their arms together. "And I think we better get back downstairs before the men come looking for us."

The men were in the living room, along with David's brother, sister-in-law and grandfather, Gus, who was as charming as Jane had insisted. He kept them laughing throughout dinner. Afterward, she and Randal and Jane and David retired into a game room where they played several games of whist, during which the conversation included airplanes. Randal's knowledge not only filled her with pride, it held her captive. He didn't just know about airplanes—he was passionate about them. She could see it on his face, hear it in his voice and feel it.

That's why he'd married her, and she knew another why. This, the airplane business, was the pirate's treasure he'd been seeking for his entire life.

She sincerely wanted him to find that treasure. He'd told her in the beginning that he wasn't looking for love, and she certainly hadn't married him for love. But she was going to help him do whatever she could to make this dream of his come true. She liked that idea, and how it made sense. Life wasn't always about your own dreams. It was also about helping others find theirs.

"What are you thinking so hard about?" he asked later, as they drove home.

"Nothing." She couldn't tell him that she was considering talking to Dad, simply asking if and when he might put his airplane business on the market.

"Didn't you enjoy the evening?"

"Yes, very much. Jane is a delightful person, and it was interesting listening to you and David talk about airplanes."

He had to stop and wait for a car to turn before driving forward again. "Would you like to invite them to our house for dinner one evening?"

"Yes, I would." That could give her a reason to call Dad, and casually bring up the topic of selling his company. "Perhaps a few others as well."

"Sure, whoever you want."

"I was thinking Dad."

His silence gave the air an odd tenseness. Then he let out a sigh. "He's out of town for a few weeks."

"Oh? I didn't hear him mention that."

"He's gone on an annual fishing trip with his sons."

"At their fishing cabin? My father went there with him all the time." Fun, warm memories filled her and she leaned back against the seat. "Our entire family went once, but Mother didn't like it, she said it was like living in the dark ages."

"I can see your mother not appreciating that. What did you think about it?"

"I loved it. We'd swim all day, cook fish over the fire outside and chase lightning bugs until we were so tired, we fell asleep as soon as we laid down. Mother only went that once, but Silas and I went almost every year. So did Chloe when she got older and Mother was certain we wouldn't let her drown. Anna was there most of the time, too, and the way she cooked that fish, oh, I can almost taste how good it was." How had she forgotten how much fun that had been? "Have you ever gone on a trip like that?"

"No. My father was always too busy working for anything like that."

That was sad and she made an instant decision. "Then we'll go someday." The prospect excited her. "I know Dad will let us use the cabin."

"Do you know where it's located?"

"On a lake with a sandy bottom and surrounded by big climbing trees." She laughed. "Dad will give us directions, tell us how to get there." More memories were filling her mind. "My father and Dad were always betting on who would catch the first fish, and the biggest fish, and the most fish. I won all three one day and was dubbed the Fishing Queen."

"That's a royal title if I've ever heard one."

His teasing said his mood had lightened. "Thank you very much, you may call me Your Majesty whenever you're inclined."

"Should I bow at your feet, or kiss your hand?"

She hadn't realized they'd arrived home until he took ahold of her hand and kissed the back of it.

The heat of his lips raced all the way up her arm. She'd missed their kisses the past couple of days. Missed the way they made her feel. "Either, or."

His smile reflected in his eyes as he opened his door. "Allow me, Your Majesty." He slid out the door, still holding her hand.

She scooted across the seat and stepped out of the car, laughing again as he gave her a deep bow.

Her laughter lodged in the back of her throat as he stood so close that if she took a step, their bodies would touch. A tingling sensation took over her entire body, especially her breasts, making her wonder if he would like to see the bras she sewed. Specifically the one she was wearing right now.

The need, the want for him to pull her close, kiss her was so great, she couldn't move. Couldn't breathe. That grew harder as he stood still, staring at her. She sucked in a deep breath while asking, "Is something wrong?"

"No. No, nothing's wrong."

"Then why are you staring at me?" That wasn't what she'd wanted to ask. It was more centered on why he wasn't kissing her, but she couldn't quite make those words form.

* * *

"I'm merely admiring the Queen." Randal forced out a laugh to go along with his answer. In truth, he'd been convincing himself not to kiss her by coming up with every excuse under the sun. Or moon. For that's what was shining down upon her. A soft, muted silver ray that highlighted her amongst the shadows surrounding them.

She was so beautiful, so...perfect in every way. The desires inside him were so strong they were painful. He couldn't pretend that she didn't mean anything to him. She did. More than anyone had in a long time. He didn't want her to get hurt in all of this, which was tearing him up inside. The two forces inside him couldn't find common ground. She hadn't wanted to marry him, she'd been forced to for money, and the idea of ending it wasn't sitting well inside him. Not just because it would be a failure.

"There's not that much to admire," she said.

"I think there is." More than he could ever have imagined, and for the first time in his life, he wished he was someone other than Randal Osterlund.

He stepped aside so she could move away from the car. Closing the door, he tightened his hold on her hand to escort her into the house.

Grandpa was sitting in the living room and waved them into the room. "How was your dinner party?" he asked.

"Fine," Randal answered. "What are you still doing up?" Grandpa was usually tucked in bed long before ten.

"Enjoying my new smoking jacket." Grandpa's gaze was on Jolie, along with a smile. "What's the use of having such a fine jacket if you don't enjoy it?"

"It certainly looks good on you." Jolie walked to Grandpa's chair and kissed his cheek. "I'm glad you like it."

"It's the finest jacket I've ever had." Grandpa rubbed one of his sleeves. "I may never take it off."

"It will need to be laundered from time to time," Randal warned as he crossed the room and sat down on the sofa.

Grandpa lifted a brow in challenge. "I see you're wearing the shirt Jolie sewed for you."

"Yes, I am. It's become my favorite shirt." Randal didn't mind admitting that. It not only was more comfortable than any other he owned, he liked knowing she'd made it for him.

Shaking her head at both of them, Jolie sat down on the sofa next to him. "You two are two peas in a pod."

"I've been called worse," Grandpa said.

Randal laid his hand over the top of hers. "Me, too." He was still waiting for the desires inside him to subside, but had to be honest enough to admit that wasn't going to happen anytime soon.

"Was Gus at the dinner party?" Grandpa asked. "I haven't seen him in some time."

That led into a conversation that lasted for almost an hour, mainly due to Jolie sharing that they would be hosting a dinner party of their own soon, and that Gus would be included on the guest list. That had lit up Grandpa's eyes and soon he'd been rattling off a list of others he'd like to invite.

By the time Randal escorted Jolie up the stairs to their room, guilt was rolling around in his stomach. "I'm sorry Grandpa got so carried away."

"I'm not." She stepped out of her shoes and carried them to the closet. "It will be good for him to see all of his old friends."

He loosened his tie while crossing the room. "It will be a lot of work for you."

"I'm not afraid of work, it'll be fun." She removed her earrings and placed them in a glass container on the dressing table. "Besides, that's part of being your wife."

His throat tightened.

"Our agreement included me performing social duties." She turned, looked at him directly, chin up as if bracing herself. "Unless you've changed your mind about that."

He pulled off his tie and unbuttoned the top button of his shirt, needing air. Her dress was white and pale green, with a large bow tied above her breasts, and all night he'd been wondering about the drawing he'd seen of a brassiere, curious if she was wearing one like that.

"Have you?" she asked.

"No." He took off his suit jacket. "I haven't changed my mind."

"Then what have you changed your mind about?"

"Nothing."

She shook her head and looked away. "I'm sorry I voiced my opinion about Danielle and James moving out. You were frustrated and I just wanted to help. I didn't mean to interfere."

Regret at how he'd acted that night struck again. He stepped in front of her. "You weren't interfering. I appreciate what you said, how you made me look at things. You were right to do so. Danielle and James are adults and they deserve the opportunity to make it on their own. Even after they got married, I still thought of them as two kids and they aren't."

Looking down, she played with the bow of her dress.

"Have I done something else that upset you? That wasn't right?"

"No. Not at all."

"So this is just..." She closed her eyes.

"Just what?"

"Part of taking it slow. Getting to know each other."

He wanted to kiss her so badly his entire body was throbbing.

"Yes."

She nodded and turned around.

He balled his hands into fists to keep from grasping her shoulders, spinning her back around to face him and kissing her.

"Oh, good grief!" Her soft exclamation included a frustrated huff.

"What's wrong?"

"Nothing." She leaned closer toward the mirror attached to the dressing table. "I just pulled the wrong tie on my bow and now have a knot."

Her reflection showed how she was attempting to see the knot in the mirror. He laid his hands on her shoulders. "Turn around. Let me see if I can help."

"I'll get it."

He could see in the mirror that her fidgeting was tightening the knot. "You're making it worse because you can't see what you're doing." He forced her to turn around and pushed aside her hands. "Lift your chin up so I can see what I'm doing."

She tilted her head back and stared up at the ceiling.

Biting back a grin, he loosened the knot almost immediately, but kept pretending that he was working on it. Even though he knew he was playing with fire, he liked it.

"Can't you get it?" she asked.

"Yes, I can get it." He loosened the knot more, letting the silky material fall through the loop.

She bent her head down. "The material didn't snag, did it?"

He undid the second loop. "I don't think so, but your face is in the way, I can't see."

She lifted her face and stuck her tongue out him.

His reaction was to laugh, at the same time his hands slid up and grasped the sides of her face. Then, he bent down and covered her mouth with his. He also took advantage of her parted lips, slipping his tongue between them. A thrill rippled over him at the warmth, the sweet taste of her, and he delved deeper, entangling his tongue with hers.

Her arms slid around his sides as she melted against him and returned the kiss, tongue twist for tongue twist.

Having her close at hand, next to him, had become natural, but holding her, kissing her, was beyond that. It felt right. So right. The thought that struck next wasn't as welcomed as others would have been, because he wondered if it felt right to her. But it couldn't. He'd told her he could never love her, and she wanted that. She may think liking each other is enough, but there will come a day when it won't be. Tonight had confirmed it. He'd seen how she'd looked at Jane and David again.

He pulled out of the kiss, and unable to meet her eyes, pulled her into a hug, kissing the top of her hair. Then he released her and walked into the bathroom, needing time to cool the raging inferno inside him.

Chapter Fifteen

Jolie was overjoyed when Peter informed her that Chloe and Silas were there to see her. She had missed them both dearly, had thought about them each and every day since moving out of her mother's house. Not worrying about them wasn't an option. That had been her role for too long, and it kicked in high gear as soon as she walked into the living room where they were both seated, waiting for her.

She forced a smile to remain on her face until after giving and receiving hugs, and they'd all settled in chairs. Letting her seriousness show, she looked at each of them. "Spill."

The look Silas and Chloe shared made her stomach sink. "What's happened?" she asked.

Slender, with curly dark hair, Silas resembled their father. Always had. Right now, she saw even more of that. It was the set of his mouth, as if he didn't want to admit to anything.

That made her turn to Chloe.

Her sister let out a long sigh. "We never realized how much you protected us from Mother."

"Not necessarily protected us," Silas interjected, always the peacekeeper. "Shielded is a better way to describe it."

Jolie clenched her teeth together. "One of you tell me what she's done."

Chloe threw her hands in the air. "She's finding people for us to marry."

"What? No. That's—" Jolie stopped before saying that's why she'd married Randal. It had been, and was working out, but she didn't want her siblings subjected to the same thing. "Not possible. It can't be true."

"It is." In his slow, calm way, Silas shrugged. "It appears that she believes it worked so well with you and Randal, that she's convinced she can get three times the amount of money Randal has promised to provide her monthly, by doing the same with Chloe and I."

Why hadn't she seen this coming? Enough had never been enough for Mother, so it wouldn't be now, either.

"I have decided to quit school and obtain employment. I'm hoping that will placate her until—"

"No!" Jolie stood and paced the floor, needing to release some of the anger building inside. "You will not quit school." She turned to Chloe. "And you will not run away. I will figure this out."

"It's no longer your problem, Jolie. You've already sacrificed yourself for us. For our family." Silas shook his head. "I shouldn't have let you do that."

"Sacrificed myself? Do I look like I've sacrificed anything?" Jolie didn't wait for either of them to answer. "No, I don't, because I haven't. Randal is truly wonderful, and I assure you, I have gained everything and lost nothing." Anger reached a new level inside her. The truth of the matter was that he'd lost, financially, by marrying her. Breathing deep to calm herself, she continued, "The only things that I miss are the two of you." And it appears, the ability to protect them from their mother.

"We miss you, too, Jolie. But if I don't act, don't obtain employment, I fear Mother will request more funds from Randal. She has already spent her monthly allotment."

Never riled, Silas always maintained his composure and spoke eloquently. Someday, he would make a fabulous teacher. Jolie had to make sure that happened. "I will fix this," she said. "I just need some time to think about it."

Holding both hands up, so they would remain silent, she sat down on the sofa. Her mother would not extort more money out of Randal. Would not. There was no way on earth that she would let that happen. She pinched her lips together, thinking of the kiss they'd shared last night when he'd untied the knot on her bow. Randal had slept on the sofa last night, but that kiss had meant something to him. She could tell by the way he looked at her. It had meant something to her, too. She wanted other things, too. In fact, she'd spent a portion of the morning wondering how she could accidentally spill water on the sofa in their room again.

Chloe jumped to her feet, took her turn at pacing, and that forced Jolie's mind back to the business at hand. If only she had a way to make money, to placate her mother until her siblings were grown and on their own.

"We've both been looking for jobs," Chloe said, "but so is half of Chicago, and the only jobs we've found expect their employees to work all day, every day. The only way we can do that is to quit school."

"You aren't quitting school. You haven't even graduated high school." Jolie looked at Silas.

"We can't let you do this on your own, Jolie," he said. "You've done enough. If we have jobs, Mother can't blame us for not contributing to the family income."

That is exactly how their mother would play on their senses. She should have known once Mother got a taste of having money again, it would only increase. "I need some time, need to discuss this with Randal."

"No, Jolie, we don't want you to ask him for more—"

"I'm not going to ask him for more money," she said, cutting off Silas. Randal would give her mother more money, and that couldn't happen. He might need it before his airline business became profitable. "This is not his problem and I won't let it become his problem. But he might know of someone who is hiring. Someone who wouldn't mind employees who must work around their school schedules."

"Do you think that is possible?"

She hoped it was a possibility. "I won't know until I ask him." She would also be talking to her mother. "Does Mother know you came to visit me?"

"No." Chloe plopped down in the chair again. "She's having lunch with Mrs. Turner at a café downtown."

Louise Turner put on airs as strongly as their mother. Jolie stood. "Well, then, the two of you will have lunch with Grandpa and I, he'll enjoy that, and when you get home, you can let Mother know that I'd invited you to lunch and that I'll be over to see her later this week. By then, we'll have a plan in place." She wasn't convinced that she'd have a plan by then, but wouldn't let them know that. She waved a hand for both of them to stand. "Come, let me introduce you to Grandpa. You met him at the wedding and will enjoy getting to know him better."

Grandpa was in his study, wearing his smoking jacket and was delighted to have company. Jolie left her siblings with him while she went to inform Mrs. Hoover that there would be two more for lunch. She knew the additions wouldn't be an issue as Danielle and James would not be home for lunch because they'd received the key for their new apartment.

Danielle and James were so excited, and Jolie sincerely hoped all went well for them. Not only for their sakes, but for Randal's. He'd done so much for so many, including her family. If only Dad was in town. She could ask him about jobs for Silas and Chloe, and ask about his business. He would be home in three weeks, but that might be too late. It had only taken her mother days to marry her off to Randal.

Ironically, that had proven to be the best thing her mother had ever done.

For her.

But it hadn't been for him.

Randal rarely came home for lunch, but the kiss he'd shared with Jolie last night still had his heart pounding, not to mention other parts. He should stay away from her. That would be the smart thing to do. Yet, here he was, driving home on the pretense of needing lunch. His office was surrounded by places to eat. Restaurants he frequented so often they knew his likes and dislikes.

He just couldn't get Jolie off his mind today. She'd tossed and turned all night. He'd heard her. It hadn't kept him awake. He'd been unable to fall to sleep knowing she was only feet away, in a bed large enough for two, while he'd been on a sofa, not large enough for one.

He'd never gone back on his word, but keeping Carl's secret was killing him. Three weeks was too long to wait. If Jolie decided she wanted out of their agreement, it should happen sooner than later, before any more damage was done.

Pulling in the driveway, he didn't recognize the old Cadillac, but heard his grandfather's laughter as soon as he entered the house. Curious as to who the visitors were, he walked down the hall to the study. As he rounded the corner of the doorway, it was Jolie he saw first, and how her face lit up.

"Randal."

His heart pounded even harder as she hurried across the room to meet him. It took a moment for him to make his voice work. "I thought I'd come home for lunch today."

"That's wonderful." She stretched on her toes and brushed her lips over his as if it was the most normal thing in the world.

He was sure it was a manufactured welcome for the others in the room, but it flooded his system with something he couldn't explain. It went beyond enjoyment, beyond joy.

"Silas and Chloe stopped by and I asked them to stay for lunch." Jolie wrapped her hands around his arm. "Your timing is perfect. We were just on our way to the dining room."

He heard her, but in his mind, was wishing that her simple kiss had meant as much to her as it had to him, even though he knew he shouldn't wish that. There was still no place for love in his life, but there was room for like, and he liked her. He was still searching for another business to purchase, while also considering ways he might be able to help her with Carl's company. For multiple reasons, he didn't want their marriage to fail, but ultimately, he didn't want anyone to think badly of her. She'd been right about that. He did care what others thought, especially when it came to her.

He greeted her siblings, and escorted her into the dining room.

If he'd expected lunch to be an awkward affair, he couldn't have been more wrong. That also had him wondering about her greeting upon his arrival. Her siblings knew about their arrangement, so there had been no need for her to kiss him.

He'd met her siblings several times, but had barely heard either of them speak. Today, there was no lull in the conversation as they ate, especially when Jolie told her siblings that Carl was at his fishing cabin. All three of them were then full of stories, reminiscing about their trips to the cabin in the past.

Grandpa joined in by sharing his own fish tales, ending one particular story with a long sigh. "I used to go fishing a lot in the old country, with my grandfather." Grandpa looked at him. "It's too bad you and I never went fishing, Randal."

"It's not too late," Jolie said. "You still can. Randal and I are going to go. I'm going to ask Dad if we can use his cabin. You can come with us."

Grandpa shook his head. "You young ones wouldn't want me tagging along."

"We would love to have you join us," Jolie insisted. "The more the merrier."

"There is plenty of room," her sister said. "There are

two bedrooms and an overhead loft, which my mother forbade me from sleeping in because she thought I'd fall off, but since she wasn't there, my father let me sleep up there. One end had a huge window and I swear, the stars felt close enough to almost touch."

"Do you remember the year you won the fishing contest?" her brother asked Jolie.

Randal grinned at how Jolie laughed as she reached over and touched his shoulder.

"I told Randal about that last night," she said.

The warmth of her hand on his shoulder spread into his chest. "Her Majesty did tell me that last night," he replied, bringing a round of laugher to the table.

She let a soft sigh as she patted his shoulder and then removed her hand. "It was my favorite place to go as a child."

At that moment, Randal wanted to put her in the car and drive to the cabin, wherever it was.

"Well, then, when are we going?" Grandpa asked.

"I'll call Dad as soon as he returns to town," Jolie said.

Though he kept it hidden, Randal's heart sank, knowing Carl's return could very well change her mind.

As soon as lunch ended, her siblings took their leave, and while Jolie was seeing them out, Grandpa planted both elbows on the table. "You've done well for yourself, Randal. I'm proud of you."

Those were words he'd never heard. He'd wanted to hear them, especially when he'd been young and striving to prove himself. A shiver tickled his spine when he noticed his grandfather's gaze was on the door that Jolie had exited moments ago.

"A man can be proud of all of his achievements," Grandpa said. "But the greatest is his family."

Those were words Randal had heard before, many times. The importance of providing for his family had been drummed into his head at an early age, and repeated over and over again.

"I remember the first time I met your grandmother. She was washing milk bottles. I'd only been in America a few months and didn't have a pot to piss in, but I told her if she married me, I'd see to it that she never had to wash milk bottles again in her life." Grandpa laughed. "That meant I had to wash them. It took more than a year before that first well hit oil."

That, too, was something Randal had never heard. His grandmother had died when he was an infant, and like his mother, no one spoke of her very often.

"There's nothing like the love of a woman to put the drive inside a man to become more than he'd ever have become on his own. Your grandmother did that to me, and your mother did that to your father. Now, it's your turn."

Randal was aware that he was expected to make more money, build the Osterlund wealth beyond what the previous generations had acquired, but had never heard it put that way. That his grandmother and mother had been behind both Grandpa and his father. He wasn't sure what to think about that.

"Well, I guess I better return to work." Randal stood. "I'll see you tonight."

"I'll be here," Grandpa said. "The one wearing the spiffy smoking jacket."

Jolie had already made a large impact on his entire family. He hadn't expected that.

Outside, he stood beside Jolie as her siblings drove away. Her smile as she glanced up at him appeared strained and, knowing it would be natural for her to miss her siblings, he put an arm around her. One more thing that their agreement had done, taken her away from her family. "There's a car in the garage you can use to go see them whenever you want."

She leaned against him. "Thank you. I may do that later on this week."

He rested his head against hers, relishing in the connection. She'd changed something inside him. Opened a part of him he hadn't realized had been closed off. That made him wary. He'd never needed anyone, especially a woman, and didn't want to consider what that meant.

This couldn't go any further. He had to tell her about Carl.

And would have, right then, if not for the two-seated roadster that pulled in the driveway.

"It's Jane," Jolie said.

He'd already recognized the blonde woman. "I see that." He wasn't nearly as excited as Jolie sounded, only because the disruption meant they couldn't talk right now. Other than that, Jane was good people and he was very glad Jolie and Jane had become friends so quickly.

"Hello!" Jane climbed out of the car. "I hope I'm not intruding."

"Not at all." He leaned down and brushed a kiss over Jolie's lips. Not for show. It was because he wanted to kiss her. "I'll see you tonight."

"All right." She tugged at his tie, straightening it. "Have a good afternoon."

He winked at her. "You, too." With a nod at Jane, he walked toward his car.

"Don't you just love when they come home for lunch?"

He heard Jane's question, and held his breath as he walked, listening for Jolie's reply.

"Yes," Jolie replied. "It's wonderful."

He couldn't have stopped the smile that tugged at his lips if he'd have wanted to.

Chapter Sixteen

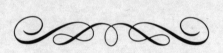

"Two dollars?" Jolie pressed a hand against the way her heart fluttered. "I couldn't possibly sell them for two dollars. Bras are only forty-nine cents in the department stores."

Jane held her arms out at her sides. "Forty-nine cents for torture devices."

No one in their right mind would pay two dollars for a bra, but to say that aloud would be saying Jane was crazy. She wasn't. She was just excited. Had been since they'd walked into the house.

"I'm telling you, Jolie. Women will pay two dollars without blinking an eye." She waved a hand toward the coffee table, where forty dollars lay. "In advance. I was going to call you yesterday, but told myself to wear the bra all day first, just to be sure, and am I sure! And David is thrilled. Not only because I'm comfortable. It's so pretty. Did I tell you that he thought I'd changed my outfit on Monday night? He said he knew right away that something was different, but was sure that I was wearing the same dress."

"Yes, you told me," Jolie replied with a laugh. It was

obvious that Jane liked her new bra, but that didn't mean others would.

Jane slapped her hands against her legs. "I can't stop telling people about it. My sisters, my mother, my sister-in-law, four very good friends, they all want bras now." She brushed her long blond hair off her shoulders. "My only request is that you make me one more first. At least one." Giggling, she added, "David told me to buy a dozen. And I will, but I'll let a few other people have one first."

Jolie rubbed her hands over her thighs, calculating how much money she'd need to buy the supplies. "I'll gladly make more, for you and the others, but I won't charge two dollars apiece for them. Fifty cents will be more than enough to buy all the material I need."

"I'm sure it will, but they are worth so much more. That's what you need to realize. Look at it this way. Besides the material, you need to be paid for your time, and more importantly, your design. It's perfect. And it's needed. Women need comfort as much as they need style. Your bras are both. Everyone who wears one is going to want more, and they are going to tell more people about them." Jane picked up the money. "This is proof."

"Two dollars seems so expensive."

"So is flying, but that doesn't stop people from buying tickets."

Jolie shook her head.

Jane nodded hers.

Attempting to compromise, Jolie asked, "How about one dollar?"

"No. I'm paying you two dollars for the one I'm wearing, and for each of the others I want you to sew for me, and that's the price I told everyone else, and they are more than happy to pay it." Jane fluttered the bills in the air. "I have my car. We can go shopping for supplies right now. I'll even come back and help you. I have everyone's measurements, told them to measure themselves just like you'd measured me."

Jolie scratched her head.

"I know you're busy, being just married and everything, but I will help," Jane offered.

"It's not that. I have plenty of time," Jolie insisted.

"Then what is it?"

Jolie huffed out a breath. "I'm not a designer, I'm not—"

"Yes, you are." Jane threw her arms in the air. "You are the designer of Jolie's dream bras. That's what I've been calling them."

"Jolie's dream bras?"

"Yes." Jane leaped to her feet. "Now, let's go shopping. I will help as much as I can between now and four. I have to be at the airport by then. I promised David."

By four o'clock, all of the patterns had been created, the material cut and several bras completed, besides the one Jane had taken when she'd left. Not only that, Jolie was very optimistic that both Silas and Chloe could soon have jobs that would work with their school schedules. Jane had to be at the airport in order to sell tickets and assist passengers when a plane landed. She'd explained that planes didn't fly in and out enough times a day to have a full-time employee manning the counter all day, but when they did land, at least two people were needed. Although many people were looking for jobs, few only wanted to work three to four hours each afternoon during the week. More planes flew in and out during the weekends, so those shifts were longer, but David was having a hard time finding people to fill those shifts, too.

Trusting her new friend, Jolie had explained that her siblings wanted to work, but were still in school. Jane had thought Silas and Chloe would be perfect for the positions, and promised to talk to David about it as soon as she arrived at the airport.

Jolie was very grateful for Jane's assistance, and was relieved that she wouldn't have to ask Randal to help her family even more than he already had. She was also grateful for the money from the sales of the bras she was making. What was left over after buying material would be enough to keep Mother placated for a couple of weeks.

Two dollars apiece seemed like an extravagant price, but again, because of Jane, and in a way, Randal, she'd accepted that price because she'd insisted that a percentage of every bra sold would go to the soup kitchen. Jane had agreed and Jolie sincerely hoped the other women loved the bras as much as Jane, because she liked the idea of how her bras were not only helping women, but those in need of food as well. Having been in that situation, though her mother would never have allowed them to visit the soup kitchen, she knew how it felt to have empty cupboards.

That led her to wonder if other married women's husbands would like the bras as much as Jane said David did, mainly because she wondered if Randal would like them.

If he ever saw one.

It was crazy, but when she thought of him seeing her

wearing one, warmth spiraled inside her body, leaving her tingling all over.

That warmth was there at other times, too, and it was a feeling that she liked. Just feeling it made her think of Randal.

A knock sounded and the door opened before Jolie had time to stand up from her sewing stool.

"I'm sorry for disturbing you, but I have to tell you about the apartment!" Danielle hurried into the room and closed the door. "I scrubbed all the floors and windows today."

Spinning her stool around to face Danielle, Jolie waved a hand toward a chair. "Sit and tell me all about it. I want to hear everything."

"There are two bedrooms, a living room, bathroom and kitchen with black-and-white linoleum. It's so cute. It's on the third floor and the kitchen window overlooks the street, the ones in the bedrooms overlook the alley." Danielle's smile never faltered as she plopped down in the chair. "It's small compared to all this, but I know we'll be happy there, even if the money is tight for a while." Sighing, she added, "I truly wish there was a way for me to help James get more customers."

Jolie wanted James to get more customers, too. Wanted this to work for him and Danielle. For them and for Randal, so he wouldn't have to worry so much about taking care of everyone. She'd been thinking about it a lot lately, including while her siblings had been here earlier. She'd told them about flying in the plane with Randal, and that had made other thoughts form. "I had a thought earlier today," she said cautiously.

"Oh? About what?"

"More customers for James."

"You did?"

Jolie nodded. "Two thoughts actually." The other idea had come about when Chloe asked if she'd hem her dress soon, so she could wear it when school started up for the class picture.

"What are they?" Danielle asked.

"The first one is about the schools, how he takes group pictures of each classroom. Perhaps he could take pictures of each child individually. The younger ones. Right now, it's just the high school students, those graduating who get individual pictures. The parents might really like that, and buy extra copies to share with family."

"Oh, my goodness, that is a wonderful idea! James knows all of the school principals, and, oh, that's just an amazing idea. I'm sure parents would like it." Danielle clapped her hands together excitedly. "What's your other idea?"

"It's very different, and has to do with Randal's friend Roger. Do you know him?"

"Roger Wayne? Yes. He and Randal have been friends for years. He uses his plane to scout new routes for the electrical and telephone companies."

"Exactly." Jolie wasn't sure about this idea, but offered it anyway. "My thoughts were about those companies. Perhaps they'd like pictures of the routes Roger finds, taken from the airplane."

Danielle's mouth fell open. "Wow. That's a very good idea. Roger says that sketching the routes, making the maps, is the hardest part. Pictures would help him immensely." She leaped to her feet. "Why didn't I think of that? Or of the schools!" She crossed the room, arms open for a hug. "You are the best, just the best."

Jolie returned her hug. "I hope one or the other of my ideas is helpful."

"I think they'll both work." Danielle hugged her again. "I can't wait to tell James about them." Stepping out of the hug, Danielle continued to stare at the sewing machine behind Jolie. "Are you sewing bras?"

Jolie spun her stool around. "Yes, I am."

Danielle picked up one of the finished bras. "It's so pretty, and soft and silky." She glanced at the table of cut material pieces. "How many are you making?"

"A few. I'll make you one, if you'd like."

"I'd like that, but how many bras do you need?"

Jolie laughed. "They aren't all for me. They are for... friends. I'll need your measurements to make yours fit properly."

By the following afternoon, Jolie had all the bras sewn, including a couple for each of Danielle and Willa. She then cut out a dress from dark blue sateen to wear to the dinner party they were hosting next weekend.

She and Randal spent Saturday helping Danielle and James move into their apartment, and on Sunday, they took Grandpa to Willa's for lunch and then to see James and Danielle's new apartment.

Randal appeared happy, but something troubled him. She could see it in his face, especially his eyes when she'd catch him looking at her for no reason. It would quickly disappear and he'd smile, even kiss her at times. Soft, sweet kisses. She liked those kisses. More than that, she liked being comfortable with him. More than comfortable. She liked the way he laid his hand on her back to escort her through a door, and held her hand to assist her out of the car, and draped an arm around her shoulders and rubbed her upper arms. Soft, gentle caresses that sent those spirals of heat throughout her body and made her wish that she'd come up with a way to spill water on the sofa again. She hadn't. He was still sleeping there every night.

She also wished she knew how long this getting to know each other time would last. They were married, there was no reason for them not to sleep in the same bed.

Not only did Jane insist that David liked her new bras, so did Danielle and Willa. Jolie wanted Randal to see her wearing one, wanted to know if he would like how it looked on her and if it would lead to what the others said it led to.

She wasn't exactly sure when she'd concluded that. Sometime over the weekend, while the orders for more bras had been coming in. Everyone who wore one wanted more, and told others, who also wanted one or two.

On Monday morning, she'd called the department store and asked them to deliver the material she needed so she could continue to sew until it was time for Randal to return home from work. She'd made sure to still spend time with Grandpa after breakfast and lunch, and to assist Mrs. Hoover and Darla with preparations for the dinner party they would be hosting on Saturday evening.

The rest of the week followed suit, with her sewing from the time Randal left in the morning, until he returned in the evening. He still slept on the sofa each night, but there was a closeness growing between them that filled her with a soft sense of contentment.

She still wanted more, but felt she understood why

Randal was continuing to take it slow. Grandpa had told her about Randal's mother's death, that his father had been angry afterward and how that had affected everyone. How Randal, especially, had never let himself get close to anyone ever since. Until her.

She'd let Grandpa believe she had cracked Randal's shell, as he'd put it, even though she knew she hadn't. She hoped time would do that, and she would give Randal all the time he needed.

He was on her mind every hour, as she continued to take more orders for bras. Jane stopped over almost daily, to pick up bras, drop off more measurements and money, and would often stay, insisting upon helping by cutting out pattern pieces while Jolie sewed.

They talked about a large variety of things, including about how David had hired both Chloe and Silas—which Jolie already knew because her siblings had called her, very excited about the jobs. Her mother had called, too, disgusted that Jolie had helped her siblings find work. To placate her mother, Jolie had driven over, visited and had given her the money. That had truly delighted her mother, as Jolie had known it would.

She and Jane also discussed the guests of the upcoming dinner party to the point that Jolie felt as if she already knew everyone who would be in attendance.

By the time Friday afternoon arrived, Jolie figured she could sew a bra in her sleep. Having made so many the past two weeks, she had it down to a very efficient system that allowed her to sew one in less than an hour. There were stacks of tissue-wrapped bras, with women's names on the little tags, ready to be distributed by Jane, Danielle and Willa, who would all be at the dinner party tomorrow night. She had just pulled the door closed on her sewing room when she heard Peter greet Randal at the front door.

Her heart raced at the sound of his voice, and she hurried down the hallway to greet him. They met on the stairway, with him going up and her going down.

He caught her by the waist with both hands. "Where are you going in such a hurry?"

Because she was still one step up from him, they were eye to eye and her entire body warmed at the way his silver-blue eyes glowed. She laid her hands on his shoulders. "To say hello to you."

"Aw, well, in that case, go ahead."

Giddy, she said, "Hello."

He lifted a brow. "Is that it?"

She wanted to kiss him, and knew that was what he was expecting, yet teasing him by not doing so was almost as delightful. "How was your day?"

He shook his head.

Acting as if she didn't know that he wasn't referring to his day, she patted his shoulder and offered her best frown. "Oh, I'm sorry that you had a bad day." Her lips tingled at the way he kept looking at them. "Is there anything I can do to make it better?"

"A kiss might help."

Not ready for the game to end, she leaned forward and kissed his cheek. "Is that better?"

"No."

She kissed his other cheek. "How about now?"

"No."

Rubbing his shoulders, she leaned close again. "It must have been a very bad day."

He pulled her hips closer, until she could feel the heat of his body. "Actually, it was a good day. A very good day." Their mouths were so close, his breath mingled with hers. "Because I came home to you."

Her heart nearly melted, as did her bones, the moment his lips met hers. It was a long, sensual kiss that left her dizzy, clinging to him and biting her lips together to keep from begging him to sleep in the bed tonight.

Chapter Seventeen

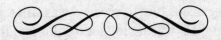

Standing there, holding her and trying to catch his breath, Randal knew he couldn't take any more. He'd tried to keep his promise to Carl, but he couldn't keep going on like this. The desire to carry her up to their bedroom and consummate their marriage was so great, not doing so might be the death of him.

Yet, he couldn't do that, not without her knowing the truth. Ultimately, making their marriage real had to be her choice. "How about we go out to dinner tonight?"

She lifted her head off his shoulder and nodded.

It might all be him, but he could have sworn he saw disappointment flash across her face. "You can wear one of the new dresses you've been sewing."

"I'm saving it for tomorrow night."

He eased his hold of her enough for them to climb the steps side by side. "I'm looking forward to seeing it. You've been sewing all day, every day, this week."

"Yes, well, the dress is done. You'll see it tomorrow."

The dinner party tomorrow night almost made him change his mind, but this living in limbo had gone on long enough. Having her so close yet so far away. Once she knew the truth, and decided what she wanted to do, he'd be able to plan his next steps. Never before had his decisions, his actions, depended so deeply on someone else. Not even his father or grandfather. Their never-ending prodding hadn't affected him the way Jolie did. His life had changed the moment she'd entered it. He didn't regret that, but was struggling with a way to make it work.

The drive inside him to succeed was still there, it was just different. He was no longer thinking of the bottom line, the money he could make. He was thinking about the people. How it would affect them.

Them.

His focus was on only two people.

Her and him.

He hoped he wouldn't regret his decision to tell her the truth.

They went to the hotel restaurant. It held good memories. She was wearing the white-and-green dress, with the bow that he'd untied. The idea of doing so again heightened his senses as they discussed the menu for the dinner party and how she'd helped Darla polish the silver, along with other preparations. He was interested, and the excitement on her face about hosting the party pleased him, and all the while he wondered about bringing up the subject of Carl's company.

He had to bring it up. Had to know if she would choose him, or the business. He was willing to help her with Carl's company, but would she want that? After they'd eaten and were sipping on cups of coffee, he did the inevitable. "I have something I need to tell you."

She set her cup down. "What is it?"

He spun his cup in a circle on its saucer. "Carl isn't interested in selling his airplane company."

Her face fell and she reached across the table, laid her hand atop his. "Oh, no." She shook her head. "I could talk to him. Find out why, or if he might reconsider."

"I know why, and he won't reconsider."

"I'm so sorry." She folded her fingers around his. "Why won't he sell?"

"Because he's already put it in his will."

Nodding, she sighed. "For his sons."

"No." He had to quit beating around the bush. "For you."

She pulled her hand off his and sat back in her chair, wringing her hands together. "Me?"

"Yes, you."

"No." She shook her head. "Whoever told you that—"

"Carl told me. The night of his dinner party. The company has been in his will, to go to you, since your father died. Per Carl, the two of them were going to be partners in the company, but then the stock market crashed. Carl bought the company, wanted your father to still be a partner, but your father died and—"

"Stop." She pressed two fingers against her temple. "I don't want to inherit it. I don't want to inherit anything."

His idea of telling her at the restaurant was failing. They should be at home, where he could hold her. "I'm sorry, Jolie."

"It's not your fault." Sadness filled her face, dulled her eyes. "I don't want to be in Dad's will."

"Well, you won't be. He plans on giving you the airplane company when he returns next week. He asked me to keep it a secret, but I—you needed to know. That's all there is to it."

Frowning, she leaned forward. "If he gives it to me—"

"It will be yours, Jolie."

"Ours, Randal."

He held back the need to take her hand. "Yours, Jolie. Carl considered giving it to you before, but was afraid that your mother might mismanage things."

"She would have."

"There was that chance," he admitted. "But the bottom line is that if he had given it to you, you wouldn't have had to marry me."

She leaned back, stared at him.

"You don't need to stay married to me, either. The agreement we had…" He shrugged, not wanting to continue. Not knowing what to say.

"Don't need to—"

"No."

Pressing a hand to her stomach, she closed her eyes, then pushed away from the table with her other hand. "Excuse me."

He stood, reached for her. "Jolie—"

"I need to go to the powder room."

Watching her hurry away, he knew he'd screwed this up tighter than a corkscrew. Why hadn't he asked if she wanted to stay married to him? Ask her opinion rather than just laying out the facts. Because he was an idiot, that's why. He was responding to this like a business deal, had been since the beginning. That's all he'd ever known. Business deals.

But this wasn't a business deal.

Not at all.

* * *

Jolie held her breath all the way to the powder room, fearing as soon as she breathed, she'd cry. She wasn't going to do that. Not here. She was responding to the idea of not being married to Randal, knowing deep down, that was the one thing she didn't want. But he didn't want to be married to her.

Thankfully the powder room was empty. She walked to the sink, leaned heavily against it, gulping for air as one thing played over and over in her mind. The same thing that had echoed in her head at the table. Dad had told Randal about the company the night of his dinner party. The exact same night that Randal had asked her if she wanted to live the rest of her life with a man who didn't love her.

She'd been so foolish.

This whole time he didn't want to be married to her.

Her hands began to shake.

The door opened and she quickly turned on the water, pretending that she'd just arrived at the sink, and stuck her hands beneath the running water.

"Well, if it isn't Miss Perfect."

Jolie's spine quivered at the same time her stomach turned. Why would *she* be here? Now?

"Aren't you even going to say hello?"

Jolie turned off the water and lifted the towel off the rack. "Hello, Amy."

"You don't appear happy to see me."

Jolie lifted her chin and did her best to not feel anything. Amy's black hair was cut short and styled perfectly, her makeup impeccable. So was her burnt orange two-piece dress. As usual. Everything about her was always impeccable.

Amy stepped around her and leaned toward the mirror to reapply her dark red lipstick. "Randal certainly was happy to see me." She smacked her lips together to set the lipstick in place. "When he met me at the airport." She dropped her lipstick into her purse. "Sunday before last. It was so sweet of him to welcome me back." Smiling at herself in the mirror, she added, "He always bent over backward for me."

Jolie's entire being was trembling and things were echoing inside her head again. Sunday before last. That's where Randal had gone after his meeting with James. To the airport. To meet Amy.

"You didn't think that would change just because I was gone for a few months, did you?" Amy made a show of slapping her own cheek. "Oh, my, are you really foolish enough to think that Randal would choose you over me? Fall in love with someone like you?" Laughing, she added, "Oh, poor little Jolie. Tricked again." Amy wiped the smile off her face. "There's only one reason Randal married you, and everyone will soon know the truth."

It took all the control Jolie had to replace the towel on its rack and leave the room without saying a word or breaking out in tears. At the table, she retrieved the purse she'd left on the floor near her chair.

Randal had stood as she'd approached the table. "I've already paid the bill."

She picked up her purse, and started for the door.

He touched her elbow.

She pulled it away and walked faster, through the room. She couldn't help but search the tables on her way to the door, looking for Amy, but she wasn't anywhere to be seen. If not for the pungent scent of Amy's perfume still stinging her nose, Jolie might have wondered if she'd seen a ghost.

She hadn't.

Amy was back and she was the woman Randal wanted. Had always wanted.

And worse yet, she was jealous. Jealous. That couldn't be. Yet, that's what the dark anger inside her was, she knew that.

"I'm sorry for the way I sprang that all on you," he said once they were in the car. "I just thought you should know."

He hadn't started the car, was twisted in his seat, facing her. She kept her gaze straight ahead. "I'd like to go home."

Home.

His home. One she'd readily accepted as hers, but it wasn't.

She didn't have a home.

Worse than that, she'd have to return to the home that drove her crazy. What was she doing? Worried about moving home when she'd been tricked. Tricked again by Amy. She'd suspected that in the beginning.

No, she'd known that in the beginning.

She should have remembered that. It explained why he said they'd take it slow, get to know each other. He never planned on her becoming his wife in every way. He just wanted Dad's company. As soon as he found out it wasn't for sale, he must have called Amy to come home.

So many things made sense now.

Except for one.

"Jolie, I—"

"I'd prefer not to talk." She drew a deep breath, but

that didn't help get her jumbled emotions under control. Nothing would. Nothing was under control. But they would be. She just needed time to figure out what she was going to do.

Do about how she'd let herself fall in love with him. That was not supposed to happen. How could it have?

She would not become her mother. Jealous and— Oh, lord. She already *was* becoming her mother.

She didn't wait for him to open her car door when they arrived home, and would have beat him up the stairs, too, if Peter hadn't stopped her at the door to inform her that Danielle had stopped by and picked up some *things* out of her sewing room.

"Thank you," she told him, moving toward the stairs.

"She also asked that I let you know both of your ideas are going to work splendidly," Peter said, sounding confused by what he was repeating.

"Thank you, again, Peter," she replied. "Good night."

Randal was beside her, taking the steps at the same pace. "What ideas?"

Her level of caring what he thought had dropped to nil. He and Amy could have each other. She was not going to turn into her mother for anyone. "Ways for her and James to make enough money that they won't ever have to worry about moving back in here with you." She upped her pace, rushed up the steps and down the hall.

He'd kept pace with her the entire way, but now passed her, opened the bedroom door and held it for her to enter. "I told them not to worry, that I would—"

"No one likes being made a fool." She walked past him, into her sewing room and closed the door, locked it before he could enter behind her.

"Jolie," he said through the wood. "I'd like to talk to you about all this."

There were plenty of things she'd like, too, starting with never having met him. Despite the fact she was shaking so hard her legs didn't want to work, she flipped on the light and moved away from the door.

"Jolie!"

Catching the side of the table with both hands, she used it to remain upright, and gave in to the tears burning her eyes. There were blurring her vision so it was no use trying to hold them back any longer.

"Jolie, please unlock the door."

She closed her eyes, bowed her head and let the pain consume her as she slowly sank to the floor. Time passed, or maybe it stood still. She didn't know or care. Eventually, the pain turned into an ache that left her numb. Her ability to feel had been all used up. There was nothing left inside her.

But she had to find something. Anger. Hatred. Something. Because lying on the floor wasn't an option. Neither was caring so much about one person that nothing else mattered.

She had to figure out what to do about that. Rising to her feet, and once again using the table to keep her upright, she glanced around the room. There had been a time when she'd dreamed of a room like this. Thought she'd have it all then.

She'd been wrong.

Or maybe she just wasn't the same person as she'd been then. Things had changed. She had a way to make money now. There was only one pile left of completed bras, the one for Jane to distribute. Danielle had picked up the ones with her name and Willa's, and she'd left a note, with measurements for more.

Would people still want to buy the bras when she was no longer married to Randal?

Flinching, she folded her arms around her midsection. She'd been wrong. She wasn't numb.

She was just foolish. A fool for being tricked again. A fool for falling—

No. That wasn't her.

But it was.

She'd told him things she'd never told anyone else. Things about Amy. Their feud had started the first time they'd met in grammar school. There had been mice in her desk, her name put on things she'd never written, lies spread...

But this was by far the worst betrayal, and it hurt so bad to know Randal was a part of it. A part of her didn't want to believe that, but how could she not see the truth? It was all there. He'd told her right from the start that the only reason he was marrying her was for Dad's company.

Her spine stiffened. He wasn't going to have it, and Amy wasn't going to have the last laugh. Not this time.

No.

She was.

She wasn't sure how, but she would come out the winner. There had to be a way, and she had to find it, because she was done. Done being tricked. Done being lied to. Done living a life everyone else dictated instead of the one she wanted.

If a person could fall in love without even realizing it, they could fall out of love, too.

Sewing had always been her escape, so that's what she did now.

Sewed.

Plotted.

And planned.

Chapter Eighteen

The click of the door being unlocked caught Randal's attention. Stiff from being on the floor all night, he wasn't quick enough to leap to his feet before the door opened. His heart, however, was fast enough to leap into his throat at the sight of her.

It also sank when she barely looked at him while stepping over his legs.

He jumped to his feet and reached for her arm. "Jolie."

She eluded his touch and entered the bathroom across the hall without a word.

Stopping himself from taking his frustration out on the door, he spun around and leaned against the wall next to it. She couldn't stay in the bathroom all day.

Then again, he'd thought she wouldn't stay in her sewing room all night, yet she had. The hum of her sewing machine had penetrated through the door deep into the night. When it had finally stopped, he'd thought she'd leave the room.

She hadn't.

He hadn't left his stance outside the door, either.

The long hours of sitting on the floor, leaning against the door, had given him plenty of time to think. He'd expected her to be confused or shocked over Carl giving her his company, but she was beyond shocked and confused.

And he was beyond knowing what to do about that.

As soon as the doorknob turned, he stepped in front of it, blocking her exit. "I'm sorry. I shouldn't have said anything, or maybe I should have told you the night Carl told me. I don't know, but we need to talk about this."

The hollowness of her eyes as she lifted her face and looked at him, nearly gutted him.

Feeling at his utmost lowest, he tried again. "I wanted you to know so you could make a decision, decide what you want."

Never pulling her gaze off him, she blinked several times. "When we entered this agreement, you said that I'd never have to do anything in private that I didn't want to do."

Nodding, he replied. "I did, and that's still true."

"Good, because I don't want to talk to you. I don't want to even see you." She waved a hand. "Step aside, please."

He could be as stubborn as her. "No. We have to—"

"I have things to see to for tonight's party."

"I don't give a rat's ass about tonight's party. Cancel the damn thing."

Her eyes narrowed. "And let you make a fool of me again? I don't think so."

"A fool of you? No. Jolie, that's not—"

"Step. Aside. Please."

Tears were starting to well in her eyes, and disgusted in himself, he stepped away from the doorway.

Careful to not so much as brush against him, she entered the hallway and walked toward the stairway, then down it.

He'd never felt so helpless in his life. Had never felt so empty and incompetent. A disgust-filled growl rumbled in his throat and he slapped the wall. How in the hell had he ended up so damned if he did, damned if he didn't?

This was by far the worst day of his life. He kept his distance from her, but that didn't stop him from hearing her laugh as she helped the housekeeper, aided Mrs. Hoover in the kitchen, directed Peter as to where to set up tables for card games and dominoes, and joked with Grandpa over whether he should wear a suit coat or his blue smoking jacket.

Randal accepted the fact that she was ignoring him on purpose. As the day went on, the craving for a simple smile, a simple touch, from her began to eat away at him, leaving his insides raw. Had he ever really believed this would work? No physical contact whatsoever while in private, yet in public, pretending to be a happy, loving couple? If that was so, he was a bigger fool than he'd ever imagined.

He'd gotten used to her in his life and... No, that wasn't entirely true. She'd made him realize what had been missing from his life. After having a sampling of it, he wanted more. He'd wanted her to want more, too.

How could he not? She was like the missing piece of a puzzle. The one, interconnecting link that made everything work.

If it was up to him, he would cancel the party, but she obviously wanted it to go on as scheduled, so it would. He would put everything inside him aside and make sure it was exactly as she wanted. Copying her persona, he planted a smile on his face and assisted Peter in re-arranging furniture, setting up card tables and doing other tasks he'd never known needed to be completed in order to host a dinner party.

As evening approached, he retreated to their room, bathed and dressed in a clean suit. He took his time in the hope that Jolie would enter the room and they could have a brief private moment. He had things to tell her. Things he now understood.

But she never entered the room, and as guests started arriving, he made his way downstairs. Both of his sisters and their husbands had already arrived, and he pulled Danielle aside after searching and not finding Jolie anywhere.

"She's upstairs getting ready," Danielle replied, as if his question was pointless.

He nodded as if he had known that, and hadn't been harboring fears that she'd somehow left without him knowing it. "So, her ideas are working for you?" he asked, once again pretending he knew all about them.

"Yes." Excitement filled his sister's face. "Roger thought it a great idea and so did the telephone and electrical companies."

"Roger...Wayne?" he asked, searching his mind for any other men he knew named Roger.

"Who else owns a plane and works with telephone and electrical companies?" She slapped his arm. "You don't have to pretend that you didn't know. The companies said pictures of possible routes was a fabulous idea and would help their engineers greatly. James will start accompanying Roger next week. And, since I'm sure Jolie told you about her other idea, too, James has already spoken to the superintendent of schools, who said he'd heard of other schools taking individual pictures of children, in addition to group photos, and would really like to try it this coming school year." Danielle stretched on her tiptoes and kissed his cheek. "Thank you for marrying her. She's the best sister-in-law I could ever have hoped for. I just love her to pieces." Lowering her voice, she added, "And the bras." She giggled. "Everyone loves them."

As he had all day, Randal kept the false smile on his face and nodded, even though he felt completely in the dark. Bras? How had that even entered the conversation?

"Oh, there's your beautiful bride now."

Following Danielle's gaze, he turned toward the staircase, where Jolie slowly made her way down each step. It reminded him of their first date, when he'd watched her come down her mother's stairway. Only this time, he recognized what the sight of her did to him. How it filled him with pride, joy and something else. He didn't want to admit that. Didn't want to go down that road.

Love could break a man. He didn't want to be broken.

A nudge in the back sent him forward to meet her as she approached the bottom of the steps.

She was wearing a long dress, made out of the shimmering blue material that he'd picked out, knowing it would make her eyes look darker, browner, but it was what was wrapped around her waist that made his heart thud harder. His white-and-gold pirate rope. She'd wrapped a long strand around her midsection several times and had it tied in a square knot above one hip. The rope emphasized her breasts, as did the V-shaped neckline, and the sleeves were layers of three triangles that barely covered her shoulders.

He held out a hand, and his insides rejoiced as she took ahold of his fingers. His elation faded as he noted the smile on her face was superficial. For show only. The dimness of her eyes proved that.

"You look stunning," he said.

She stepped off the last step. "I didn't care for the way the waist looked, so I borrowed your rope to cover it up. I hope you don't mind."

"Not at all." He kissed her cheek. "It looks lovely."

"Well, it's homemade." She withdrew her hand from his and stepped around him to greet Danielle, and then the others.

The rest of the guests soon arrived, and as she had all day, Jolie kept her distance. She would grant him a smile when she knew others were watching, but it was little consolation.

Shortly before dinner was to be served, she and Jane disappeared up the stairway.

"Another bra order, I'm sure," David said, standing next to him.

What was up with bras? Why did everyone keep mentioning them? Besides Danielle, and now David, he'd heard others whispering the word.

David slapped his shoulder. "And her siblings are working out great."

Randal shook his head to clear his mind from bras. "Siblings?"

"Yes. Jolie's brother and sister are both working for me, selling tickets at the airport. I should have thought about students. The hours work perfectly for them and for me."

Silas and Chloe were working at the airport? When did they get jobs? Why did they get jobs? He would have given them money.

David chuckled. "Your mind is still on the bras. I know. Jane loves them, and, well, they are..." Slapping his shoulder again, David said, "Well, you know."

No, he didn't know. It appeared as if there were a lot of things he didn't know.

Getting through the evening was far harder than Jolie had thought it would be. The day had been tough, but she'd been able to escape to another room each time Randal had gotten too close. That wasn't possible with a houseful of people who thought she and Randal were a happy married couple.

They weren't.

She wasn't sure if that made her mad, or sad, or just so frustrated she wanted to scream.

Which she couldn't do.

All she could do was keep a smile pasted on her face and not punch Randal in the stomach every time he took her hand, or rested a hand on her back, or draped an arm around her shoulders. This was all his fault. If he wasn't so...so perfect in every way, she could walk away, forget she'd ever known him.

This was not turning out as she'd planned last night, while locked in her sewing room, sewing bras. She'd thought she could simply not care. Simply fall out of love.

That thought had been shattered as soon as she'd opened the door, and realized he'd been in the hallway, in front of her door, all night.

Then, he'd had to help with the preparations for the party tonight. Happily!

Even her dress had fought her plan. The side zipper had gotten snagged on a thread. Rather than take the dress off and snip off the thread, she'd tried to snap it off, and had broken the zipper. His stupid pirate rope was her only option of saving her outfit because people had already started to arrive.

Damn it all! And damn him!

She had to get everything back in focus. Remember that he and Amy had been in on this together. That was a real stickler. How could she win? She couldn't, because Amy would end up with Randal, and that was what she wanted.

She shouldn't, and was trying hard not to.

"Excuse me, big brother," Willa said. "I need to steal your wife for a moment."

Randal tugged her closer to his side and looked down at her rather than at his sister. "Only if you promise to bring her right back."

Jolie chided her heart for defying her by skipping a beat as he kissed her temple.

"I promise," Willa said. "We won't be long." She looped an arm through Jolie's and led her out of the den where they had been watching Gus Albright and Grandpa play dominoes.

Once in the hallway, Willa apologized. "I'm sorry, but Don and I must leave soon. The babysitter can only stay until nine and I have a proposition that I need to talk to you about."

"A proposition?"

"Yes, it's something my mother-in-law and I came up with, and I promised her I'd discuss it with you tonight."

"What is it?"

Music was coming from the front room, where the radio was playing a popular opry show, and the laughter and conversations from the other rooms made the hallway loud. "Could we go upstairs?" Willa asked.

"Sure."

"You know, you did the one thing I never thought possible," Willa said as they walked.

"Oh? What's that?"

"Made my brother happy."

Willa was tall and slender, with sandy blond hair and big blue eyes that were much darker than Randal's, but right now were glowing the same way his often did. Looking at them made Jolie's voice lock up.

"Even as a kid, all he did was work," Willa said. "Because that's what our father expected. Randal never complained. The only time he was defiant was when it came to something to do with me or Danielle, then he'd tell our father to leave us be and he'd take care of whatever it was. I always felt sorry for him, how hard he worked to take care of us, and how little he got in return. He acted as if he didn't want appreciation or love." Willa shrugged. "Because of you, I've seen Randal laugh more, be more relaxed, happier, than I've ever seen him. So thank you."

Jolie cleared her throat. "It's nothing I did."

"Yes, it is. You taught him about that one thing that Osterlunds aren't real good at finding, because it was never really shown to us growing up."

"What's that?"

Willa laughed. "Love."

Jolie stubbed a toe on the top step and grabbed ahold

of the railing. She was the last person to teach anyone what love was about. Furthermore, Randal didn't love her.

"Are you all right?" Willa asked.

"Yes, just, ah, caught the hem of my skirt," Jolie lied while stepping off the stairway.

"Your dress is gorgeous, and I love the silk rope. It's adorable. How did you come up with that idea?"

"To be honest, it was a last-minute repair. My zipper broke."

"Oh, my gosh, I wish I had your ingenuity."

"I wouldn't call it that."

"I would, and that brings me to my proposition. Alice, my mother-in-law, and I both love the bras you make, and as you know, the other people we've told about them love them, too. We are wondering if you would be interested in selling them at the drugstore?" Willa paused and drew in a breath. "We were thinking that you could make half a dozen bras or so, of various sizes, for women to try on in the powder room at the drugstore and then determine if they wanted to order one, or more. Of course, they will want to order, once they try them on. Seriously, what's not to love about them? So...what do you think?"

Jolie thought this was a way she could bring in money regularly, which she would need once she moved back in with her mother. She had thought to stay here, just to thwart Amy and Randal, but she wasn't good enough at pretending for that to work. "Well, um, last night, I couldn't sleep and sewed a few extras. You could take those until I get a chance to sew a few more."

"That would be perfect, can I take them now?"

"Of course." In her sewing room, Jolie wrapped the bras in tissue paper, put them in a bag and gave them to Willa. She and Don left a short time later, and others soon followed suit.

With her nerves dancing, because she wasn't sure what would happen after everyone left, Jolie stood beside Randal. His arm was around her waist, tight enough to let her know escaping wasn't going to be easy. Part of the problem was that she didn't want to escape. She'd tried so hard to be mad at him, but every time he looked at her, smiled at her, she had a hard time believing, or maybe just accepting, that he'd been in on this with Amy right from the start.

But he had been, and that explained why he didn't expect love from their marriage. He was already in love. With Amy. The jealousy inside her peaked again. She hated how she couldn't stop it.

As the last guest left, leaving an invitation to their own dinner party soon, Grandpa closed the door. "That was the best party I ever attended."

"Yes, it was a good party," Randal replied, tightening his hold on her waist even more. "Good night."

She dug her heels into the floor as he turned. "I need to clean—"

"No, you don't." With a solid, steady stare that didn't falter, he continued, "You either walk up those stairs on your own, or I'm carrying you, because we are going to talk. Now."

Short of making a scene in front of Grandpa, and Peter, who was discreetly staying out of sight, other than the toes of his shoes poking around the corner leading into the living room, she had no choice. "Fine."

Randal's hand never left her waist as they crossed the foyer. "Don't even think about escaping. I will not spend the night on the hallway floor again."

"That was your choice."

They started up the stairs, side by side. "And it was your choice to not talk to me all day."

"I didn't have anything to say. Still don't."

"I do. Plenty."

Chapter Nineteen

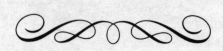

Now that he had her where he wanted her, Randal wasn't sure where to start with all he wanted to say. There was plenty. He locked the door and dropped the key in his pocket before turning to face her.

She stood near the sofa, arms crossed.

"Would you care to change first?" he asked.

"No."

"Would you care to sit down?"

"No."

One-word answers. Her defenses were up, making broaching the subject all the more unfavorable. He shrugged out of his jacket, tossed it and his tie on a chair, and chose to bring up another subject first. "Your brother and sister are working for David at the airport."

"So?"

"Why?" he asked.

"They needed jobs. Ways to make money."

"That's why you married me, so they would have money. If they need more, all you had to do is tell me."

She pinched her lips together and lifted her chin. "They wanted to earn their own money."

He was trying his best not to be angry, but couldn't do much about the other emotions. That of being hurt that she'd gone to someone else, rather than come to him. "I'm your husband, I could have found jobs for them."

"You'd already done enough."

He rubbed the back of his neck, where tension was building. "And Danielle and James, you took it upon yourself to find jobs for them, too? Taking photos of Roger's routes and schoolchildren?"

"They were just ideas I provided them."

"Why?"

"Because they, too, want to earn their own money."

"You're trying your damnedest to make sure no one needs my help, aren't you?"

She shrugged.

"Why?"

The way she shrugged again got his ire. "Damn it, Jolie, we aren't going to solve this if we don't talk about it."

"Maybe there's nothing to solve."

"Yes, there is. You're my wife, and—"

"Am I? Or am I just means to an end?" She planted her hands on her hips. "Fine, you want to know why I helped them? Because no one should take advantage of someone else." Breathing so fast her breasts rose and fell, she added, "No one should enjoy making a fool out of someone, either."

"You aren't a means to an end and I wasn't trying to make a fool out of anyone."

She let out a false laugh. "Dad's company is why you married me."

The truth stung, and he hated that. "It was, and that's why I thought it was only fair for you to know about

Carl's intent to give you the company before our relationship went any further."

"Fair?"

Her voice grew louder each time she opened her mouth. So did his. "Yes!" He threw his arms out at his sides. "I thought you should have all the facts before deciding if you want to stay married or not."

She spun around, stomped along the length of the sofa. "When we discussed this arrangement, I seem to recall you stating you had no intention of seeking a divorce."

"I don't."

Turning, she glared at him. "You mean didn't, until you found out you can't buy Dad's airplane company."

"No, I mean I don't." He kept his gaze locked on hers. "A divorce will be totally up to you."

She planted her hands on her hips again. "What about infidelity?"

He shook his head, momentarily lost by her question, then a hard knot formed in his stomach. He had said that in the beginning, but there was only one reason for her to bring it up. "Infidelity?"

"Yes, infidelity!" She spun around, walked across the room. "You know. When a man is married to one woman, but in love with another."

His entire body went rock-hard. No wonder she was so willing to marry him. So willing to not want love. "Who is it? Who are you in love with?"

"Spare me!" She pivoted, pointed a finger at herself. "I'm not talking about me! And you know it! Well, I know things, too! I know everything. How you and she set this all up to make me look like the ultimate fool! A wife who can't keep her husband happy, a wife whose husband divorces her for another woman!"

"Stop it!" He grasped her upper arms. "What are you talking about?"

She shoved his arms aside. "The jig is up, Randal. Amy told me everything."

His anger hit a new level, and he let out a curse under his breath. He should have known that as soon as Amy hit town, so would trouble. He'd been so focused on Jolie, on how he'd fallen in love with her, he'd forgotten Amy was back. "Whatever she told you is a lie, Jolie. That's what she does. She lies and she hurts people."

"Did she lie about you meeting her at the airport the morning she arrived?"

He shook his head in disbelief. Amy would have told her that for sure, and made far more out of it than there had been. Damn it. He spun around, paced the floor.

"As soon as Dad told you about the airplane company not being for sale, you came home and called Amy, then met her at the airport the next day. I'm sure the two of you had a good laugh that day!"

"No, I didn't! I didn't come home and call Amy. When Carl told me, all I thought about was you, and how I couldn't force you to stay married to me when you didn't have to. Didn't need to."

She swiped at her cheek. "I suppose you *didn't* meet Amy at the airport, either?"

"I saw her at the airport, but I hadn't gone there to meet her. I'd gone to see Carl, to tell him that I couldn't keep a secret like that from you. That he was going to give you his company. He'd already left his house, so I drove to the airport to see if his plane had left." Could this get more jumbled? Not that he could imagine. He crossed the room, to his dresser. "Amy's flight landed while I was there. She told me I could give her a ride home. I told her no." He opened the drawer. "And I bought these."

She glanced from his face to the tickets in his hand.

He walked closer, holding out the tickets. "They are for our flight to South Dakota, to see Mount Rushmore. It's still a couple weeks away, but it was the earliest a plane was flying up there."

She was looking at him, but her eyes were still full of skepticism. He couldn't blame her. The entire thing was a mess. He should have told her right away. Should have told Carl. Should have done so many things differently.

He tossed the tickets on the table, held up both hands. "Other than that brief encounter at the airport, I haven't seen or talked to Amy since she left town months ago. And I didn't marry you to make a fool out of you!"

"Then how did she know we'd be at the restaurant last night?"

"I don't know!" He was so mad he couldn't think straight, but he was sure he hadn't seen Amy last night.

Shaking her head, she walked away from him, around the edge of the sofa. "She said someone like you would never fall in love with someone like me. She was right."

The coffee table and sofa were between them. Using the table as a launch, he leaped over the sofa, landed in front of her. "She lied!"

"No, she didn't!"

She attempted to sidestep around him, but he moved so she couldn't.

She gave his chest a hard shove. "You said so yourself the night of Dad's party. That you could never love me. I didn't expect you to, and—"

"I lied! I didn't want to fall in love with you!"

"I didn't want to fall in love with you, either!"

They had been yelling loud enough for the entire house to hear, and everyone probably wondered about the silence that filled the house now.

His ears were ringing, wondering if they'd just heard right.

Both breathing heavy, they stared at each other. He took a single step closer, not wanting to frighten her, but needing to be closer. He loved her, and wanted to love her. Wanted her to love him in return more than he'd ever wanted anything. "But I did fall in love. With you."

She pinched her lips together, closed her eyes for a moment, before saying, "And I fell in love with you."

He couldn't take it any longer, had to touch her. Gently, he rubbed her upper arms. "I didn't want to fall in love because I've seen it hurt too many people." His stomach sank. "And now it's hurting you."

Tears trickled from her eyes. "I've seen it hurt people, too. Make them jealous and not care about others."

He pulled her close, hugged her. "I know. After my mother died, my father hated everyone. Everything. Because he'd loved her so much."

Her arms went around his waist. "My mother quit caring about anyone else after my father died, and before he died, she was so jealous he couldn't speak to someone else without her being mad and upset."

He tightened his hold on her, rocked her gently. "You are nothing like your mother."

She buried her face against his shirt. "Yes, I am. I was so jealous at the thought of you and Amy that I—" She let out a little sob.

He tightened his hold even more. "There's nothing to be jealous about." Yet, because he'd experienced a large bout of jealousy only moments ago, he admitted, "The idea of you with someone else makes me jealous, too, because I love you so much. Love you in a way I never thought I could love anyone."

She lifted her head, looked at him with tears in her eyes. "I love you, too, and I can't stop." She shook her head. "What are we going to do?"

He laughed and framed her face with both hands, kissed her lips. "We are going to love each other, for the rest of our lives. We both know what we want and what we don't. It's that simple."

Jolie's heart pounded so hard it hurt to breathe. He loved her, and she loved him, so very much. Would for the rest of her life. Not loving him wasn't an option. She'd tried that, and it hadn't worked. But it couldn't be that simple. Not after all of her fears. "But what if—"

He pressed a thumb against her lips, shook his head. "We'll make it work. No matter what, we'll make it work. I love you, Jolie. That will never change. I'll love you tomorrow, and the next day, and the one after that. Forever."

The tears flowed from her eyes. Tears of joy and happiness. She believed him, wholly, completely, because everything he'd said was reflected in his eyes. Maybe it was that simple.

She laid her hands on his shoulders, those broad, wonderful shoulders that she'd admired since their wedding night when she'd wiped the rice off his back. She already had so many wonderful memories of him, and she wanted more. So many more.

"I'll love you tomorrow, and the next day, and the day after that." Emotions made her voice crack. "I also loved you yesterday, and the day before that, and the one before that. I don't know exactly when it happened, but it did."

She had more to say, more to admit, but his lips stopped her. What happened next was like nothing she'd ever experienced. Something inside her broke open. Like it had been given wings.

Their kisses grew. The air between them became charged, hot and intense. Their arms, their hands, their lips, were frantic, touching, caressing and coming together over and over again.

All the wants, all the desires of becoming his wife in every way, hit with ten times the force as before.

When their lips had to part so they both could gasp for air, his hands were on the sides of her face again, keeping their gazes locked.

"You've made me happy since our first date. Without you, my life means nothing. I know that for a fact, because it's meant nothing for years. Until now. Until you." He pressed his forehead against hers. "You're my pirate's treasure, Jolie."

Nothing he could have said would have meant more. Her heart was still pounding, her body still burning with need. "And you're mine."

He ran his hands over her shoulders, down her arms, and then hooked them inside the rope looped around her waist. "I knew this pirate rope would be lucky."

He was so handsome. So wonderful. She regretted thinking badly of him for even a moment. "I'm sorry for doubting you. I will never do that again. I'm sorry I didn't tell you about Silas's and Chloe's jobs, and the ideas for Danielle and James, and—"

"And the bras?"

Her cheeks heated up. "You know about them, too?"

"I've heard mention, and am curious to know more."

The way he glanced down at her breasts made them tingle and grow heavy. The swirl of heat was elsewhere in her body, and so strong, her toes curled.

His hands slid to the knot in the rope. "If you want to tell me."

Her entire being reacted, pulsated, as he began untying the knot. An eagerness filled her, recalling how others had stated their husbands liked the bras. "I've always sewn my own bras, and so I made one for Jane. She liked it so much she asked me to make some for other people, so did Danielle and Willa after I made them each one, and now Willa wants to sell them at the drugstore."

The knot let go and he began to slowly unwrap the rope from around her waist. "Are they like the one in your sketchbook?"

She'd forgotten all about that sketch, but it excited her that he'd seen it. She tightened her hold on his shoulders against the thrill happening inside her. "Somewhat. That was my first attempt."

He dropped the rope onto the floor. "They've gotten better since then?"

The teasing, the heightened senses between them was so exhilarating, she felt emboldened. She lifted one shoulder in a playful way. "Would you like to see?"

His hands slid upward, brushing the sides of her breasts. "Very much."

With the rope gone, and the zipper broken, her dress was loose. She took a step back, slipped one sleeve and then the other off her shoulders, and held her breath as her dress slowly slid down her body, into a pile around her feet.

She watched his expression, the lift of his brow, the shimmer of his eyes, but the way his smile grew was the best part.

He slowly slid a finger across one cup and then the other, making her nipples grow hard.

"I've never seen anything more..." His eyes met hers. "Enticing. You are a very talented seamstress."

Her breath came out in a gush.

"I already knew that." He took her hand, guided her steps over the gown at her feet. "But now I'm completely convinced."

"Do you like it?"

"I intend to show you how much I like it." He pulled her close, covered her mouth with his.

From that moment on, she was lost, fully absorbed into a world so wonderful, she hoped it would never end. Before long, they were on the bed, naked and glorifying in their open admissions of loving one another. His touch was so loving and gentle, she truly felt as if she was the treasure he'd searched for his entire life.

He was hers. A treasure she hadn't known she'd been searching for, but certainly had discovered. He kissed her, tasted her, touched and teased her, and filled her with a pleasure that was all-consuming. There was no room for her to be self-conscious or worried about what to do next. He guided her, enticed and encouraged her so thoroughly, that when the moment came, when she became his wife in more than name, it was a true coming together. The one thing they both wanted more than all else.

She'd imagined what the moment might be like, but it was so much more. The only thing she had to compare it to was their wedding chase, when they'd been speeding toward the hotel. It was as if they were once again racing to a finish line, the two of them, together. Her heart was pounding, her breathing hard and fast, and exhilaration filled her.

The feel of his bare skin touching hers, of him filling her, of the friction that was taking her on what could only be called an impossible journey filled with indescribable pleasure, left her unable to think. All she could do was feel.

And she felt wonderful!

Amongst all the excitement, a moment hit when she felt her entire body go tense, lock up. She looked at Randal, momentarily stunned. The smile on his face told her there was nothing to fear. That he was here with her. Forever.

Believing him, she let herself go, and embraced the way everything inside her burst into something that was even more pleasurable, more satisfying, than anything she'd ever known. It was as if their bodies had become one, their souls, too, dancing together on some magical waves of blissful love.

As everything slowly faded into pure contentment, her body was so lethargic, she couldn't move, just lie there, breathing and smiling.

Slowly, her mind returned, and the happiness that filled her made her laugh out loud. She flipped onto her side and snuggled close against him. Content, free to not hold anything back, she used the tip of one finger to draw a heart on his chest. "Had I known the outcome I would have shown you one of my bras long before now."

Still basking in the aftermath of their lovemaking that had been so utterly fulfilling he was completely drained, Randal let out a groan, not wanting to think of the past few weeks of tortuous nights of being so close to her, yet so far. "I was at my wits' end as it was. If I'd seen you wearing that bra, my final bits of control would have snapped."

Her fingertip was still roaming across his chest. "You always appeared to be in control."

"I wasn't." He shifted enough to look at her upturned face, and feasted on her beauty as strongly as he had when she'd let her dress fall to the floor. A formfitting, delicate garment made of shimmering white silk, the bra had been pretty, but her wearing it had nearly sent him over the edge. Had he truly considered letting her go? It would never have worked. He'd been too enticed, too smitten, right from the start. From the moment he'd seen her walking down the stairway at her mother's house. He just hadn't wanted to admit it. He'd been too afraid of failure, yet the ultimate failure would have been not falling in love with her.

She stretched, kissed him and sighed sweetly. "I think that's my favorite part."

Confused, he asked, "What is?"

"That I can kiss you whenever I want."

Her honesty made him smile, and touched his heart like nothing ever had. He traced a finger over her lips. "That's one of my favorite things, too." He let his fingertip trail over her chin, down her neck. "Another is touching you, and yet another is looking at you and thinking how lucky I am."

She blushed and bowed her head. "Can I ask you a question?"

"Of course." He lifted her chin so they were again eye to eye. "You can ask me questions whenever you want. I'll tell you anything you want to know."

"Did you ever do what we just did with Amy?"

After the way Amy had treated her, he understood why she'd want to know. "No. I never had any feelings toward Amy. Especially none that would lead to making love to her. Nothing even closely related to what I feel for you."

"Then why did you date her?"

"Because it was safe. Amy guaranteed that I'd never fall in love. She's the complete opposite of you. You're beautiful, smart, caring, and most of all, lovable." He kissed the tip of her nose. "It's impossible not to love you."

"That's how I feel about you."

His body had just known the greatest satisfaction imaginable, but his desires were far from appeased. After one taste, he wanted more, but was also concerned about her. "How are you feeling?"

"Wonderful."

Despite her bravado of dropping her gown, he'd sensed her shyness, and had gone slow introducing her into lovemaking. "Are you sore? Did I hurt you?"

Twisting a leg around one of his, she kissed his chin. "No, in fact, I was wondering... Now that I know what to expect, maybe we should try it all again."

His answer came through in the kiss he gave her. Their first time had been amazing, but with experience came confidence, and his wife was soon a very confident woman.

Chapter Twenty

Familiarity, closeness, grew between them throughout the weekend, to the point Randal was late going into the office on Monday morning, and every other morning that week. Waking up next to Jolie was just too enticing to immediately climb out of bed. Once at work, all he could think about was returning home, of having Jolie in his arms, her perfect body molded and melded with his.

That's where his mind was on Friday morning when his secretary knocked on the door, and then opened it. "Telephone. It's a Mr. Blocker—Carl Jansen's butler."

Randal thanked her and picked up the receiver.

"Good day, sir," the butler said. "Mr. Jansen would like you to know that he will be home this afternoon, and would like to invite you and Mrs. Osterlund to join him for dinner at seven o'clock this evening."

"Thank you, Mr. Blocker," Randal instantly replied. "Mrs. Osterlund and I are honored to accept the invite."

"Very good, sir. Good day to you."

"And to you." Randal hung up, grabbed his jacket and told his secretary he wouldn't be back until Monday morning. He and Jolie had discussed her inheritance several times and he knew how difficult it would be for her to face Carl. Tell him no. That was her decision, and he'd support her in upholding it. Not so long ago, all he'd wanted was Carl's company, but now Jolie's happiness is what he wanted above and beyond all else.

She wasn't expecting him home so soon, because he'd left for work only a couple hours ago, and he found her in her sewing room, head bent over the sewing machine and pumping the treadle with her feet. He stood in the doorway, watching for several minutes, until she must have sensed she was being watched and looked over her shoulder.

The joy on her face stirred the love inside him that just kept growing and growing.

"What are you doing home?" She rose from the stool and met him in the center of the room.

"I missed you."

She lifted her face for him to kiss her.

He obliged.

As the kiss ended, she sighed. "I missed you, too."

She fit into his arms so perfectly, as if she was made just for him to hold. He kept his arms around her as he glanced at the machine behind her. "More bra orders?"

"Yes." Her smile brightened even more. "Willa sold another ten yesterday."

A tinge of guilt struck him at interrupting her sewing. Orders had come in every day this week. "Is there anything I can do to help?"

"No." She frowned slightly. "Maybe."

"What? Just tell me, other than sewing. I've never done that, but I suppose I could learn." He nuzzled the side of her neck. "You could teach me."

She laughed. "I could, but right now, I just need your brain."

He nibbled on her earlobe. "Are you sure that's all you need?"

She let out an encouraging little moan. "You're going to make me forget what I needed help with."

Giving in, he lifted his head. "Okay, what can my brain help you with?"

The smile in her eyes promised what he wanted would come later. "Willa wants a name for the bras, so people can ask about them and not be embarrassed."

He ran his hands up and down her sides. "Your bras aren't embarrassing."

"It is a delicate subject for some women. Jane has been calling them Jolie's dream bras, but that's…" She shrugged. "Not very discreet."

He grinned. "It's a fitting name. I dream of you every night." He cupped her backside with both hands. "Sometimes you aren't wearing anything."

She blushed and gave his chest a playful slap. "I'm trying to be serious about this."

He loved teasing her, but could also tell the name was a real concern for her and grew thoughtful. "What would you like to call them?"

"I don't know. I like Jane's idea, because it proves I am a designer. That I designed them, but it could be embarrassing if word got out and people pointed at me, saying that's Jolie from Jolie's dream bras."

He'd never be embarrassed by her. He was proud of her, but could relate to what she was saying. "So you don't like your name or the word *bra*?"

She nodded, then shook her head. "I don't know."

Taking a shot in the dark, he said, "How would you

feel about JO's Dream Wear? JO as in capital *J*, capital *O*, for Jolie Osterlund, and dream wear instead of dream bra?"

"JO's Dream Wear. JO's Dream Wear." Her smile grew a little each time she repeated it. "I like that, and it would leave it open for me to design other things."

"Yes, it would."

She slid her arms inside his coat, wrapped them around his waist. "You really are a smart man."

He brought their bodies tighter together. "The smartest thing I've ever done is marry you."

With a tiny, sweet moan, she kissed him. Which led to another kiss, and another one, each one more passionate. He'd been ready to take her to bed the moment he'd walked in the room, and with the encouragement she was demonstrating, stating that she wanted the same thing was impossible to ignore.

Pushing him backward, toward the door, she said, "I think we should go to our room."

Thrilled, and more than willing, he walked backward, kissing her the entire time. Unable to dismiss the opportunity to tease her, he waited until his back was up against the door before asking, "What for?"

With a teasing grin, she reached around him and turned the doorknob. "Because I want to show you something."

"Will I like it?" He would, that was a given.

She shrugged, and gave him a slight shove so she could open the door.

Following her out the door, he caught her around the waist as they hurried down the hallway and into their bedroom, laughter floating in their wake.

* * *

Jolie hadn't known she could be so happy, or that her body could respond so quickly to nothing more than the sight of her husband. Her husband! There were times when she sat by herself, sewing, that she'd laugh, so happy that she'd gotten over her fears of loving him. She couldn't even remember why she'd been afraid.

After he locked their bedroom door, she held up a hand. "Stay there."

He frowned slightly, which made her pinch her lips to keep another giggle inside. When she'd put the new bra on this morning, she'd been excited, and thought she'd have to wait until tonight for him to see it. "I said I had something to show you."

Eyes shimmering, he nodded.

She began unbuttoning her dress. It was amazing how confident she'd become, because of him. He made her feel so loved, so beautiful. "You bought some blue silk material when we'd gone shopping." She'd only made white bras, but he'd bought so much blue material, she figured that was his favorite color. "And I used some of it to make a new bra."

"You did?"

"Yes." Biting her bottom lip, she watched for his reaction as she pulled the front of her dress wide for him to see the bra. "What do you think?"

"I like it, but I need to see more." He stepped forward and grasped the bottom of her dress, lifted it over her head. Tossing her dress aside, he ran a finger under one strap. "It's beautiful. Almost as beautiful as you."

Her body knew his touch so well, and that's all it took. One touch, and she was filled with need, with want, that only he could satisfy. Making love with him was far more than she'd ever imagined, far more thrilling and exciting. She'd been so wrong when she'd once thought that liking him, liking each other, would be enough. She'd love him for the rest of her life, and still want him as badly as right now.

He picked her up by the waist. Her shoes fell off her feet and she wrapped her arms around his neck and her legs around his waist. "I want you. Now."

"I want you, too." He laid her on the bed and slid her panties off. "You should make some of these to match your bra."

"Would you like that?"

"Very much." He kissed her bra, the very tip of each cup, making her nipples harden.

Barely holding on to keep from spiraling into the unknown world he took her to every time they coupled, she pushed his jacket off his shoulders. "Then I will, but right now, you have too many clothes on."

He continued to kiss her in sensitive spots, pausing only long enough to remove another article of clothing. When he finally stood naked, she indulged in the glorious sight.

Anticipation spiked as he climbed on the bed, positioned himself, and her eyelids fluttered at the pleasure of him entering her. It was no wonder that she'd fallen so deeply in love with him. There wasn't anything in the world that could have protected her from not falling in love with him. He was such a good man, kind and caring, and loving. Falling in love with him had been so easy, and continuing to love him was even easier. It was as natural as breathing.

There were times when their lovemaking was fast and furious, and other times when it was slow and so sensual it was as if every bone in her body melted. She loved all of it, every minute, and had learned a lot since their first night, and that was empowering.

Wrapping her legs around his, she arched into him and increased the tempo, increased the glorious friction that would soon overtake her ability to think of anything, send her heart racing and cause her breath to become locked in her lungs. Before that happened, she cupped his face with both hands. "I love the way you love me."

"I love loving you. It consumes me day and night."

"Me, too," she admitted, and then let herself go, soak up every nuance of the waves of pleasure that led her to the ultimate peak, where gratification struck with a burst that left her gasping as she sank deep into the softness of the mattress and reveled in just how lucky she was to be married to him. To be loved by him.

A warmth spread across her stomach at the idea of how their actions might someday cause her to become pregnant. She'd cherish that moment. Wholly.

Reality was slowly returning when he touched the center of her bra. "I like the little bow right there."

She was still wearing the bra. He, however, was stripped of all clothes, except his socks, which made her giggle. He was lying on his side, and she flipped onto her side, so they faced each other. "I hoped you would." She had sewn on the tiny silk ribbon bow to make the bra prettier, just for him.

"When did you start sewing bras?"

"For myself, shortly after I started wearing them. The ones my mother bought for me were just flat strips of material that flattened and squished everything. They weren't very comfortable, and there was only one set of hooks, so you couldn't adjust anything. I tried a few designs before finding one I liked. I made some for my sister and a couple of elderly neighbors, but Jane was the first other person."

"Do you like sewing them?"

It was her dream, to be a designer, yet, with him she had to be honest. "Yes, and no. I'd always wanted to be a clothes designer, and I love sewing, but I have to admit, sewing bras all day, every day, can get tedious. It is still exciting to know so many people like what I've designed and want them, though."

"You need to hire people to sew for you."

"Maybe someday. I don't have the money to do that yet."

"I do."

"You need your money for your airline."

He ran a hand up and down her side. "No, I don't. I think we should focus on JO's Dream Wear instead. It has as much potential as an airline."

She forced the smile on her face to not falter. She knew an airline was still his dream, and was going to make sure it came true for him. If it meant giving up her dream of being a designer so he could have his airline, she would do it. Do it in a heartbeat. Leaning forward, she kissed him.

His smile said he was aware of her attempt to avoid his suggestion. "Carl's home. He's invited us for dinner tonight."

Her plan had been to go see Dad as soon as he was back, so tonight was fine with her. She scanned Randal's face, taking in his handsomeness, as well as who he was. A proud man, who had only ever had one goal, that of taking care of his family, financially. That's what had driven him and she loved him for that. For who he was. And she didn't want that to change, because that would change him—the man she'd fallen in love with. "Okay. What time?"

"Seven."

"Then we have plenty of time."

"For what?"

She scooted closer to him, nuzzled his chin. "Nothing."

"Nothing?"

Shrugging, she trailed a finger along his side. "Unless you can think of something you want to do."

Chapter Twenty-One

"That fish tasted as good as it used to over the campfire," Jolie said as the meal concluded.

"I caught them this morning," Dad answered. "Cleaned them, wrapped them in a wet towel and stuffed them in my tackle box so they'd stay cold all the way home." He laughed. "There were some wrinkled noses on the airplane when people got a sniff of them." Winking at her, he added, "I remember how much you liked eating fish."

"I had forgotten how good they taste when they are fresh caught." She smiled at Randal across the table from her. They'd spent a large portion of the day in bed, and the contentment of that still lived inside her. "I've told Randal all about your cabin."

"It's never locked and you know how to get there," Dad said.

She laughed. "I'm afraid I don't. I was too excited to arrive and never paid attention as to how we got there."

"I've missed having you kids with me, as much as I've missed your father," Dad said. "We'll all have to go down there together someday." He set his napkin on the table. "For now, shall we retire to my den?"

Jolie waited for Randal to arrive at her chair and held his arm as they followed Dad down the hall and into his den.

As soon as they were seated, side by side on a brown leather sofa, Randal patted her knee and said to Dad, "I owe you an apology, Carl."

Seated in his wingback chair, Dad lifted a bushy, gray brow. "Oh? How so?"

"For breaking a promise of silence." Randal took hold of her hand. "My vows to Jolie take precedence over all else and so I told her about your intention of a possible inheritance."

"I see." Dad leaned back in his chair and settled his gaze on her. "So you know I have willed my airplane company to you?"

Her heart softened as she thought of all the years she'd known Dad and how generous he'd been over those years. "Yes, and I'm honored that you think so highly of me, but I hope you will understand when I say that I can't accept a gift like that. You've already been more than generous by paying for the wedding."

"I bought that company with every intention of sharing it with your father," Dad said.

"I understand that." She also understood some of the actions her mother had taken, and why. Her mother had refused to ask Dad for help because she'd felt that would mean Jolie's father had failed his family, and she wasn't willing to let anyone believe that. Jolie would never allow someone to believe that about Randal, either. "And I appreciate your kindness and friendship. It's my greatest wish to maintain that, and I hope we can come to an understanding about this."

Dad sighed. "I do understand. I should have given you the company before now, back when you needed it."

"No, you shouldn't have," she said, "because I wouldn't have been able to accept it then, either. No more than my father would have been able to accept it."

"You certainly are your father's daughter," Dad said.

"Thank you, I consider that a compliment."

"Do you agree with her, Randal?" Dad asked.

"Yes. I will always support every decision she makes." Randal tightened the hold on her hand. "Jolie has created her own clothing design business that is well on its way to being extremely successful. I'm very proud of her, very proud to be her husband."

There had been a point in her life when she'd thought that falling in love would make her vulnerable, change who she was and wanted to be. Now she knew it did just the opposite. Because of him.

Dad cleared his throat, making them both look at him. "Congratulations, I'm not surprised. You always had get-up-and-go. That's why I wanted to give you the company. Once you married Randal, I knew the two of you could turn that company into something I could only dream about."

Jolie smiled to herself as she looked at Dad. This was her chance to make Randal's dream come true. She'd told him she wouldn't accept the company as a gift, but hadn't fully explained why. Randal was a man of principle and would never accept the company as a gift. But he wanted it. Wanted to create an airline, and she wanted to help him in every way she could. "I agree, and though I can't accept the company as a gift, I am interested in knowing if you'd be willing to sell it to us."

Dad frowned. "What about the clothing design company Randal just mentioned?"

Not surprised by his question, she shook her head. "I'm just sewing for friends and family. Randal is the true businessman and will take the plane company to new levels in no time, and I'll be there with him every step of the way."

Dad let out a chuckle. "Oh, Joey-girl. Right now, I know your father is looking down on you, smiling." Leaning back in his chair, he looked at Randal. "I'm not ashamed to admit that I was aware that you were interested in buying my company for some time, and that's why I told you about my plan of willing it to Jolie. I wanted to know how you'd react to that news, because it would prove to me whether or not you had ulterior motives for the marriage. That may not have been any of my business, but I felt I had to look out for Jolie. Thankfully, the two of you have proven that I have nothing to worry about."

"I love Jolie," Randal said. "Her happiness is what is most important to me."

She leaned against his shoulder. "Your airplane business will be our saddle shop, Dad."

Randal wasn't sure what she meant about a saddle shop, but he now understood why she'd been so adamant about not accepting Carl's company. She'd planned on them buying it. Them as in both of them. The idea would have excited him, if he was just thinking of himself. But he hadn't been doing that in weeks now. Her bras were amazing, and he believed in her talent, was prepared to provide whatever support she needed to achieve success. It bothered him that she made it sound like it was nothing by saying she was just sewing for friends and family. It had grown well beyond that. Yet, right now, she was beaming and he couldn't take her joy away from her. In order to buy some time, he suggested to Carl, "Perhaps we could set up a time to meet and discuss this further next week?"

"Of course," Carl answered. "Whatever is convenient for you. I'm interested in hearing what your thoughts are for the company."

"He has it all planned out, Dad, and it's amazing," Jolie said. "Air America will become the largest airline in America, mark my words."

Randal's heart thudded. He loved the way she looked at him, with such pride and confidence. Not very long ago, he'd have been as excited as she was about buying Carl's company, but his focus was different now. His entire life was different now. He still wanted to succeed in business, but he wanted her dream to come true, too. That dream was JO's Dream Wear, not Air America. "I think we've taken up enough of Carl's time tonight."

They left a short time later, and he'd barely started the car when she asked, "Why do I have the feeling you aren't happy about buying Dad's company?"

He countered with, "Why did you belittle your design company?"

"It is little. I'm just sewing for friends and family."

He put the car in gear and drove around the curved driveway. "No, you're not. Your bras are being mailed to women in other states."

"Friends and family of friends and family."

He shook his head. "It's more than that. It has real potential. With salesmen and advertising, you could soon be selling thousands of bras each week. We'll hire workers, find a building and—"

"Selling thousands of bras a week won't compare to an airline," she interrupted.

"Yes, it could, because it won't be just bras. You can design all sorts of women's clothing."

"But an airline is something people need."

"So are women's underclothes."

"Why are you refusing to talk about it? You had the chance to tell Dad all about your ideas and didn't."

His spine stiffened. He didn't want to argue with her, but wasn't going to let her give up her dream of designing clothes. "Why are you refusing to talk about your design company?"

"Because we weren't at Dad's to discuss that. We were there to talk about his company. I thought you'd be happy about buying it. Not argue about it."

"We aren't arguing," he insisted.

She let out a loud *humph*. "Aren't we?"

"No." He turned on the dark, empty road that would take them back to town.

"I say we are. Just like the last time we left his place."

Randal huffed out a sigh. They had argued last time they'd left Carl's, and he didn't want to do that again. "I'm just curious as to why you want us to buy it so badly?"

She was staring out the passenger window and didn't answer.

He shifted the car into a higher gear, still waiting for her to answer. When she didn't, he asked, "Are you going to tell me?"

She sighed again, but this time it sounded different. Sadder.

"Jolie?"

"The truth?" she asked.

"Yes, the truth."

"Because I want you to have it. I want your dream to come true."

"And I want yours to come true."

"I know you do, but mine isn't as important as yours."

"Yes, it is."

"So, that's what we are arguing over?" she asked. "Whose dream is more important?"

He was about to say they weren't arguing, but they were. Why? Last time they'd left Carl's it was because he thought he was giving up his dream, now it's because he didn't want it? He'd thought he'd come to grips with it all, made sense of everything.

Downshifting, he slowed the car and pulled it to the side of the road. "That's a stupid thing to be arguing over."

"Yes, it is."

They sat there, staring at each other for a moment. He knew she wouldn't give up, and reached over, took ahold of her hand. "My entire life, I've been afraid of failure. Even more after I sold the lawn care business. That's why I said no divorce, no infidelity, because that would have been failure. I don't want to fail you, Jolie. Not ever."

She wrapped her other hand around his. "You will never fail me."

"Yes, I would, by not helping you bring JO's Dream Wear to its full potential so that it becomes everything you dreamed it could become."

A tiny smile tugged up the sides of her lips. "You've already made my dream come true."

"And you made my dream come true."

"Maybe it's time we start to focus on a dream we share." She scooted closer to him, kissed him. "The only true failure is not trying at all."

He had to smile at her fortitude. She was not one to give in easily. He never had been, either. "It would be a lot," he said, "building up two businesses at the same time."

"Two?"

"Yes." She was right, giving up was the only true way to fail. Furthermore, he already had all he wanted, so truly didn't have anything to lose. It sure had taken him long enough to figure that out. "We'll buy Carl's company, but JO's Dream Wear will be just as important. It won't be one or the other, it's both."

Smiling, she shook her head and then nodded. "I'll agree to that."

He folded his arms around her, hugged her tight. "But neither will come before you."

"Before us." Lifting her face, she reached up, cupped his jaw. "I love you."

Pure contentment filled him. They could turn both companies into multimillion-dollar enterprises, but they'd never be worth as much as she was to him. She was his everything. His dream come true. "I love you, more than anything."

"So I guess we aren't arguing anymore," she said.

He planted a quick kiss on her lips. "No, we aren't."

She slid her hand inside his jacket and fiddled with the buttons on his shirt. "We probably should completely make up."

He knew what she meant, yet asked, "How would we do that?"

She was still unbuttoning his shirt. "I can think of a way."

He was more than willing to comply, but did have to point out, "You do know we are on the side of the road."

Her hand moved to the waistband of his pants. "Yes, and I know we haven't seen another car since we pulled onto this road."

He was growing harder by the second. "One could come along at any moment."

She undid his pants. "I guess we could wait until we get home." Her hand slid inside his underwear and her fingers wrapped around him. "But it's a long drive."

He found the lever, pushed the seat back, so there would be room for her to straddle his lap. "Too long of a drive."

Jolie felt as if she was floating on air the following week. They'd met with Dad, bought the company, which was exciting, but she was more excited about her and Randal's trip to see Mount Rushmore tomorrow.

She had already packed their suitcases, and just had to deliver the bras she'd made for some of Willa's customers. Evidently, there had been a party where one of the women had been wearing a JO's Dream Wear bra, and the next day, the drugstore had been overrun with women ordering bras. She'd be sewing for a straight month once they got back from their trip.

A hint of chagrin washed over her as she picked the bag off the seat of the car she'd just parked near the drugstore. When she'd discovered who one of those customers was, she'd gotten a glimmer of satisfaction knowing who had made a specific request to have several layers of padding sewn in the bras. Willa had suggested charging the person extra, and extra again to have the order rushed. Jolie could have declined the rushed order, but had agreed, because of the satisfaction it provided, even though she and Willa were the only ones who knew.

A moment later, as Jolie stepped up on the curb, that very customer walked out of the drugstore. Despite all she knew, her stomach sank as it always did upon seeing Amy.

"Well, well, well, look who it is," Amy said. "Little Jolie Cramer."

Jolie wished that Amy couldn't get her goat so easily, but it was hard to break a habit that had been with her for years. "It's Osterlund now, but you know that."

Amy stepped closer. "Not for long."

Telling herself to just walk away, Jolie attempted to step around the other woman.

Amy sidestepped, not letting her pass. "Your *husband* never told you about meeting me at the airport, did he?"

Jolie's spine stiffened.

"Afraid to face the truth?" Amy continued. "That your husband only married you to make me jealous."

Jolie cracked a smile, stared directly in the other's woman's face, but didn't say a word. There was plenty that she could say, but nothing she said would penetrate Amy's thick skull. She'd been a bully too long, had gotten away with too much. Jolie knew the truth, and the truth was, Randal was hers. Would be forever, and knowing that left her with absolutely no reason to be jealous, but a lot to be proud of. She had no doubt of Randal's love for her. Of their love for each other.

"He'll get tired of your cute, sweet little innocent

act sooner or later," Amy sneered. "And want a real woman."

Jolie looked at Amy and was a bit surprised that all she felt was pity. She began to walk away.

"Go ahead, run away," Amy jeered. "But just know, I'm not going anywhere."

Jolie stalled her steps. This wouldn't stop until she put an end to it. She reached into the bag and grasped ahold of one of the special-order bras. "Of course you aren't going anywhere, because you are here, at the drugstore, to pick up the bras you ordered. You know, JO's Dream Wear bras."

"How do you know that?"

Jolie pulled the bra out of the bag. "Because I design and sew them."

Amy's eyes widened and her jaw went slack.

Jolie feigned surprise. "You didn't know the *J O* in JO's Dream Wear stands for Jolie Osterlund? It does. Randal suggested using my initials in the name. He loves everything I design and sew. Loves it even more when I model them for him." She spun the bra by one strap with a finger. "I must admit, yours were the first ones that I've had to sew in several layers of batting, because, well, you know."

"Give me that!" Amy reached out to snatch away the bra, but Jolie was quicker, held it out of her reach.

"You haven't paid for them yet." Jolie dropped the bra back in the bag. "And special orders like this are twice the price, to pay for the extra materials. Padding, so it looks like you have boobs…" She lowered her voice. "We wouldn't want that getting out, now, would we?"

"You…" Amy let out a growl. "You can't go around talking behind people's backs."

"I'm not talking behind your back." Jolie stepped closer. "I'm talking to your face."

Amy's neck and face had turned beet red. "They are terrible bras. I don't want them."

"That's fine. I understand that they might be too expensive for some people." She smiled. "As you know, they've become quite the rage. Everyone is talking about them and I'm sure Willa will be able to sell these to someone else. Of course, she'll let them know that I'll take out the extra padding that you'd ordered."

"You can't do that."

"Yes, I can."

"Those are mine," Amy insisted.

"No, they are mine." Jolie's heart skipped a beat as she noticed a car fly around the corner, hit its brakes and pull up next to the curb. A dark blue Cadillac. "Mine," she repeated. "And so is Randal. I suggest you remember that."

He was already out of the car and arrived at her side within seconds. His arm instantly went around her shoulders and he pulled her up against his side. "Are you okay?"

"I'm fine. Just delivering some bras," Jolie answered, smiling up at him. Then, because she could, she stretched on her toes and held her face near his. He promptly responded to her unspoken request, and she was overjoyed by how he extended the kiss into far more than a simple hello.

"You do know you're not alone," Amy snarled.

"Yes," Randal said as he ended the kiss. "Feel free to leave."

"Oh!" Amy huffed. "You two deserve each other."

Jolie bit back a grin.

"You're right," he answered, but his eyes were on her, not Amy. "We do. That's why we married each other. I knew I couldn't live the rest of my life without her."

"And I couldn't live mine without him," Jolie replied, releasing a smile that was so big her heart doubled in size.

He kissed her again, and when that kiss ended, they were alone. It was a moment before Jolie caught her breath, because his kisses always left her breathless, then she asked, "How did you know I was here?"

His gaze went over her shoulder.

She twisted, saw Willa and Don standing beneath the awning of the drugstore. "They called you?"

"Don did. He knew you were on your way to drop off bras and Amy had been there for half an hour, complaining because her bras hadn't arrived yet."

"And you came to my rescue."

"Yes, and I always will." He rubbed her shoulder. "Are you all right?"

"I've never been better." She kissed his chin. "Except for this morning, and last night, and the night before that, and tomorrow, and the day after that, and—" She let out a sigh of happiness. "Forever."

He laughed, picked her up, spun around and hugged her tight. "Me, too."

Epilogue

Jolie leaned closer to the window and watched as the huge monument disappeared behind a cloud. They were too high up to see much, but having seen it, not once but twice, from the ground level, she knew the carvings were majestic and grand. The changes between the carvings of faces from last year to this year had been inspiring.

She continued to stare out the window. The beauty of sky, the clouds, and of the fact that they were flying high above the ground never failed to amaze her. This trip was even more amazing than last year's because they were flying in an Air America airplane.

The past year had been a whirlwind. A magnificent one. Starting two companies simultaneously had been a challenge at times, but also fun and exciting. There was still a lot to do to bring Air America and JO's Dream Wear to their full potential, but it would happen because they believed it would. She and Randal believed in each other, and in their love.

She turned and looked at him. Unlike many others, Air America planes had two seats, instead of only one, on each side of the center aisle, so traveling companions could sit side by side. Customers liked that, and so did she. The smile Randal bestowed upon her melted her insides, and she had no doubt it would be that way for the rest of her life.

He rested a hand on her stomach. "We don't have to wait a year before coming back."

Covering his hand with both of hers, she said, "This little one will only be a few months old a year from now." The life growing inside her was their greatest accomplishment.

"They'll grow up flying the skyway," he said.

"It's so exciting, isn't it?"

"Yes, it is." He kissed her cheek. "Every day with you is exciting."

"Excuse me."

Jolie glanced past Randal to smile at the stewardess.

"Mother asked me to give you this." Chloe handed her crackers wrapped in waxed paper. "She has more if you need them."

"Tell her I said thank you, but also that I'm fine," Jolie said, taking the crackers. Her bout with morning sickness had ended last month, but her mother had been concerned flying might make it return. "My stomach isn't upset." This was the first flight for Air America, therefore, all members of her and Randal's family, including Dad, were aboard. "What do you think of being a stewardess?"

"I think it's going to be the best job ever," Chloe answered. "I'm not going to want to go back to school in the fall."

"You can work shorter flights around your school

hours," Randal told Chloe. "And your college schedule after graduation."

Chloe rolled her eyes as she replied, "Yes, sir."

Randal shook his head, and looked at Jolie. "I hope our children aren't as impetuous as her."

"Ha, good luck with that," Chloe said. "Look at who you married."

Jolie laughed at both Chloe and Randal, because teasing like this is how they always reacted to one another. "Is the dress comfortable?" she asked her sister. It was navy blue, with red piping, white cuffs and brass buttons. She'd designed them for all the Air America stewardesses and similarly colored suits for the pilots.

"Very, and it makes me feel so official." Chloe straightened and squared her shoulders. "I need to go check on other passengers." She gave Randal's shoulder a playful slug. "Do what I'm getting paid to do."

That was another thing that both of their companies had done, provided jobs. Good jobs, and many of them. Ironically, even for her mother. She was a top salesperson for JO's Dream Wear, and loved it.

"You know, that's a good idea," Randal said.

He was staring at her purse that she'd just picked up and put the crackers in. "What is a good idea?"

"Giving passengers something to snack on," he replied.

Letting the idea settle, she set the purse back on the floor by her feet. "It is. We'll have to look into how we can do that."

Randal winked at her. "Every once in a while your mother has some very good ideas."

She leaned closer to him. "That you instantly go along with."

He kissed her and rubbed her stomach. "Look how well the first one turned out."

She had to agree with him, but also insisted, "I'll never force one of my daughters into a marriage."

Randal would never force one of his children to do anything they didn't want to do, but couldn't not take advantage of the opportunity to tease Jolie. "Even if he's the most wonderful man on earth?"

She hugged his arm. "Even if he's the most wonderful man on earth."

He chuckled. His children would have a very different life than he'd had. They'd grow up knowing they were loved and encouraged to follow their dreams. If one or the other, God willing that he and Jolie had several, would be interested in taking over an airline or a clothing company, they'd be welcomed, but they'd also be welcomed to pursue their own hopes and dreams.

Jolie leaned her head on his shoulder and closed her eyes. He shifted in order to wrap an arm around her so she'd be more comfortable using him as a pillow. She had completed his life in so many ways, and the future of his family was now brighter and broader than he'd ever imagined.

He leaned his head back and let his eyes close as his own drowsiness grew, smiling as he drifted off to sleep, thinking about the little baby Jolie was carrying.

Uncertain what had woken him, he sat up straight, heart pounding. The first place he looked was at Jolie. She was staring at him, eyes wide. "What is it?" he asked.

She pressed a hand to her chest. "I had a dream."

His senses were returning, and noting that everything about them was fine, he realized that's what had woken him as well. A dream. "I did, too."

She laid a hand on her stomach the same time his gaze landed there. "It's a girl," she said.

That's what he'd dreamed about, too, but wasn't convinced he wanted to share that. Or anything else about what he'd just dreamt about. He laid his hand over the top of Jolie's.

"She'll get married someday, to a man she loves," Jolie said.

His dream had been about that, too, but there had been more. Much more. His spine shivered, yet he wasn't about to cause Jolie any concern. "We have years and years before we need to worry about that."

"Years go by quickly."

He swallowed, hard, and took ahold of her hand. "They do, and we'll be together the entire time."

"Through thick and thin."

Remnants of his dream, of their daughter, pregnant and unwed, flashed in his mind again as he repeated, "Through thick and thin." A resolution formed. He was putting too much into one fleeting dream. Laughing to lighten the mood, he said, "Look at us, the baby isn't even born yet, and we're worrying about things that don't even exist."

She smiled up at him. "You're right."

Turning the conversation even lighter, he said, "If it's a boy, we should name him Joseph, after your father."

Her eyes shone. "Boy or girl, this baby will be named after you."

"A girl named Randal? No. She wouldn't like that."

"I was named after my father. Jolie, for Joseph, and my daughter will be, too. Her name will be Randi, with an *i*."

He laughed, and gave in for now. "If you say so."

"I say so."

He still couldn't say no to her, so kissed her instead.

Twenty-two years later

"Mother, Father."

Randi Osterlund pressed her lips together and forced herself to keep her chin up. She was about to tell her parents something that would cause them to be disappointed in her. Severely disappointed. She wasn't married. Didn't even have any prospects in that direction. Yet here she was. Pregnant. By a man she'd been told to steer clear of for years...

* * * * *

THE HEIRESS
AND THE
BABY BOOM

To Jean.
Thanks for the lunches, road trips and laughs.

Chapter One

1956

The deep breath of fortitude that Randi Osterlund drew in was full of chilly January air, and she begged the brightness of the sun to give her strength as she ran her hands up and down the front of her red wool coat.

All she had to do was knock. Just knock.

Then say hello.

Then... Her entire body drooped.

Oh, good grief.

She squared her shoulders, nodded to herself and almost took the last step toward the front door, but then she envisioned the unopened letter. The one he'd written *Return to Sender* on.

Her hands began to shake and she balled them until her nails dug into her palms. That had been years ago. She'd thrown that letter away. Was over it. Over him. All she needed was his land.

She checked the double row of brass buttons on the front of her coat, made sure they were neatly fastened and flipped her hair off her shoulders.

Time to get this over with. Knock on the door.

It was just Jason Heim.

With a motorcycle, a hot-rod car, slicked-back sandy-brown hair, dark brown eyes and a physique that would make the greatest male movie star jealous, Jason had been the James Dean of Chicago long before the real James Dean had hit the big screen.

He was also the reason she'd locked up her heart and thrown away the key.

Her family and his had bad history, as her father had wanted to buy the one hundred sixty-acre plot of land Jason's father owned, but Heim had refused to sell.

That had been years ago, though. Now Jason owned that land, and she was going to acquire it. Prove she had what it took to be a woman in the corporate world. She might only be twenty-two, but she was ready, and fully capable. After all, the Queen of England was only thirty and had already been queen for three years.

Not that Randi wanted to be a queen, but she did want to prove that women could do more than get married and have children.

She took another deep breath in preparation to take that last step and knock on the door, but chose to make sure the big rhinestone R pinned on her coat was straight first.

"Are you going to stand there primping all morning, or are you going to knock on the door?"

Startled from her thoughts, her heels slipped on the concrete. She caught her footing, but seeing the man peering over the fence next to the house made her heart pound so hard it hurt and enough butterflies erupted in her stomach to make her take flight.

Jason's grin showed off the dimple in his right cheek, and his elbows propped on the gate were a sign that he'd been watching her for some time.

He was as handsome as ever.

Maybe this hadn't been a good idea.

No. She was no longer a schoolgirl. She was a grown woman. "No, I—" Quickly deciding that ignoring his comment would be a more mature choice, she lifted her chin. "I don't know if you remember—"

He laughed. "Everyone who ever stepped foot in Westward High School remembers *the* Randi Osterlund. The princess who would one day become queen."

The bitterness of his laugh sparked ire. She loved her family, loved her parents for all of their successes, but she was more than just Randal and Jolie Osterlund's daughter. Head up, she stepped off the concrete porch. "No more than they remember *the* Jason Heim."

"Aw, yeah, the rebel who was sent to reform school."

That was another thing that connected their families and not a subject she'd intended to bring up. "I would like to speak to you about—"

"Buying my land? It's not for sale."

And then he was gone, disappeared behind the fence.

She would not let him get away that easily. He'd not only walked away without an explanation years ago, he'd returned her letter of apology unread. This time he'd hear her out.

The snow crunched beneath her shoes as she stepped off the porch and was deeper than the low sides of her kitten-heeled black pumps, but she kept walking. She reached the gate and gave it a push. Then a second push, much harder. The snow on the other side gave way and she nearly fell through the opening. Catching herself, she let out a growl. "If you—"

"I said it's not for sale."

This time he disappeared around the house. Her pumps

were already snow packed, so she moved forward, stepping in his footprints as much as possible.

Rounding the corner of the house, she spied a concrete slab completely clear of snow and made her way to it. Her nylons were soaked through and her toes were becoming ice cubes. Shivering, she stood on one foot, emptied one shoe and then repeated the process with the other shoe.

"They're just going to get full again when you make your way back out the gate."

She would not let him affect her, in any way, and let her gaze start at his feet, which were covered with leather boots, before working upward. His pants were dark blue denim, cuffs rolled. The material hugged his thighs and hips. The jeans met a brown leather jacket that was zipped halfway up his chest, and the collar was turned up around the back of his neck. When her gaze met his, it took nearly all she had to keep it there, chin up. She wasn't sixteen and would not let her nerves get the best of her.

She had to get that land. Prove she was not only fully capable, but that nothing would get in her way from running Air America.

He was the first to look away, and that gave her an ounce of triumph. Something she needed greatly. Using it, she started, "The taxes alone on your prop—"

"Are none of your business. The land—"

"Isn't for sale." Holding up a hand, she continued. "You already said that. However, I would appreciate it if you'd let me get a complete sentence out before you interrupt."

He folded his arms across his chest.

"You are aware that your parcel of property is something Air America has been interested in purchasing, and I understand, from what you just said, that you are not interested in selling it."

He didn't so much as twitch.

She, however, was shivering from head to toe. Both from the cold and from being face-to-face with him. The dreams she'd had years ago kept trying to flash forward. Of her and him riding on his motorcycle, burning rubber in his hot-rod car and kissing. Blast it all, but that dream was stronger right now than ever. To the point it made her throat go dry. He'd matured. Was even better-looking, and the things she'd felt for him years ago were taking sprout all over again.

That couldn't be. Gathering her thoughts, she reminded herself that she had to get that land, despite all obstacles. Including those deep inside her. "I believe we could still come to an agreement, or arrangement of sorts, if you would give me the opportunity to explain."

Of all the people in the world who could have shown up on his front porch, Randi Osterlund was the last one Jason would have imagined. Well, he might have imagined it, but that would have been a fantasy. However, she was the last person he would ever make any sort of agreement or arrangement with in this lifetime. What was her father thinking, sending her over here to talk to him? Randal Osterlund was not the kind of man who would use his daughter— Jason's thought stopped right there.

"Does your father know you're here?"

Her entire body seemed to slump, but only for a moment before she caught herself and straightened her spine.

Bingo. Her father didn't know.

With her pert little chin lifted high, she said, "I am employed by Air America and have full authority to conduct business in their name and—"

He waved toward the fence as he walked over to collect the shovel and pail he'd left by the tree when he'd heard a car pull into the driveway. "You know where the gate is." She might claim to be employed by Air America, but there was more to it than that. She was an heir to Air America, and a multimillion-dollar lingerie company that her mother owned, JO's Dream Wear. Besides her mother, Randi Osterlund was one of, if not the, richest women in Chicago. He'd learned his lesson when it came to her years ago and didn't need a repeat. That was one thing his father had been right about. Thinking he would have ever had a chance with a girl like her had been stupid. Very, very stupid.

"Do you ever let someone finish a sentence?" she asked.

"I let you finish several." That had been a mistake. But not his first one. That had been speaking to her when she'd been preening on his front porch. As soon as he'd seen her climb out of her car, he'd known it was her. Other women may have chestnut hair like her, thick and long, but no one had the same shade of eyes. A pale blue, that captured and held attention. He should have kept his mouth shut, let her knock and believe he wasn't home. She would have left, but he'd opened his mouth and now she was standing on his back porch instead of his front one. He'd managed to steer clear of her for years and needed to continue to do so for the rest of his life.

He picked up the shovel, scooped a pile off the ground and dropped it in the bucket.

"Why are you shoveling snow into a bucket?"

He grabbed the bucket by the handle. "Why are you still here?"

"Because I'm not leaving until you hear me out."

Hands on her hips, arms akimbo, she continued. "I can wait until you get your bucket full of snow."

His jaw tightened. He'd worked hard to forget her. Forget the huge crush he'd had on her. He'd been a gangly teenager with pimples the first time he'd seen her. They had gone to different primary schools, but the same high school, and for two years he'd thought of little else than catching her attention. He finally had, and then had dug deep to find the confidence to ask her out. Bitterness filled him recalling how she'd laughed at him. His hands tightened on the shovel and the bucket handle. "It's shit, not snow."

"Excuse me?"

"I'm shoveling shit, not snow."

"Really?"

"Yes, really." He let out a whistle and a moment later, Tanner bounded out through the rubber flap installed in the back door for the yellow Lab to enter and exit at will.

As if taken aback by her beauty, Tanner slid to a stop at her side, plopped on his haunches and stared up at her with stars in his big brown dog eyes.

Letting out a cooing sound, she knelt down beside the dog and scratched him behind his ears. "Hello, big guy. You are a handsome one. What's his name?"

At that moment Jason figured *Traitor* would be a good name for the dog. "Tanner," Jason answered, growling out the name.

She leaned back and cupped the dog's head with both hands. "Tanner, is it?"

Tanner barked.

She laughed.

Jason carried the bucket to the back of the yard and dumped it over the fence, into the trash can placed there for just that purpose. After putting the bucket and shovel in the shed, he walked to the porch, where she and the dog were still fawning over each other. "Tanner, inside."

He could have sworn the dog curled a lip at him as he stood, turned and with his tail between his legs, reentered the house through his doggie door.

She stood, too. "You should take lessons from your dog. He listens."

"He's a dog."

Both of her finely arched brows lifted as she stared at him.

If he wasn't so irritated, he might have been impressed at her boldness. As things stood right now though, he wanted her gone. Needed her gone. He had tried, but the moment he'd seen her step out of her car, he'd known he'd never gotten her out of his system. "You need to leave."

"No. You ran away from me once. That won't happen again."

"Ran away? What the hell are you talking about?"

"I'm talking about the night you jumped on your motorcycle and sped away before I could—"

"Stop laughing?" He knew the night. It was forever scorched in his brain. An hour after she'd laughed in his face, he'd been arrested, and by the following Monday, he was in reform school.

"My toes are cold. I am going inside." With that, she turned, opened the door and marched straight into his house.

Chapter Two

Letting out a curse, Jason followed. "You're trespassing."

She stepped out of her shoes and walked to the table, unbuttoning her coat on the way. "Have me arrested."

With smooth, graceful movements, she removed her coat, laid it over the back of the chair and sat in one of his padded chrome chairs. His eyes betrayed him by refusing to pull his gaze off her white blouse, or how it was neatly tucked into a blue skirt at her narrow waist, or the way she crossed one leg over the other at the knee. Mad at his inability to stop staring, and at his dog who was at her side again, Jason turned around and shrugged out of his coat. "That's your family, not mine."

Her silence made him feel like an ass, and his statement made him sound childish.

Damn it. He'd made it through six years. Six! And in a matter of minutes, she'd brought back every thought he'd ever had about her. As well as some new ones.

He walked into the laundry room off the kitchen, hung his coat on the rack nailed to the wall and grabbed a pair of socks out of the pile of clean clothes he hadn't yet put away.

Back in the kitchen, he laid the socks on the table while walking past her on his way to the sink.

"Thank you."

"You're welcome." He washed his hands and then grabbed the electric percolator, emptied and refilled it to make coffee. As he set the pot back on the counter, something inside him flinched. The countertops were blue, as was the tabletop, and the chair cushions, appliances and walls. It was called turquoise, but it was a pastel shade of blue, much like the color of her eyes.

"Your kitchen is very nice, very modern," she said, as if reading his mind.

He opened a cupboard door, which he'd stained rather than painted, and lifted down the can of coffee. "Thanks."

"You built it, didn't you? The entire house?"

It was no surprise that she'd know that. Her father had probably been keeping track of him, especially since his father had died. He glanced over his shoulder, to voice that the land wasn't for sale again, but instantly realized he'd made a mistake when he saw how she was rolling one nylon down over her knee, down her shin. She must have reached under her dress to unhook the little plastic hooks that held it in place. The idea of watching her unhook the other silk stocking was what made him turn around. Not because he didn't want to see it, but because he did.

"Your craftsmanship is excellent," she said.

He spooned coffee grounds into the percolator, put on the top and plugged the cord into the wall, all while trying not to envision her taking off her second nylon.

"Do you live here alone?"

He chanced a glance and tried to convince himself that he was glad that she was pulling on the second sock of the pair that he'd given her. "No."

"So you had a woman's help," she said, sounding as if that explained everything.

"No." He opened another cupboard door and took down two cups and two saucers. They were white with blue rings around the edges. Light blue. Damn it. She'd been stuck in his head for years, but he hadn't realized just how deeply.

"Who lives here with you?"

He turned around, leaned his backside against the counter. "Tanner."

She smiled down at the dog, who, with his head on her lap, was looking up at her with pure devotion.

Damn dog.

"Poor puppy," she said.

The dog barked and Jason considered changing the dog's name to Traitor again. He pushed off the counter. "I'll go put your shoes near a furnace grate." With a nod toward the nylons as he crossed the room, he asked, "You want me to put those there, too?"

She picked up the nylons. "No, thank you. They have holes in them now. Where is your trash can?"

"Under the sink." He picked up her shoes, carried them into the laundry room and turned the grate all the way open after setting them in front of it. Her perfume filled his nose; had since he'd walked into the house. He'd been trying hard to ignore the soft, floral scent as much as he'd been trying to ignore the things going on inside him.

Chicago was full of women, good-looking chicks. He'd dated a good number of them. Why the hell couldn't one of them have affected him the way she did? Why the hell wasn't she married to Gus Albright? Living in some ivory tower, eating with silver spoons and throwing money out the windows.

Enough was enough. He needed to get rid of her. Out

of his house. Out of his life. Things were going well. His construction company was thriving, thanks to the housing boom, and there were four work sites he had to visit today. He would have already been gone if he hadn't spent a few hours this morning working on the plans for the racetrack. Drag racing was in his blood, and this summer he'd be building a real strip on the land she wanted.

There would be no arrangements, agreements, or anything else between the two of them. Not over the land or anything else.

He left the laundry room, ready to stand his ground, but stopped at the sight of her standing near the stove, running a hand over the handle on the oven door. It was as if he was seeing a dream that he hadn't known lived inside him, coming true before his eyes.

She completed the area. As if it had been built just for her.

Damn it. It had. She'd been the image in his mind the whole time he'd been designing and building the entire house.

Right down to her wearing his clothes.

It was only a pair of socks, but it made him want to claim her, to wrap his arms around her and kiss her as badly as he'd wanted to in high school when he used to imagine her wearing his jacket.

That had never happened, and he'd been a fool to think it ever would. He was older now, wiser, and more importantly, not the fool he'd been back then. Money divided people. Always would. He'd accepted that and the fact that the Randi Osterlunds of the world had no place in his life, or he in theirs.

Randi willed all the old feelings she'd had for Jason to go back down, deep inside her, where she'd kept them hidden for years. She should never have come here. Never thought she could face him and not remember how crushed she'd been when she'd ruined everything. He had reasons to hate her.

Swallowing hard, she reminded herself that she didn't have a choice. She needed that land. Had to have that under her belt when her father became a senator, otherwise, no one would respect her role at Air America. They'd go on believing she was only there because she was an Osterlund—the next in line to take over the helm because of her last name, not because she could truly do the job. Everyone thought she should be focused on taking over her mother's company. A woman could run a lingerie company, but not an airline. Never an airline. She should leave that for her brother.

Well, her mother wasn't running for senator and her brother was still in college. So that left her. She'd been soaring through the skyway in an Air America airplane since before she'd been born—while still in her mother's womb. Taking over the helm would prove she was more than just Randal and Jolie's daughter. She was her own woman.

"How's Gus these days?"

She blew the air out of her lungs and turned about. Jason was leaning one hand on the door frame that led into a laundry room. Her heart started racing all over again. Damn him for being even more handsome than ever. And damn him for being such a major hurdle in getting what she needed. "Good. He's out in California and loving it. Says he'll never move back." Gus Albright was a safe subject, so she continued. "He has a lot of family out there. Aunts and uncles, cousins, grandparents."

Jason pushed off the wall. "I figured the two of you would be married by now."

"Me and Gus?" She laughed. "Why would you think that?"

He shrugged. "The two of you were always together."

"Because he was my ride before I got my license. His parents and mine have been best friends since before either he or I were born. He's as much of a brother to me as Joey." She bit her lips together at the mention of her younger brother. Joey was another subject she wasn't going to bring up with Jason.

He stopped near the refrigerator. "Do you want cream or sugar in your coffee?"

"Both, please," she answered with a laugh. "I keep thinking I'll acquire a taste for it black someday, but it hasn't happened yet."

He nodded, and then shook his head.

Embarrassed because her joke failed, she turned back around to face the counter. That was what had happened years ago. She'd laughed. Not because he'd said something funny, but because she'd been so nervous and happy. He hadn't thought so, nor had he let her explain, and that had been the catalyst that had led to her never seeing him again, until today.

The days, weeks and months following that event had been the saddest in her life. Deep inside she'd felt that if she could just explain why she'd laughed, Jason might forgive her and her family for all that had happened afterward. She'd put out an olive branch in the letter she'd written to him, only to be heartbroken again when it had been returned unopened.

There had been no denying the inevitable then, so she'd tried to move on, and had. She'd put her focus on Air America. And that was where it had to stay.

The coffeepot was in front of her, perking. Assuming it was done by the color of the coffee in the glass bulb on top, she unplugged it from the wall and filled the two cups he'd set out. While he carried a bottle of cream out of the fridge and a sugar bowl from a cupboard, she carried the cups to the table in the center of the room.

He set the cream and sugar, and a spoon, in front of her and sat down across the table from her. She put both in her coffee and stirred, wondering what to say. "I—"

"Look—" he said at the same time.

"Sorry," they both said.

"You go ahead," they again said at the same time.

She shook her head and looked at him, waited for him to speak first. He didn't look exactly like she remembered. His hair was still sandy-brown, his eyes still as dark as the coffee in his cup and there was still that dimple in his cheek, but his features were more defined. His body, too. There was a power about him, a determination, that made him even more alluring. She used to stand in the hallways of the school just to get a glimpse of him, and she'd been on cloud nine the first time he'd said hello. She'd been in tenth grade and had been infatuated with him for almost an entire year by then. Everything she'd been so attracted to then was still there and fueling all of her old feelings for him tenfold.

"I have plans for my land," he said. "There is no sale, arrangement, or agreement that I'd be interested in."

So much for apologizing. That was what she'd been going to do. For the past. But he didn't want to hear it any more than he had back then. Accepting that, she took a sip of her coffee. "All of it? Forty acres is what I'm interested in. Possibly leasing it?"

"Leasing it?"

"Yes. Every one of our airplanes needs to be washed at least four times a year. Currently, we don't have space for that. Therefore, we pay other carriers to provide those services, which isn't cost-effective."

"You want to build a facility on land you *lease* from me to wash your planes?"

"No, I wouldn't build on leased property, but I would use it for storage, freeing up space that we currently own to build a washing station. The forty acres I'm interested in is the plot of land that butts up to the rear of our property." His acreage was in an L shape and her plan would still leave him one hundred and twenty acres for whatever plans he had.

He took a drink of coffee and set the cup down on the saucer before saying, "None of my property is available for sale or lease."

Growing frustrated by his stubbornness, she drew in a breath. "As I said—"

"I heard what you said, but you don't seem to have heard what *I* said. I'm not interested. Not in leasing or selling anything."

"Well, I think it would behoove you—"

"Behoove me?"

"Yes, it means—"

"I know what it means." He stood, picked up his cup and saucer. "I may not have gone to an Ivy League college, but I have a good grasp on the English language." He walked toward the sink.

"I didn't mean to insult you. If you would just listen to my offer, you'd see it would be beneficial. You'd have extra money and—"

"You didn't insult me." He set his cup and saucer in the sink and turned, looked at her with a somewhat scathing glare. "I'm used to your kind."

Her spine stiffened. "My kind?"

"Yes."

"And exactly what is my kind?"

He let out a bogus laugh. "The kind that believe I need your money. I don't."

"I wasn't implying—"

"Weren't you?"

Her last nerve was about to snap. "No. I wasn't." Unable to stop herself, she continued. "If you would have listened to me that night, maybe we'd be friends now."

He laughed again. "I'd rather be your enemy."

The response inside was so swift and unexpected, she pressed a hand to her breastbone, against the pain that sliced through her heart. No one had made her heart hurt, not like this, except for him. She wouldn't put herself through that again. "Fine, if that's the way you want it."

"It is."

She stood, grabbed her coat. Kept her chin up. "Thank you for the coffee, Mr. Heim."

"You're welcome, Miss Osterlund."

The living room and the front door were visible through the arched doorway of the kitchen, and she marched toward it, slipping on her coat as she walked through the living room and then out the front door. It wasn't until she stepped off the porch that she realized she didn't have any shoes on. Just his socks. She clamped her teeth together and kept moving. Walking through the snow stocking footed was better than facing him again.

She marched forward, along the shoveled walkway, to her car parked in the driveway. To her great distress, Jason arrived just as she opened her car door.

"You forgot your shoes." Holding out her pumps, he glanced at her feet. "You can keep the socks."

"I intend to." She grabbed her shoes and climbed in the car, slamming the door extra hard.

Chapter Three

 F our days later Randi's temper was so close to the boiling point, she might actually break something. It was either that, or complain to her father, which she wouldn't do. Sam Wharton knew that, which was precisely why he was purposefully not providing her a copy of the profit and loss sheets for December. He was her main adversary in the company, because he knew, when—not if—she took over for her father, he'd be out the door. Or at least demoted. She wasn't so mean as to cause someone to completely lose their job.

Sam was one of the people who thought she couldn't do anything except spend her parents' money, and was trying his damnedest to make sure she failed. She wouldn't, but also had to be cautious because Sam would go to her father and complain. He already had. Several times over the years, against both her and her brother.

She understood that Sam had been working for the company for years, and that he was interested in taking over for her father, but he wasn't what the company needed. He took no initiative, had no drive to make changes that could grow the company. It was 1956, the world was changing and Air America had to, too, in order to remain on top.

Frustration had her slapping her desk with both hands, and she glanced out the window of her corner office, only to instantly pull her gaze away because her windows overlooked the very land that Jason wouldn't sell or lease to her.

He was stuck in her mind enough already.

She pushed her chair back. Without those P&L reports, she couldn't complete her reports, which were due by the end of the week. A deadline Sam didn't want her to meet.

Removing her shoes, she put them in a satchel and slid on her boots. They were black, heeled, lined with sheepskin and had black wool cuffs around the tops that stopped near her ankles. After getting her shoes wet at Jason's, she'd worn her boots every day and carried her shoes.

She put on her coat, slipped the satchel strap over her shoulder, picked up her purse and left her office.

"I'm leaving for the day, Carol," she told her secretary in the outer office. "Please inform Mr. Wharton, once again, that I expect those reports to be on my desk first thing in the morning."

Carol had been with the company for years, and knew what Sam was attempting to do. "I will, Miss Osterlund. Have a good evening."

"You, too." Once out the office door, while walking down the hall, Randi hooked her purse over her wrist to pull her gloves out of her pockets. Only to discover they weren't there. She dug in the satchel and pulled out a pair of socks rather than her gloves.

Jason's socks. She'd washed and dried them, and rolled them together like they'd been when he'd set them on the table.

Her insides sank at how that visit had gone. Everyone always wanted something from her, but not him. Jason didn't want anything to do with her.

She dropped the socks back in the bag and dug until she found both of her gloves and pulled them on as she walked down the steps to the front door of the big Air America office building.

It was spitting snow. Not a lot, just enough to leave a thin coating of the white flakes on the ground and on her car. There was also a sheet of ice covering her windshield from sitting in the elements since she'd arrived early this morning.

After putting her purse and bag in the car, and starting the engine, she grabbed the metal ice scraper and cleared the windshield, side windows and the rear one. By the time she climbed inside she was shivering from head to toe. Her gloves were wet, and she pulled them off, stuck them in her coat pockets and put her hands up on the dash, over the warm air blowing out.

She sat there until her fingers were warm, then shifted the car into First and drove out of the parking lot.

Her father hadn't yet announced who would be his successor when he was elected senator, because he claimed his bid was a long shot. In her mind, though, he was a shoo-in. He also claimed that he would continue to oversee the operation, even if he was elected, but everyone knew he'd need someone here on the day-to-day basis and she needed to be that person. Otherwise, besides being her mother's daughter, her father's daughter and her brother's sister, she'd also be the senator's daughter. Never her own person.

She had to get that land from Jason. That was all there was to it. The problem was facing him again. Seeing him had brought back more than memories. Just thinking about him made her heart beat faster. Dreams had formed again, and that scared her. He was so handsome. So fit. So iconic...

If only there was a way for them to be friends, so she could explain why she needed the land, not just for the washing bay, but for her. So she would be recognized as her own person. He'd done that. His construction company was very successful. He'd been his own person in high school, too, and she'd admired that.

She had to try. Had to do something. The socks were in her bag. She could drop them off to him.

That might work, and she already knew how he felt about her, so there was no reason for her to worry about having her heart broken again. She'd learned her lesson on that. No one would fall in love with someone who wanted to be their enemy. Furthermore, her focus was Air America, nothing more.

At one time Air America had been a distance from town, but the suburbs now extended farther out of the city, and in less than twenty minutes, she turned down Jason's street and wondered why he'd built his house here rather than on his land. That was where he'd lived when they were in high school, and as far as she knew, the house was still there.

She pulled into the driveway and took a moment to stare at the windows, looking for some sign of movement. It was only late afternoon. He might still be at work. The garage was on the far side of the backyard, in the alley, like the others in the neighborhood, so she couldn't tell if there was a vehicle here or not. She wasn't even sure what type of car Jason drove. He used to drive a motorcycle and a red hot-rod car with a ball of fire painted on the hood.

There was only one way to find out if he was home

or not. She shut off her car and pulled the socks out of the bag, stuffing them in her coat pocket while opening the car door.

There were no footprints in the thin coating of snow on the sidewalk, but there wouldn't be if he parked his car in the garage. Arriving at the door, she forced herself to not check her clothes like she had the other day and knocked.

A bark sounded and she smiled. Tanner's friendliness had already stolen her heart. He was much bigger than other Labs she'd seen and so very sweet.

When no one opened the door, she knocked again, heard Tanner bark again and waited until she had no choice but to believe Jason wasn't home.

She could leave the socks, but doubted he'd contact her to acknowledge their return. However, if she did leave them, she could stop by later to make sure he got them.

That was far more probable than him contacting her.

She lifted the door on the mail slot, but the slit was too narrow for one, let alone a pair of rolled socks. Closing the slot door, she glanced around, realizing he might not find them if she just left them on the porch.

Tanner barked again, and she smiled. The doggie door. Jason was sure to find the socks if she dropped them through it. Proud of her own ingenuity, she walked off the porch, proceeded to the gate and entered the backyard.

She was grateful she was wearing her boots because her feet were sinking into the snow, even though she was stepping into the footprints she'd left the other day.

On the back patio, she knelt down, pulled the socks out of her pocket and pushed open the doggie door to drop them in. The flap was made of rubber, and heavier than she'd expected. She held it open with one hand and, reaching in with the other, dropped the socks. As they fell, she realized one of her gloves had also been in her hand and tried to catch it, but it was too late. It had fallen inside the doggie door with the socks.

Shoot!

She tried to find the floor, feel her glove, but couldn't. Leaning closer, she shoved her entire arm inside the doggie door, right up to her shoulder, and then, able to feel the floor, searched for the glove, blindly, using only her fingers.

Not feeling anything—not the socks or glove—she pulled her arm back out and looked at the door. It was big. Big enough for Tanner, and therefore, big enough for her head.

With no other option, she got down on her hands and knees.

Jason shot a glare at Tanner, telling the dog to stay quiet as the slender hand, complete with manicured nails, painted pink, slipped back out of the doggie door. He'd been stepping out of the shower when he'd heard Tanner bark, but by the time he'd gotten dressed, no one was at the front door. However, he'd recognized the blue-and-white Bel Air parked in his driveway. Assuming Randi had walked around to the back, he'd entered the kitchen and had been about to open the door when a pair of socks and a woman's black leather glove had landed on the floor through the doggie door.

A moment later he'd bit back a smile and watched as the hand had slid through the door, searching for the glove.

He hadn't been able to help himself and had toed the glove and the socks out of her reach.

Eyes on the doggie door, he waited for the hand to return again. To his surprise, when the flap moved again, a full head of dark hair popped through the opening.

He knelt down, picked up the glove and dangled it where she'd see it as soon as she pushed the rubber flap up high enough.

As soon as that happened, he asked, "Is this what you're looking for?"

Her head snapped around so fast the rubber slapped the side of her face. Flinching from guilt at causing that to happen, and at her pain, he grabbed the flap, held it out of the way. "Are you okay?"

Light blue eyes blazing hot enough to light a good-sized fire glared at him.

He wanted to laugh at how adorable she looked, yet was concerned that she might be hurt and repeated, "Are you okay?"

"Why didn't you answer your front door?"

"I was in the shower."

"Oh." Her gaze went to his bare feet and then she glanced around, as if not sure what to say or do.

Still holding the flap with one hand, he balled the glove in his other hand, and used that one to reach up and turn the doorknob. "Hold still, I'm going to open the door."

She didn't answer, but did hold still as he slowly opened the door, until her head was no longer in the doggie door. He then released the flap and held out a hand to help her up.

There were still flames in her eyes, but she took his hand and gracefully rose to her feet.

His hand, where hers touched it, was on fire, shooting flames up his arms and igniting other flames.

She slowly pulled her hand away, ran it over her coat,

then, chin up, said, "Thank you. I—I'll take my glove, please."

The opportunity was too great to ignore. He dangled the glove. "This one?"

She reached for it.

He quickly pulled it out of her reach. "How do I know it's yours?"

"Because I have the other one right here." She pulled a matching glove out of her coat pocket.

"Oh, and here I was thinking it was yours because I watched you drop it through the doggie door."

"Because you didn't answer your front door."

Closing the door, he replied, "Because I was in the bathroom." He'd pulled on jeans and a white T-shirt, but was barefoot. "Didn't even have time to put on socks in my hurry to get to the door, but by then you were no longer at the door." He picked up the socks she'd just delivered and walked over to a kitchen chair, sat down and proceeded to put them on. "Your car was in my driveway, so I figured you'd walked around to the back, but I didn't expect to see you climbing through the doggie door. I wonder if that's considered breaking and entering?"

"I wasn't breaking and entering. I was returning your socks. Now, if you'll just give me my glove, I'll be leaving."

He should give her the glove, let her leave, but teasing her was so much fun. Little else had consumed his thoughts since she'd stormed out, wearing only his socks on her feet. Then again, she'd had a permanent place in his mind for years. "Nice boots," he said, nodding toward her feet. "You should have been wearing those the other day."

"I hadn't planned on trudging through snow the other day."

"But you did today? Planning to come around to the back, to sneak in through the doggie door?"

"No. I—" She shook her head. Sighed. "What were you doing taking a shower at four in the afternoon?"

"If you must know, Miss Nosy—" he stood up, handed her the glove "—I just got off of work and need to be in Downers Grove by five."

"I wasn't being nosy. Just curious."

"What's the difference?"

She smoothed the fingers of the glove he'd given her with one hand. "There is a great difference."

"Do tell. I'm listening."

She rolled her eyes at him. "You know the difference."

He did indeed, and he was curious about her, even though he shouldn't be. "Came over to ask about the land again, did you? My answer hasn't changed."

"No, I didn't come to ask about the land," she said. "I heard your answer the other day. I just wanted to return your socks."

He wasn't sure he could believe that. "I said you could keep them."

"I don't have a need for a pair of men's socks."

"In that case, thank you." He wiggled his toes. "I do have need for them."

"Why do you have to be in Downers Grove?" She stuffed her glove in her coat pocket and shot him a saucy look. "I'm simply curious."

"A birthday party." He waited until she met his gaze before adding, "For a lovely young lady."

"Oh." She fidgeted, smoothed a hand over the front of her red coat that had the big rhinestone R pinned below one shoulder. "Well, then, I should be going so you can finish getting dressed."

His mouth moved before his brain engaged. "Would you like to go with me, meet her?"

"Oh, I couldn't, I—"

Had he just asked her on a date again? And been turned down again? Was he that stupid? "That's all right, I get it." Shaking his head at himself, he turned to lead her to the front door.

She caught his arm. "No, you don't understand. I would like to go, but I wouldn't want to impose."

Her touch was soft, yet he felt it as strongly as he had her hand earlier. "If it was an imposition, I wouldn't have asked."

They stood there for a moment, doing nothing but staring at each other, as if they were each trying to read the other's mind. At least, he was trying to read hers. His own was in too big of a jumble to make hide nor hair out of what he was doing. And his eyes kept flicking toward her lips, making him wonder what they tasted like.

"In that case, yes, I'd like to go with you."

His heart skipped several beats. So many he was damned near breathless. "All right, I have to put on my shirt and shoes and feed Tanner, then we can leave."

Stroking the dog's head, she offered, "I could feed Tanner for you."

Completely taken with her, the dog looked up at him with pleading eyes. "His dishes are by the door and there's a bag of dog food in the laundry room."

As she cooed over the dog, Jason hurried out of the room and down the hall. Within minutes he'd put on a blue-and-white button-up shirt, slipped his belt through the belt loops of his cuffed jeans and put on his shoes. On his way to the door, he grabbed his leather coat off the bed, all the while wondering what the hell he was doing.

This was Randi Osterlund—*the* Randi Osterlund—and he was the rebel her father had sent to reform school.

He flinched, knowing that wasn't true. There was no one to blame for his stint in reform school except for himself. And that was another reason he needed to stay clear of her. His past was more jaded now than it had been back in high school.

She was still in the kitchen, petting Tanner as the dog ate. "I wasn't sure how much to give him, so I filled the bowl."

"That's fine." He nodded toward the back door. "We'll take my car." His Buick was bigger, heavier, which meant it would maneuver the snow-coated roads better than her smaller Bel Air. Furthermore, the dollhouse and furniture he'd built for Rachelle were already in his car. "Unless you've changed your mind."

"I haven't changed my mind. Your car is fine."

He must have lost every last marble that he'd had, because he was excited to take her to the party. Then again, he wanted the event to be a huge success. Rachelle deserved that after all she'd been through.

"I need to get my purse out of my car." She moved away from Tanner, but on her way to the doorway, she stopped and smiled at Jason. "Thank you for inviting me to join you."

He nodded and fell into step beside her. "I hope it didn't interfere with other plans." He didn't even sound like himself.

"No. Just going home to an empty house. My parents are in New York."

"What for?" he asked as they walked toward the front door.

"A fashion show. Some of my mother's designs are being showcased."

He'd seen some of her mother's designs and wasn't convinced that women's underwear would be a good topic to have floating around in his mind right now.

As if knowing his thoughts, she said, "She designs uniforms for several airlines."

He opened the front door. "I wasn't aware of that."

"Most people aren't."

He walked her out to her car, and then back through the house, the backyard and into the garage. They talked of several things, just small talk, but he found it interesting to learn more about her. That she found fashion shows tedious and that she'd never had a dog, but had had a cat for several years while growing up.

In the garage he held the passenger door open as she slid inside his car. Then he swung open the garage door before climbing in the driver's seat.

"How old is this lovely young lady?" she asked with a glance toward the backseat that said she'd noticed the two large wrapped boxes.

He grinned at her. "Six."

Chapter Four

Going out with Jason had been a dream of Randi's for years, and she was having a hard time convincing herself that this was not a date as he drove through the spitting snow. He looked so handsome, smelled so good, that every part of her body was alive, tingling with excitement.

"The party is at a café that my aunt works at," he said. "We'll eat there, if that's all right."

"Of course it's all right. What's the birthday girl's name?"

"Rachelle. She's my cousin's daughter."

"What are in the boxes?" Huge, they took up the backseat and were gaily wrapped and hosted big blue bows.

"You'll have to wait and see," he said.

He flashed her one of his grins that made her want to drop dead twice. That was a silly saying that had stuck with her since high school, but when it came to him, it held a whole different meaning. He could stop her heart with just one of those grins. If she let him. Which she would not do.

"I might need you to carry in the smaller one, if you don't mind. It's not too heavy."

"Aw, you had an ulterior motive in asking me to join you. You needed a helper."

"Free labor is nothing to scoff at."

She laughed. "How do you know it's free?" Embarrassed that he might take that the wrong way, she pointed to the radio. "Oh, I love this song."

He turned it up. "You're one of those?"

"Girls who love Elvis?" she asked. "Yes!" She then proceeded to sing along with the song about blue suede shoes.

He was tapping a hand on the top of the steering wheel, and she gave him a playful slap on the arm. "You like him, too."

"He has a few good songs."

"Like every one of them!"

He laughed and they talked about songs and performers for most of the drive, and her insides were nearly glowing when he pulled into a parking lot of a small café with a lighted sign in the shape of an arrow saying Mama's and pointing at the building.

She reached down and picked up her satchel. "I'm going to switch my boots for my shoes so my feet don't get hot."

"Oh, yes, hot feet would be a terrible thing."

"Very funny," she said while giggling because she was enjoying herself.

Perhaps too much, but it really couldn't be helped. He was fun and made her feel comfortable.

As they entered the café, with its black-and-white tiled floor and red-and-white booths, a tall blonde woman met them. "What's buzzin', Cuzzin?"

"Not much," Jason replied, carrying the large box that nearly covered the bottom of his face.

The woman lifted a brow. "Really?"

The woman was looking at her, grinning, and Randi, carrying the smaller box, smiled in return.

"Randi, this is Lottie, Rachelle's mom," he said.

"Yes, I am," Lottie said. "I'm also this cat's cool cousin."

"You wish you were as cool as me," he said.

Randi rolled her eyes toward Lottie, and teasingly asked, "Doesn't everyone wish they were as cool as him?"

"Ooh, I like you, Randi," Lottie said. "Someone who can rattle his cage is exactly what Jason needs."

"Ha ha," he said.

"Jason! Jason, I knew you'd come!"

Randi's attention was instantly drawn to a tiny, dark-haired girl moving toward them in a small wheelchair.

"I wouldn't miss this party for anything in the world," Jason replied.

Randi's heart swelled at how the little girl gazed up at Jason with adoration shimmering in her big brown eyes. It appeared that he still had the ability to steal a young girl's heart.

"Are both of those presents for me?" Rachelle asked, stopping her chair before them.

While holding the big box, Jason knelt down. "I don't know. Is someone else having a birthday party here to-night?"

"No!" Rachelle replied.

He kissed the girl's forehead. "Then they both must be for you, kiddo."

"Can I open them now?"

Lottie rested a hand on her daughter's shoulder. "Let's give Jason and Randi a chance to get their coats off first."

Not deterred in the least, Rachelle nodded. "Okay!" She quickly maneuvered the wheelchair around. "Follow me. You can sit at my table, and put the presents on it so I can open them right away."

Randi giggled at the girl's excitement.

"You heard her," Jason said, nodding for Randi to walk in front of him.

With her heart nearly flowing over, Randi followed the girl and said to Lottie, "Your daughter is adorable."

"Thank you. As you can tell, she adores Jason." Lottie glanced over her shoulder at Jason following them. "He visited her every day while she had been in the hospital with polio last year."

A deep sense of admiration for Jason grew inside Randi, at the same time empathy formed for Rachelle. "How long was she in the hospital?"

"Ten weeks," Lottie answered. "She was in an iron lung for over a month."

Randi knew the devastation polio caused and served as the chair of the local fundraiser to collect dimes to pay for every school-age child to get vaccinated, but mass inoculations had only started last year. They still had a long way to go before every child would receive the vaccination. "I'm glad she's recovering so wonderfully."

"Thank you. We are, too, and credit a lot of her healing to Jason. There were days that she wouldn't eat, like she was giving up." Lottie cleared her throat, as if choked up. "But Jason would find a way to get her to eat. To smile. I know it made a difference."

Randi's eyes stung, and she had to blink quickly to keep the tears inside.

"I need to stop," Lottie said. "Before I make myself cry again."

"Yes, you do, Cuz," Jason said. "And you need to step away from the table. This box is heavy."

Lottie laughed. "All right, you can put them right here on this table."

Rachelle had already wheeled her chair up to the end

of the table, and Randi stepped aside so Jason could put his package down first.

He set it in front of Rachelle and then took the package from Randi and set it near the back of the table.

"Can I open them now?" Rachelle asked.

"Not everyone is here yet," Lottie said.

"I arrived early, just so she could open these before everyone got here, then we can move it aside so it doesn't take up so much room," Jason said.

"Please?" Rachelle asked her mother.

"All right. Let me get Grandma," Lottie answered.

"I'm coming! Don't start without me!" a voice shouted from the kitchen area behind the long counter across the room from the booths.

"I'll take your coat," Jason said.

Randi was so enthralled, she hadn't even unbuttoned her coat yet, but did so quickly, and let him lift it off her shoulders.

He carried it over to hooks on the wall past the counter, where a jukebox sat, and hung up her coat and his. Before his return, a plump older woman with short, dark hair arrived at the booth and introduced herself as his aunt Marla.

After an exchange of greetings with his aunt, Randi slid into the booth, leaving room for Jason to sit on the edge, next to Rachelle.

Marla and Lottie slid in on the other side, and as soon as Jason sat, he said, "Go ahead, kiddo, rip it open."

Rachelle didn't waste a moment tearing away at the paper.

An adorable blue-and-white dollhouse was instantly revealed. Completely finished with shingles on the roof and shutters on the windows, tile and carpets on the floors, and each of the rooms was painted a different color.

Randi was in awe. The house was a work of art. Built with such skill and precision, it was truly extraordinary.

Jason stood and lifted the house. Seeing what he was doing, Randi slid the other box forward so there was room for him to set the dollhouse down behind the second present.

"Now this one?" Rachelle asked.

"Now this one," he answered.

Rachelle tore off the paper and opened a box full of miniature furniture that was handcrafted as perfectly as real furniture found in stores. The little chairs even had cushions attached to them, and the beds had mattresses. The amount of love Jason had put into the gifts had Randi's heart expanding, and her hands trembling. Her parents had showered her and Joe with their love, as well as each other, and she'd told herself she'd never settle for less. She'd been young, but there had been a time when she'd imagined Jason loving her like that.

He stood and lifted the house off the table. "Wheel your chair away from the table. I want to show you something."

Rachelle wheeled her chair backward, and he flipped down folded-up legs from the bottom of the house and locked them in place with metal brackets, and then set the dollhouse in front of her.

"I made it so you can wheel your chair right up to it," he said.

"This is the best present ever," Rachelle said. "Ever, ever, ever!"

"Oh, Jason, that is so perfect," his aunt said. "And so like you. You're amazing."

"Yes, he is." Realizing she'd said that aloud, Randi's cheeks burned when he looked at her, yet she couldn't look away. Nor could she deny that he was becoming the man of her dreams all over again.

* * *

Jason knew he should, but for the life of him, he couldn't pull his gaze off Randi, not with the way she was looking at him. It was causing a good case of chaos inside him. And desire. Strong desire to kiss her.

The ringing of the bell over the front door, signaling the arrivals of others, is what forced him to look away. He glanced down at Rachelle. "Let's move this over by the jukebox so it's not in the way."

"All right, but leave room so we can dance later," she said.

He ruffled her dark hair. "I will."

While he carried the dollhouse, Rachelle followed in her chair, as did Randi, carrying the box of dollhouse furniture. He set the house near the corner, where it wouldn't get bumped if there was dancing later, and made sure the legs were locked in tight.

Rachelle rolled up to the dollhouse, and as Randi handed the girl furniture, one piece at a time, Jason was once again questioning his sanity. He shouldn't have brought Randi with him. They were as opposite as night and day. No one in his family had ever had anything handed to them. They'd worked hard, and continued to, for every loaf of bread put on their table, whereas she'd probably never wanted for anything in her life.

He had. He'd wanted her and was wanting that again.

"This is a beautiful dollhouse," Randi told Rachelle.

"Jason could build one for you, too," Rachelle said.

"I might have to ask him," Randi replied.

She was wearing a red dress. Tailor made. Had to be. It enhanced every area of her body to perfection before it flowed into a wide skirt. Her hair was hanging loose, in soft curls, down her back. She looked eloquent, beautiful and had every part of his body alive, pounding with desires that he couldn't ignore. Couldn't control. Every fantasy he'd imagined about her seemed to float across his mind, filling his chest with abnormal sensations.

"He builds real houses, too," Rachelle said. "He could build you one of those, too."

"I'll remember that when I need a house," Randi said.

"He fixes houses, too," Rachelle said. "He fixed our house so my wheelchair can fit through the doors and he—"

"Hey, kid," he interrupted. "You have other guests arriving and should go say hello."

"Okay." She spun around and wheeled away.

Randi stepped in front of him, close enough he could smell her perfume, see the sparkles in her gorgeous blue eyes.

"I always knew your bad-boy persona was just an act," she said.

Needing to ground himself before he said or did something he'd regret, he pulled up the only reason for her to have agreed to come with him tonight. "The answer is still no."

She frowned. "Answer to what?"

"To buying my land."

Shaking her head, she said, "I wasn't thinking about your land, and I wish you weren't, either."

The sadness in her tone and in her eyes gutted him as she turned. He grasped her wrist. "I'm sorry. I was just teasing."

She glanced from him to where people were staring at them, walking in through the door two at a time. Everyone was sure to want to know who she was and why she was with him. For a moment he considered getting their coats and leaving, taking her to her car so she could go home. He couldn't do that to Rachelle. Didn't want to do that to Randi, either.

Rubbing the inside of her wrist with his thumb, he said, "Honestly, I was only teasing, and I'm sorry."

Her eyes fluttered closed for a moment. "I'm sorry, too." Sighing, she looked up at him. "I shouldn't be so prickly."

"Prickly?"

"Yes."

Of all the ways he could describe her, *prickly* wasn't what came to mind.

"I'm just nervous," she added.

"Why?"

Her one shoulder shrug was cute, charming. "Of meeting your family," she whispered. "I wouldn't want to embarrass you."

He had to laugh at that, which brought more curious stares from onlookers. "That will never happen." He took a hold of her hand and held on, even as his palm felt as if it was being licked by flames. "Come on, I'll introduce you to everyone."

Aunt Marla had worked at the diner for years, ever since her husband had died, and the owner, Elwood, who was also in attendance, had shut the diner down to the public tonight, so the entire family could celebrate Rachelle's birthday. And no one in the room was immune to Randi's charm, including him.

She was soon giving back one-liners about being with him as quickly as some of his cousins tossed them out. Her laughter, teasing comments and the way she'd touch his arm or dip her head against his shoulder, filled him with a lightheartedness that he hadn't felt in a long time.

Several family members worked for him, including

Stu, Rachelle's father, and Randi asked him about his company, appearing truly interested in his answers.

When the time came for Rachelle to open her gifts, he found seats for them on the stools at the counter to watch.

Randi leaned closer to him. "Rachelle is adorable. It had to have been hard, seeing her so sick. In an iron lung."

"It was." The past year had been hell, and tonight was an event that at times he'd worried might never happen. "She was so little, so sick, there were times I didn't know if she'd win."

Randi's fingers wrapped around his. "She did win. Tell me how you convinced her to eat."

The memory made him smile. "Ice cream. I took her milkshakes."

Randi giggled. "She must have loved that. What flavor was her favorite?"

Watching Rachelle rip open another present, he answered, "Strawberry, but chocolate was a close second."

"You took her one every day?"

"Yes."

As presents continued to be opened, Randi quietly asked more simple questions, and he ended up telling her things that he'd never told anyone about how concerned he'd been over Rachelle's illness and gradual climb to health. Ironically, talking about it to her felt right.

The last gift had been opened and he stood, pulled her off her stool. "What's your favorite milkshake?"

"I don't know. Why?"

He led her around the counter, toward the freezer and milkshake machine. "Because we'll make it."

"We can't go back there to make our own milkshake."

"Where do you think I got the milkshakes that I took to Rachelle?"

The smile on her face was reflected in her eyes. "You made them?"

"Yes."

A hint of challenge added to her expression. "Prove it."

He gently flicked the end of her nose, then grabbed a metal cup and slid open the top of the ice cream freezer.

A short time later, while eating hamburgers and French fries that Elwood had placed in front of their stools while they'd been making the strawberry milkshake, Randi let out an adorable sigh after taking another sip from one of the two straws sticking out of the glass.

Jason popped a French fry into his mouth, chewed and swallowed. "Still not going to admit it, are you?"

She gave him a cheeky grin. "I'm still deciding."

"If I should have made two?"

Giggling, she took another sip before setting the milkshake between them. "No, it's been so long since I've had a milkshake, I can't tell if it's that good, or if I'd just forgotten how tasty they are."

He picked up the glass, and not knowing which straw was hers and which was his, simply chose one and took a drink. "It's that good. I know. I have them all the time."

Her eyes were twinkling. "You do?"

"I do." He popped another French fry into his mouth.

She dipped a fry in ketchup and made a show of biting off the end. "I suppose you have hamburgers and French fries all the time, too."

He picked up his hamburger, said, "I do," and took a big bite.

The room was full of gaiety, laughter and music from the jukebox, but it was the sound of her giggle he liked the best. Her beauty had struck him years before, but tonight he'd discovered she was just as beautiful on the inside.

They continued eating and talking and laughing. He felt as if he'd been given a gift. A once-in-a-lifetime gift of her company, and wanted to make the most of it. "Want to dance?"

"Yes, I do." Eyes sparkling, she leaned closer. "But I'll wait."

"For what?"

"Until after you dance with Rachelle. It's her party."

It was Rachelle's party and he had promised her a dance, but it was the fact that she understood how much Rachelle's happiness meant to him that touched him deeply. "You won't mind?"

"Not in the least." Giggling, she picked up the glass. "I'll finish our milkshake."

Laughing, he stood. "I'll make you another one before we leave."

"I might hold you to that."

Giving her a wink, he spun around and crossed the room. To Rachelle's delight, he lifted her out of her chair.

Her arms latched around his neck as he carried her to the dance floor. "Thank you for the dollhouse. I really, really like it."

"I'm glad," he said, bumping his forehead to hers. "Because I really, really like you."

Her giggle floated on the air with the music about rocking around the clock. "I really, really like Randi, too. She's pretty."

"Yes, she is pretty."

"She's nice, too."

"Yes, she is nice."

"She likes you, too."

"How do you know that?"

"Because of the way she smiles at you. Like seeing you makes her happy."

As nice as that sounded, he wasn't going to hold much credence in what a six-year-old thought. "Seeing you makes me happy." He swung around quickly, making her laugh, and continued to do so until the music ended.

"Want to dance again?" he asked.

"No, you can dance with Randi now."

"Maybe she doesn't want to dance," he suggested while carrying her back to her chair.

"She will if you ask her," Rachelle said.

He set her in her chair, made sure her legs were straight and her feet on the little metal plates.

"Do you want me to ask her for you?" she offered. "I will."

"I'm sure you would, kiddo." He winked at her. "But I can manage on my own."

A short time later he wasn't overly sure if he could manage on his own. Randi was in his arms, swaying to the slow song about an earth angel and being a fool in love. He wasn't in love, would never be in love; his childhood had closed his heart to that ever happening. However, having her body pressed up against his had his mind nose-diving into what people called making love. That, with her, would be the ultimate.

He should have been glad when the song ended, but evidently, he hadn't tortured himself enough, because he stayed on the dance floor; kept her there, too.

Another record fell into place on the machine and began to play.

"I love this song!" She grasped one of his hands and started tap stepping to the beat of the music, making her skirt flip and flop around her knees.

He thought the fast beat of the song might clear his mind and so he matched her steps, twirled her beneath their clasped hands. "Every song is your favorite."

She laughed. "How can they not be?"

They danced several dances, some fast and fun, others slow and sensual. It was during one of those slow and sensual ones, where their bodies were touching from hips to shoulders and the singer was singing about being in paradise, that she lifted her face, looked at him with eyes glowing.

"I wasn't laughing at you that night, Jason, when you asked me out." She kept her gaze locked with his. "I was happy, so excited that all I could do was laugh because I'd thought you'd never notice me. Never ask me out. You walked away, got on your motorcycle and left, before I could explain."

He'd practiced, refined every single movement, on nearly every other girl in high school, all in order to build up the nerve to ask her. Yet, even though dozens of other girls had gone out with him, he'd expected her to say no, and had his escape route already set in his mind before he'd even approached her. They'd been from two different worlds then, and still were. He knew that, but it didn't stop him from admitting the truth. "I'd noticed you long before then."

Her arms tightened around his neck. "I'd noticed you long before then, too."

His resolve about not kissing her was dissolving like a sugar cube in hot coffee as the music played on, slow and low. She was looking up at him and dipping his head, touching his lips against hers, filled his thoughts.

She licked her lips, bit down on the bottom one, and every muscle in his body went tight. He'd wanted to kiss her for years, and at this moment knew without a doubt she wanted that, too.

He had to pull his gaze off her, look away. Had to,

because he couldn't kiss her. Not here. With his entire family in attendance.

He'd wait until the night ended, and then he'd kiss her because he had to experience that. Had to.

Randi's entire being was humming with such an all-encompassing excitement that she had to keep telling herself to breathe. The entire evening had been truly magical, as exciting as she'd imagined going out with him would be. However, he was more than she'd imagined. More charming. More kind and caring. From the time she'd been fourteen and seen him for the first time, she'd never looked at another boy because she'd known, somehow, deep inside, that he was the only one who would ever see her for herself. That her last name, her family's wealth, wouldn't make a difference to him.

She'd been nervous to meet his family. They all had to know it had been because of her family that he'd been sent to reform school, but right from the start, he'd made her feel comfortable. Hadn't even mentioned her last name, as if it didn't matter. She was just Randi, and she liked that. Liked him, so very much.

She'd never wanted to kiss someone so badly in her life. For a moment she'd thought he might kiss her, right here on the dance floor. He hadn't, but the way he'd looked at her gave her hope that it would happen before the night was over.

Heavens to Betsy, she hoped it did.

The music ended, and she slowly lifted her head, looked up him, and his smile sent a delectable tingle throughout her system.

"It—" he cleared his throat "—looks like the party girl is getting tired. I'm going to help Stu load up her presents."

The idea of leaving meant the kiss she wanted might happen sooner rather than later. Releasing her hold on his neck, she said, "I'll help, too."

"You don't have—"

"I want to."

With the help of so many, it didn't take long before the diner was put in order and the gifts all loaded in Stu and Lottie's car.

Jason retrieved their coats and as he was holding hers for her to slip her arms into the sleeves, Rachelle rolled in front of them.

"Thank you for coming to my party, Randi."

Kneeling down in front of the chair, Randi replied, "Thank you for having me. It was the best birthday party I've ever attended."

Rachelle touched the rhinestone pin on Randi's lapel. "Our names both start with an R."

"Yes, they do." After unpinning the pin, Randi removed it and pinned it on Rachelle's coat. "Happy birthday."

Rachelle's adorable eyes grew larger as she looked down at the pin. "I've never seen anything so pretty." She looked up at Jason. "Have you, Jason?"

"No, I haven't," he replied.

Randi's heart flipped at the way he was looking at her rather than Rachelle or the pin.

He held her elbow as she stood and then his hand slid down her arm, until their palms met and his fingers threaded between hers as they walked to the door. She was so giddy she could barely think.

The feeling continued long after they'd climbed into his car and were driving toward his house. She had to bite her lips together to keep the excitement inside her, and bit down harder as she wondered if he would kiss her in the car or at his house.

"Thank you for giving Rachelle your pin. She really liked that."

Trying to sound as normal as possible, she replied, "I'm glad she liked it, but nothing will ever compare to her dollhouse and furniture. That had to have taken you months to make."

"No, just a few weeks of evenings and weekends in my basement. I like working with wood."

"It shows, but I thought you liked cars and motorcycles."

"I do, but they are more of a summer hobby. I can't fit motorcycles and cars in my basement." He shot her a quick glance. "What about you? What do you do?"

"I work." She pinched her lips together, wishing she hadn't said that because she didn't want him to think she was thinking about work. She wasn't.

"What about for fun?"

"Tonight was fun." Oh, good grief. That made her sound like an idiot. A desperate idiot. Sighing, she searched her mind for an honest answer. She knew how to sew, that was a given considering her mother's company, but she wasn't very good at it and luckily her mother had never pressured her into getting better. "I like to bake, to cook." Shrugging, she went with the truth. "But mainly I work. I've worked at the airline since I was twelve."

"You have?"

"Yes, I started out cleaning my father's office and just kept moving into other jobs. Someday I will take over running the entire company." There was no one, especially not her parents, that she could tell about Sam, yet, for some reason, she felt comfortable telling Jason. "But I'm being sabotaged."

"Sabotaged?"

"Yes. By Sam Wharton. He's worked for my father

for several years and thinks that he should be the one who my father appoints to handle the day-to-day oversight of the company when my father is elected senator. He hasn't announced that he's running yet, but he is. For US Senator, not the state senate. Sam knows, and since learning about it, he's started to withhold reports that I need in order to complete my work, and other little things. Like claiming that he didn't get expense or wage reports from me on time and other things like that just to make me look bad. He's always wanted that—for me to look bad—but it's gotten worse lately."

"Have you told your father?"

"No."

"Why not?"

She twisted, just enough to be able to look at him. "Because that's what Sam wants me to do. He wants everyone to think that I run to my father with every little issue. Wants everyone to believe I only have a job there because of my last name. That I'm not capable of actually doing the work. I am, and I'm going to prove it. To everyone."

"You sound pretty determined."

"I am. I'll do anything I have to." Thinking about work was too irritating, and she didn't want that right now. Not tonight. It had been too wonderful. "Thank you for this evening. It was good to not even think about work. I really enjoyed that."

"Maybe you should do it more often." He slowed the car down to stop at a red light. "Go out and eat hamburgers and French fries."

"And drink milkshakes."

He looked at her, smiled.

Her toes curled inside her shoes at the bolt of excitement that shot through her at the connection she felt between them. One that grew the longer they looked at each other.

The sound of a horn honking had them both looking at the light that had turned green, but the connection was still there. She could feel it, and wished tonight would never have to end.

"And dance," he said.

The memory of dancing with him made her sigh with contentment. "How many other dollhouses have you built?" she asked as other memories of the night flowed through her mind.

"That was my first, but I have built a doghouse that a certain dog never uses."

She laughed. "Because he has a doggie door. That you built for him."

"I did."

They laughed, talked about Tanner and other things, until he pulled up next to his garage and climbed out to open the doors.

The headlights shone on a pickup truck, with Heim Construction painted on the door, and two motorcycles parked in front of it. "Why did you build your house here instead of on your land?" she asked once he climbed back in the car to pull it forward.

"Because I needed to make money. No one wants to live that far out of town, so I bought this entire block of land, one lot at a time, and built all six houses. Mine was the last one I built here, and if someone comes along and wants to buy it, I'll sell it."

"Where will you live then?"

He parked the car and shut it off. "Wherever. I have other houses I'm building, and an apartment complex."

"Where?"

"The apartment building is downtown, the houses in other suburbs." He opened the car door.

She collected her purse and satchel and opened her door.

They met in front of the car. He took a hold of her hand, and her heart started pounding again.

"Sounds like Tanner is at the door," he said.

She hadn't heard anything, but he was right. As soon as he opened the door on the side of the garage that led into the backyard, the dog was there to greet them, and walked ahead of them to the house.

"I don't have a milkshake maker, but I could make some coffee," he said while closing the door. "If you want."

She didn't want coffee, or a milkshake, but didn't know how to voice what she did want. Setting her purse and satchel on the table, she turned, looked at him. "Jason, I—"

"I'll go start your car. Clear off the windshield."

She looked at the hand he held out. If she gave him the keys, the night would be over. She didn't want that. Frustration and a hint of fear filled her. There was no experience that she could draw upon for this. She'd been kissed before, but had never initiated it, or wanted it to continue, because it had never been him who had been kissing her.

What if this was her only chance for that to happen? She'd regret not doing something. A need was pulsating inside her, a desire she'd never felt to this degree before, but it felt right. She took a hold of his hand and stepped closer.

He was looking at her, watching her. The heat between them was still there, making her feel as if the air was sizzling.

Taking a breath, she laid her other hand on his chest. "I don't want to leave yet."

His eyes landed on her lips.

Her heart was pounding, her body full of that magical electricity, and she couldn't wait any longer. She slid her hand to the back of his neck, stretched on her toes and pressed her lips against his.

The first touch made her knees go weak, then a surge ripped through her as their lips merged perfectly, naturally, and his arms encircled her. It was as if more than their lips were kissing. His entire body seemed to be kissing her. There was nothing even close to the way he made her insides feel. Crazy, and wild and wonderful.

He held her tighter, met her kisses over and over again, but she still wanted more. When his tongue slid across her lips, she opened her mouth, inviting him in.

A groan of pleasure rumbled in her throat. Tightening her hold on his neck, she held nothing back as their tongues met, twisted and teased each other's.

When their lips parted, they were both breathing hard, sucking in air. She tried to catch her bearings, but when their eyes met, she knew that wasn't going to happen.

The air between them was even more charged, sparking with an energy she'd never experienced.

Fervently, mutually, their lips met again, in a heated, nearly frantic way that somehow included getting rid of their coats. She'd never wanted to feel someone, to be so close to, so connected to, someone as she did him. All of her dreams about him were accumulating into this very moment, planting her in the place she'd wanted to be for years.

He let out a low, sexy-sounding groan and pulled his lips off hers, stared down at her.

A splash of fear rained upon her that he might say they had to stop before things went further. She wanted things to go further. Her heart was slamming against her breastbone with anticipation that it might. She could have had sex before but had never wanted to. Had never wanted anything like she did right now. Every part of her was alive, throbbing, begging for more, and she knew why.

Wanting him to know that she trusted him, and herself to continue, she touched the side of his face. "I still don't want to leave."

Chapter Five

Jason cupped her cheek. "Are you sure?"

She ran her hands down his upper arms, feeling the hard muscles beneath. He was leaving the choice up to her. She could leave now, knowing what it was like to kiss him, be kissed by him, but the want inside her had grown beyond kissing. The need to know what that would be like was growing by the second, making her toes curl. He was who she wanted to do that with, had always been who she'd wanted to do that with. "Very sure." She wanted a night to remember, even if it was just one night. With a boldness she didn't know she had, she pressed her hips against his. "We're adults, and both know what we want."

He let out a low growling sound as his arms tightened, holding her hard against him. "I've never wanted someone like I want you."

The thrill that shot through her was indescribable and confirmed she'd made the right choice. "Me neither," she admitted, and was instantly lost in another round of kissing.

She didn't have time to think about being nervous, not even when they made their way into his bedroom. It all felt too right, too perfect.

As he kissed a line down her neck, to the very top of the vee in her A-line dress, his hand slowly unzipped the zipper running down the back of the dress. She bit her bottom lip as every part of her body hummed, tingled. Her breasts grew heavy as her nipples hardened, and at this moment she was excited about the lingerie her mother designed. The bra and panties set beneath her dress was made of red lace, with a black silk under layer. So was the matching garter belt that held up her nylons.

She waited until the zipper had reached the very bottom, and then slowly slid her hands off his upper arms and took a step back, until she had enough space to shrug the dress off her shoulders.

He grasped the material as it reached her elbows, then guided it downward, until it slipped over her hands, and fell to the floor.

Randi held her breath as his gaze scanned her from head to toe, leaving a trail of heat that made her insides sizzle.

He trailed a hand down her arm, to her elbow. "You are so beautiful."

The heat swirling in her most private places increased; so did her confidence. He wanted her. She could see that in his eyes. This was her dream come true. "I'm glad you think so."

He threaded his fingers into her hair, combed it back, away from her face. "So beautiful."

Reaching up, she unbuttoned his shirt, all the way to the bottom, then pushed it off his shoulders. When that fell, she grasped the hem of his T-shirt and pulled it over his head. Her breath caught at her first sight of his chest, rippled with muscles and splattered with dark hair. "And you are extraordinarily handsome."

He let out a sexy-sounding laugh and grasped her waist, picked her up and pulled her tight against his body.

She looped her arms around his neck, and her legs around his hips, gasping at the sensations of her bare skin feeling the heat of his body. He buried his face between her breasts, and she was too focused on the pleasure to be self-conscious over the way a pleasure-filled moan rumbled in the back of her throat when he kissed her nipples through the material of her bra.

He laid her on the bed, and as he continued to kiss and touch her most sensitive areas, she knew all of her dreams about him didn't compare to the reality. The real Jason was far more consuming, far more enlightening, than her dream Jason.

As he slowly, teasingly removed her nylons, then garter belt, underwear and bra, Jason continuously watched her, making sure she was in agreement and enjoying everything he was doing.

She was. There was no doubt about that. She'd never known anything so exhilarating. It was like being on a carnival ride. Out of control, but loving every moment, and wanting more.

"Jason." It was hard to talk with so many sensations rippling through her body, making her muscles contract and her toes curl.

"Hmmm?" he asked, once again kissing her breasts.

She had to groan at the pleasure erupting from the feel of his lips on her breasts and his hand that was between her legs. "You still have your jeans on," she said with yet another sound that was nearly a growl.

"I know."

Nearly desperate, she said, "Take. Them. Off."

"Is that what you want?" he asked.

"Yes. Now."

With a laugh, he gave her a final, long kiss and then crawled off the bed. "I'll be right back. Don't go away."

"I won't." She attempted to use his absence as a reprieve, but was missing him too much for that. It seemed like forever before he returned, climbed on the bed and covered her with his warm, amazing body. She luxuriated in the weight of him, the feel of his skin touching hers, and ran her hands over every part of him that she could reach. Felt the hard muscles beneath his heated flesh as they kissed again, and again.

He lifted his head, stared her right in the eye. "You're sure about this?"

She had never been more sure of anything in her life. "Yes."

He reached between their bodies and guided his way inside her. The pressure, the way her body stretched to accommodate him, was delightful, amazing, until a sharp snap caused her breath to catch.

He went completely still. "Randi?"

The pain was gone, or maybe it had never been there. Maybe it had just been more pleasure than she'd ever known. She wasn't sure, but knew the schoolgirl crush she'd had on him had entered an entirely new dimension.

Grasping the sides of his face, she kissed him, using her tongue, and arched her body into his. She felt the moan that rumbled in his throat as much as she heard it, and following her inner instincts, began to move her hips. He moved with her, kissed her intensely. Who knew what tomorrow might bring? But tonight, here, now, in his bed, she was in a paradise she'd never dreamed about.

When she found something she liked, something she wanted, she never held anything back, and didn't this time, either. She gave all she had, fully joined him in riding the glorious storm they were creating. It was all so new, so wild and pleasurable, she embraced every nuance of feeling him inside her.

When an inner crescendo built to a point where she knew something else had to happen, but didn't know what, she looked at Jason in question.

His mouth covered hers and a moment later, an explosion let loose inside her, washing her with a great gush of pleasure, followed by miniature waves that encompassed her entire being. He continued to kiss her until every last wave faded, leaving her body feeling boneless as it sank deep into the mattress.

She'd known making love with Jason would be magnificent, but when he lifted his head, the glorious feeling of happiness inside her doubled again because of the smile on his face.

It had taken every ounce of control he'd had to bring Randi to completion before he let himself be consumed by the way her hot, slick body was clenching his, causing more intense pleasure than he'd ever known. The smile on her face was the straw that broke his last ounce of reserve. With a final thrust, he closed his eyes as the first wave of bliss washed over him, and then fully surrendered to the best release of his life. The best sex of his life.

He'd thought about kissing her, touching her, making love to her, for so many years, it had been as if he'd already known her body. Knew exactly where to touch, when to kiss and how to bring her to the utmost pleasure. Doing so had been an awakening. He'd put his entire soul into being with her, and it had paid off in ways he'd never imagined.

He was completely drained by the time the final wave dissipated. Bracing himself on his arms, to keep his full weight from crushing her, he opened his eyes. She was still looking at him, still smiling. His lungs were seeking air, and he sucked in a deep breath, held it. He'd never believed this moment, of him and her, making love, would ever come.

Her smile faded, and a slight quiver raced over his shoulders, hoping she wasn't on her way to regretting what had just happened. He could handle anything but that.

She touched his face and then giggled slightly and her eyes shimmered as if she'd just won some sort of contest.

The real world. The one he'd lived in, returned with the strength of a gut punch. Not a contest. Land. That's what she wanted. Not him. His land.

He rolled off her, lay on his back and covered his face with one arm as it all entered his mind. A mind that had been filled with fog since the moment he'd seen her poking her head through his doggie door this afternoon. No, before then. Ever since she'd shown up on his front porch, she'd been the only thing on his mind.

How stupid could he possibly be? He climbed off the bed, headed to the bathroom across the hallway. There he took care of the condom, thanking his lucky stars that he'd had one in the house. He never brought women home. Never. He slapped the sink with one hand and mumbled a curse.

Taking a virgin wasn't his thing, either.

Damn it! The way she'd kissed, rubbed against him, offered herself, he figured she was experienced. That this was...was what? A casual encounter?

No, it was her way of getting to him, thinking he'd give in to her, sell her his land. He didn't have anything else she'd ever want. Didn't have anything else to offer her.

His stomach sank even farther.

Was her plan to use the fact he'd taken her virginity to blackmail him into selling her his land?

The rich were like that. They'd do anything to get richer.

He grabbed a washcloth out of the cabinet, wet it with warm water and carried it back into the bedroom, all the while keeping his temper in check.

She was sitting on the edge of the bed, and without making eye contact, he handed her the washcloth. "The bathroom is across the hall."

"Oh, all right, thank you." She took the washcloth.

Jason kept his gaze averted, but knew the moment she left the room. He got dressed, quickly, and went into the kitchen, where her coat, purse and bag holding her boots were piled on the table. Knowing her car keys were in her coat pocket, he found them, slipped on a pair of shoes from the closet near the front door and went outside to start her car.

The cold air helped tremendously in cooling down his body, but his temper was still smoldering. He'd never learn when it came to her.

She was in the kitchen, fully dressed, when he returned to the house. "I started your car."

"Thank you." She ran a hand over the back of a chair, looked around the room and then back at him. "I'm not sure what to say. Did I upset you?"

"No." He walked to the counter, leaned back against it.

"Then, um…" She shrugged.

Man, he hated how cute she was. How downright beautiful. It was going to take more than six years to forget how perfect her body was, and longer yet to forget making love to her. "There's nothing to say." His anger got the best of him and he added, "My answer is still no."

She frowned. "No to what?"

"Selling you my land."

"Jason, this had nothing to do—"

"Right," he interrupted. "You just wanted to return a fifty-cent pair of socks." The flash of hope inside him shattered as her face fell. "You will do anything for Air America, even sleep with a reform school rebel." As soon as the words were out, he hated himself for saying them. It made it sound like all of it was her fault, and it wasn't.

She spun around and grabbed her coat off the table.

He watched, remained silent. On the outside. On the inside he was berating himself for being so stupid. What the hell was it about her that made him want things he knew he'd never have? Few men would ever be good enough for Randi Osterlund, and he sure as hell wasn't one of those few men.

Coat on, she picked up her purse and bag, then crossed the room, stopped directly in front of him. Eyeball to eyeball, she stood there for a moment, breathing hard and fast. Then she hauled off and slapped his face.

It stung, but he didn't so much as flinch. Let her be mad at him. He sure as hell was pissed. Pissed at himself for forgetting what he'd known for years. He could earn money, succeed in some things, but his past had set his path and that would never change.

He counted to ten after hearing the front door slam shut, then walked into the living room and peered out the window. As soon as she climbed into her car, she put it in gear and backed out of the driveway.

It was cold out, and her car hadn't had time to warm up. She probably couldn't even see out of her windshield. It was snowing again, too. Damn it!

He turned, jogged across the house, grabbed his coat from the laundry room and ran across the backyard, to the garage.

Within a few blocks, he recognized the taillights of her Bel Air, and kept back far enough that she wouldn't realize she was being followed. He followed her all the way to her big, brick home in one of the richest neighborhoods in all of Chicago.

Christmas lights still surrounded the windows of her house and a big evergreen wreath hung on the front door. The shack he grew up in had never been decorated for Christmas. After his mother left, there had been no Christmas presents, no Thanksgiving dinners, Easter eggs or birthday celebrations.

No love had filled his house, either, which was the ultimate stark reality. He'd never be able to love a woman like her the way they deserved to be loved. He didn't know how, and that would never change.

She parked her car in the driveway and ran into the house through a side door.

He should leave. Knowing that she'd made it home safely should be enough, but he couldn't stop himself from continuing to stare at the house, telling himself he'd never see her again and should be happy about that.

A smart man would be.

He definitely wasn't smart. If that was the case, he would never have slept with her.

In her bedroom Randi threw her coat in one direction, her purse in another. She'd given herself a night to remember all right. A nightmare. She had told him she'd do anything, but hadn't meant sleeping with him. His land had been the last thing on her mind, but evidently, the only thing on his.

Why had she thought he was different? Thought he'd see her for herself. No one else did, so why should he?

And why did it hurt so bad that he didn't? She was used to it. Used to being invisible other than her last name.

Knowing the answer, she threw herself on the bed. It hurt because she'd let herself believe in a dream that would never come true. Other than her family, people either hated her, or wanted something from her, all because of her last name.

Jason had more reason than anyone to hate that last name. Hate her.

She curled into a ball, told herself she'd hate him in return. Would hate him for the rest of her life.

She could live with that. Live with being nothing more than an Osterlund.

After a very sleepless night, she set out to prove that when, still filled with anger, she walked in and still didn't have the P&L report.

Her footsteps echoed off the walls as she made her way into Sam Wharton's office. He was sitting behind his desk, his black hair full of beeswax pomade and combed over his ever-growing bald spot. The glower he cast at how she threw open the door had her anger hitting the boiling point. "Where's the P&L report?"

He shrugged.

She stomped over to his desk. "My father will be home tomorrow and expects every department report to be on his desk for review."

"Every department report was couriered over to your father's house last evening. Except for yours. You weren't in your office when I collected them. Your secretary said you'd left early."

"Because I didn't have a P&L report so I couldn't complete mine."

"Everyone else did."

She glared at him.

His green eyes narrowed. "Maybe it's time you realize being your father's daughter doesn't get you everything you want."

After everything that had happened last night, his remark cut to the core. She slapped her hands on his desk and leaned toward him. "Perhaps it's time you learn exactly what it means to go against my father's daughter." With that, she spun around and marched out of his office, purposefully leaving the door of his office open purely out of spite.

She'd get that P&L report, and she'd find another way for Air America to have their own washing bay. One that had nothing, absolutely nothing, to do with Jason's land.

Chapter Six

Three weeks later Randi had more than one new plan in place, and was making good progress on both of them. Setting up a washing bay in California had never crossed her mind before, but nearly all of their planes landed in LA several times each year, and logistically, she could make it work.

The plan of using her status for her instead of against her was also working. She'd requested copies of every report Sam sent down to typing to be delivered to her upon completion. Sam had balked, and had gone to her father, but much to her delight, her father had said he appreciated the initiative she'd always taken to know what was going on in all aspects of the company.

The only plan not working was getting Jason out of her mind. Despite how the night had ended, she couldn't forget the wonderful aspects of their time together. Out of the blue, specific moments would flood her mind and body, and leave her aching.

There was also another issue. She was two weeks late on her monthly.

It had to be something other than *that*.

Had to be.

She couldn't be pregnant.

Absolutely could not.

Jason had used a condom. She'd seen it.

Glancing in the mirror above her bathroom sink, she patted her cheeks, trying to put some color in them. It didn't work. She looked awful.

Sick.

That had to be it. She was sick.

She didn't have time to be sick. Not right now. She was flying out to California next week to look at land for the washing bay—a project that no one but she knew about.

By that afternoon, when the sandwich she'd attempted to eat for lunch threatened to come right back up, she called Dr. Spencer's office. Olivia Spencer had been her doctor since childhood and would be able to give her something to make her feel better.

Being told to come right over to the clinic, Randi left her office, telling Carol that she had an errand to run and would be back within the hour.

However, an hour later she was still in the doctor's office, wearing an ugly green cover-up as she sat on the examination table. Her heart was in her throat and she had her hands clasped together in an attempt to hide how badly they were shaking. "How can that be? We used a condom."

"They aren't one hundred percent effective," Dr. Spencer said. "One tiny pinhole is all it takes."

There were so many thoughts flowing through Randi's mind that it was hard to focus on any particular one. Other than Jason, and how he was sure to believe she'd done this on purpose, too. "You're sure?"

Dr. Spencer closed the folder in her hand. "As I said, we'll know for sure when the test results come back."

"When will that be?"

"A few days. I can call you with the results."

"No!" Randi bit her lips together. She couldn't have the doctor calling either her house or office. "I'll come back in."

"All right, I'll set up an appointment. You can get dressed and I'll be back in with a prescription."

"For what?"

"Vitamins. I want you to take them no matter what the results of the test are. You've lost weight since your last visit. If we aren't careful, you'll soon be nothing but skin and bones."

Randi waited until the doctor left the room before she allowed a sob to escape. Jason would have even more reason to hate her now.

She climbed off the table and got dressed, noting how loose the waistband of her red-and-black skirt was, even with her blouse tucked in. If not for the added decorative belt, that she could tie tight, the skirt would have slipped right off her hips.

After stepping into her shoes, she put on her red cardigan, and then with her coat and purse in her lap, she sat in the chair, waited for Dr. Spencer to return. As much as she wanted to believe that she wanted the test to come back negative, she couldn't deny that the idea of a baby, of Jason's baby, made her heart beat faster. She pressed a hand to her stomach. If things were different, she'd be the happiest woman on earth.

Dr. Spencer returned, but as she held out the slip of paper, another thought hit Randi. "I can't have that filled. Not at my aunt's drugstore, or anywhere else. Every drugstore in Illinois could recognize my name, put two and two together."

"I suspect that is correct." Dr. Spencer wadded up the prescription. "I'll get some vitamins for you before your next visit." Dr. Spencer then handed her a small note card. "Here's when you are to return, but until then, I want you to get some rest. I've been taking care of you for years, and I'm concerned that you aren't taking care of yourself the way you should be."

Randi took the card and tucked it into her purse. "I will. Thank you."

It felt as if the air was locked in her lungs. The tightness wouldn't ease, no matter how deeply she attempted to breathe, even after exiting the clinic, stepping outside in the cold air. Most likely because of her thoughts. If the test came back positive, she couldn't tell Jason about the baby. That was all there was to it. Not ever. It wasn't as if they ran into each other. In the past six years the only time she had seen him was when she'd sought him out, and she would never, ever do that again.

The idea of that made her sick because she wasn't a deceitful person, but what else could she do? He hated her.

She walked the half a block to the lot where she'd parked her car, and was about to climb in when she heard her name.

She froze, could barely swallow, at the sight of the pickup truck with Heim Construction painted on the door. It was black, not red like the one in his garage, and the little arm waving out the window certainly wasn't Jason's, but she couldn't see who was driving the pickup, and that frightened her.

"Randi!" Rachelle repeated as the pickup stopped near the back of her car. "It's me, Rachelle."

"I see that, how are you?" she asked, stepping close enough to see that it wasn't Jason driving, but Stu, Rachelle's father.

"I'm fine! We had to bring some lumber to Jason after Dad picked me up from school. Is that why you're here?

To see him?" Pointing across the parking lot, Rachelle continued. "He's in that building over there. Working. He said Dad doesn't need to work any more today and we are going to Mama's to have a milkshake!"

Randi's glance across the parking lot revealed another pickup. A red one with Heim Construction painted on the side. "That sounds wonderful," she replied, trying her hardest to sound cheerful. "What flavor?"

"Strawberry!" Rachelle giggled. "You should have Jason bring you there for a milkshake, too. He would if you asked him to. I know he would."

Randi knew Jason would never take her anywhere, ever again, which made her eyes sting all over again. "Well, you enjoy your milkshake. It was good seeing you again." She nodded at Stu and then turned, hurried to the driver's door of her car and climbed in before the tears broke loose.

There wasn't time to let them flow, not with Jason's truck on the other side of the parking lot. He was so caring, so loving, toward Rachelle, Randi could only imagine what a wonderful father he'd be to his own child.

Blinking against the blurriness of tears, she started her car and left the parking lot, wondering what she was going to do. How she was going to live through having his baby and never telling him.

Jason flinched at the pain of putting on his coat. Between the swelling and the bandage, his hand was twice its normal size. He was frustrated with himself for not having the injury looked at before now, and at how he'd managed to nearly slice his hand in two in the first place. It had been nearly a week ago. He should never have looked out the apartment house window while using a skill saw.

If he hadn't looked out and if he hadn't seen Randi, he wouldn't have cut himself, and then wouldn't be here now, leaving the doctor's exam room after having the cut cleaned, bandaged and a penicillin shot jabbed into his backside, while a tetanus one had been shot in his arm. He'd thought his hand would get better on its own, but infection had set in, and the doctor had given him a good talking-to about that, about taking better care of himself.

A large part of him wanted to blame Randi. If she hadn't rounded the corner at the exact same moment that he'd looked out the window, he wouldn't have cut himself.

As usual, the mere thought of her set his imagination wild, to the point he heard her voice. Which was impossible.

Growing madder at himself, he twisted the doorknob to leave the room, only to pause from pulling the door all the way open.

It *was* her voice.

"Yes, thank you," she told the receptionist while entering the room directly across the hall from him.

Concern filled him at the idea of her being hurt or sick. He'd thought of little else but her the past four weeks, but that was nothing new. He'd been thinking of her for years. It was just that now he had more memories. Vivid ones.

The receptionist dropped a folder in the metal rack beside the door that Randi had entered and then walked down the hall, toward the waiting room. He checked the hallway for spying eyes, then left the room and pulled out the folder, opened it.

His entire body froze as if his heart had stopped, drained all the blood from his system. Shaking, he returned the folder to the rack, headed down the hall and didn't stop until he was outside, in the icy February air.

There he gulped for air as the words he'd read continued to race through his mind.

Pregnancy Test: positive

She was pregnant.

Randi was pregnant.

It couldn't be his. He'd used a condom.

Had it ripped? Been too old?

"What did they say?"

Jason shook his head, blinked and stared at Stu.

"Your hand," Stu said. "What did they say?"

Jason rubbed his forehead, trying to collect his thoughts.

"Have you been waiting long?" Stu asked. "I went next door, into the café and had a cup of coffee while waiting. Just saw you out the window."

Remembering that he hadn't been able to drive and shift with only one hand, Jason recalled that Stu had given him a ride to the doctor's office, and that Stu would soon need to pick Rachelle up from school. The bus couldn't accommodate her wheelchair, which meant he couldn't stand here and wait for Randi to exit the building, ask her about being pregnant.

He couldn't do that, anyway. Not until he got his head around it all.

"Are you all right?" Stu asked.

"Yeah, I'm fine." He started walking toward the lot where the pickup that Stu drove was parked.

"What did they say about your hand?"

"It's infected. They gave me a shot of penicillin."

"That'll take care of it, but your ass is going to be sore for a few days."

He had deeper worries than his ass or his hand. Pregnant. That had to be why she'd been here last week, at the doctor's office, the day he'd seen her out the window.

"Do you need to stop anywhere else?" Stu asked as they arrived at the truck.

Jason's eyes were on the Bel Air parked in the lot. "No, just take me home." That was where he'd be when she showed up. To tell him that she was pregnant.

He had to have his response ready.

Chapter Seven

Jason waited a week for Randi to stop by his house. When that never happened, he tried to contact her. Called her home and her office. The answers were always the same. She wasn't available, but if he cared to leave a message, she would get back to him.

He hadn't *cared* to leave a message. He wanted to know what kind of game she was playing now. How the hell could she not be available for an entire week? He'd called every day, at different times. She was avoiding him, that was what she was doing.

It was time that stopped.

He glanced into the rearview mirror, smoothed back his hair on both sides. The slice across the top of his hand was still red, the skin puffed and tender, but was healing. He had full use of his fingers again.

Her car wasn't in the driveway of the big house, but that didn't mean it wasn't in the garage. He hadn't seen her car all week. Not here or at the Air America offices and was tired of looking for it. Tired of waiting for her to contact him.

He climbed out of Lottie's car, having borrowed it because he knew if Randi saw his, she'd avoid him. That had to stop. She'd been a virgin. It had to be his baby.

He walked to the door, anxious to know what was going on with Randi, and nervous to see her father again. He'd met Randal Osterlund twice. Once when the man had come to the reform school, told him that he'd discovered the truth and that he'd told the judge to withdraw the charges, and a few years later, at his father's funeral, where Randal had offered his condolences.

His father had been a stubborn man. Hateful at times. Though the money they would have obtained by selling Osterlund a portion of their land would have made a significant difference in their lives, his father had refused to sell. His father had found an odd pleasure in knowing he'd owned something a rich man wanted.

The massive door opened, and an old, gray-haired man, dressed in a black suit, gave a slight nod. "Good evening, sir, may I help you?"

Jason cleared his throat. "I'm looking for Randi—Miss Osterlund."

"I'm sorry, sir," the man said loudly, "she is not available this evening."

Jason's back teeth clamped together. That was the same voice as the one on the phone, the same answer he'd received for a week.

"Who is it, Peter?" a female voice sounded somewhere in the background of the house.

"A young man to see the young miss," the man answered.

A trim woman, wearing a fashionable pale green dress, appeared behind the old man, and though he'd never met her, Jason knew it had to be Randi's mother. She may have gotten her pale blue eyes from her father, but the rest of her beauty was inherited from her mother. "Good evening," he said. "I need to speak to Randi."

"I'm sorry," her mother said. "She's not home right now, but should be shortly. You'd be welcome to wait."

He nodded. "I'd appreciate that."

She nodded toward the old man. "Thank you, Peter."

The man bowed and walked away.

"Do come in, Jason, isn't it?"

He paused in the doorway. "Yes, Jason Heim."

"I'm Jolie, Randi's mother. She's been in California all week, but her plane should have landed about fifteen minutes ago." She waved a hand and repeated, "Do come in."

He stepped into the foyer, where a large stairway on the left swept upward to the second floor. The home held an old-world style that was elegant, without being ostentatious. Many of the older homes had been remodeled, and, appreciative of old craftsmanship, he was impressed to see how well they'd preserved the home rather than making it look more modern.

"This way," she said. "Randal is in the front room. I was on my way to join him when I heard Peter answering the door." Her smile grew. "He's getting hard of hearing, but answering the door has been his job for over forty years."

Jason nodded as he walked beside her to a framed doorway. A butler. One they'd had for over forty years. Jason's stomach sank. He was so out of his league. Yet, he was here, and would stay until he talked to Randi.

"Randal," Jolie said as they entered the room. "You remember Jason Heim."

Tall, with dark hair sporting gray near his temples, Randal Osterlund rose from the chair. "I most certainly do." He held out a hand as he crossed the room. "How have you been, Jason?"

Jason shook his hand. "Fine, thank you. And you?"

"Can't complain." Randal laid a hand on his wife's back. "Come sit down. To what do we owe this pleasure?"

Jason drew in a deep breath. "I'm here to speak to your daughter."

Randal aided his wife in sitting on the sofa, and waved for Jason to sit in an armed chair before he sat down beside his wife. "Randi?"

Jolie laughed slightly. "She is the only daughter we have, dear."

Randal chuckled. "I know that. I'm just surprised."

Jason felt his spine stiffen.

"Surprised only because she doesn't receive many callers," Jolie said.

Jason doubted that was the reason her father was surprised. "Randi had been interested in purchasing, or leasing, some land from me."

Randal frowned. "She had?" He shook his head. "I apologize. I've made it clear that your land isn't for sale and no one was to pursue you about it." He leaned forward, rested an elbow on his knee. "I know there were rumors upon your father's death that our land dispute had something to do with his heart attack. I assure you, that wasn't the case. I hadn't spoken to your father in months."

"I know that, and I know they were rumors brought on by my father," Jason said. He'd tried to quell the rumors back then, but his father had already spread that there was a feud between their families so wide that the lie had become the truth to many. Not so unlike the night he'd gotten arrested for trespassing. The truth was, his father had hated everyone who'd had more than he'd had and that was just about everyone. Very few people were poorer than they'd been.

"Why would Randi be interested in buying land?" Jolie asked.

Randal shook his head. "I don't know."

Jason considered not mentioning more, but changed his mind. "I believe it's due to a man named Sam Wharton."

"Sam?" Randal asked.

"Yes, it appears he's, well, Randi called it sabotaging her."

Both husband and wife sat up straighter, stared at him.

"She claimed Sam refused to give her reports she needed in order to complete her work, and I believe she was interested in buying my land so there would be room to build a place to wash your airplanes, proving she was fully capable of taking over for you when you win the senate seat."

Randal folded his arms across his chest. "It appears that you and Randi have discussed far more than a land deal."

Over the past few weeks he'd gone over every single conversation, every word they'd said to each other. Mainly during times when regret had been eating him alive. "Yes, sir, we have. She's determined to do whatever it takes to gain that position."

"Randal, if Sam is—"

"Don't worry, dear," Randal interrupted his wife. "I will be talking to Sam, and this explains why Randi asked for copies of every report the typing pool creates." He nodded. "You are right, Jason, my daughter is very determined, has always been very determined. She takes after her mother in that sense."

"I believe that is a mutual trait she inherited," Jolie said. "I'm assuming you refused to sell her your property?"

"Yes, I did," Jason replied. "I have plans for it."

Randal was rubbing his chin. "Now we know why she went to California."

Jason frowned. "Why?"

"To build a washing bay facility there," Randal replied. "It's something I've considered, but never pursued for various reasons."

Jolie laid a hand on Randal's arm. "You don't think she's considering moving to California, do you? Is that why she's been so quiet, so sad, lately?"

"I don't know," Randal said. "But she certainly hasn't been herself."

The idea of her moving to California struck Jason deeply. Is that what she was thinking? Moving there, with his child, without ever telling him? For all he knew, she could go out there, marry Gus Albright and pretend the child was Gus's. That wasn't going to happen. He wasn't going to let someone else raise his child, nor would he deny a child the right to know both parents. What he did next was the last thing he'd ever thought he'd do, but it was the only one thing he could do. "Sir—" he moved his gaze to glance at Jolie for a second "—ma'am, I'd like to ask permission to marry your daughter."

Jolie pressed a hand to her chest, while Randal lifted his brows and glanced at his wife before saying, "We could grant our permission, but the answer would need to come from Randi. That's her decision to make."

Jason had a good idea of what her answer and decision would be. He was also fully aware that he would not be living his life without knowing his child. He'd grown up with one parent, having no idea where the other one was, and would not let that happen to his flesh and blood. "I do apologize for being so blunt, and although precautions were taken, I believe that Randi is pregnant with my child."

"Mother, Father." Randi bit her lips together, and forced herself to keep her chin up. She was about to tell her parents something that would cause them to be disappointed in her. Severely disappointed. She wasn't married. Didn't even have any prospects in that direction. Yet, here she was, pregnant. By a man she'd been told to steer clear of for years.

The steam seeped out of her and she slumped her head against the steering wheel. "Oh, Lord, how am I going to do this?"

She'd already put it off for nearly two weeks and couldn't for much longer. Maybe she should have stayed in California. The one plot of land she'd looked at would work for a washing bay, and she could live out there, oversee the project. Which would work into her plan of never telling Jason that she was pregnant.

A plan that would never see fruition because she couldn't see it through. She had to tell him, just like she had to tell her parents. Each day brought the time closer of when her father would announce his bid to run for senate. Having an unmarried, pregnant daughter was sure to cause a scandal. Even if she was in California.

She lifted her head, leaned back against the seat of her car and stared at the airport. Her parents knew when her return flight had been scheduled to land.

She hated the idea of disappointing them. Hated the idea of Jason believing she'd gotten pregnant on purpose. And she hated the idea of having to ask him, trust him, to keep the pregnancy a secret until after her father announced his senate bid.

Leaning forward, she started her car and stared at the sky "Give me strength. Please. Lots and lots of strength."

Far sooner than she was prepared to face him, she arrived at Jason's house. There were no lights on, but that didn't mean he wasn't home. She wasn't going to be caught unaware this time. She backed out of the driveway and drove around to the alley. There, she climbed out and opened one of the garage doors.

The pickup and two motorcycles were there, but his car was gone.

She could wait, but her parents would start to worry if she didn't arrive home soon. Her plane had landed well over an hour ago.

First thing in the morning she'd drive back over here. It would be Saturday. Surely, he'd be home. She'd tell him then. And tell her parents after that.

The idea of waiting a few more hours offered a small amount of relief. Which only caused the guilt inside her to increase.

She closed the garage door, got back in her car and drove home.

There was an unfamiliar car in the driveway, but that wasn't all that unusual. Her parents often had company. She climbed out, got her suitcase out of the backseat and entered through the side door.

Peter met her in the hallway, took her coat. "It's good to have you home, Miss."

She kissed his cheek. He'd been their butler since long before she'd been born. "It's good to be home."

He reached for her suitcase. "I'll carry that up for you. Your parents are in the front room."

She wrapped her hand around the handle of the suitcase that she'd set down while removing her coat. "Thank you, Peter, but I'll take it up myself. I saw a car in the driveway. I know Mom and Dad have company."

"The company is here to see you."

"Me?"

"Yes, Miss. They are in the front room."

Having no idea who it might be, she checked her hair, made sure the scarf holding it in a ponytail was still tight and then smoothed a hand over the front of her printed green-and-white pencil skirt, checking for wrinkles from sitting so long on the plane. There were a few, but there wasn't anything she could do about it, and after making sure her blouse was neatly tucked into the waistband, she walked down the hall, to the front of the house.

Laughter echoed across the foyer. She instantly recognized her mother's and father's, but it was the third one that made her footsteps falter. It sounded like Jason. She closed her eyes, told herself that wasn't possible, that her mind was simply playing tricks on her, and continued onward, into the room, where her footsteps did more than falter.

They stopped dead in their tracks.

The entire world stopped.

The next thing she knew, she was lying on the sofa, afraid to open her eyes. Could things get any worse?

No!

She sat up, swung her feet over the edge of the sofa.

"Whoa." He grasped her shoulders. "Slow down, or you'll faint again."

Pressing a hand to her temple, at the dizziness in her head, she asked, "What are you doing here?"

"Right now I'm making sure you're okay."

"I'm fine." She lifted her head, looked around, testing to make sure the dizziness had truly faded. The dizziness was gone, and the room was empty. "Where are my mom and dad?"

"They left us alone, so we can talk."

She refused to look at him. "I don't want your land."

"Found some in California, did you?"

There was a hefty dose of sarcasm in his voice. She bit her lips together to keep from responding. No one, not even her father, knew that was why she'd gone to California.

"Your father said he'd told you to not attempt to buy or lease my property."

"Then it's a good thing you didn't agree with me, isn't it?"

"He'll also be speaking to Sam, about how he's been sabotaging you."

She twisted, stared at him. All of him. His dress pants, his neatly pressed white shirt, his tie and suit coat. It seemed odd to see him dressed in a suit. He looked as handsome as ever, but she liked the way he looked— She stopped the thought right there. What he was wearing, or not wearing, was of no importance. "You told him?"

He gave a nonchalant shrug that raised her ire even more.

"How dare you! I told you that in full confidence. Trusted—" She leaped to her feet.

He grabbed her arm. "You're not going anywhere."

"Yes, I am. I'm going to talk to my father."

He shook his head.

"They are probably concerned that I—"

"Fainted? Your mother said that's not uncommon in your condition."

Her blood turned to ice right then, making her shiver as it ran through her veins.

He lifted a brow.

She shook her head.

He nodded.

There was no way he could know. No one knew, other than Dr. Spencer, and she didn't know Jason was the father. No one knew that.

"When were you planning on telling me?" he asked. "Or, let me guess. Never."

Her blood was heating up fast, with anger. "I was going to tell you tomorrow. I stopped by your house tonight, but you weren't there."

He laughed. "Likely story."

"I don't care if you believe me or not."

"Good, because I don't believe you."

Her mind snagged on something else he'd said. About her mother. "No. No! You didn't tell my parents—"

"That you're pregnant with my child?" He nodded. "Yes, I did."

"Why? Why would you do that?"

"Because it was apparent that you weren't going to tell anyone." He eyed her, with anger blazing on his face. "You were going to move to California, probably marry Gus Albright and pretend the baby was his."

No one could make her as mad as he could. It was utterly inconceivable for him to know everything! Everything! Other than that stupid mention of Gus. "Gus? Get real!"

"I am. You've lied about everything else, why not that?"

"I haven't lied about anything, you've just got such a big chip on your shoulder, you don't want to know the truth!"

"I'll tell you the truth. Your parents gave me permission to ask you to marry me, but I'm not asking, I'm telling you, we are getting married, because I'll be damned if you are going to keep me from seeing my child."

"I wouldn't marry you if you were the last man on earth!"

"Yes, you will."

"No, I won't." She was so mad she was shaking. "I'll never forgive you for this. Never!"

"I don't care. This isn't about you or me. It's about

the child you're carrying." Glaring at her, he held up one hand, two fingers. "You have two days, until Monday morning, to decide when and where, or I'll decide."

Chapter Eight

Randi was lying on her bed, with one arm over her eyes, wondering how she'd managed to completely screw up her life beyond repair when the knock sounded on her door. She knew it was coming from the moment Jason had stormed out of the house and she'd run up the stairs. There was no sense putting off the inevitable. "Come in."

She sat up, watched her mother walk in and close the door. "Where's Dad?"

Her mother crossed the room. "Downstairs. Pacing the floor. Thinking he should be the one up here talking to you."

Randi glanced away as tears formed. "I don't think I can face him. I never thought I'd disappoint him like this. Or you."

Her mother climbed on the bed, cupped her cheeks with both hands. "You haven't disappointed him or me, not now, not ever."

"I'm pregnant, Mom. Not married. That could hurt Dad's chances at the senate, and—"

"Stop right there. This is about you."

"I don't want it to be about me."

"Well, it is, and about a baby that will arrive before Christmas."

Laying a hand against her stomach, Randi said, "November."

Her mother laid her hand over the top of hers. "And it's about Jason."

The flood hit so fast, there was no stopping it. Randi laid her head on her mother's shoulder and cried until there were no tears left. When she lifted her head, her mother had a tissue in hand. Randi used it and balled it in her hand, while sucking in air. "I don't even know how it happened."

"Yes, you do. We've talked about how babies are created many times." Her mother wiped the residue of tears off Randi's cheek with one hand. "And I know you. I know you've never had sex with anyone else."

Her mother had been open and honest about sex, said when it was with the right person, it was wonderful. It had been wonderful. Jason had made her body come alive and the way he'd looked at her had made her feel so special. "I never wanted to."

"But you did with Jason."

"Yes, so badly."

Hugging her close to her side, her mother said, "I remember the crush you had on him in high school."

"I never told you I had a crush on him."

"You didn't have to tell me. There were all sorts of signs, even before the night that your brother got Jason in all that trouble. You insisted Jason wouldn't have been trying to break into the office building, and didn't give up until you made Joey admit that it had been him and his friends who had been trying to break in to steal the pop."

That had happened right after she'd laughed when Jason had asked her out. "Joey had done that before. Numerous times." She pressed the heavy air out of her lungs. "By the time Joey admitted it, it was too late. Jason had already been sent to reform school." She'd thought she was done, but another sob hit. "He hates me, Mom. Hates me and has a right to."

"How do you feel about him?"

She didn't want to admit it, couldn't admit it. How could she love someone who hated her? Broke her heart. Betrayed her.

Her mother kissed her temple. "Your father and I will never force you to marry someone you don't want to marry."

"I'm pregnant, Mom." That was the reality of it all.

"There are far worse things in this world than being pregnant outside of marriage."

At this moment in time, she couldn't think of anything worse.

Her mother hugged her tight, kissed her temple. "Jason was out of his chair and across the room before your father and I even realized you were fainting. The look on his face, when he caught you, was not that of a man who hates you."

Jason couldn't sit still. Hadn't been able to since he'd left the Osterlund house on Friday night. He'd told her she had until tomorrow morning. What if she left town again? She could get on a plane, go anywhere in the world. He'd never find her.

He reached the kitchen counter, spun around and paced toward the laundry room again. Maybe that would be best. He didn't know anything about being a parent. Other than he didn't want his child to have a repeat of his childhood.

Reaching the laundry room, he walked back toward the counter, and upon arriving, picked up the receiver of the telephone hanging on the wall, just to make sure there was a dial tone, that the phone was working.

She might call.

She might be in Haiti by now, too.

He hung up the phone and leaned his head against the wall. He shouldn't have betrayed her the way he had. Shouldn't have told her she had to marry him. Asking would have been... No, she would have said no if he'd asked.

Tanner barked and Jason ran into the living room, looked out the window. His heart slammed against his rib cage at the Bel Air that was in the driveway. She was alone, wearing her red coat, and left the car running as she climbed out. He could see the exhaust coming out of the tailpipe.

Not sure what that signified, he walked to the door, opened it before she knocked.

She stopped, stared at him until Tanner shot past him.

Giving the dog a pet with one hand, she held out her other hand, handing him a piece of paper.

He took it but didn't look at it.

"That's where and when. I'd like a list of names and addresses for the invitations by Tuesday. There are a few other things. It's all listed there."

His throat was dry. His heart pounding. "Do you want to come in?"

"No." She gave Tanner another pet, then turned, walked to her car.

"Randi." He stepped onto the porch but wasn't sure what he could say in order to make any of this better.

She didn't look his way, just climbed into the car, backed out of the driveway.

"Tanner!" He held the door, waited for the dog to walk into the house with his head down and tail between his legs. Jason followed, feeling as downtrodden as Tanner looked.

That shouldn't be how a man feels when he's about to get married. He glanced at the slip of paper in his hand, read it, then walked into the kitchen to make a few phone calls.

His first call was to Stu, and if the other man was surprised, he didn't let it come through in his voice. Instead, he sounded excited upon agreeing to be his best man.

Jason's second call was to Aunt Marla. She'd have all the addresses that Randi needed. His aunt didn't sound surprised, either, and her excitement came through the phone line so loudly Tanner perked up.

Jason faked it well, even put on a good laugh for his aunt before he hung up. Other things on the list included where he needed to be and when, the location of the church and hotel for the reception, and the size of clothing he wore, with measurements. Actually, the measurements she asked for weren't really necessary. He owned a suit but would buy a new one. After wearing it the other night, he realized the one he owned was too tight through the shoulders.

He taped the note to the front of the refrigerator and went downstairs, hoping to focus on a project rather than her. Rather than marrying her. It went against everything he knew to be true, and that meant one thing. It wouldn't work.

Within an hour he was back upstairs and his house was being bombarded with family members, carrying in platters, kettles and pans full of food.

"You can't call with that kind of news and not expect a celebration!" Aunt Marla said. She had six kids, and they were all there, along with the respective mates of those that were married and their children.

Including Rachelle, who was the first to ask, "Where's Randi?"

"She left a short time ago," he said, making it sound like her visit had been longer and more affable than it had been.

"What's her phone number?" Lottie asked.

Jason shook his head. "She's busy. Has things to do."

"I know! That's why I want to call her, to let her know that I'll help with whatever she needs. We all will. Two weeks isn't much time to get everything done. What's her number? Tell me or I'll call information."

Randi might need help, and if so, he wanted her to have it, so he rattled off her home number. He'd memorized it last week, and her office number.

Later, after everyone had eaten, the women were sitting at the table, making lists from Aunt Marla's address book and the men were in the living room, giving him marriage advice when Tanner ran to the front door, tail wagging.

Upon peering out the window, Jason was out the door in ten seconds flat, meeting Randi on the sidewalk. "Hi."

"Hello," she replied stiffly.

He glanced at the house, at the faces looking out the window. "They—"

"I know. Lottie told me everyone was here. When I asked if Rachelle could be the flower girl, Lottie suggested that I drive over and ask Rachelle myself." She sighed. "So here I am."

He hated how stiff, how prickly and strained, things were between them. Letting out a sigh, he said, "I'm sorry."

She averted his gaze for a moment, and then looked at him. "For what? Did you tell them about the baby, too?"

Stung, he rocked on his heels. "No."

"Thank you for that."

His jaw muscles tightened. "Don't thank me too soon. They all think we're happy about this. About getting married."

"I assumed as much." With a smile that only he knew was fake, she waved at those still gawking out the window. "Don't worry, unlike some, I know how to keep secrets."

She was working hard at getting his goat. It was working, too. "Secrets or lies?"

Leveling her fake smile on him, she shrugged. "I'm sure that difference ranks right up there with nosy and curious in your world."

It appeared that she, too, remembered every conversation they'd had. Not about to remember certain ones right now, he stepped aside so she could step onto the porch. "Might as well go in, get this over with."

"Might as well."

He crossed the porch at her side and opened the door, let her step over the threshold first, and into the room that erupted with clapping and cheering.

"I have to see your engagement ring," Lottie said, rushing forward.

Jason draped an arm around Randi's shoulders. "She just agreed to marrying me. Give me a little time, will you?"

"You asked her without a ring?" Lottie laughed. "You're slipping, Cuz. Either that or head over heels."

Randi laid a hand on his chest and looked up at him. If he didn't know better, he'd think the shine in her eyes was real.

"He wants me to help pick it out," she said. "I told him any ring would be fine, but you know how stubborn he can be."

"Don't we all," Lottie said.

Someone in the background agreed, and others soon joined in with laughter and jokes. Jason returned the teasing with his own jokes and kept his arm around Randi as if all was right in the world.

Lottie broke into the noise by saying, "Rachelle is in the kitchen, Randi."

"No, I'm not, Mommy, I'm right here, behind you."

The room quieted more as Lottie stepped aside and Rachelle rolled forward.

"Mommy says you and Jason are getting married!"

Randi knelt down in front of the chair. "We are, and that's why I drove over here, to see you."

"Me? What for?"

"To ask if you'd like to be in our wedding," Randi said. "Be the flower girl."

The room went completely silent, and Jason's heart swelled as he saw Rachelle's face light up.

"You mean it?" Rachelle asked, eyes wide. "Me, in a wedding?"

"Yes, I mean it." Randi reached into her coat pocket and held up a tape measure. "I need to get your measurements so my mother can sew you a new dress to wear."

Rachelle's little face scrunched up, and she rubbed one eye with a fist. "But, Randi, I can't walk."

Jason stepped forward, ready to say that was just fine, but Randi had already taken a hold of Rachelle's hand.

"That makes it even more special," she told Rachelle. "We can decorate your wheelchair with flowers. All sorts of them." She touched the tip of Rachelle's nose. "You are going to be the most beautiful flower girl ever."

Lottie grasped a hold of his arm, squeezed it tight and whispered, "No wonder you fell in love so hard and fast. She's an earth angel."

Jason's stomach sank. He wasn't going to be able to pull this off. Neither was Randi, not with the way she hated him. She probably thought he got her pregnant on purpose, just to have access to her money.

She said something about measurements, and soon all the women were in the kitchen again, and the men in the living room. Including him. And holding the smile on his face was growing harder by the minute.

He had to put a stop to this, before it went any further, but what could he do? She was pregnant. There was nothing else that could be done, other than getting married, and being miserable for the rest of their lives.

It wasn't long before Randi walked into the living room, took a hold of his arm. "Your turn."

"My turn for what?"

"Measurements. My mother is sewing you a suit for the wedding."

"I already have a suit."

She tugged on his arm. "Now you'll have two."

With cheers and jeers from his male cousins, he let her pull him into the kitchen, where he had to remove his shirt, hold his arms out and be exposed to all sorts of giggling as Randi proceeded to measure his arms, neck, chest and waist.

"Are we done now?" he asked after she measured his biceps.

Aunt Marla, who had written down the measurements as Randi had taken them, said, "No, she has to measure you for the pants now."

His insides quivered. "No, she doesn't."

"Yes, I do," Randi said with a challenge in her eyes.

He'd been measured before, and didn't want her hands in the vicinity of his inseam. His body had a hard enough time behaving when she was near; having her touching him would put flame to fire.

"It won't hurt," she cooed.

She was enjoying this too much. He caught her by the waist, whispered in her ear, "It's not me I'm worried about."

"Then who?" she whispered in return.

"You."

"Me?"

"Yes, you might find something you want."

She laid a hand on his bare chest, making the skin tingle. "I've already found that and wasn't impressed."

He could tell by how her breath caught that she was far more affected than she was willing to admit. That made him grin, outside and inside. "All right, go ahead. Measure away."

She did, and he had to tighten every muscle in his body, especially when she measured his inner thighs, one at a time, more than once.

Standing up, she pressed a finger to the tip of his chin. "All done. You can put your shirt back on now."

Her smile said she'd thought she'd won. She hadn't, and she would pay for this. His jeans were now a full size too small and walking wasn't going to be pain-free.

It took time, but he found his moment of payback while everyone was preparing to leave. She was in the laundry room, collecting her coat. He walked up behind her, reached around and cupped both of her breasts while nuzzling the side of her neck.

She flattened her coat against her front, pushed at his hands. "Jason, stop it. Someone might see."

He nibbled on her ear. "I'll shut the door."

"No, you won't." She spun around. "You'll—"

He covered her mouth with his and kissed her until he felt her melt against him. Then he deepened the kiss, used his tongue, growing more and more satisfied as she returned the kiss, twist for twist.

Then he broke the kiss, turned around and left her, standing there, breathing hard and holding on to the counter.

She was steaming mad when she exited the room. Her eyes told him so. He laughed, took a hold of her arm, walked her to her car. It was parked behind others, who were waiting to leave.

"That will not happen again," she hissed while climbing into her car.

"You started it."

She glared at him and slammed her door shut.

He laughed.

Chapter Nine

He wasn't laughing now, a week and a half later. The contest that had ensued was killing him. Anytime they were together, they tried to make the other one as hot and bothered as possible, as if that would make them the winner. Jason knew the truth. He wasn't winning. Neither was she. They were doing little more than making each other miserable.

Life itself was miserable.

More than that, he was worried about her. He hadn't seen her every day, but often enough and for someone who was pregnant, she was losing weight rather than gaining it. He could tell each time he touched her.

It was not quite noon when he pulled up next to her car in the Air America office parking lot. He'd driven by the place thousands of times but hadn't pulled into the lot since that night years ago, after Randi had turned him down for a date.

He'd been mad at the world and had been driving like a bat out of hell on his motorcycle. After almost laying the bike down on the last corner, he'd slowed down, and his teenage mind had been questioning his life. How nothing had ever gone right, when he saw four people jump out of a car and run to the building. He'd slowed his bike, watched them check the doors and then run around to the back of the building. Randi had still been on his mind, and still wanting to impress her, he'd sped around to the back of the building, climbed off his motorcycle and yelled at the kids.

They'd been young, he could tell that, and one of them had smashed a window with a tire iron. He'd run over, taken away the tire iron. The night watchman had shown up right then. The other four ran, got in their car and sped away, and he'd been the one left holding the tire iron.

The one the police hauled off.

The one the judge sentenced to reform school, because his bad-boy reputation had preceded him. A teenager with no mother, a drunken father and a list of drag-racing tickets.

He'd been a month away from his eighteenth birthday, and that had set his sentencing. Thirty days of reform school.

If he'd been smart, he'd have gotten over Randi that very night.

But he hadn't.

Now he was about to be married to her.

He climbed out of the car.

A receptionist on the ground floor told him where Randi's office was located on the second floor. He chose the stairs over the elevator. Halfway down the long hall on the second floor, someone yelled.

"You there! What are you doing up here? What do you want?"

Jason looked over his shoulder at the man behind him in the hallway.

Tall, yet pudgy, with greased-back black hair and

squinting eyes, the guy said, "Yes, you. What do you want?"

Jason would bet dollar to dime that this was Sam Wharton, and deep loathing rose up inside him. Randi was going through enough and the idea of this guy making her life worse had his hands balling into fists with wanting to smack Wharton's smug face. He let his feelings show on his face, in his glare. "I'm not here to see you." Jason gave the guy a final glare before adding, "Not today."

He turned, continued down the hall and entered the room with Randi's name on a plaque by the door.

An older woman with short, dark hair was behind a desk. "Is Miss Osterlund available?" Jason asked.

With a smile, the woman stood. "Yes, she is. One moment please." She walked over to a door, knocked and opened it. "Mr. Heim is here to see you."

It seemed even here, his reputation preceded him, because he hadn't said his name. He walked forward, entered the room. His steps faltered slightly when he saw her sitting behind a large desk, wearing a dark purple-and-white blouse, or maybe it was a dress, he couldn't tell. She was a beautiful woman. The very one he went to bed thinking about and woke up thinking about. This morning it had been different, though, and right now he was seeing what he'd seen become prominent the past few days. An unnatural paleness, darkness under her eyes, even her face was growing thinner.

"Hello, Jason."

He tugged his gaze off her, and saw her father sitting in another chair.

Jason stepped into the room. "Sorry to disturb you," he addressed both of them before looking at Randi again. "I stopped by to see if you had time for lunch."

She shook her head. "I—"

"That is a splendid idea," Randal said. "I was just telling her she needed more time off."

"I'll be taking several days off," she told her father. "And have things to finish before then."

While she'd been talking, a ruckus was coming through the door the secretary had closed moments ago.

The door flew open and Sam Wharton barreled his way through the doorway, followed by two other men. "Right there! That's him!" Wharton said.

"What the hell is going on?" Randal asked.

"This hoodlum's casing the joint," Sam said.

Randi slapped her desk as she stood. "He's not casing the joint!" She marched around her desk. "Get out of my office! Now!"

Jason hooked her by the arm when she would have marched past him.

Randal stepped up on Jason's other side. "I'm assuming you haven't met Randi's fiancé, Sam," Randal said. "Jason Heim, my soon-to-be son-in-law."

Jason didn't need either Randi or Randal fighting his battles and met Wharton's glare with one of his own. The other man was taking note of his jeans, boots and leather jacket, and was definitely finding them lacking. With Randi filling his mind all morning, he hadn't given his clothes a second thought. He was dressed for work, and after checking on the crews at his different building sites, he'd gone back home, made lunch for her and then drove here to pick her up.

Wharton mumbled something under his breath.

Jason ignored the insult. The guy wasn't worth his time. However, he couldn't ignore the way Randi stiffened. He stepped forward, putting himself between her and Wharton.

The man took a step back.

"Jason." Randal slapped his shoulder. "You and Randi enjoy your lunch. You men go back to work, and Sam, I'll see you in my office in five minutes."

The two other men flew out the door like birds espying a cat, and Wharton's face turned red as he pivoted on one heel and left.

"Collect your coat, honey," Randal said.

She huffed out a breath, but spun around, walked to the coat hanger behind her desk.

Randal gave his shoulder another slap. "She has always jumped to your defense."

By the time Randi was in the front seat of Jason's car, the boost of energy the anger at Sam had given her was waning. It wouldn't be if Wharton was still in front of her, accusing Jason of casing the joint! At that moment she'd wanted... She wasn't sure what she'd wanted, other than to blister Sam within an inch of his life. Jason was ten times the man Sam would ever be, in every way. If only she was bigger, stronger, she would have taken Sam out.

She wasn't bigger, though, or stronger, and pinched her lips together, not sure there was enough energy left inside her to go another round with Jason. Since the day she'd agreed to marry him, they'd gotten caught up in some kind of game to see who could drive the other one crazy first.

She was on the losing end.

He didn't even have to touch her to make her body beg for more. A single look from him was capable of doing that, and it was exhausting. To the point it kept her awake at night. When she did manage to sleep, dreams of him woke her.

Going to work had become the only time she could escape him, but it was also exhausting because Sam had increased his antics. He was twisting everything she did to make it look wrong. She didn't want her father involved, nor did she want Jason involved.

Add all the wedding preparations, and she was nearly worn out. Her mother, grandmother and Lottie were taking on the brunt of the planning, thankfully. She wouldn't have been able to get everything done without them.

When she'd told her parents that she wanted to marry Jason, they'd said the wedding could be whatever she wanted. Large. Small. Here in Chicago or on some exotic beach.

She hadn't been able to tell them that all she really wanted was for Jason to want her as his wife. Really want her. Not because she was pregnant, but because he loved her. Loved her for herself. Loved her like her parents loved each other.

That would never be, and because others would expect it, she'd said the wedding should be here, in Chicago.

"I have to get back as soon as possible," she said. "I have a lot to get done at work and I have to pick up Rachelle to try on her dress this evening."

"It won't take long to eat," Jason said. "I have it staying warm in the oven."

"You made lunch?"

"Yes. You sound surprised."

"I didn't know you cooked."

"How do you think I eat?"

That had never been a part of all of her thoughts about him.

"I've cooked since I was eleven," he said.

That had been something she'd thought about. Marla was his mother's sister, but no one spoke of his mother. "What happened to your mother?"

"I don't know."

"How can you not know?"

He shrugged and sent her a quick glance. "She was there one morning when I went to school and gone when I came home that afternoon."

"What do you mean *gone*?" Compassion filled her. "Dead?"

"No, just gone. Some of her clothes were gone, a few other things. My father said she went to Florida. I don't know if that was true or not."

He sounded nonchalant, noncaring, but he couldn't be. "How old were you?"

"Eleven." He kept his eyes on the road as he continued. "My father wasn't an easy man to get along with, he was very stuck in his ways. She couldn't take it any longer and left, and I figured out that if I wanted to eat, have clean clothes, clean sheets, I had to do it myself."

She'd had no idea his childhood was so...sad. It made her heart ache and she wished she could touch him, hug him, even just hold his hand, but that could only happen when they were around others, playing their game of intense attraction that was nothing more than a superficial facade. His admission wasn't a facade. She could feel the honesty in his words. "You never heard from her again? From the time you were eleven?"

"No, but I've heard she's doing fine."

"Heard? From who?"

"My aunt." He turned the corner that led to his street, and had to slow down, stop for someone backing out of their driveway.

A plethora of questions filled her mind, along with empathy. "Jason, I—"

"I'd like to call a truce," he said, interrupting her.

She stared at his profile, wondering where his comment had come from. "A truce?"

"Yes, between us. We are getting married in two days, and…" He drove forward, following the car that had backed out. "I don't think marriage is easy even for people who are in love, who love each other. I think we should try to get along, make things as easy as possible, for the baby's sake if no one else's."

His honesty wasn't brutal, but its effect on her heart wasn't tender. A loveless marriage hadn't been her goal. Getting pregnant hadn't been, either. Yet, that was what had happened and she had to make the best of it. "I agree."

He turned into the alley and drove to his garage. Stopping there, he looked at her. "I know the position this has put you in, and know there will be times, at the wedding for instance, that we'll have to pretend…"

That we're in love, she finished silently.

"But we don't have to do that all the time. We can just—" He shrugged. "Be who we are when we're alone. No pressure. No faking."

No pressure? No faking? She wished that were possible. Wished so many things were possible.

"Is that okay with you?" he asked.

She nodded, more to herself than to him. "Yes, that sounds fine."

He shut the car off. "I'll give you a ride back to work when you're done eating."

She nodded again, and opened her car door, climbed out.

Tanner met them in the backyard and she was grateful that there was nothing fake about the dog. He was happy to see her, and she didn't have to pretend that she adored him.

"Oh, you poor dog," she told Tanner once in the house.

"Poor dog?" Jason carried her coat into the laundry room. "He has a pretty easy life."

"Easy? It smells delicious in here. He's probably been drooling for hours. What are you cooking?"

"Stick-to-your-ribs stew. Sit down and I'll get you a bowl." With a grin, Jason winked at her. "I'll even give him a bowl if you eat all of yours."

"Is that called bribery?"

He chuckled. "Possibly."

"More like probably." She rubbed Tanner's ears one last time. "Don't worry, I'll make sure you get a bowl." On her way to the sink, she asked, "What is stick-to-your-ribs stew?"

"The only stew I know how to make," he replied, carrying additional plates to the table. "It fills you up. Sticks to your ribs."

Her laughter came easy. His truce idea must be making her feel at ease, because she did. After washing her hands, she sat down at the table, and pressed a hand on her stomach as it growled. Besides the meaty stew, there was bread, milk, cheese and a plate of cookies. "You've been busy."

He sat down across from her. "Aunt Marla made the cookies." Nodding at her bowl, he said, "Eat up."

She took a bite of stew and nearly moaned over how delicious it tasted. "This is scrumptious."

"I'm glad you like it. You've lost some weight."

Not wanting him to think that was on purpose, she quickly chewed and swallowed. "Dr. Spencer says it's not unusual for women to lose weight at first. That it'll all come back sooner than not."

"What else does she say? Is there anything that you should be doing or not doing?"

It was the first time they'd discussed the baby, her pregnancy. "No, not really. Other than I shouldn't reach my hands over my head because that could make the umbilical cord wrap around the baby."

"It could?"

"Yes, that's what she said." Dr. Spencer had said a few other things, about hemorrhoids and breast soreness, but those weren't subjects she wanted to share with him. Not when she was more curious about something else. "How did you find out? Dr. Spencer was the only person who knew."

"By chance. Being in the right place at the right time."

His secretive grin made her smile. "What place?"

"The clinic. I'd heard your voice when the receptionist put you in the exam room across the hall from me. Your folder was in the holder on the wall. I took a peek. It said the rabbit died."

She shook her head at him. "It did not say the rabbit died." Then, truly curious, she asked, "Did it?"

He chuckled. "No. It said positive, but that is how they test. Rabbits."

"I know, isn't that crazy?"

"Actually, I recently read that they are using frogs for the testing more and more, because it doesn't kill the frog."

"Really? Where did you read that?"

"In a magazine I bought."

"What sort of magazine?"

His face slightly pinkened. "A women's magazine about pregnancy. It's in the bedroom, on the nightstand. You can read it if you want."

Her insides warmed that he was interested enough to buy a magazine. However, something else did concern her. "Why were you at the clinic?"

"I'd cut my hand."

He didn't point to it, didn't need to. She'd already noticed it and had been watching it, without letting on, to make sure the redness and puffiness were going away. It looked far better now than the first time she'd noticed it. "How had you cut it?"

"Bumped it with the skill saw."

Her heart leaped in her throat. "Skill saw! Good Lord, Jason, you could have cut your hand off!"

"It wasn't that bad and it's fine now."

She could see the scar, how it went all the way across the back of his hand. "It had to have hurt."

"The tetanus and penicillin shots hurt worse."

"I hate shots," she admitted.

"The needle isn't so bad, it's when they shoot the serum in that burns, and hurts for days." He nodded at her bowl. "Ready for seconds?"

She glanced down, unaware that she'd eaten the entire bowl, and the bread and the cheese. Her stomach felt fine. Full. But fine. No queasiness. There was still some milk in her glass, and she picked a cookie off the plate holding several. "No, thank you, but I am going to eat this with the rest of my milk."

He took a cookie off the plate and held it toward her. Laughing, she clicked her cookie against his as they both said, "Cheers."

A short time later she was helping him clean the kitchen when the phone rang. He answered it, and his question a moment later—about what supplies were missing—let her know it was about one of his building sites. She finished cleaning and putting away everything, including rinsing out Tanner's dish that Jason had filled with stew as promised.

"I have to make a couple of phone calls real quick, then I will give you a ride back to your office," he said.

"That's fine." She had a lot to do, but was no longer in a hurry to do it. While he dialed the phone, she walked down the hall and used the bathroom. When she exited, she could hear that he was still on the phone. Curious, she glanced in his bedroom and saw a magazine on the bedside table.

She entered the room, picked it up and grinned at the title of an article claiming everything a woman needs to know about pregnancy on the cover. Flipping through to the page indicated, she sat down and started to read.

When Tanner jumped up next to her, she swung her legs onto the bed and leaned against the headboard, petting the dog as she continued to read.

Chapter Ten

Jason hung up the phone, feeling guilty that it had taken him so long to find out where the materials that Stu was missing had been delivered. They were now on the way to the right site. The lumberyard was usually spot-on, but a new driver had put a wrench in the morning deliveries. All was in order now, and he went looking for Randi.

He found her in the bedroom, snuggled up against Tanner, sound asleep, with the magazine lying on the bed beside her. He'd bought it at the drugstore, while picking up bandages for his hand shortly after seeing her chart at the clinic. The article had said weight loss in the beginning wasn't unusual, but whoever had authored that article hadn't seen her. She'd lost too much weight. In his mind, anyway, and he was glad she'd eaten as much as she had at lunch.

Tanner lifted his head. Jason pointed at the dog, silently telling him to stay put. Tanner didn't seem to mind that command and laid his head even closer to Randi.

Jason collected a blanket from the linen closet in the hallway, removed her shoes and carefully draped the blanket over her. After watching to make sure she was still sound asleep, he left the room, closing the door behind him. A nap would do her good. The article had said rest was also needed for expecting mothers.

He checked on her regularly, and when she was still sleeping by four in the afternoon, he called Air America and spoke to her father, explaining how she'd fallen asleep and was still sleeping.

"Thank you, Jason, her mother and I have been worried that she hasn't been sleeping enough. There's nothing here that she needs to worry about. Would you like me to have her car delivered to your house?"

"No," Jason replied. "You can have it delivered to yours. I'll give her a ride home when she wakes up. I just wanted you to know so you weren't worried about why she hadn't returned to the office."

"I appreciate that very much."

He bid Randal farewell and then placed a call to Lottie. Once again explaining how Randi had fallen asleep and was still sleeping. Lottie assured him that she'd drive Rachelle to the dress fitting.

When he checked on Randi again, Tanner was sitting near the door, but she was still sleeping. After making a trip outside, the dog lay down in the hallway, outside the bedroom door.

"Sorry, boy, I don't want you to wake her by jumping on the bed."

Tanner covered his eyes with both paws.

"Nice try, but I don't feel sorry for you," he told the dog and went back into the living room, where he was using the coffee table to draw up plans for a cradle and a crib. Normally, he'd use the table in the basement, but wanted to hear when she woke up.

As a builder, he knew the sturdiest buildings would fall if the foundation hadn't been properly set, and so far, he wasn't creating much of a foundation for him and Randi to build upon.

He'd failed before. Not in building, but in life, and didn't want that again. He had to find a way to make this work. To make her not regret marrying him. Not regret having his child. He'd do whatever he had to in order to make sure his child knew they were loved, by both parents. Even if those parents were from two different worlds.

The part that was hard to swallow was knowing what it was like to live with parents who didn't love each other. He knew what that was like, and had to find a way to make sure that didn't show. Not to anyone. He didn't want Randi to be embarrassed, to be hurt.

Around seven the phone rang and he ran to catch it on the first ring.

"Hey, Cuz," Lottie said. "Rachelle and I are getting ready to leave Randi's house and want her to know the dress fits to a T. Rachelle is ecstatic over it, and it looks absolutely adorable on her."

"I bet it does." He was happy to have Rachelle in the wedding. "I'll let Randi know when she wakes up."

"She's still sleeping? She must have been exhausted."

He started to answer, but heard Lottie speaking to someone else.

"Hey, Cuz, Jolie wants to speak to you," Lottie said. "Talk to you later."

Jason shifted his stance, not sure why Jolie would want to speak to him.

"Hello, Jason. I just want to say thank you. I don't know how you did it, but I'm so thankful you managed to get her to take a nap."

She sounded so sincere he was comfortable admitting the same. "I am, too." Then he added a joke. "I'm just hoping it wasn't food poisoning from my cooking. She fell asleep right after eating."

"You got her to eat, too? You are a miracle worker." She laughed. "And don't worry. If it was food poisoning, she'd be throwing up not sleeping."

He chuckled. "Good to know."

"All right, dear, I'll see you tomorrow."

"Tomorrow?"

"Yes, I need you to try on your suit. Maybe you can do that when you bring her home?"

"Tomorrow," he repeated, not sure what her mother was suggesting.

"Yes, tomorrow. If she wakes up this evening, you tell her to go right back to sleep."

"Okay," he said hesitantly.

She let out another soft laugh. "Jason, the two of you will be married in a couple of days. I think it's okay if she spends the night."

Stunned that he was having this conversation with his soon-to-be mother-in-law, he couldn't help but wonder how his mother would have reacted to the situation. He knew how his father would have reacted, and it wouldn't have been good. "Okay, I'll tell her that, but—"

Jolie laughed louder. "But she may argue. You do know my daughter so well. Goodbye, now, see you tomorrow."

"Bye," he got in, just as she was hanging up. Replacing the receiver on the metal hook, he shook his head. The Osterlunds were proving to be nothing like he'd expected. He wasn't sure why, but had thought they'd be standoffish, rude, prude. Especially to him. There was no justification for why he'd thought that, other than the bias he'd grown up with about the differences in the rich and the poor. The haves and the have-nots. His father had

had plenty to say about that. About how the two worlds can't mix. Can't get along. And how he'd better stop mooning over *that rich girl*.

He'd tried more than once to discuss the property Randal had wanted to buy with his father, but that topic had been volatile, and he'd given up.

It had been his short stint in reform school that had given him the kick in the butt he'd needed to put himself on a different track. He'd accomplished a lot in the past six years, things he could be proud of. Was proud of. But he'd never be in the same category as the Osterlunds. Which was exactly what his father had always said. Right up until the day he'd died.

That may have been because of his mother. His father claimed that she'd run away with a rich man because money had meant more to her than her husband and son.

Rubbing the back of his neck, he walked back into the living room. He couldn't believe he'd told Randi all about his mother. That was a subject no one brought up. Not even Aunt Marla. Yet, he'd told Randi.

Tanner sat up, looked at the bedroom door. Jason walked to the door and carefully opened it to peer inside. The light was off, but the one in the hallway gave enough light for him to see that she'd moved, rolled from her side to her back.

"I think I fell asleep," she said groggily.

"Yes, you did."

She let out a tiny groan. "Why is it so dark? What time is it?"

"About seven thirty."

She shot upright. "Seven thirty!" Kicking her feet, she tried to get the blanket off her legs.

He sat down on the bed beside her, laid a hand on her

legs. "Slow down. You don't have anywhere you need to be."

"Yes, I do. I have work to do and Rachelle! I was supposed to pick her up at six o'clock. Oh, why didn't you wake me?"

"Lottie took Rachelle to your mother's, and the dress fits perfectly. Rachelle loves it and Lottie said she looks adorable in it." He smoothed the blanket over her stomach now that she had lain back down and was no longer trying to get out from under it. "Your father said there is nothing that you need to worry about at the office, and he had your car delivered to your house. Your mother said when you wake up, I'm supposed to tell you to go back to sleep."

She looked at him. "Is there anyone you haven't spoken to?"

"Is there someone you want me to call?"

"No." She sighed. "I can't believe I slept so long. So hard."

"You were tired."

"But I have so much to do."

"Not tonight. Are you hungry? There's plenty of stew left over." He searched his mind for quick meals. "Or I could make you some scrambled eggs or oatmeal and toast."

"Oatmeal?"

He chuckled silently at the way she said it.

"That sounds good, doesn't it?" she asked. "With cinnamon and sugar."

"I have cinnamon and sugar. I'll go make you some."

She laid a hand on his arm before he stood. "No, that's okay. I just need a ride home."

"That is the one thing I can't give you."

"Why not?"

"Your mother."

"My mother?"

"Yes, she told me you are to spend the night."

Smiling, she closed her eyes. "She would." She stretched her arms over her head and sat up again. "Don't worry. Her bark is worse than her bite. She won't be mad if you give me a ride home."

He couldn't quite imagine her mother angry. Nor could he imagine Randi looking more adorable. The desire to kiss her was so strong he had to get off the bed. "I'm not worried. I'm going to make you some oatmeal." At the door, he added, "With cinnamon and sugar."

A few moments later, while he was in the kitchen, waiting for water to boil, he heard her talking to Tanner.

"You're the reason I fell asleep, silly old dog," she said. "You were so warm and snuggly it was impossible not to."

Tanner let out a bark. She laughed, and then told him, "No, you don't, I don't need your help in the bathroom."

As smart as he was, Tanner still hadn't mastered privacy.

The old saying *a watched pot never boils* was coming true, because Jason was still waiting for the water to boil when she walked into the kitchen.

"May I use the telephone?"

"Of course." He nodded toward the wall. "There's that one, or the one in the living room, on the table by the window."

"Thanks." She nodded toward the stove. "The water's boiling."

"Hi, Mom." Randi leaned against the wall and watched Jason pour oatmeal into the pot on the stove.

"Hello, honey. Did you have a good nap?"

"Yes, I just woke up. I'm blaming it on Tanner."

"Tanner?"

"Yes, he has yellow hair, big brown eyes and his snuggles put me to sleep."

Her mother laughed. "I'm assuming this Tanner has four legs."

"Yes, he does, and he's about as big as a small horse."

"You sound happy, dear."

She was happy, a content happy. "I feel so much better. You were right, I needed to eat and sleep."

"Yes, you did, and you need to do that again."

Smiling at him, she said, "Jason is making oatmeal right now."

"One of your favorites."

"I just wanted to call, ask about Rachelle's dress."

"Oh, honey, she is so adorable! Your father didn't want to let her go home. He was prepared to play checkers with her all night. Right now he's attaching wire to the silk flowers I had the girls at the shop make so they can be attached to Rachelle's wheelchair. He was adamant that if we just tied them on, they might fall off."

That was her father. Both the checkers and finding a way to make sure the flowers wouldn't fall off. "He'll have them twisted on her chair so tight that they'll never fall off."

Her mother laughed. "That could be his plan."

"And the dress? She liked it? It fit?"

"She loved it, and it fit perfectly. The rosy pink of the silk was perfect for her complexion. Just like you said. It had been so long since I'd sewn a little girl's dress, I'd forgotten how fun it was to work with all that lace and ribbons. I'm making her a little veil as a surprise. I'm sewing the pearls on it right now."

And that was her mother. They truly were really, really good people. "Thank you, Mom. She'll like that."

She heard background noise before her mother said,

"You're welcome, dear. Your father says hello and that he needs my help with something, so I need to go. We'll see you in the morning. I told Jason he can try on his suit when he brings you home. We love you."

"Love you, too." Randi hung up the phone. Her mother was fully convinced that everything would work out fine between her and Jason. Randi didn't want her mother to be disappointed, but she wasn't convinced her mother was right this time.

"Everything okay?" Jason asked.

"Yes. Mom is sewing a veil for Rachelle, and Dad is putting wire on the silk flowers for her wheelchair."

"That was really special of you to ask her to be the flower girl."

"She is a very special girl." Randi pushed off the wall and walked toward the fridge to get the milk. "I wish she'd been able to receive the vaccination."

"She wasn't in school yet, and that's the only place they are inoculating children."

"That's just where they can inoculate the most children at one time, it's expanding to clinics and other facilities, but it takes time."

"How do you know that?"

"I've served on the fundraising committee for several years and collect a lot more than dimes." Fundraising was one time her last name was a blessing, and she appreciated that.

"Thank you for doing that."

"You're welcome." As she opened the door of the refrigerator, she saw the note taped there and frowned. It was his wedding, too. "Was there anything specific about the wedding that you wanted?"

"No. Whatever you want is fine."

She lifted the milk off the shelf and turned around. He was spooning the oatmeal into bowls. "You're sure?"

"Yes." He looked at her. "Just that you're there."

Her insides nearly melted. She'd never forget what it felt like to be kissed by him. Touched by him. She had to take a deep breath and hold it in order to carry the milk to the table. "You said no faking while we're alone."

"I'm not faking. You will be there, won't you?"

Her face grew flush. "Yes, I'll be there."

He set the bowls on the table. "So will I. Nothing fake about that."

That was true. They talked about different people who would be at the wedding, and a variety of other things while eating the oatmeal and washing the few dishes they'd used. Tanner got the last of the oatmeal, as well as a good portion of dog food, before they all went into the living room.

She debated asking him to take her home. There was a lot to be done before Saturday, but she didn't want to go out in the cold. Truthfully, she didn't want to leave. Now that her stomach was full again, she was trying not to yawn.

"Want to watch the television set?" he asked. "I think *I Love Lucy* is on tonight."

She sat down on the sofa. It was dark brown and soft. Tucking her legs beneath her, she eyed him closely. "You like that show?"

"I figured you did."

"My mother and I love it, my father, not so much. He says it's too silly."

"I'd probably be on his side, but we can watch it if you want to," he answered while gathering several papers on the coffee table into a pile and setting a ruler and pencil on top of the stack.

"How about we watch whatever you want?" Gesturing to the pile, she said, "Or you can work on that if you need to."

"No, they are just some plans I'm drawing."

"For a new job?"

"No." He filtered through the papers, handed her one and then walked to the television on a table near the far wall and turned it on.

Her heart thudded as she recognized the drawings. "It's a crib and a cradle."

"I figure we could stain them, or paint them, whichever you'd like. Whatever color you'd like. I thought I'd make a rocking chair, too. And a high chair later on."

"Jason…" Her heart was thudding at his thoughtfulness. "I don't even know what to say."

"We could buy furniture instead, the—"

"No. This is so thoughtful. You making it for the baby is wonderful. Truly."

He nodded, then shrugged. "The furniture store has mattresses that will fit both the cradle and crib."

She had to pull her eyes off him before her mind went to other things. "What's this down in the corner?" She pointed at the bottom of the drawing.

He sat down beside her. "That's the pattern of the spindles for the legs."

"They are going to be beautiful."

"I thought I'd use maple, it's a good hard wood. Won't nick or scratch."

She continued to ask questions, and listened intently to each of his answers, using her imagination and the drawings to see each piece in her mind. "I'm looking forward to watching you build them."

"You'll be building the important thing."

She laid the drawing on the table and flatted both

hands on her stomach. A deep warmth filled her. Leaning her head against the back of the sofa, she asked, "This truce between us, what does it entail?"

"What do you want it to entail?"

"I don't know, I've never called a truce before."

"I haven't, either." He leaned back.

Everything felt so complicated, and it was, but there was also this baby growing inside her and she couldn't believe that was anything short of wonderful. Her greatest hope was that he thought that, too. "I did stop here, at your house after my plane landed that night, so I could tell you that I was expecting. Your car wasn't in the garage, so I left and planned on coming back the next morning."

He laid a hand over the top of one of hers. "I believe you, and I'm sorry. I should have handled things differently. I should have been more patient and waited for you to contact me."

Though it was hard to admit, she had to. "No, you shouldn't have. I was afraid to tell you and petrified about telling my parents. You saved me from having to tell any of you."

She huffed out a breath in preparation of telling him that she hadn't gotten pregnant on purpose, but didn't want to disrupt things more than they already were. Therefore, she stuck to the topic of her parents. It was hard for people to understand what it means to be the daughter of such a successful couple. "My parents are wonderful people, the best, and the idea of disappointing them—" She pinched her lips together.

"Scared you."

"Yes." Her breath grew heavy again. "I shouldn't have been, but couldn't help it, and now they are so excited about the wedding and everything, I don't want to disappoint them again."

He released her hand. "You won't. That'll be part of our truce. We'll get through the wedding just fine, and no one else needs to know about the baby until we decide to tell them. I think that shouldn't be until after your father announces his senate bid."

It was all so complicated and weighed so heavily inside her, she was grateful for his truce, even if it was only for a short time. Hopefully, it would be enough time for her to figure out how to make all of this work out. That was what needed to happen, for the baby's sake. "Thank you."

"You're welcome." He nodded toward the television. "Your program is coming on."

Chapter Eleven

"Hey, sleepyhead, it's time for bed."

She didn't want to move, didn't want to open her eyes, and snuggled closer to the warmth at her side.

"You're going to end up with a crook in your neck if you sleep like that much longer."

Letting out a sigh, she opened one eye, realized it was Jason's shoulder that she was using for a pillow and it was his warmth that she was snuggled against. "Hmm?" she asked, still not wanting to move.

He rubbed her shoulder. "Come on, Miss Rip Van Winkle. It's time for bed."

Sighing, she opened her eyes, sat up. "Is Lucy over?"

"About two hours ago."

She stretched, rubbed the back of her neck with both hands. "I remember seeing the beginning."

"You made it through the first five minutes." He helped her stand and kept an arm around her as he escorted her down the hallway. "I don't have a nightgown to loan you, but I have a pair of long johns and a T-shirt."

At this point she didn't care what she wore, she just wanted to sleep. All of her sleepless nights seemed to have caught up with her. "That'll work."

"Do you need to go to the bathroom?"

"Yes." She stumbled slightly.

He chuckled softly. "Are you going to be okay by yourself? Or are you going to fall in?"

She wasn't totally sure and forced her eyes to open wide. "I'll be fine. But I'll take those clothes so I can change in there."

"Okay." He walked her into the bathroom and set her down on the toilet seat. "I'll be right back."

She rubbed her eyes, trying to force herself to wake up enough to get undressed.

He was back in no time and set clothes on the edge of the sink. "Do you need help getting undressed?"

She was tired, but could still remember how dangerous his help might be. "The last time you helped me undress, I got pregnant."

"Well, that won't happen again."

Her heart thudded. "Ever?"

He lifted her chin with one hand. "Are you half-asleep or half-drunk?"

What had made her ask that? And why wasn't she embarrassed to have asked it? "I don't need any help."

He released her chin. "I'll be in the hallway. Yell if you do."

She didn't need help in undressing. The help she needed was in making sense of all this, but she was too tired to think. Too tired to think about anything but going to bed. To sleep.

Yawning, she removed everything except her panties, draped it all over the rod holding the curtain that hid the bathtub and put on his long johns and T-shirt. Then she used the toilet and washed her hands before opening the door.

He was in the hallway and looped an arm around her

waist, walked her into the bedroom, where the covers were folded back. She crawled in, rolled onto her side and sighed at the comfort. Then, feeling chilled, asked, "Can Tanner sleep on the bed again?"

"No."

"Why not?"

"Because then there wouldn't be room for me."

"I hope you snuggle as good as he does."

A moment later the bed shifted as he climbed into it. One arm went under her neck, the other around her waist and his body aligned itself against her back. "Will this do?" he asked.

His warmth surrounded her. "Yes. That's nice. Very nice."

"Good night, Randi."

She covered his hand that was resting on her stomach with hers. "Good night, Jason."

Jason counted sheep, estimated how many boxes of nails were in his basement and tried to recall how many episodes of the *Red Skelton* show he'd seen, but none of it helped. Every part of him was still responding to holding her. Not just his body and mind, but his emotions. He felt things for her. Deeply. Should he have told her that the reason he'd gone to her parents' house was because he'd been worried about her? He had been. She'd been the only thing he'd thought about for days, weeks, and not being able to get a hold of her had driven him crazy. He hadn't planned on telling her parents she was pregnant, but the idea of her leaving town had struck him like a bullet and he'd responded out of fear.

He wasn't proud of that, or of forcing her to marry him. All he'd been able to think about was her, and what she'd go through being unwed and pregnant. What that would do to her reputation. He was to blame, not her. If he'd have had more self-control, he would have stopped before making love to her. He hadn't, and not taking responsibility for that had never been an option.

The baby, their baby, would be his responsibility for the rest of his life. He'd be responsible for Randi the rest of his life, too. He accepted that completely, but what about her? That wasn't what she wanted. Had never wanted, and he didn't know what to do about that. Other than to make it as easy upon her as possible. That was all he could do.

If he could love, could learn to love, he'd do it, for her, but that could never happen. He was his father's son and everyone knows that the apple doesn't fall far from the tree.

The trouble was, desire and love were two different things, and he desired her. More every day.

However, what he desired, what he wanted, wasn't as important as what she needed.

He repeated that over and over, until he fell asleep and then repeated it when he woke up. His body was definitely reacting to how she was snuggled up against his side and had one leg thrown over the top of his thighs.

In the midst of repeating it one more time, he felt her shift, and then watched her eyes open. There were no dark circles under her eyes and her cheeks were flushed pink.

He was happy to see that. "Morning."

Her lips curled into a smile. "Good morning."

"How do you feel?"

"Wonderful." She rolled onto her back and stretched. "Completely refreshed."

The white T-shirt she was wearing didn't hide things

very well. He should climb out of bed, but if she glanced at him, she'd see something he couldn't hide very well.

Flipping onto her side so quickly the bed shook, she kissed his cheek. "I'll go make coffee, and then I'll make you breakfast." She tossed aside the covers. "It's only fair, you did all the cooking yesterday."

She bounded out of the bed, and he had to swallow a groan at how cute her butt looked wearing his long johns. No truce on earth was going to make this easy. Not with the way his desires had his blood pounding stronger than ever.

As soon as she disappeared into the hallway, he leaped out of bed and pulled on a pair of jeans. He couldn't wake up like this every morning for the rest of his life. He'd have to buy a bed for one of the spare bedrooms and sleep there.

She already had the percolator filled and plugged in when he arrived in the kitchen. Once again, it struck him at how perfectly she completed the space.

"I'm going to get dressed before I start cooking," she said, patting his chest as she brushed past him.

He grasped her hand, held it. She was so pretty, so… above him. She raised money for the organization that had helped Rachelle while she'd been in the hospital. Her father was running for the senate. The only thing his father ever ran for was town drunk. He wanted to apologize for who he was, but it wouldn't do any good. It wouldn't change anything.

She smiled up at him.

It wouldn't make him not want to kiss her, either. Nothing would do that. He gave her hand a squeeze and released it.

"Don't touch anything," she said while walking toward the doorway. "I'm cooking breakfast."

"I won't," he answered while walking to the refrigerator to get the cream she'd need for her coffee.

She returned to the kitchen, once again wearing the purple-and-white dress and looking not only refreshed, but also gorgeous. There was a shine in her eyes and on her face, and her energy was boundless as she fluttered around the kitchen.

"My cousins are arriving today," she said while they were eating eggs, bacon and toast. "You might remember Wendy. We were in the same grade and she's my very best friend. Was the entire time we were growing up. Her dad is a photographer. His company takes all the school pictures. He'll be taking pictures at the wedding."

The name didn't ring a bell. Not surprisingly. The only girl he truly remembered from school was her. "What does she look like?"

"My height. Short blond hair. She looks like Doris Day, and she laughs all the time. Makes everyone else laugh, too. She's my maid of honor. Both her and her sister Sandy are going to school out east. Wendy is going to be a doctor and Sandy a veterinarian. Sandy is younger by a few years. They were home for Christmas but only for a couple of days and I'm excited to see them both."

By the time she was done talking, he could no longer hold back a grin. "I can see you're excited, and I hope you don't wear yourself out within the first hour of the day."

Her plate was empty and she jumped up to carry it to the sink. "There's no chance of that. I feel amazing. Better than I've felt in weeks. I guess I really was tired."

He stood, stacked and carried the rest of the empty plates from the table to the sink, where she was running water to wash them. "That was delicious, thank you."

"You're welcome." She glanced up at him and scrunched up her face.

"What's wrong? It really was good."

"I'm glad you like it, but um…" She glanced around the room. "My bridal shower is at noon today."

He knew that. It was on the note she'd given him and he'd taped to the front of the refrigerator. A hint of nervousness struck. "Do I have to be there?"

She giggled. "No, but it's at my aunt's house, and I'm wondering if I could bring the gifts here, rather than to my parents' house after the shower. That way we don't have to move them twice."

He grabbed the towel to dry the dishes she was stacking in the rack. "Sure. What time?"

"I'm not sure. It could be around three or four, I really don't know."

After opening a drawer, he pulled out the spare key to the front door and laid it on the counter. "Here's a key so you can come and go as you please." He winked at her. "And not have to use the doggie door."

She punched him in the arm with a soap-covered fist. "Very funny, but thank you for the key."

The urge to kiss her just wouldn't go away. He grabbed another plate to dry. "You're welcome. I'll try to be here to help carry things."

"You don't have to. I'm sorry I kept you from your work yesterday."

"You didn't."

"I think I did, and I thank you. I really do feel much, much better."

"I'm glad."

They finished washing, drying and putting away the dishes, and she picked up her engagement ring from where she'd set it on the windowsill in front of the sink. She turned, looked at him. "Thank you for the truce, too."

The day after she'd agreed to marry him, he'd gone to

the jewelry store and had been at a loss as to which ring to buy. He'd settled on one with a diamond in the center, and two sapphires on each side. None of the stones were overly large, but that had been why he'd liked it. Its delicateness reminded him of her. At the time he hadn't been sure how to give it to her, so had had it sent to her office.

He stopped her from sliding the ring on her finger. Took it. Held it between his thumb and forefinger. "We could go to the jewelry store this morning and you could pick out whatever ring you want."

"Why? I like this ring."

"You could pick out a bigger one."

"This one fits perfectly."

"I mean a bigger diamond. Or a different-shaped one, different stones, or—"

"Jason, I like this ring exactly as it is. Don't you?"

"Yes, I do. It reminded me of you the moment I saw it." He wanted to ask her to marry him. Really ask her, not tell her, but it was a moot point. Their wedding was the day after tomorrow, and it wasn't like her answer would mean she wanted to marry him.

"It reminds me of you every time I look at it," she said.

He took her hand, slid the ring on her finger. Then, because he wanted to kiss her, have her kiss him in return, he released her hand. Neither of them moved, just stood there, staring at each other. The air, the energy between them, was shifting, growing electrifying, and he stepped back. "I'll go start the car so it can warm up."

Randi stared at the door to her father's den, waiting for Jason to exit. He'd looked so handsome in his suit her heart was still pounding. Just as it had been doing since she woke up next to him in his bed.

She felt so much better today. It could have been because she'd finally eaten and slept, but those things had happened because of him. Therefore, he was the reason she felt better. Him and his truce. She didn't know exactly what that all entailed, but it felt as if she wasn't alone. That they were in this together, which they were, but it felt different now.

The sound of the front door opening had her turning about, and she squealed upon recognizing a familiar voice. She ran down the hallway to the front foyer, where she and Wendy met, and hugged and squealed at the happiness of seeing each other.

"I couldn't wait!" Wendy pointed to the suitcases on the floor. "My plane just landed. I haven't even been home yet. Sing! Now! Asking me to be your maid of honor, but not telling me who you are marrying has been driving me crazy!"

"I couldn't tell you," Randi said, giving Wendy another hug. If she'd told her cousin who she was marrying, she'd have had to tell her everything, and she didn't want even Wendy to know why Jason was marrying her, or that he didn't love her.

Wendy's blond hair was brushed back in waves, making it look like Doris Day as always, and her blue eyes narrowed slightly as she asked, "Why?"

Just then, as if he'd known the exact moment to appear, Jason stepped into the hallway. He'd used her father's den to try on his new suit, and was wearing his jeans again now, cuffed, and his leather coat was hooked on a finger and flung over his shoulder as he walked down the hall, toward the foyer where she and Wendy stood.

"DDT!" Wendy hissed. "Drop dead twice! Again and again! You're marrying—"

"Yes!" Randi hurried to meet Jason as he reached the foyer.

"I left the suit in the den," he said.

"That's perfect." She wrapped a hand around his arm and nodded toward Wendy. "This is my cousin Wendy."

He gave Wendy a nod. "Hello."

"Hel—lo," Wendy replied, elongating the word in a way only she could do.

Randi laughed at the way he looked down at her, one brow risen.

"Jason Heim," Wendy said, nodding. "Jason Heim. How have you been?"

"Fine, thank you," he replied. "You?"

"Fine. Just fine." Wendy crossed her arms and tapped a toe on the floor as her eyes widened to look at Randi. "Meanwhile, back at the ranch."

Jason glanced from Wendy to her and asked, "Do you need anything else from me right now?"

"No," Randi said.

He swung his coat off his shoulder. "Then I'm off to work."

Wendy had moved to the other side of the foyer, where Peter was waiting to take her coat, and Randi walked with Jason to the door.

"You go slow today," he said while putting on his coat. "Don't wear yourself out again."

"I will, and I won't." She giggled at her own nervousness. "You know what I mean. I'll be fine."

He stopped at the door, zipped up his coat and gently touched her side. "I hope so."

She was fine in many ways, but in others, not at all. If she hadn't agreed to his truce, she could kiss him right now, in front of Wendy. She'd been able to do that when they'd been playing their game, but now, with the truce, she couldn't. Why didn't anything seem to work out in her favor?

"What's the matter?" he asked.

She reached up, flipped his collar up around his neck and leaned close, so no one could hear. "Can I ask a favor?"

"Yes," he whispered in return.

She bit down on her bottom lip, hard, not wanting to break the truce because yesterday, last night, this morning, had all been wonderful, in a comfortable, easy way. She'd eaten, slept and felt better than she had in a long time.

"What is it?" he asked.

"Will you kiss me goodbye?" she whispered quickly, before she lost her nerve, and then attempted to explain, "It's just that Wendy—"

"I get it," he said. "Big or little?"

The bigger the better, but she wanted it to look real. "Medium?"

"Medium?"

She nodded. "Is that okay? Little would—"

"Medium is fine," he said while cupping her face with both hands.

The next moment his lips met hers with such tenderness, it sucked the air right out of her lungs. She buried her hands in his collar and arched against him as his lips moved across hers, giving her several small, tender kisses that accumulated into a very special feeling that settled deep inside her.

When the kiss ended, she was floating on cloud nine.

He gently bumped his forehead against hers. "I'll see you later."

"Okay." She knew she had to release his collar, but couldn't quite make her fingers uncurl.

He kissed the tip of her nose, then gave her lips another single, quick kiss.

She forced herself to release his coat and patted his chest. "Bye."

As he opened the door, he winked at her. "Bye."

She barely had time to shut the door behind him, when Wendy let out another squeal and ran across the foyer.

"I can't believe you didn't tell me! I didn't even dare ask my mother, because I knew if it was anyone except him, I'd have to object to the wedding! DDT! He's even better-looking now! I knew it! I knew it, knew it, knew it. Knew that you'd find a way to make him marry you! You said you would, and you did!"

Randi's stomach fell. She had said she would find a way to make him marry her, years and years ago.

"Sing! Girl! Sing!" Wendy continued. "I need to know everything!"

"Um, well, let's go up to my room. I have to get ready for the bridal shower, and I'll tell you everything."

"You better believe you will."

No, she wouldn't. Not everything.

Chapter Twelve

Randi hadn't told Wendy about being pregnant, but had told her about going to his house to ask about buying his land, and about how she'd left, mad, wearing only his socks, and how she'd returned and dropped her glove, along with his socks through the doggie door.

Standing in his kitchen, she was in the midst of telling her other cousins that same story, when Jason opened the back door. She sidestepped closer to him. "I was just telling them about when I accidently lost my glove in the doggie door."

"I heard the laughing from the garage." Glancing at the others, he asked, "Did she tell you she lost her glove, or dropped it on purpose?"

She slapped his shoulder. "It was not on purpose!"

Her cousins, however, found his question hilarious, and because not a one of them was shy, they instantly started asking him questions about the event, which he answered with such humor and charm that every woman in the room was swooning. Including her.

She finally ended the storytelling by shooing everyone out to the cars to carry in another load of gifts she'd received at the bridal shower.

Once the room was empty, she told Jason, "I'm sorry, I was hoping we'd have everything put away before you got home."

"And I was hoping you'd wait for me to carry things in for you. I'll go help."

"No, none of it is heavy." She lowered her voice. "I wanted to mention that I moved your drawings off the coffee table. I put them in the laundry room."

"Sorry. I forgot I'd left them there."

"No, don't be sorry. I just—"

"I know, and it's okay."

She pressed a hand to her stomach. In a way, she had done exactly as she'd vowed—found a way to make Jason marry her. She hadn't gotten pregnant on purpose, but she had come to his house. He would have never searched her out. He would never have searched her out if he hadn't been at the clinic that day, either. Knowing all that made her feel awful. She had vowed to marry him, but she also wanted him to love her.

"What's wrong?" he asked.

"Nothing."

He rubbed her upper arms. "Are you not feeling well?"

"No, I'm fine."

"No, you're not."

The front door opened, filling the house with chatter and giggling. She glanced that way and swallowed against the burning in her throat. "Yes, I am. I'm fine."

In the next instant his arms were around her and he was kissing her, in the same, wonderful way he had this morning. It was so different from their kisses before they'd become engaged. Those ones had been hot, full of unrefined passion. His kiss now, and this morning, were affectionate, caring. Loving. Which made her feel better and worse at the same time.

By the time the kiss ended, feeling better won out, and increased when he held her in a long hug.

"What are your plans now?" he asked.

Her arms were around him, inside his unzipped coat, and she kept them there as she leaned her head back, looked up at him. "We are going back to my house, to paint our fingernails and toenails and practice how we want our hair to look for the wedding. Want to join us?"

He brushed the hair away from the side of her face. "No."

"It'll be fun," she teased.

"For some."

"We are also going to be packing up my bedroom, and will drive it over here tomorrow, and then we have to be at the church at five for rehearsal."

Clearing her throat before she spoke, Wendy said, "Sorry to interrupt, but we put everything in the spare room down the hall, and are just sort of standing around, twiddling our thumbs, trying not to stare. You know, in a sort of, take-a-picture-it'll-last-longer kind of way."

"I do remember her," Jason said.

Randi gave him a quick hug. "I thought you would." Wendy had always made everyone laugh, and she needed that to get through the next few days. When Wendy was near, it was easy to pretend that Jason loved her and was marrying her because he wanted to, not because he had to.

Jason closed the front door as Randi and the other women drove away in two cars. He did remember the cousin, because he remembered her telling him to take a picture once when he'd driven past her and Randi walking across the school parking lot. He'd been embarrassed at being caught staring.

He'd gone out with dozens of women since then, but none of them had left the lasting effect that Randi had on him. Still did.

The air in his chest seeped out slowly. This truce idea was backfiring on him. Kissing her before had been a challenge, and though it had left him heated, wanting more, his heart hadn't been in them, not like it was today. It made something deep inside him ache.

Tanner let out a bark.

Jason turned, looked out the window on the door, disappointed to not see Randi's car. "No one's out there."

The dog barked again.

"She's not coming back tonight."

Tanner lay down on the floor with a solid thud and sighed.

Jason shook his head at the dog, but admitted aloud, "I know the feeling." The house felt empty. She'd never been here for a full twenty-four hours, yet had left her mark. Just like she had on him.

"Come on, bud. It's leftover stew and *Red Skelton* for us."

Tanner didn't lift his head. Jason figured he wasn't hungry, either, and sat down on the sofa. With his feet on the coffee table and his hands clasped behind his head, he stared at the television set that he hadn't turned on. Last night, when she'd told him about being afraid to disappoint her parents, he'd been surprised. Had never thought about how hard it must be for her. To have such successful parents.

He knew the exact opposite. For years he'd been determined not to become his father and had hit the workforce. Hard.

He'd done well so far, and the future looked good, but he was still the boy who'd grown up in a shack on the edge of town. Still the boy whose mother had left because... Well, because not even love lasted forever.

Money won out. His mother had left because she was tired of being poor.

The phone rang and his thoughts instantly went to Randi. He leaped to his feet, answered it before the first ring completed.

"Hey," Stu said. "Since we are both home alone to-night, do you want to hit a burger joint and then hit a tavern for a couple of beers?"

"Why are you home alone? Where's Lottie and Rachelle?"

"Heading over to Randi's. Rachelle is in her glory. Lottie let her miss school this afternoon so she could attend the bridal shower and now they are on their way to get their finger- and toenails painted. It's really great how she's being included in everything. That doesn't happen a lot for her. So what do you say to the burgers and beers?"

"I say yes," he replied, even as his thoughts continued to remain on Randi, and how special it was that she was including Rachelle in everything. Too many people, who didn't understand polio, thought Rachelle was contagious and shunned her.

"Meet you at Rolly's in twenty?" Stu asked.

"I'll be there."

Stu was there as promised, along with nearly every male member of his family. They ate burgers and then headed across the street, where they had more than a couple of beers.

There were plenty of stories told, some good old-fashioned ribbing and a few serious conversations before the night ended well past midnight.

Then he spent a sleepless night feeling alone in his own bed.

* * *

Shortly after noon the following day Randi appeared, and rather than two carloads of women, it was two cars and a pickup.

"I brought help," she said, giving him one of her adorable grins as she stepped onto the porch. "I didn't want to take up all your dresser space, so I brought my own. And a dressing table, and a few other things."

The back of the pickup was heaped full and tied down with heavy ropes. "I see that."

"Is there any particular place you want it?" she asked.

It was still February and cold. "You can decide that while staying inside where it's warm."

"I won't argue. It's freezing out." She grasped his arm. "Just let me introduce you to everyone first."

Her cousin Wendy was with her again, along with a couple other women who had been with her yesterday, and the men were two other cousins and her brother, Joe.

They unloaded the cars first, so the women could stay inside, and then attacked the load in the truck with gusto in order to get it all inside before anyone ended up with frostbite.

The women were busy, finding places for everything with only a small amount of rearranging, and soon the men's work was done.

Joe approached him. "Hey, Jason, could we talk—alone—for a moment?"

Joe had returned home from college for the wedding, and assuming he wanted to put in his own two cents concerning his sister's choice of marriage, Jason nodded. "Sure."

His house was one of the top-selling models on the market, with three bedrooms, living room, kitchen and other necessary rooms, but there were women in every room, reorganizing and putting things away.

"We can go downstairs." The doorway was off the kitchen. Jason opened it, turned on the light and led the way down the stairs.

"Man," Joe said, stepping off the last stair. "This is quite the workshop."

"Thanks." The basement was the entire size of the house above, and unfinished other than a workbench that ran the length of one wall. He'd carried the plans for the crib and cradle down here this morning, and slid them out of the way while clearing a spot near a stool. "Have a seat."

"Thanks." Joe looked a lot like his dad, tall with dark hair, but had his mother's brown eyes.

Jason sat down on another stool.

"I want to apologize for what happened that night years ago," Joe said. "Young and dumb, that is what it was, and I've felt bad about it for years. I hadn't known that you had gotten caught and blamed for everything until the next week, when Randi almost killed me."

Jason had figured the topic would come up. "It's in the past, forgotten." However, he was curious as to why Randi would have been so mad. Other than thinking he'd been vandalizing her family's business. That would have been enough. She loved Air America.

"The night watchman always left a door unlocked," Joe said, "and I'd take people there to get free soda pop, which was stupid, I know, but kids, you know, they always want something to make them stand out. Free sodas got me rides when all I had was a bicycle."

Jason nodded, though he couldn't figure out why a rich kid would want to steal sodas, especially from his own father.

"Sam Wharton had figured out it was me and wanted me to get caught. He hired a different watchman, ordered the doors locked. I thought that I'd show him and break a window." Joe shook his head. "You know how that worked out."

"Sam Wharton has worked for your father for a long time," Jason said, thinking aloud. After meeting Wharton, he didn't want the man anywhere around Randi.

"Yes, he's an ass, but he knows numbers inside and out. Most people wouldn't have missed a few bottles of soda, but Sam could tell you how much each ounce was worth. Like I said, I hadn't known you got caught until Randi nearly cut my life short, and then I fessed up to Dad. I think that was the only time I was truly afraid of my father. He was furious. I went to the judge with him, explained everything. My dad insisted that you be released, but—"

Jason held a hand up to cut him off. "There wasn't any more your father could have done. My father wouldn't let them release me." His father had wanted him to hate the Osterlunds as badly as he had. "I was a minor, with a notebook full of drag racing tickets, which was enough to keep me there until I turned eighteen."

"Aw, man, I'm sorry. I didn't know that." Frowning, Joe asked, "Why didn't you return to school when you got out?"

"I couldn't. Westward High wouldn't allow it. There was only a month left, so I went to night school."

Joe let out a low whistle. "Man, I know it's a lot to ask, but I'm hoping you can forgive me for what I did."

Jason wasn't sure what he'd expected from Randi's family; Joe's sincere apology, her parents' full acceptance of him, their wedding, along with the rest of her family's friendliness was proof of one thing. They loved Randi and would do anything for her. Even accept him into their family. "Like I said, it's forgotten, with no hard feelings."

Joe's cheeks puffed as he let out a breath. "You have no idea how much that means to me. Just between us, I love my sister, but she can be brutal."

"She told you to apologize to me?"

"No, the subject hasn't come up for years. I apologized for me. So there wouldn't be bad blood between us." He chuckled. "And because if the two of us couldn't get along, she'd disown me."

"Jason? Are you and Joey down there?" Randi's voice echoed down the steps.

"Yes, I'm showing him my workshop," Jason replied.

"Do you have a hammer?" she asked.

Jason picked a hammer off the table. "Yes."

"May I borrow it, please? The leg came loose on my dressing table."

Joe shook his head. "Don't let her borrow it," he whispered. "She and tools are a dangerous combination."

Having carried in the dressing table, and the attachable mirror earlier, Jason also picked up a screwdriver, knowing the legs had screws, not nails. "I'll remember that warning," he told Joe before shouting up to Randi, "We're bringing it up!"

"Thank you!" she responded.

Joe slapped his shoulder as they stood. "Welcome to the family, man. It's a little bit crazy, awkward at times, but we all get along and know how to have fun."

Jason laughed as they walked toward the stairway. "Sounds like mine." Ironically, it did sound like his family. Now, at least. After his mother had left, his father had refused to let him see his aunt or cousins.

Randi was waiting for them at the top of the stairs. "I

didn't mean to interrupt, but the leg needs to be nailed tight before we can put the mirror on."

He held up the hammer. "Will it also need a screwdriver?"

Her face scrunched up. "Oh, maybe."

He held up the screwdriver in his other hand. "I got you covered."

She laughed, then whispered, "I had them put it in your bedroom."

"Okay," he whispered.

Chuckling, he headed toward the bedroom. Halfway there, his thoughts shifted to something that wasn't humorous. Her whisper must mean she wanted separate bedrooms.

Chapter Thirteen

"How are you doing, sugarplum?"

Randi pressed the side of her face against her father's shoulder as he tugged her closer to his side. "Good. How are you doing?"

"I can't lie. I need a drink." He kissed the top of her head. "I don't like the sound of giving away my daughter."

The two of them were waiting for their turn to practice walking down the aisle to the altar, while anyone not in the wedding was decorating the church with flowers and big bows made of white netting. "You can have a drink when we get home after the rehearsal. And I'll just be a few miles away. We'll see each other all the time."

He looked down at her, seriously. "You know you can always come to me for anything."

"I know that, Dad."

He nodded. Sighed. "Marriage isn't an easy thing, darling. It takes work. Hard work. On both sides. Give and take. But there is nothing more rewarding than living life with someone who loves you completely. For who you are and who you become. Everyone changes over time. Grows older. Wiser. More handsome." He winked at her. "Love changes over time, too. It grows and becomes wiser, as long as you let it. That's the hard part. You have to let go of what you expect it to be and let it become what it is."

If there was anyone who truly knew what love was, it was her parents. Randi's gaze went to Jason. From what he'd said about his parents, he hadn't grown up with the kind of love that she had.

He was capable of it. She saw it in his eyes as he watched Rachelle roll her wheelchair along the aisle, pretending to throw flower petals. But would he ever love her? *Could* he? There was so much between them that they'd had to call a truce to get through their wedding. She'd said she wouldn't settle for anything less than the kind of love her parents had, yet she was. She had to.

"You two are next," the pastor's wife said.

Randi looked up at her father. If she said she couldn't do this, he'd accept her decision, and call the wedding off, whether she was pregnant or not. She was certain of that, because he loved her. Without love, could she ever be certain of Jason?

"Ready?" her father asked.

She nodded. There was no other option. As Jason had told her, this wasn't about him or her, it was about the baby.

They started down the aisle, one slow step at a time.

By the time they arrived at the altar and her father handed her off to Jason to practice the words they'd vow to each other tomorrow, her entire being was trembling from the inside out.

Jason smiled as he took her hand.

She tried smiling in return, but her lips were trembling too hard. They were sealing their fate, putting themselves into a loveless marriage because of one night. It didn't seem right, didn't seem fair, but it was to the baby inside her. It would need both of them.

* * *

The rehearsal went off without a hitch, even the part where Pastor Williams told Jason he could practice kissing his bride, and before long, everyone, his family and hers, was gathered at her parents' house for dinner and drinks.

She'd lived here her entire life, and loved the big, old house, but as she and Jason roamed from room to room, saying hello to everyone in attendance and making introductions, she couldn't help but wish they were at his house, sitting on the sofa watching television.

Her younger crowd of cousins, and Jason's, were gathered in the dining room near the food and drink tables, and as they arrived in that room, Jason asked, "Why didn't you go out east to college? Joe and all of your cousins have."

Before Randi could answer, Wendy laughed.

"Because all she ever wanted was here," Wendy said.

Although she wanted to give her cousin a glare to shut her up, Randi couldn't. Wendy thought this all was on the up and up, therefore, she had little choice but to shrug at Jason.

The conversation quickly changed to another topic, and another and another.

The entire group was in the midst of laughing, when someone shouted, "Late but still great!"

Randi instantly recognized the voice, and so did half of the others in the room because shouts of "Gus!" echoed off the ceiling.

The big blond buffoon that he was, Gus made a beeline for her and lifted her off the floor into one of his big bear hugs. "My flight had a layover in Minneapolis and was delayed because of snow."

She returned his hug. "You should have flown Air America."

He laughed and put her down. "I did!" He then shook Jason's hand. "Hey, man, still agitating the gravel?" Slapping Jason's shoulder, Gus continued. "Do you still have that souped-up red Chevy with the V-8?"

"Yes," Jason answered.

"Dig it! That car's cherry! Still drag racing?"

"When I have time," Jason replied.

"Me, too. You should bring that Chevy out to California. We got some screaming drag racing out there, and we can ride motorcycles along the coast year-round." Gus looked at her again. "I can't believe you didn't tell me about this when you were in California."

"Because you can't keep secrets," she lied.

"I kept your secret for years." He chucked her under the chin. "Congratulations, kid. I'm happy for you." Turning to Jason, he said, "Good luck, man." Winking at her, he added, "You'll need it." Laughing at his own joke, Gus moved on, saying hello to others by shaking the men's hands and giving every girl a big bear hug, whether he knew them or not.

"He always makes an entrance," she told Jason, who was looking at her quizzically. She'd never told Gus she'd had a crush on Jason, but had the gut feeling that Gus had known. Just like her mother had. Perhaps she hadn't been as discreet about that as she'd thought.

Jason's gaze followed Gus, with a somewhat contrite expression. "He's a likable guy."

"If you like someone who doesn't have a serious bone in his body," she replied. "He'll never grow up."

His gaze shifted back to her. "Is all this getting to you?"

"No—" The air left her lungs. "Yes. I've never liked parties, not even when I was little."

"Where did you hide out then?"

She had no idea how he knew she'd done that, but he was right. "Why?"

"We can't cut out, but no one will notice if we're gone for a few minutes."

A short break would be wonderful. She took a hold of his hand, led him out of the dining room and to the very end of the hallway. "This is my mother's office now." She opened the door and clicked on the light to reveal the large desk near the windows that overlooked the backyard as well as walls of bookcases and file cabinets. "But it was my great-grandfather's bedroom when I was little. He and I used to sneak in here and play checkers when the house was full."

Jason closed the door behind them. "Why didn't you go to your bedroom?"

She plopped down on the powder-blue sofa across from the desk. "Because it was more fun to play checkers."

He sat down next to her. "I'm sure it was."

Checkers or not, it had been the escape she'd liked. "He died when I was eight, but I still snuck in here, even after it became Mother's office."

"Didn't you want to play with your cousins?"

"Family gatherings were fine. It was dinner parties and other events when people would make their requests that made me want to escape."

"Requests? What sort of requests?"

A knot had formed in her chest, like she'd swallowed something hard and it burned while going down. She'd never told anyone about how those requests had made her feel, but it was pressing to get out now. She knew the benefits of being who she was, had lived with those benefits every day, but those benefits also had their downfalls. "From money to band uniforms and everything in between."

"People asked you for—" He shook his head, staring at her as if he didn't believe her.

"All the time, everywhere I went. My parents are very generous, but the expectations..." It was hard to explain. Hard to understand. "It's always been like that. Even kids. I never knew if they wanted to be friends with me, or my parents' daughter." She looked at him. "You were the only one who acted as if my last name didn't mean anything."

"Really?"

"Yes." She sighed. "I should be used to it by now, but parties always give me a hard knot in my stomach because I know before the night is over, someone will expect something from me."

He touched her chin with one knuckle so softly, was looking at her so tenderly, her heart flipped. Her mouth went dry, too, because she was sure he was going to kiss her. Not because others were nearby, but because he wanted to.

Disappointment flooded her when a knock sounded on the door. She huffed out a sigh. "Come in."

Joe opened the door just wide enough to stick his head inside. "I thought I'd find you here. Uncle James wants to take some family pictures."

"Okay. We're coming."

Jason tugged at the tie around his neck. It wasn't tight—the suit, shirt, all of it fit him perfectly and was comfortable. As comfortable as anything could be for a man who couldn't breathe.

It was here.

His wedding.

To Randi Osterlund.

He was standing at the altar, watching Rachelle roll down the aisle in her flower-coated wheelchair, looking happier than he'd ever seen.

He should be that happy.

Would be if he belonged here.

He didn't.

The reasons went beyond the pomp and circumstance surrounding him. The few minutes he'd spent alone with Randi in her mother's office last night had been an eye-opener that he hadn't expected. He'd always assumed growing up wealthy would have been a walk in the park, but it hadn't been for her. What she'd said had him understanding why Joe had stolen pop from Air America. As payment for rides, to friends who hadn't been friends except for what they could get.

He'd thought of little else after going home last night and wished he could have told her that her last name hadn't mattered to him. But it had. It still did. It had been the reason he'd been afraid to ask her out and the reason he shouldn't be standing here, about to marry her. He hadn't wanted anything in exchange for her friendship back then. It was the opposite. He hadn't had anything to give her. Still didn't. Not in comparison to what she'd always known.

Jason sucked in another breath, held it. He wasn't the poor kid he'd been growing up. In all rights, he had plenty of money, but he wasn't wealthy. Not like the Osterlunds and Albrights and most of the other people in the pews. There was more wealth in this church than rocks on the shores of Lake Michigan. Hell, just the gifts she'd received for her bridal shower filled one of the bedrooms at his house. Her clothes, shoes and other personal items filled the other bedroom and half of his.

There was nothing that he could ever give her that she didn't already have. Ever.

But not even all that made his stomach sink as much as the other thing she'd said last night. People always expected something from her. He hadn't expected anything from her after Rachelle's party, but he'd taken it.

And now, because of that one act, he was taking even more from her.

The music changed, the crowd stood and his heart crawled its way into his throat, completely blocking off his airway as his gaze settled on the couple walking down the aisle. She had a hold of her father's arm, and a long veil covered her face, but he knew how beautiful her face was underneath the lace. The long white dress with lacy sleeves fit her like a glove, and all he could think was that he was going to disappoint her. He didn't want to, but he would.

He already had. In one selfish act. He should have stopped as soon as he'd realized she was a virgin.

He'd stayed away from her for six years, knowing that he wasn't good enough for her and should have continued to stay away from her. This was her wedding, and because of him, she was having to pretend to be happy. Pretend this was what she wanted.

She and her father arrived at the altar, her father handed her off to him, shook his hand and all Jason could think was that being married to him was going to ruin her life. She could have done anything, become whatever she wanted to be, but now she was stuck with him for a husband, and a house that was a fourth of the size of what she was used to, with a child on the way. The pregnancy was an accident. An accident that was his fault.

What if this pregnancy was too much for her? Too much for her delicate frame? What had he done?

The preacher talked, people chuckled and prayed for them.

It wasn't going to help.

He repeated the vows, because there was nothing else that he could do; he put the wedding band on her finger that he'd bought along with the engagement ring, and when told, he kissed her. However, when she melted against him, he held back, didn't let himself get lost in the touch of her lips, because this shouldn't be, and he had no idea how to make this right for her.

As they left the church, he tucked her close to his side in order to shield her from the rice pelted on them while they ran from the church to the limo waiting to give them a ride to the hotel.

It was black. A Cadillac, with tin cans tied to the bumper and Just Married painted on the windows with shoe polish. The seats were leather. Soft. Warm, because the car had been running so they wouldn't need coats.

Horns started honking as the driver pulled the car away from the curb and continued honking as cars pulled in line behind them to follow them all the way to the hotel.

"I guess we did it."

The tone of her voice, the way it cracked, struck him hard. This wasn't her fault and he had to make her life as easy as possible.

"We did." He kissed her forehead. "You look beautiful." That wasn't pretend. There was no one more beautiful. "Really beautiful."

Color tinged her cheeks. "You look very handsome." She laid her head on his shoulder. "And Rachelle was so adorable. It was hard not to cry as I watched her roll down the aisle."

The blaring of a horn filled the car.

"Oh, shirts! Look!" She pointed out the window. "It's Gus and Joey!"

The two guys had pulled their car up next to them and were gesturing for him to roll down the window. Jason did.

"Here! We bought you a present." Joe tossed a box through the window. "Don't use them all before you get to the hotel!" he shouted as Gus hit the gas and swerved in front of the limo just in time to get out of the way of an oncoming car.

"What is it?" Randi asked.

Jason had caught the box, and held it out, showing it to her.

Frowning, she read the label. "It's a box of—"

"Condoms," Jason supplied.

"Those two will never grow up! Buffoons! That's what they are."

He was trying hard not to, but it had been a funny gesture and his smile broke loose.

"I told you it was like I had two brothers," she said. "When one wasn't trying to embarrass me, the other one was."

"Are you embarrassed?" he asked.

"No. It just irritates me that I can't get them back."

He opened the box, took out a package and opened it.

"What are you doing?"

Removing the condom from the packet, he stuffed the condom back in the box and held up the empty packet. "I'm going to give this to them and say thank you."

She giggled. "Good idea."

"Unless you want to give it to them."

Her eyes lit up. "Oh, I do!" She pulled the bottom of her dress over her knee and slid a lacy blue garter down her leg. Kicking off a shoe, she completely removed the garter and handed it to him. "And you can show them this."

He laughed. If this was real—could ever be real—he'd be the happiest man on earth. She was not only the most beautiful woman on earth, she was also fun, charming and had gumption. "You sure?" he asked.

She slipped her shoe back on and took the empty condom packet. "Very."

They arrived at the plush hotel downtown a few minutes later, where Joe and Gus were standing just inside the door, grinning from ear to ear.

With her arm hooked through his, she walked straight to the two of them. Holding up the packet, she said, "Thank you both. That was so thoughtful." She slid the packet in front of the pocket square on Joe's suit, making sure the packet was visible. "A little backseat bingo is exactly what we needed."

With an astonished look, Joe lifted the packet out of his pocket. "It's empty."

"Of course it is," she said.

As Gus and Joe looked at each other, Jason twirled the garter around his index finger. "Bingo."

She giggled and leaned her head against his biceps as they walked toward the ballroom door. "Thank you, I've never seen them speechless before."

He read her eyes, the way she was looking up at him, and knew what she wanted. A kiss. Like she had in front of her cousin the other day. He had to oblige, and told himself once again that it was only for show, and that he was a very good actor.

He kept telling himself that over and over again

throughout the evening. The massive room was decorated as brilliantly as the church had been. Flowers and bows made of netting were everywhere, as were bottles of champagne that were soon filling long-stemmed glasses. The sky was the limit when it came to what her parents were spending on the event, including the impressive meal that was served before the dancing started with music performed by a live band.

Kissing her on demand when someone shouted, "Kiss!" or when she turned her face up toward him, became second nature for the next several hours; so did acting like they were truly in love and the happiest couple in the world.

He kept up the act, all the way to the end, when it was time to leave. In front of the excited crowd bidding them farewell, he scooped Randi into his arms, and carried her out the door, to the once again awaiting limo.

Chapter Fourteen

Randi stood in the bedroom, staring at the door, wondering what she should do. Nothing about the wedding could have been more perfect. It had been glamorous, beautiful and fun. The way he'd carried her out of the hotel, to the car, had been like a fairy tale.

The end of a fairy tale.

That was how they all ended, with the prince carrying his princess into happily-ever-after. That part wasn't true for her and Jason.

The ride to his house had been completely silent.

When she and her mother had started planning, her mother had suggested renting the wedding suite at the hotel for their wedding night, but Randi had declined. She hadn't wanted Tanner to be home alone all night.

She patted the dog's head, who was sitting near her feet, and glanced down at her dress.

It was gorgeous. Her mother had paid seamstresses to help with the sewing of dresses and suits the past two weeks, but not this dress. Although people often begged, her mother always refused to sew wedding gowns. She'd sewn only her own, and now this one.

The dress had long lace sleeves, a fitted bodice with

scalloped neckline, and a layered skirt that was puckered and adorned with dozens of miniature pearls. And it buttoned up the back. There was no way she could get out of it by herself.

Barefoot, because she'd removed as much as she could by herself, she left the room and headed to the basement, where Jason had disappeared upon their arrival home over half an hour ago.

He'd removed his jacket and tie, had the sleeves of his white shirt rolled to the elbows and was sitting on a stool at a large wooden workbench. He was still wearing the golden-brown silk vest and looked as handsome as he had all day.

She stepped off the bottom stair. "What are you working on?"

"Just some plans."

"For the crib and cradle?"

"No. A house. It's work."

His quick, clipped answers stung. "Is our truce over?"

"The truce included no pretending while we're alone."

It had. She pinched her lips together to prevent any sound from emitting.

"It's late," he said. "You should be in bed."

A fair amount of pity washed over her. Pity for herself. Caused in part by pretending all day. There was no one to blame but herself. "I can't unbutton my dress."

He set down the pencil and spun on the stool. "Turn around."

She turned her back to him and grasped a hold of the scalloped neckline as he started unbuttoning the row of silk-covered buttons near her waist.

Her heart was pounding by the time he undid the last button between her shoulder blades. Not only that, her body was throbbing with desire. Wedding night desires.

He didn't say a word, but she heard the stool creak as it spun back around. Silently, she walked back up the stairs, to the bedroom, and got ready for bed. It was foolish to want love when there wasn't any there. No hope for it.

Hours later, and surprised that she'd slept, Randi rolled over, checked the other side of the bed. Empty. The covers, the pillow, untouched.

She rolled onto her back and stared at the ceiling until a thud sounded in the hallway, then she threw back the covers. This was her life. She might as well start living it.

Tanner was lying outside the bedroom door, in the hallway. She gave him a quick pet and, wearing a housecoat over her nightgown and a pair of house slippers, she entered the kitchen to find Jason making coffee. He had on jeans, a white T-shirt and socks, and the mere sight of him made heat swirl deep inside her.

Hero-worship, that was what Wendy called it. Her cousin thought that hero-worship had turned into real love. Trouble was, hero-worship was always one-sided.

"Good morning," she said, walking to the refrigerator to collect the cream.

"Morning," he replied. "Coffee will be done shortly."

She closed the fridge door, and the note stuck on the front made her stomach sink. She'd nearly forgotten.

"What is brunch?" he asked.

He hadn't forgotten that they had to be at her parents' house by ten for brunch and the gift opening. "A meal between breakfast and lunch."

The look on his face was classic, and she couldn't stop a tiny laugh from escaping.

"Why would anyone need a meal between breakfast and lunch?"

"It's for those days when you don't eat breakfast or

lunch, and for special occasions," she replied while carrying the cream to the counter.

He lifted down two cups. "Like gift openings."

"Yes."

He poured coffee into both cups, handed her one and then a spoon. "You already have a room full of presents."

While adding cream and sugar to her coffee, she explained, "Those were from the bridal shower. These are wedding gifts, for both of us. After we eat brunch, we'll open them."

He was leaning against the counter and his cup paused before his face. "We?"

She nodded.

"Before or after we haul them home?"

She took a sip of coffee. "Before."

He grimaced. "I knew you were going to say that."

Giggling, she asked, "Then why did you ask?"

He emptied his cup in little more than one swallow. "Because I was hoping I was wrong."

As she watched him set the cup on the counter, she wondered when he'd been in the bedroom to get the clothes he was wearing. While she'd been sleeping, obviously, but why hadn't it awoken her? He had to have been in the closet and the dresser, and had to have let Tanner out of the room. "Look at the bright side."

He lifted a brow.

"We'll never have to buy a set of glasses, or dishes, or pots or pans, or towels or sheets, ever." She'd already received a large supply of those things for her shower. "I'm going to go get dressed. Do you need to use the bathroom first?"

He shook his head.

If there were other people here, all she'd have to do was lift her face to him and he'd kiss her. Even knowing all she did, she wanted that to happen. Then again, there was nothing different about that. She'd wanted to be kissed by him for years.

She'd vowed to marry him, too. Guess she'd proven that she couldn't have her cake and eat it, too. Carrying her coffee, she left the kitchen and after using the bathroom, returned to the bedroom to get dressed.

Hoping to look bright and cheery, she chose a shimmering pink dress with red ribbing, and red shoes. After brushing her hair, she added a wide red headband and put on a set of string pearls and earrings that her father had given her one year for Christmas.

Before they left the house, Jason changed into black pants and a white shirt under a V-neck black-and-red sweater. He looked so handsome she bit her lip to cover up a tiny moan that rumbled in her throat.

The ride across town didn't take long, and the house was already full of people. Jason's hand cupped her side as they greeted everyone, and though she knew they'd both gone into acting mode again, she found solace in the closeness they portrayed throughout the event.

"Man, I don't know how you sat through that," Joe said while lifting a box out of the trunk. "All that gushing over towels and sheets. I had to cut out, went and talked to Peter."

"Randi enjoyed it," Jason replied, trying to sound diplomatic as he grabbed a box. Truth was, he'd have sat there all day, just for the chance to have her look at him the way she did at times. With her eyes all bright and glowing.

"Good answer, Jason," Randal said, as he, too, took a box out of the trunk. "Take note, Joe, once you get married it's no longer all about you."

Joe guffawed.

"Your mother wrote thank-you notes for the entire first week we were married," Randal told Joe as they walked toward the house.

"It's going to take Randi two weeks to write notes for all this crap," Joe muttered.

Randal shot Joe a look before asking, "Do you have a certain place you want us to put all this stuff, Jason?"

"One of the spare bedrooms for now," he replied. "I'll build some shelves in the basement to store some of it. I have no idea what we'll do with five coffeepots."

Randal laughed. "Are you sure it was only five?"

"No." Jason shifted the box in his hand to unlock the front door. "I lost count after the third one."

"This is a nice house," Randal said. "I understand that you built it."

"Yes." Jason opened the door, and instantly told Tanner, "Stay."

The dog sat, tail thumping as Jason held the door open for the others to enter.

"Nice job, nice craftsmanship," Randal said, walking inside. "I like it. Good-looking dog, too."

"Thanks. That's Tanner. His bark is far worse than his bite."

"You have to see the workshop in the basement, Dad," Joe said. "It's impressive. And I warned him not to let Randi borrow tools." As he walked past, Joe added, "I didn't mention why—that she once flooded our house with only a hammer."

"Down the hall, second door on the right," Jason directed as he stepped into the house behind them.

"In her defense," Randal said, "our house is old. The plumbing had been very old."

"She took a hammer to the sink, Dad," Joe said.

Randal chuckled. "She couldn't get the water to turn off, the handle was stuck, and she thought she could just tap it with a hammer. Suffice to say, she hit it a little too hard."

"Suffice to say you had to have the entire house re-plumbed," Joe said.

"Jason won't have to worry about that happening here, everything is new." In the bedroom, which was already half full of gifts, Randal set down his box and looked around the room. "Did you hand-make all this trim work? The molding?"

Jason set down his box. "Yes." The small amount of work that it took to put up ceiling moldings was well worth it when it came to selling houses. People were willing to pay for the little extras that made his houses unique.

"It looks sharp," Randal said, "really sharp."

If the other man hadn't sounded so sincere, so truly impressed, Jason might have wondered if Randal was only saying that because he was now his father-in-law and this was the house his daughter would now be living in. "Thanks."

Randal continued to point out things he liked about the house as the three of them carried in box after box out of the car. Randal and Joe had ridden with him in his car, and Randi and her mother arrived in another car, also full, before the first one was empty.

"We packed up some of the leftover food," Randi explained as he opened the car door for her. "There was too much for them to eat, and we didn't want it to go to waste. We will carry that in first and then be back to help."

"No, stay inside where it's warm," he told her. "It won't take long for us to get everything hauled in."

After about another dozen trips, both cars were empty,

and he, Randal and Joe were shivering and blowing into their hands as they set down the last of the boxes in the bedroom.

"Come into the kitchen and have some hot coffee," Jolie said, stepping up beside her husband.

Randal put his arm around her shoulders, and Jason noted how Jolie looked up at Randal, and how Randal bent down and kissed her.

That was how Randi had perfected that look, that silent request for a kiss. She must have seen that between her parents her entire life. He'd never seen anything like that growing up. His mother and father had done little more than fight. Day in and day out.

When it came to his children, his child, he knew which one he wished they'd see, and which one they wouldn't.

Randi sidled up next to him, and shivered. "Brrr. Your coat is cold. Take it off."

Laughing and shaking his head, Joe said, "That makes sense, Sis, take off your coat because it's cold."

"It does make sense," she said. "His coat is cold on the outside."

"It's cold outside," Joe said, tossing her a sneer over his shoulder as he walked out of the room.

"Brat!" she hissed.

"Coffee sounds good," Randal said.

As her parents walked out of the room, Randi turned to follow them, and on impulse, Jason wrapped both of his arms around her from behind and pulled her back up against his chest.

She giggled and lifted her shoulder as he nuzzled the side of her neck. "Your face is cold, too."

"I know," he said. "I'm hoping you can warm me up."

She turned around, slowly, cupped his cheeks and whispered, "I'll try."

The kiss she started, and he completely gave in to, raised the temperature of his blood by a good ten degrees. Or more.

"Better?" she asked.

"Much." Questioning if he should have done that, he released her and shrugged out of his coat. "This sure is a lot of stuff."

"It is." Her face scrunched up. "I'm not sure where we are going to put it all." Her hands were on her stomach. "Eventually, we are going to need this room."

"I'll build shelves in the basement," he said, laying a hand on her back to escort her out of the room.

"But that's where your workbench is."

"That's only half of the basement. The other side is empty. I already have the wood down there. It won't take long."

"That would be wonderful! Thank you!"

Her face was alight with excitement. He was amazed that such a little thing could delight her so much. That excitement continued as they entered the kitchen.

"Mother," she said, "Jason has figured out the dilemma. He's going to build shelves in the basement. I won't even have to unbox things. Just store them down there until we need them."

"That is the perfect solution," Jolie replied.

Jason wasn't sure that Randal and Joe had been prepared to build shelves, but by the time they were done drinking their coffee, it had been decided the three of them would work on the shelves while Randi and her mother decided what should be stored on them.

He'd planned on putting shelves in that area. Had the lumber stacked in the basement, cut and ready to be assembled, but had never completed the project because he'd needed someone to hold the long boards in place while he nailed them.

It turned out to be an enjoyable project, and the stories that Randal and Joe told him about Randi during her growing-up years had them all laughing.

"You men have been laughing the entire time you've been down there," her mother shouted down the steps while they were putting away the tools. "Come upstairs and eat and tell us what's so funny!"

"Not on your life," Joe whispered. "Randi will kill me if she knows I told you about how awful her cooking was."

Randal slapped Jason's shoulder. "Don't worry. It's gotten much better."

Supper continued to be a fun family affair. Jason had known those, but only after his father had died and he'd started spending more time with his cousins. The differences between his father and Randal were stark, and embarrassing. He'd been ashamed of who he was for years, of who his father was and how his mother had left them. The humiliation of that had been tough for a kid. He'd thought he'd gotten over it but knew he hadn't. Some things were just too embedded in a person to ever go away.

After the meal the men helped him carry the boxes that Randi designated downstairs, and then the others prepared to leave.

While giving him a hug goodbye, Jolie whispered, "Thank you for making my daughter so happy."

Jason nodded, but wasn't convinced he would be able to make Randi happy. Not completely. Not ever. The time would come when she would regret marrying him. Living in his small house instead of the huge one she was used to. How could she not? There was nothing that he could ever give her that she hadn't already had.

"I'm sorry that took all day," Randi said as he closed the door. "But the good news is that the bedroom is cleared out except for a stack of towels that I want to wash before putting away."

Last night when they'd arrived home, he'd headed straight to the basement, because the want to carry her into the bedroom had been overwhelming, and was feeling much the same right now. Taking her to bed again would only make him want her more, want it to happen again and again.

"Jason?"

Giving his head a clearing shake, he said, "That sounds good, about the room, the towels." Then, needing an excuse, and escape, he walked past her. "There's a shelf in the basement that I need to reinforce. There are some heavy things on it."

"Do you need any help?"

"No. None."

Chapter Fifteen

Randi forced herself not to follow Jason as he disappeared into the kitchen. Every time they were alone, he didn't even want to be in the same room as her. If this was a work issue, she'd walk up to him and lay down how things are going to be, period. She'd had to learn to fight her own battles and wasn't afraid to do so, but this was so different. She didn't want to fight with him.

Feeling the frustration clear to her bones, she walked down the hall into the bedroom to collect items to take a bath before going to bed.

Reclined in the tub, with her eyes closed and fully submerged in warm water, she could hear the pounding of a hammer below her, in the basement. If only...

What? If only she wasn't pregnant?

She didn't wish that.

She laid her hands on her stomach, thinking about exactly how that had happened. Every aspect, and a groan rumbled in her throat as heat swirled inside her and specific parts tingled with their own memories, creating desires she couldn't control.

The ringing of the phone shot her upright. She'd forgotten to call Wendy, set up a time to meet her cousin before she flew out tomorrow.

Leaping out of the tub, she grabbed a towel to wrap around her torso as she hurried to answer the phone.

She pulled open the door, rushed into the hallway and collided with something hard. It took a brief second to realize it was Jason she'd run into, who'd caught her by her arms.

Jason without a shirt on.

Her palms were plastered against his bare flesh, and her mind instantly returned to where it had been in the bathtub. So did her body. She had to swallow against how certain muscles contracted.

She could feel the rise and fall of his chest, of how his breathing quickened.

"Are you okay?" he asked.

She wasn't, but nodded.

He released his hold on her. "The phone—" He stopped because the ringing had stopped.

Not sure what to do, she pressed her hands harder against his chest, pushing herself backward as she took a step back, separating them. The action wasn't thought out. Without her holding it up, her towel fell, exposing her breasts. Exposing all of her.

They both acted at the same time, bending down to retrieve the towel, and smacked heads so hard it sent them both stumbling backward, against the walls of the hallway, with the towel on the floor between them.

He bent down, picked up the towel and as he straightened, mumbled something.

Randi wasn't sure what, but didn't care, either, because then his lips were on hers. His hands cupping her face, holding it as his tongue entered her mouth, igniting the flames that had been smoldering inside her for weeks.

A storm erupted, one of passion, of unmet desires, needs that had been building every time they'd kissed, touched, the past several days. It was mutual, his hands were as frantic as hers, touching, feeling, caressing.

He was the only man she'd ever craved, ever wanted, but had never known something could overtake a person so fully. Nor had she ever known such desperation. Nothing else mattered. Just this. Him and her, coming together. She found the waistband of his pants, unfastened them.

"Randi—"

She stopped him from saying more by covering his mouth with hers. It would be impossible to live with him and never kiss him, never— She pulled her mouth off his, took a step back. Her breathing was coming hard and fast, so were her thoughts. "I know you don't love me, Jason. I don't expect you to, but we are married, and married people have sex."

Silent, he stared at her.

She couldn't read his face, didn't know what he was thinking, but kept her chin up, even as her insides began to tremble. Their marriage had to have something or it would never last. "We both have needs and there's no reason for us not to satisfy them."

He let out a low growl, picked her up and carried her into the bedroom. They landed on the bed together, arms locked around one another and kissing wildly.

A crinkling sound reminded her that she still had on her shower cap. Any other time, that might have embarrassed her, at how she must look, but Jason didn't seem to care. Therefore, neither did she.

His hand was between her legs, teasing her, pleasing her, making her body feel fully alive, but it wasn't enough. She knew the full pleasure of having him inside her and nothing except that would ever be enough. "Now, Jason. Please."

He separated them long enough to remove his pants.

During that time, because even the cap felt like a restraint keeping them apart, she tore off her shower cap.

"You are so beautiful," he whispered as he lowered himself on top of her, entering her at the same time.

Overwhelmed with the pleasure, she couldn't speak. Memories and instinct had already taken over. She met his hips with hers, thrust for thrust. Met his lips kiss for kiss. The perfect connection and friction of their bodies made tension grow inside her like a balloon getting bigger and bigger. Every stroke of him moving inside her thrilled her more and more, knowing she would soon reach her limit.

She bit down on her lip, trying to hold off, because she didn't want this to stop. Not yet. It was too wonderful. He smelled so good, felt so good. It was enough to make her believe there could be hope for their marriage. But that wasn't what this was about. This was just him and her, and what they had right now.

The tension reached its peak inside her, she arched into him, held on to him and welcomed the burst of pleasure that consumed her.

During that moment she comprehended it wasn't the pleasure, the act of making love, that thrilled her, it was the fact that neither of them was pretending. At this moment everything between them was real.

Jason refused to let anything else in while losing himself in bringing Randi to full pleasure. She'd wanted him, needed him, and despite knowing it wasn't going to change anything, he couldn't deny giving her exactly what she'd wanted.

He'd wanted it, too, and the pleasure of being inside her, of having her warm wetness cloaking him, the smell of her surrounding him, was beyond bliss. It was out of this world like nothing he'd ever known.

Her body tightened, clenched onto him and then shuddered as she gasped, moaned his name.

It was his undoing and he succumbed to the waves of pleasure that washed over him as his release hit, and lingered, sucking all of the strength out of his body until he felt completely spent. Completely satisfied. Completely content.

She made him feel like that. Content. She made him feel other things, too. Things he'd never felt before. At times that made him feel helpless, like he was sinking into an abyss, and if he went too deep, he'd never be able to climb out.

It was a struggle, because he wasn't sure that he wanted to climb out.

Still breathing hard, he rolled off her, knowing that any moment now regret would strike. For her sake, he wished he were someone else. Someone who could love her, provide for her, in the way she deserved.

She snuggled up to his side, kissed his shoulder blade, laid a hand on his chest. "Don't leave. Please. Stay here next to me."

He covered her hand with his, squeezed it.

She kissed his shoulder blade again, then rested her cheek there and sighed sweetly.

Jason lay there, half wishing he'd stayed in the basement, and half-glad that he hadn't. He'd figured she was in the bathroom when he saw the door had been closed.

He'd decided to take advantage of the empty bedroom and change out of his shirt and sweater, and put on a T-shirt, fully prepared to sleep on the couch again tonight. That was where he'd be right now, if the phone hadn't rung, and if she hadn't barreled out of the bathroom like the house was on fire at the same time that he'd left the bedroom.

She'd looked so adorable with that bright pink-and-white polka-dotted plastic cap covering her hair, wearing nothing but a towel. He'd gone hard instantly, and when her towel had fallen to the floor, he'd started throbbing like nobody's business.

The rest had been inevitable. The past few days of kissing and hugging had left them both with unmet needs. He hadn't wanted to complicate things more than they already were, but that was impossible. And they were married, going to have a baby together. A little tiny life, a child, who would deserve to grow up happy, being loved and not wanting for anything.

Like she had.

He could make that happen for their baby. He would make that happen. The baby would have everything that he'd never had. That included a mother. For the baby's sake, for Randi's sake, he had to do everything he could for them.

Lifting her hand, he kissed her fingers that were curled around his.

She let out a soft, sweet-sounding little moan, and then rolled so that portion of her upper body was lying across a section of his chest. Running her fingers through his hair, she looked him in the eye. "I didn't plan a honeymoon because I didn't know what we'd do with Tanner."

Blood rushed to his groin so fast air hitched in his lungs. "He could stay with Lottie and Stu." Her hair was flowing over the front of her shoulders, hiding her breasts from his sight. But he could feel them. One against his upper arm, the other against his chest. Sucking in a breath of air, he asked, "Where had you wanted to go?"

"Nowhere in particular." She hooked a leg over his thigh. "Where would you have wanted to go?"

"Nowhere in particular."

Still combing her fingers through his hair, she asked, "Could you have taken the time off work?"

Parts of him were starting to throb, jolt. "Yes, I could spare a few days. What about you?"

"I already took this week off work, I thought there would be things I'd need to do."

"Like what?"

She wiggled her hips closer to his. "Putting things away, writing thank-you notes, little things like that."

"Do you want to go somewhere?"

She kissed the side of his jaw. "Packing, traveling, would take time."

He was following her thoughts completely, and her actions. "And we'd have to drop off Tanner."

"He might get lonely for you."

Jason ran his hand down her back. "And you."

She giggled, and slid a bit more of her body on top of his. "We could have a honeymoon here."

He was more than ready for round two. Grasping her hips, he lifted her, settled her body on top of his. "Starting when?"

She tapped her chin. "I'm not sure. When do you think we should start?"

He ran his hands down her sides, across her lower back. Their game of questions was intensifying every touch. "Probably not now."

She wiggled against him, kissed the side of his neck. "Probably not."

"And probably not like this." He reached between them, guided himself into her and wasn't sure which was more gratifying, entering her slick heat, or watching the way her eyelids fluttered.

Arching upward slowly, she lowered onto him fully. "Probably not."

He began to move. "Or like this."

"Or like this." Rising and lowering, she matched his every movement.

Her face glowed with the pleasure she was receiving and giving. He took it slow, taking time to fully experience every nuance, but before long they were both breathing hard, working together to reach their completion.

Knowing she was as close as he was he covered her mouth with his, kissed her deeply as completion struck, shrouding them in intense pleasure.

First thing the following morning he called Stu, told him to let the crews know that he was taking the week off, and that they could call him if needed, but he hoped they wouldn't. Other than later that day, when her cousins and brother stopped by to say goodbye before flying back to school, he and Randi were in full honeymoon mode.

The entire week was one that Jason figured would have fulfilled every man's dream. The closeness and familiarity that grew between them enhanced all aspects of living together. Including in the bedroom. Randi was not only receptive, she was also adventurous and demanding in a way that not only suited him, it thrilled him as well.

She was spontaneous, too. Showed it by joining him in the shower, sitting down next to him on the sofa wearing nothing but a robe and bringing him breakfast in bed stark naked.

More than once, the thank-you cards that he helped

her complete by licking stamps and envelopes had been left on the table as other needs overtook them.

He enjoyed listening to her sing along to the radio as she cooked, her body swaying to the rock-and-roll songs, and how when a particular favorite song of hers would come on she'd make him dance with her. He'd soon learned that many songs were particular favorites of hers.

They left the house a few times, to go out and eat and buy groceries, but for the most part, they stayed home, ate, slept and made love.

He couldn't say he was pretending, and neither was she, yet it felt that way, as if they were playing house with adult actions.

Lots of real adult actions.

So real that when the following Monday rolled around, they were both so used to staying up late, enjoying each other, they overslept.

It was a mad dash of dressing, brushing teeth and eating toast while drinking coffee. The only time they slowed was for a long, leisurely kiss in the garage before they climbed into separate vehicles and left for work.

At the parking lot of the apartment complex he was remodeling, Jason climbed out of his truck, tossed his keys in the air and caught them while closing the door.

Then the location hit him, and it was like being hit with a bucket of cold water. He remembered the day he'd watched Randi walk to her car. A week later he'd found out she was pregnant with his child.

A shiver rippled his spine. She'd become a part of his life since then. A major part of his life, but nothing else had changed. Nothing about him.

The passion between them was electrifying, but that wouldn't always be enough.

Chapter Sixteen

Randi was on cloud nine. An entire week of living with Jason had been exactly as she'd dreamed it would be for years. She even smiled at and said good morning to Sam—after she'd dropped off a stack of thank-you notes in the mail room—which made her laugh, because he'd done little more than scowl at her.

She was still going through phone messages when her father entered her office. Jumping to her feet, she met him in the center of the room, returned his hug and kissed his cheek.

"You're looking more radiant than ever," he said.

"Just happy."

"Then I'm happy, too." He lifted a brow. "Other than the fact that, since seeing your house, your mother is talking about having Jason build us a new house."

"I might be able to pull some strings." Pride filled her as she walked around her desk and sat in her chair. "But it will be a long wait. He's juggling several job sites at the moment. Besides building a couple of houses, he's remodeling an apartment building downtown."

"He told me about that while putting up the shelves in your basement." Her father sat down across from her desk.

"Thank you for that, Dad. Thank you for everything."

"You're welcome. It was my pleasure and your mother's." He leaned back, glanced around the room. "Were you surprised to see this place still standing after being gone over a week?"

"No, I knew it would be fine. You were here."

"And others."

She'd expected this to be coming when she'd returned from California. Other things had taken precedence.

"I know you and Sam haven't always seen eye to eye," her father continued. "And I've talked to him about a few issues lately, but if you're interested in running this place someday—"

"Of course I am," she interrupted. "Why wouldn't I be?"

"You're married now, with a husband to consider and a baby on the way."

"That's not going to change anything. Jason doesn't expect me to quit my job. Mom worked while Joey and I were growing up."

"I know. That was a decision that she and I came to together, as all of our decisions have been."

"Jason and I will—"

"That," he said, cutting her off, "will be between you and Jason. What I want to talk about is you. If you do end up overseeing things here, you need to realize what an asset Sam will be to you. He's been here a long time. He can be brash and opinionated, but he knows what he's doing. There's not a dime that rolls in or out of this place that he can't account for, and I rely on that. Whoever is overseeing things will need to rely on that, too."

She'd had talking-tos from her father before, and a part of her knew she needed to hear this. Yet, at the same time, she wanted her father to understand her frustration. "I know he's great at accounting, and I'll try harder to appreciate that. But I believe we can do other things that if done right, will not only cut costs in some areas, but could increase overall revenue."

"A washing bay?"

"Yes."

"On Jason's land."

"No. I admit, I considered that, but then did more research. That's why I went to California. Not just to visit our ticket sales office there, but to look at land. If we were to build a bay there, we could not only wash our planes at a significant savings, we could wash planes for other airlines."

Elbows on the arms of the chairs, he tapped his fingers together, an action he was known to do. "Land costs? Construction costs?"

"I've put estimates together. It'll be an investment, but one we should be able to recoup in three years." She'd heard numerous times about how, when he'd bought the original plane company from Carl Jansen, he'd expected it to take five years to recoup and start generating income. It hadn't taken him that long, and it wouldn't take her three years to recoup the costs of the bay, either. "The preliminary numbers could shift slightly once we actually buy the land and contract the construction, but not by much."

"What about the companies that wash our planes now? And those of other airlines?"

Frowning, she asked, "What about them?"

"Have you spoken to any of them? Remaining competitive is important, but while doing so, it's imperative that you think of the overall industry. We've worked with some of the companies a washing bay would affect for years. They depend on our business to meet their goals, just like we depend on them to make ours. Receiving without giving never works out in the long run. Not in business, or life. It has to balance out, honey, everything does."

She understood what he was saying, and hadn't looked as deeply into things as she should have, but she would. "You're right. I'll look into that. Put some more planning in place before going any further."

"Take your time." He gestured toward her desk as he stood. "You have a lot of work to catch up on, so I'll let you be."

Although she was disappointed, she'd rather have learned mistakes now than later. "Thanks, Dad. I was getting ahead of myself."

With a nod, he winked at her and walked to the door. Before opening it, he said, "Your mother will be calling you later, wants to know if you and Jason could join us for dinner one night this week."

"Okay." She picked up her messages again, to start reading through them. "Any night will work."

"She's going to ask you to check with Jason, and I suggest you do."

"I will, but I know any night will be fine."

He acted as if he was going to say something more, but didn't.

She stared at the door for a moment, wondering what he hadn't said, until she figured the dinner date was to let them know he'd chosen the date to announce his bid for senate. That had to be it.

As she turned back to her messages, she thought of one thing her father had said. That everything had to balance. Give and take. Jason had given her everything, but she hadn't given him anything. She didn't have anything to give. Didn't own anything.

She stood, moved to the window and stared out it. The

only thing she could give him would be proof that she didn't want his land.

Her phone rang, she answered it, listened to the fire brewing over the backlog in licenses being renewed and promised to see to it right away.

The good thing about all the work that had piled up was it made the day fly by, and as if they'd timed each other, she and Jason arrived at the turn onto his street, each from a different direction, at the same time. He waved for her to go first, and when they arrived at his garage, he jumped out of his truck, told her to stay put as he opened the garage door.

A mutual welcome-home kiss was shared before they left the garage, and Tanner greeted them as soon as they entered the backyard. Jason asked about her day as they walked to the house. She told him about a few things, but not the washing bay or talking with her father, and then asked about his day.

He told her that a representative for an investment company had stopped by the apartment building, interested in buying the property once it was completed.

"That's wonderful," she said.

"Maybe, but we'd make more money in the long run by renting out the apartments."

"That's true, but you'd have the expense of managing the renters."

He said he was aware of that and they continued to discuss the options, along with a few other subjects while preparing supper. She also told him that her parents would like them to come over for dinner one night this week.

"I can make any night work," he said. "Whatever is good for you."

She kissed him. "I knew you'd say that. Should I tell them Friday?"

He kept his arms around her. "Friday will be fine." He kissed her again. And again. Until supper was forgotten and she was too happy to care.

The bliss filling her remained all week, and well into the month of March, until Sam walked into her office one morning and tossed an old expense report on her desk. "All flight tickets need to be approved by the immediate supervisor. Your ticket to California wasn't. Without approval, the ticket price will be deducted from your next paycheck."

Her immediate supervisor was her father, and she had never needed to get a ticket approved before. A single ticket was not the issue he was making it out to be, and she wasn't going to make it be, either. "All right. Take it out of my pay."

He stared blankly for a moment, then sneered. "Your father gave up on the Heim land years ago. The cost of keeping a washing bay heated during our winters would be counterproductive."

Her spine quivered. "Exactly what is your point?"

He shrugged, turned, but stopped at the door. "Does your father know you married Heim just for his land? Or is it the other way around? He married you for what he can get?"

Anger filled her and she jumped to her feet, but he was already gone. Grabbing the expense report, she balled it up and threw it at the door, then her knees gave out. Sam was an ass, knew how to strike a nerve, but that was too close to home.

That afternoon Sam's comment was still twisting her mind in knots. Jason was also in those knots. She'd thought she could deal with him not loving her. That what they had was enough, but was it? Would everyone think like Sam did? That the only reason Jason had married her... No, they'd soon learn it was because she'd been pregnant.

Her door opened and her father stepped in. "Got a minute to talk?"

She tried to clear her mind. "Sure."

"Are you okay?"

"Yes." She tapped the stack of papers on her desk. "Just have a lot going on."

"I want to discuss a couple of decisions I've made," her father said.

"Okay." Hands clasped, she set them on her desk. She'd been in contact with several other airlines about her California washing bay, and was proud of the collaborative efforts that were now in place. Her father would be impressed when it all came together. There was still a lot to do, but she was feeling even better about it than before. Especially after Sam's comment. Once she was his supervisor, she'd put Sam in his place. But that wouldn't help the issue between her and Jason.

"Your mother and I started this business shortly after we got married," her father said while sitting down in front of her desk. "It would never have been this successful without her. We started her clothing business at the same time, and found out she was pregnant with you in the midst of it all. Every decision we made, we made together, and after we found out you were on the way, we agreed on the importance of hiring people to help us with both companies, because dedicating time to each other and to you and Joe was always at the top of our list. My bid for senate is a decision we both made, too. Win or lose, we are in it together."

"I know you'll win, Dad, and that you'll do good things for our country."

"I hope to." He leaned forward, set his hands on the top of her desk. "You are a great asset to this company, and I'll be extremely proud to see you at the helm of it."

Her heart skipped a beat.

"Someday."

A hint of shiver tickled her spine.

"I want you to know that on Saturday, when I announce my run for senate, Wayne Klein will be in attendance." He paused for a moment. "I'll be announcing that he'll be the interim president until I make a more final decision after the election in November."

Her heart sank and she forced herself to sit straight, to breathe. Wayne Klein oversaw flight acquisitions and sales and was not someone she would have considered for the position.

"I know that's a disappointment to you, and I'm afraid this next one is going to be, too."

She lifted her chin.

"I want you to put off the washing bay project. Wait until next year. You have a lot happening in your life, and should be enjoying this time, not making extra work for yourself."

Put off the washing bay? She couldn't do that. She had to open that bay in California to prove to Jason that she doesn't want or need his land. Prove to others, too.

"As long as I'm here," Jason said to the banker, Adam Freeman, "I wanted to let you know that I've added a name on the title of my land." He'd borrowed against the land in order to buy the apartment building downtown, and while at the courthouse, paying taxes on the building, he had them add Randi's name to all of his properties.

"Always good to have things in order. We appreciate you letting us know. Let me get your file." Freeman pushed a button on the phone, requested the file through an intercom system and clicked off the button. "How is the remodeling of the apartment building going?"

"Ahead of schedule, planning on having tenants in the building by June instead of August," Jason replied. "I just stopped by to make a payment on my loan, but like I said, thought I'd go ahead and have you note the name change." He only had a few payments left, but if anything were to happen to him, he wanted things in Randi's name. His worth wasn't close to her father's, and he certainly wasn't planning on anything happening to him, but when his father had died, he'd had to jump through hoops to hold on to the property and get it changed into his name. That had been due to owed back taxes, which he'd kept current ever since.

"I was down near that building a couple of weeks ago. Prime location. With the shortage of housing right now, that could be a real moneymaker."

"I'm counting on that," Jason replied. He'd declined the offer to sell the building to the investment group. He'd bought it with the long-term plan of it generating a regular income. That had been his plan when he built his first house, to rent it out, but the first people to look at it wanted to buy it instead. He'd sold it to them, and invested that money in the next one and so on and so on. He didn't need that quick turnaround of cash now. His company had a solid, comfortable base and the only reason he didn't pay off the loan on the land was because it kept an open line of credit if he needed it. That had taken years to build up. Though the land was worth it, the banker had been cautious of loaning him more than a portion of the value.

A woman entered the office and laid a file on Freeman's desk and left as quietly as she'd entered.

Freeman, a middle-aged man with salt-and-pepper hair and thick, black-rimmed glasses, flipped open the folder and shuffled through the papers. "Here it is. What name have you added?"

"Randi, spelled R-A-N-D-I. Last name Heim."

Freeman's frown grew as he wrote the name. "Randi, that's a unique name. I've only heard it once before. A local girl."

"Randi Osterlund."

"You've heard of her?" Freeman asked.

Jason had to hold back his grin. "I married her." Married life had suited him well the past few weeks. Coming home to her every night and waking up next to her was paradise. One he didn't want to disrupt.

Freeman's brows were raised. "I heard she got married. Congratulations."

"Thank you." Jason stood. "And thanks for adding her name to that."

"Wait a minute." Freeman held up a hand. "Looking at your loan here…"

"Is there a problem?"

"No, other than we certainly can increase the amount, and I'm sure we can do something about the interest rate as well."

Jason gritted his teeth together at the quiver that raced over his neck. Three years ago he'd practically had to beg to get the loan. "No, I'll have it paid off shortly."

"Well, perhaps there's another project you're looking at? Another apartment complex? We could write up the loan today, deposit it into your account, so it's there when you need it."

Jason would bet the Osterlunds didn't bank here, and

Freeman would love to have them as customers. Them. Not him. "No, that's not necessary."

Freeman closed the file. "I understand your financial situation has changed since your wedding, but our bank has enjoyed doing business with you, and hope you will continue utilizing our service."

Jason had to pull his jaw apart to say, "Have a good day."

He left Freeman's office, left the bank, and once in his truck, pushed the hot air out of his lungs. Freeman had merely been doing his job of drumming up business for the bank. That didn't surprise him, nor had Freeman's comment.

He'd spent years digging himself out of the poor house he'd been born in, and before that he'd spent years hardening his heart. He'd had to. Watching his parents verbally tear each other apart day after day, night after night, had been hell. The two, the lack of money and the fighting, had merged into one, making him into who he'd become. It had also provided him with the ability to build an armor around himself, one strong enough that everything bounced off him. Except for one thing.

Randi had put a kink in that armor years ago. Even from afar, she'd touched something deep inside him. Made him want things, dream of a different life, to the point he'd given in, and had failed. Ended up in reform school.

He'd rebuilt that armor, swore he'd never be that weak again, never give someone that much control over him again, but once again, she'd put a kink in his defenses the day she'd shown up at his house asking to buy his land.

Since then she'd completely penetrated the armor he'd built around himself. He could feel her inside him, all the time. Her smile, her touch, her sighs of pleasure, were like sledgehammers battering that armor until she'd gotten inside him.

That scared him. If he couldn't protect himself, how could he protect her? Not from him, but from his reputation, his past. Which were one and the same.

Jason started the truck.

He'd already failed to protect her by getting her pregnant.

With his gut churning, Jason shifted the truck into gear and headed toward his accountant's office to give her the receipts for the taxes and loan payment. He'd hired Brenda Owens to do all of his book work three years ago, and it had been the best move he'd made.

For his business.

If only he could get his personal life in order.

It had been in order, had been rowing along just fine. Until Randi had shown up out of the blue. Is that how she'd leave, too? He'd come home to an empty house one day. Have to learn how to live without her like he'd had to learn to live without his mother. Randi didn't need to leave him for a rich man. She had more wealth at her fingertips than he'd ever have.

At some point she'd get tired of him.

Of all the pretending.

Living with her was amazing. All parts of it. But it was pretend.

Her car wasn't in the garage or the driveway when he arrived home, but the phone was ringing. Concerned, he rushed inside to answer it.

"Hey, Jason, it's Gus, how are you doing?"

Jason was relieved and frustrated at the same time. It

was past the normal time she usually got home. "Fine. You?"

"Can't complain. I got Randi's message, is she there?"

"No." He glanced at the back door. "She's not home from work yet."

"I just called her office, there was no answer." Gus paused before asking, "Will you be coming to California with her?"

Jason's entire body went stiff. "No."

"That's a drag. Maybe next time. Tell Randi I'll call her tomorrow."

Knots were forming in Jason's stomach. "I will."

"Thanks! Later, gator."

"Later." Jason hung up the phone and stilled himself, trying to keep his thoughts at bay. Her father had said a washing bay, here or in California, wasn't on the agenda right now, yet she must be pursuing it. There was no other reason for her to go to California. If she'd defy her father, she'd defy anyone. Especially him. And what did Gus have to do with it?

He'd been jealous of Gus for years. Not because of Albright's money, but because of the fact that Randi had always been with Gus. She claimed it was because of their families' friendship, but friends could become more a whole lot easier than enemies could.

He didn't want to jump to conclusions and wouldn't. They were married. There had to be a modicum of trust between them. Trust. Not love. Their marriage wasn't based on love.

It wasn't based on trust, either.

It was based on sex. The outcome of sex. No matter how amazing that was, it wasn't a solid foundation. Or enough to keep her happy.

Tanner barked and shot out the doggie door.

Jason walked to the door, held it open as she walked toward the house. His body reacted to seeing her, filled with a familiar warmth that he had no control over.

"Hi." She held up a bag. "I stopped at the meat market. How do pork chops sound for supper?"

"Fine."

She arrived at the door. Kissed him before walking inside. "How long have you been home?"

"Just a few minutes." He closed the door.

"That's why you still have your coat on." She set the bag on the table and unbuttoned her coat.

He removed his coat and took hers, hung them both up in the laundry room. "Gus called for you."

She stiffened and paused in emptying the bag.

He leaned against the wall, crossed his arms. "He tried your office first."

"Okay. Thanks." She lifted out a package of wrapped meat. "Baked or fried?"

Any other day, he'd be helping her, but today he forced himself to stay put. "Doesn't matter."

She lifted out a few other items, carried them to the refrigerator. "How was your day?"

"Fine. Yours?"

"It was fine. I think I'll bake the pork chops and some potatoes."

He pushed off the wall to cross the room and help her. "Gus mentioned you going back out to California."

She stood with the fridge door open for a few seconds before closing it. "Possibly. I won't know for a while. Maybe you could go with me. See a drag race or ride Gus's motorcycle along the coast."

She'd just come up with that. He could tell by the way she was fidgeting.

The phone rang and the way she nearly ran across the room to answer it, confirmed there was something going on. Something she didn't want him to know about.

Chapter Seventeen

Randi's relief at hearing Lottie's voice was massive. After listening, she said, "Just a minute, I'll ask Jason." Covering the mouthpiece, she told him, "It's Lottie. Everyone is meeting at Mama's for hamburgers in an hour. She wants to know if we can join them."

He shrugged. "I don't care."

"We'll be there," she told Lottie, and hung up the phone. "I'm going to change my clothes."

He nodded while putting the package of pork chops in the fridge.

She questioned telling him about her day, about her plans to continue with the washing bay project, but despite how wonderful things were going between them, they were pretending. The only time they weren't was when they were making love. There were no barriers between them then.

But there was something missing. She could feel it. Knew what it was.

Love.

He didn't love her, and he didn't want her to love him. Therefore, she wouldn't. She'd save all of her love for their baby. But she'd still prove that she didn't want his land.

No matter what her father said, she wasn't going to give up on that project. He could appoint anyone he wanted to oversee the company. In a way, he was right. She wasn't ready for that commitment. Didn't have time. She had to get this washing bay built, in California.

After quickly changing into a pair of hem-cuffed blue jeans and blue paisley-print blouse, she brushed her hair into a ponytail, secured it with a white scarf and put on a pair of black-and-white saddle shoes.

As the radio filled the car with rock-and-roll music while they drove to the café, her thoughts continued to twist and turn. Everything from wondering if their baby would have Jason's amazing brown eyes to estimating how quickly she could find a construction company in California to build the washing bay. Gus had connections out there, and she was counting on him helping her.

The moment they walked into the café, all of her other thoughts vanished and she grabbed a hold of Jason's arm. "Look at her!"

Jason nodded and swallowed, as if he couldn't speak. Together, they rushed to where Rachelle, fitted with leg braces and using crutches, stood near a booth.

"The doctor said it's time I can start walking again," Rachelle exclaimed. As if further explanation was needed about her wearing her flower girl dress, she added, "Mom said I could wear my wedding dress to celebrate."

Kneeling down in front of her, Jason gave Rachelle a hug. "This certainly requires a celebration."

Randi hugged Rachelle as soon as he released the girl. "Yes, it does, and you look so beautiful!"

The party became a real celebration with food and dancing—that included Rachelle, albeit for only a short time because just standing with the braces tired her out after not being able to use her legs for so many months.

That didn't stop the little girl from making the most of the evening, though, nor anyone else, and the party was still on Randi's mind the following day as she drove home from work.

Jason's entire family accepted her, treated her like family, but they had to know her family was the reason why he'd been sent to reform school. Had they forgiven her because they thought he loved her? Would that all change when the truth came out? It would eventually. Once the baby was born, anyone who could count would figure out why they'd gotten married.

That thought hung on, stuck in her head. Left her unable to think of anything else.

Later that night, after they'd climbed into bed, she couldn't remain silent and flipped on her side, stared at the moonlit shape of his back as he lay on his side, facing away from her. "Jason?"

"Hmm?"

"Did you ever think of getting married? Before I became pregnant," she quickly added.

He lay there, silent for a moment, and then flipped onto his back, looked at her and then at the ceiling. "I never thought I would get married."

Her heart sank a bit more. "Why?"

"Probably because of my mother."

"Because of how she left?"

He nodded. "I guess a lot of people get tired of who they are at some point in their life. What they'd once wanted changes and they get stuck. Trapped. Feel they have to get out."

She swallowed and the lump in her throat nearly choked her. Trapped. That was what their marriage had done to him. Trapped him.

Tears pressed hard and knowing she couldn't keep

them at bay, she kicked the covers off, flung her legs off the bed.

"Where are you going?" he asked.

"The bathroom," she managed to say on her way to the door.

Once inside the bathroom, she leaned the back of her head against the door, closed her eyes and kept them closed until the burning eased. Until she could swallow. Until she could breathe.

"Randi? Are you all right in there?"

She shot across the room and flushed the toilet even though she hadn't used it. "I'm fine."

"You didn't even turn on the light."

After crossing the room again, she opened the door. "Didn't need to. There's a window."

"It's dark outside."

She entered the bedroom and crawled back into bed. "Not that dark." It was far darker inside her.

He got under the covers, curled an arm around her waist. "Are you okay?"

Her body reacted to his touch. That wasn't pretend. Her body craved him. Worse yet, so did her heart. Could she go on pretending that wasn't the case? Forever? That thought hurt. Badly.

The following evening, at a dinner party where her father announced he was running for senate to the wider group of the Osterlunds' friends and family, Randi realized just how big the trap was that she'd put Jason in. She'd been in it her entire life.

She'd been trying to escape it her entire life, too. Though her parents were amazing people and her home life wonderful, she had always felt trapped, confined. That that was the way she had to live. Not dictated by her parents, but from outside forces because of their social standing. Everyone always expected something from them.

She loved her parents and was proud of them, proud to be their daughter. Her family were the only people who loved her for who she was, and all this pretending that Jason was now having to do, too, was eating away at her.

Beneath the table, he grasped a hold of her hand, bringing her attention back to what was happening just in time to hear her father announce that Wayne Klein would be filling in for him at Air America for the time being.

But not even that held her attention. As his fingers threaded through hers, her mind went completely to him. This was all so unfair to him.

So very unfair.

"I'm sorry things didn't turn out like you wanted," Jason said while backing out of the driveway. He'd tried to get her out of there as soon as possible after her father had mentioned she wouldn't be taking over the helm of Air America. He knew it had to be a great disappointment.

"It was my father's choice."

She hadn't seemed to be surprised, or overly upset by the announcement, and he could guess why. "I take it he told you about his decision in advance."

She stared out the side window. "Yes, he did."

"When?"

"Earlier this week." She sighed. "Wayne will do a good job."

Taking over at Air America was her dream. If he'd have leased her his land, that might have happened tonight.

The rest of the ride home was completed in silence, as was the walk into the house. He took off his coat and reached to help her, but wrapped his arms around her instead. "I know you're disappointed—"

"Stop." She pushed his hands aside and stepped out of his reach. "We're alone. You don't have to pretend to—" She shook her head. "We don't have to pretend."

He took a step back, held his hands up at his sides. "Okay."

She kept her back to him. "I'm not as good at it as you."

He thought of the past few weeks, of their lovemaking. "You're wrong about that."

She turned, faced him. "This isn't going to work, Jason. It's just not."

"We don't have a choice of it not working. You're pregnant. Or have you forgotten that?"

"Of course I haven't forgotten that! How could I? It's the reason you married me."

That may be true, but there was far more that she wasn't saying. "Just because you didn't get the job you wanted right now doesn't mean—"

"Air America has nothing to do with this."

He was still mad at himself for what he'd said in bed last night, about being trapped. Her question about getting married had caught him off guard, and he hadn't been able to tell her the truth. That she'd been the reason he'd thought he'd never get married. Every woman he'd ever dated he'd compared to her, and they'd come up lacking. Therefore, he'd never thought he would get married.

But he was married and he hated arguing. Didn't want to argue with her, but was growing more frustrated by the minute. "It has everything to do with it. It's the reason you showed up on my doorstep in the first place."

She threw her hands in the air. "And ended up pregnant and trapped you into marrying me!"

"I didn't say you trapped me." No one on earth would

believe that. "It's the other way around. The richest girl in high school marrying the poorest boy."

"You aren't poor! And I'm not rich."

He may no longer be poor, but she was still rich. "Yeah, right."

"I'm not. My parents are rich, but I'm not. It's no different than your father was poor, but you're not."

Tired of that subject, of the entire argument, he said, "It doesn't matter. The fact is we are married and we are going to have a baby. So what are we going to do about it?"

She ran her hand through her hair. "I don't know. I just know I can't go on pretending we're in love when we aren't. Pretending everything is fine, when it's not."

Bingo. It was only a matter of time before she left. "Okay, then we don't pretend."

She stared at him for a long, somber moment. "Including when we are alone."

A sudden need for air struck and he pulled off the tie around his neck. He'd worn a suit and tie more in the past two months than he had his entire prior life. That was as fake as everything else. "Fine."

She spun around and marched out of the room.

Tanner got up off the floor, where he'd been lying, and followed her out of the room.

Jason squeezed his temples with one hand, wishing there was something he could say, something he could do, but there wasn't. It would all be for naught. He'd expected this. Her to get tired of it all.

He slept on the sofa that night, and the next night because no stores were open on Sunday, but first thing Monday morning, he went to the furniture store, bought a bed and hauled it home, set it up in one of the spare bedrooms.

Their marriage became another masquerade. This time

of not speaking, not even seeing each other, except for bumping into each other on mornings when she'd venture into the kitchen before he'd left for work. He tried to leave prior to her waking each morning, and each evening he stayed late, long after sending the crews home at the apartment building or the houses. There was always something that he could do by himself.

People noticed, and questioned him working every night and weekends, especially Stu, but he was the boss, therefore, no one pressed him for more of an explanation than he was willing to give. Not wanting Randi to be blamed for his shortcomings, the reasons he gave often related to her father's campaign. That she was doing something for it. Which she did on a regular basis.

So did he, and oddly enough he found solace in spending time with Randal. He accompanied his father-in-law to union meetings and job sites, listening to questions about laws and regulations that workers felt would benefit them and their families. Randal was serious about helping people and committed to making changes nationwide that would do just that. Jason had learned how down-to-earth and sincere Randal was, and knew if anyone could make a difference, it would be his father-in-law.

It all gave him food for thought, and the ability to look at things differently than he had in the past. Money wasn't the root of all evil. It was the love of money that was. When used in the right ways, everyone benefited.

Being with Randal also helped Jason with what he was missing most.

Randi.

Randal had all sorts of tales about her, when she'd been young, and it seemed like that was the only connection Jason had to her right now.

Living, yet not living with her, was complex, and

every week that passed their separation grew wider, deeper, darker.

She didn't seem to mind, so he kept his wish of trying to fix it to himself.

It had been almost a month, when one Sunday late in April, he found himself with nothing to do. The sun was out, had been for a few days straight. The grass was getting greener and the puddles left by the melting snow in March and the rainy days of April were drying up. He considered taking Tanner with him, but not wanting Randi home alone, he left the dog at home and pulled one of his motorcycles out of the garage, drove out to his property.

He stopped the bike as he pulled off the highway and got off to check the mailbox. No one had lived here since his father had died, but there was still mail in the box every so often. Catalogs, advertisements and the occasional letter from a Realtor interested in the property.

The dirt road needed to be graded. He had to dodge a few deep puddles before reaching the turnoff to the old homestead. He'd rebuilt the barn a couple of years ago, turned it into a functioning garage for his cars. Three of them. Souped-up to run a quarter-mile drag race in record time. He was going to take the red Chevy out today. Run the strip. Hoping that might make him feel better.

His plan had been to start working on an official drag race strip this summer, complete with bleachers for spectators and electric timers. It would be the first in the state and a draw for drivers. Real drivers. Not just teenagers.

That was who used the strip he had now. He'd had gravel hauled in, with a clay base to keep it from getting rutted, and ran his cars on it during the summer months regularly. But it was his cousin Wally and Wally's friends who used it more often.

Wally was Lottie's younger brother, and like him in his younger days, Wally had ended up with a couple of tickets for drag racing. Knowing what could come of that, and knowing that simply telling Wally to stop wouldn't work, Jason had told him to use his track. Drag racers were going to race, and without someplace to do it, they'd end up with tickets or worse, cause accidents that could get people hurt and killed.

So far Wally had kept his part of the agreement. Nothing had been trashed or damaged, and because it was private property, the cops had left the drag racers alone.

Jason stopped the bike near the garage. His plan was to build the strip on the piece of land Randi had wanted for her washing bay. He could give her that chunk, build his drag strip on another section.

However, the other section was low land. He'd have to haul in a lot of fill and have a culvert put in for the creek. That would more than double his costs, and the work would put him back at least a year, but it would work. He'd thought about it a lot lately, and the fact that he didn't want to go against Randal by supporting her washing bay project.

Yet, she was his wife, and far more important to him than anyone else. Anything else.

He huffed out a sigh. Things couldn't keep going as they were. That was for sure.

With nowhere to stash the junk mail on his motorcycle, he pulled up next to the house. It was looking worse for wear every year. Hardly any paint left, the roof of the porch sagging. He'd only been inside a half a dozen or so times since his father had died.

The key was on top of the door frame, he used it to unlock the front door. Dust, cobwebs and more than one sign that mice had moved in, greeted him. The house wasn't large. Kitchen, living room area, two small bed-rooms and a bathroom you could barely turn around in. He'd cleaned out anything worth keeping long ago, and should just set a match to what was left, including the house, but for whatever reason, he hadn't.

He was thankful for a lot of things in his life, and right now one of them was that this hadn't been the house Randi had shown up at. She was right in the fact that he wasn't as poor as his father had been, but it might have been better if this had been where she'd first found him. She'd never have returned to give him back his socks or for any other reason.

There were times when he'd arrive home, late, after she was already in bed, and open the bedroom door to let Tanner out, when he'd just stand there. Staring at her, wanting to crawl into bed beside her so bad every part of his body and soul ached. The want to hold her, feel her in his arms again, was torture.

There were times when he wondered if he should just give up. Being half Osterlund, his baby wouldn't ever want for anything, especially not love.

But he couldn't stomach the idea of not being there, of not knowing his child.

Pushing the dead air out of his lungs, he looked around, wondering if instead of burning the shack down, he should remodel it. Give the house in town to Randi and he could live out here. Bring his child out here, give him or her rides in his hot rods and motorcycles, then take them back home to their mother.

He crossed the small living room area to the kitchen table, where years of junk mail had piled up, and fig-ured this place would be more work than it was worth. He could build a new house, on the other side of the barn. A big one. Nice one. That, too, would take time.

His crews had just broken ground on three more houses that already had buyers lined up. Too bad he'd already rented out all of the apartments in his building, or he could have moved there.

That would really fit his reputation. Cutting out on a pregnant wife. That was something a reform school guy would do.

He glanced around the house. Selling this place, all of it, was what he should do. His cars, too. Drag racing wasn't for married men. Neither was a drag race strip. He could give Randi the acreage she wanted and sell the rest. Be done. Completely done with his past.

Tossing the mail from his hand onto the table stirred up dust, and as he pivoted to get away from it, the toe of his boot caught the table leg, jostled it enough that a pile of mail slid onto the floor.

Prepared to leave it, because it really didn't matter, he turned away, but a gut instinct had him twisting back around to look at a catalog that had landed on the floor. It was flipped open, and between the open pages there was an envelope. With his name on it.

There was something familiar about the handwriting. He wasn't sure what and picked it up. No return address, but the postmark was from four years ago.

He slid a finger under the flap and pulled out a card.

A sympathy card from when his father had died.

He almost tossed it on the table unread, but folded it open instead.

There was a check, and a folded-up letter. His heart stopped for a fraction of a moment at the signature on the card.

Your mother,
Scarlet (Heim) Crosby

Chapter Eighteen

Randi buried her face in the pillow on the bed Jason slept in, breathing in the scent of his aftershave, of him. How a person could live with someone and miss them as much as she missed Jason was unfathomable. She tried to stay busy, working and helping on her father's campaign, but Jason was on her mind no matter what she was doing.

All she had ever wanted was Jason Heim and now that she had him, they were both absolutely miserable.

Letting out a groan, she flipped onto her back, stared at the ceiling.

She missed his grin. That bad-boyish hooded grin that made her heart skip. She missed the butterflies in her stomach when he'd wink at her, but mostly, she missed the way he'd looked at her when they'd made love.

The number of nights that she'd heard him come home, and lay there, wishing instead of just opening the bedroom door to let Tanner out that he'd come in, lie down beside her.

That hadn't happened and it was stupid to keep wishing.

It was just that wishing was all she'd known to do when it came to him. She'd wished he'd noticed her. She'd wished she'd run into him somewhere. She'd wished. Wished. Wished.

The phone rang and she considered not answering it. Her mother knew things weren't going well, and was probably calling, going to try and talk to her again, even though she and her father were in Springfield this weekend. Randi didn't want to talk to anyone, but as the ringing continued, and not knowing where Jason had gone on his motorcycle hours ago, she leaped off the bed and ran into the living room to answer it.

"Hey, girl!" Wendy exclaimed. "I haven't talked to you in ages. I hope I'm not interrupting anything. Like you and your husband having a moment."

There hadn't been any type of *moment* in over a month. As she did at work, Randi put a smile on her face and attempted to sound as normal as possible. "You aren't interrupting anything. I'm home alone." She patted Tanner's head as the dog sat down beside her chair. "What are you doing?"

"Studying. I'll be so glad when this quarter is over. Why are you home alone? Where's Jason?"

Forcing the smile to remain on her face, Randi said, "It's nice out today. He took his motorcycle out for a ride."

"Why didn't you go with him? That sounds like fun."

It did sound fun, but she hadn't been invited. "I had things to do. What about you? What have you been up to?"

"Studying. Going to class. Studying. Going to class. I did go to a movie two weeks ago, fell asleep. The usher woke me up and told me I needed to leave because they were closing."

Flinching for her cousin, Randi said, "Uh-oh."

"Yeah, worse yet, I'd gone to the five o'clock show. They close at midnight."

"Oh, Wendy!"

"Yeah, so meanwhile, back at the ranch, how about you? Any news?"

"No."

"No? Like no...baby on the way?"

Randi rubbed a temple. She'd have to tell people soon.

"DDT!" Wendy exclaimed. "I hit it, didn't I?"

Why had she answered the phone?

"Randi!"

"I don't know, Wendy," she said for lack of anything else.

"What do you mean, you don't know?"

"It's...it's too soon."

"No, it's not! You go to the doctor, get a test. If the rabbit dies..."

"They use frogs now."

"Oh, my God! You did have a test!"

Randi smacked herself in the forehead. "I read that in a magazine."

"Have you missed a period? Experienced morning sickness? Tired? Emotional? Fuzzy headed? Dizzy?"

Wendy continued listing off symptoms until Randi interrupted her. "Do you have a medical journal in front of you?"

"Several," Wendy answered. "When was your last period? I'll calculate your due date."

"No!" Randi drew in a deep breath. "Can we just change the subject?" Knowing that wasn't likely, she added, "When the time is right, telling people is something Jason and I will do together." She and Jason hadn't done anything together lately. Not even drink coffee.

"All right, I can respect that." Wendy gasped. "But I have to know as soon as possible! I have a baby shower to plan! Oh, this is so exciting! How fun is that going to be?"

Randi had to swallow at the burning in her throat. "I— It's going to be fun." She squeezed her eyes shut at how her voice broke.

"Oh, Randi, I'm sorry. I didn't mean to make you cry. It's just emotions. That's very normal, your body is producing a baby."

"I know."

"Tell me about Jason," Wendy said in her happiest voice. "I bet he's excited."

Her cousin was attempting to cheer her up, but Randi was slipping further into sadness, regret, despair. "He's drawn up plans." The tears hit and a full sob emitted. "To build a crib and cradle."

"Oh, I'm sorry, now you're really crying," Wendy said. "When will Jason be home?"

"I don't know," Randi sobbed.

"Do you want me to call your mom?"

"No."

"Do you want me to shut up, and still be on the line when you're done crying?"

"I wish you were here, Wendy."

"I wish I was there, too, but Jason will be home soon, and he loves you so much."

"No, he doesn't."

"Yes, he does."

"No, he doesn't."

"I don't believe that," Wendy said. "But I'm not going to argue, because I know how much you love him."

She couldn't love him. He didn't want her to. The tears flowed faster. Harder. She couldn't talk, sobs were all that came out. Wendy talked, reminded her of how beautiful and fun the wedding had been. How Jason had carried her out of the hotel.

Tanner barked, stood and ran into the kitchen.

Knowing what that meant, Randi's head snapped up. "I—I have to go."

"Why?" Wendy asked. "Is Jason home?"

"Yes. Bye."

"No! Wait! Let me talk to him."

"No! And don't tell anyone anything! Nothing!"

"Ran—"

"I mean it! No one!" Randi hung up, and swiping the tears from her face, jumped up to run to the bathroom.

Jason walked into the living room, blocking her way to the hallway. "What's wrong? Why are you crying?"

If she looked at him, the tears would increase. She kept her eyes downcast. "Nothing."

He didn't move, repeated, "Why are you crying?"

"I was talking to Wendy on the phone." She wiped her cheeks again.

"Is something wrong with her? Did something happen?"

"No. She's fine. It…it's just me. It's just—" A sob escaped.

His arms folded around her, and she had no control over her response. Her body melted against him; she wrapped her arms around him and held on.

He rocked her back and forth, kissed the top of her head, rubbed her back and whispered that everything would be okay in her ear.

She cried harder because nothing would be okay.

He continued holding her, whispering, and she tried hard to make them stop, but the tears wouldn't stop. Not until after several minutes of being in his arms.

Her breathing was still shaky when he framed her face with both hands, forced her to look up at him.

"We can't keep living like this," he said.

He looked so sad, so glum. It was her fault and she

didn't know how to fix it. To make anything better. All she could do was agree. "No, we can't."

"What do you want to do?"

She had no idea and shrugged. "What do you want to do?"

"Right now?"

She nodded.

"This."

Air locked in her lungs as his lips met hers. Warm and soft and perfect, the kiss made everything inside her become more complicated because this was the last thing she'd expected. While also being what she'd wanted the most. She told herself to be cautious, to proceed slowly, but that was impossible. She'd missed him so much. Missed being with him.

Arching into him, she parted her lips and took the kiss to the next level. Within seconds pent-up desires exploded between them. They practically tore off each other's clothes while stumbling toward the bedroom, sharing openmouthed kisses and feasting on any inch of exposed skin while sucking in enough air before another mating of their lips.

There was no time for a moment of thought to form, other than how much she needed him.

They made it to the bed, ripping off any last bits of clothing, and came together with the same frenzy that had struck in the living room. There was no holding back, not on either of their parts. Her body knew the pleasure he provided. Her heart knew neither of them was pretending. And that was what it was all about.

Emotions exposed. Bare flesh upon bare flesh. Hands touching, feeling. Lips meeting. The indescribable pleasure incited by their joined bodies.

The velocity never slowed, even as the tension inside

grew to the point they were both gasping so hard for air that kissing was impossible. Randi couldn't pull her eyes off him, reveling at how he was watching her with just as much intensity.

When the commotion inside her broke loose, she clung to him, holding on to him as his body stiffened and she knew his time had come, too. They collapsed into the mattress as one, still gasping, still holding on to one another, still kissing whatever skin their lips touched.

His lips were touching hers, and as they parted, he chuckled.

All she could do was smile as he lifted his head.

"The phone's ringing again."

"Again?" she asked.

"Yes, again." He planted his hands on the mattress near her shoulders and straightened his arms, pressing upward.

She grasped his shoulders. "It's probably just Wendy again."

"It must be important. That's the fourth, maybe fifth time it's rung."

"It is?" She had no recollection of hearing the phone ring.

He kissed her nose. "I'll be right back."

Reluctantly, she let him go, but as he disappeared into the hallway, she remembered her conversation with Wendy and leaped off the bed.

He already had the phone to his ear when she arrived at his side. Giving her a wink, he wrapped an arm around her waist and held her against his side as he said hello to the caller.

"Fine, how are you today?"

She could tell it was a man's voice, not Wendy's, and let out a sigh that was a mixture of relief and delight as she laid her head on his shoulder.

"That's good," he said into the phone.

His hand caressed her side as he listened to the speaker. "Okay. When?"

She glanced at him as his hand stilled and his frame stiffened.

"Okay. Thanks for calling," he said, followed by, "Good day to you, too."

"Who was it?" she asked as he hung up the phone.

With his arm still around her waist, he tugged her across the room at a quick pace. "Your parents are on their way over."

"My parents are in Springfield this weekend."

"Their plane arrived half an hour ago." He started picking up their discarded clothes. "They called. When we didn't answer, they called Peter and asked him to keep trying, to let us know that they were stopping by."

She started grabbing clothes, too. "They could be here any minute!"

Their underclothes were in the bedroom, and they ran into the room, dashed around, finding pieces and tossing them to each other, getting dressed as fast as possible.

Having already pulled on his jeans, Jason had just put on his white T-shirt when Tanner barked.

She only had on her panties and jeans. "They're here."

He handed her the bra he'd tossed on the bed moments ago. "I'll go meet them outside."

Hopping on one foot while putting a sock on the other, he left the room, taking the time to close the door behind him.

She would have liked to relish the moment with a laugh, but there wasn't time. Once dressed, she tightened her ponytail by separating her hair and pulling it tight, then quickly straightened the pillows and bedspread.

Jason's coat was on the floor. As she picked it up,

tossed it on the chair near the closet, an envelope fell out. She picked it up, carried it to the chair. It appeared to be a card, mailed to Jason, but not at this address. She slid it under the coat and hurried to the kitchen, where she quickly filled the coffeepot, giving herself an excuse to not have met her parents outside with Jason.

When she heard the front door open, she said, "I'm in the kitchen, putting on coffee."

"It's just me," her mother replied. "Your father and Jason went to the garage to see his motorcycles."

Randi plugged in the percolator and spun around just as her mother entered the kitchen. "How was Springfield?"

"Fine." Her mother crossed the room and kissed her cheek. "You must have been outside with Jason when we called. Your face is glowing, as if kissed by the sun."

Her face had been kissed, but not by the sun.

"I'm happy to see that," her mother said. "I've been worried about you."

"I told you that I'm fine."

"I know, but just because you'll soon be a mother, doesn't mean I stop being yours." Her mother's lace-trimmed blue blouse was tucked into her black slacks, and her long hair was pulled back on both sides, held in place by a barrette.

When she'd been little, she'd thought her mother was the most beautiful woman on earth. Still did. "You don't look old enough to be a grandmother," Randi said.

"That's what your father says, but I am, and I'm happy about it." Hooking their arms, she said, "It is a beautiful day. Let's sit outside on the patio while the coffee perks."

Randi curled her bare toes against the linoleum. There hadn't been time to put on her socks or shoes, and she wondered about Jason wearing only his socks until she remembered he had shoes in the closet near the front door. "Let me just slip on a pair of shoes."

She collected a pair of white canvas shoes that didn't need socks from the closet near the front door, glad to notice that Jason's brown-and-white penny loafers were missing.

Once seated in the outdoor chairs on the patio, her mother said, "Your father and I have been worried about both you and Jason."

Randi sucked in a breath. Nothing had changed between her and Jason, other than satisfying one particular need. If only they were as good at other things as they were at that.

"I've never told you, but your father and I only knew each other for two weeks before we got married."

Stupefied, Randi said, "What?"

Her mother nodded. "Your grandmother arranged it because we were about to lose our house. Your father thought a wife would give him a better chance at buying Dad's airplane company, and I agreed, because besides my family needing money, I wanted to be a clothing designer. I thought everyone would see the wedding dress I sewed for myself and want one. That didn't happen. I became a designer because Jane was pregnant with Gus and needed a bra that fit."

Randi knew about Jane's needing a bra, but not the rest. She'd always assumed her parents had been as in love as they are now when they got married.

"It didn't take long before I realized what an amazing man I'd married and was completely in love with him." Her mother reached over and took a hold of her hand. "What did take a little bit of time, was figuring that together we could do anything, as long as we put our love for each other first."

Despite what had just taken place between her and Jason, Randi knew she and Jason didn't have love to put first. "I'm afraid, Mom."

"Of what?"

Her throat thickened. "That he feels trapped. We had to get married because I'm pregnant."

"People get married for a lot of reasons. That's the easy part."

That was true. "I don't know what to do," she said, desperate.

"I can't tell you what to do, honey, but I do know that you've never given up on something you've wanted."

"Except a pony," she said, just to lighten the mood.

Smiling, her mother replied. "Riding lessons was a compromise on both sides."

"Dad only won because he's a better negotiator than I am." Those negotiations had resulted in her agreeing to clean her father's office once a week to pay for a portion of the lessons. She sighed. "Once I started working at Air America, everyone assumed I'd take over someday."

"Yes, people did, but it's your choice, always has been. Your father and I have told you that."

"I know you have."

"And I know being our daughter hasn't always been easy for you. We've been fortunate, very fortunate, and along with that comes expectations. Large and small ones."

Randy huffed out a breath. "Like free band uniforms."

"For your brother, it was free soda pop."

Randi's gaze went to the garage.

"Your father has always been a generous, caring man. During the Depression, when others were unable to give to the soup kitchen, he increased his donation. We've been blessed and have found joy in helping others. Look at Rachelle. All the work you've dedicated to raising money for polio research helped her when she needed it. The iron lung she needed was there because of the work you'd put in."

Randi understood that, but it had nothing to do with her and Jason.

"What I'm trying to point out is that there is balance in everything, honey. Even in being our daughter. I know the expectations have weighed heavy on you. You've always taken everything to heart. But there are good things about being our daughter that I hope outweigh the others."

"Yes, there are, Mom." Once again, she thought about how different her and Jason's lives had been growing up.

"It's that way in other things, too. I didn't know anything about airplanes when I met your father, but his dream was to own an airplane company and I wanted that for him, more than I wanted to become a designer."

"You did both."

"No, *we* did both, your father and I, because he wanted my dream to come true more than he wanted his." Her mother touched her hand. "I sense there is something bothering you, and Jason, and though I'm your mother, and I love you, I know it's none of my business. However, I can't help but wonder if the two of you have taken the time to get to know each other? Do you know his hopes and dreams? Goals for the future? Does he know yours?"

Randi had her assumptions, but she really didn't know what Jason wanted, other than for her to not love him. "No." She huffed out a sigh. "Right now I don't even know what mine are."

Her mother squeezed her hand. "That might be a good place to start. The two of you might have more in common than you imagine. You could even want the same thing."

* * *

"I've test driven several motorcycles, but never pulled the trigger," Randal said, running a hand over the leather seat of the motorcycle. "This is a Black Hawk Chief, isn't it?"

"It is," Jason replied, leaning against his other motorcycle. "So is this one. I've had other bikes, but like the Indian the best. You can take her for a spin if you want."

Randal grinned. "I do want to do that. Take Jolie with me. She thinks they're dangerous, but I'm sure if she rode on one, she'd change her mind."

"You're welcome to it," Jason said. His breathing was finally under control. Making love to Randi had stolen every last breath in his body, and it hadn't returned before they'd both been running a marathon to get dressed before her parents arrived.

"Changing a woman's mind isn't an easy thing," Randal said. "Not my wife's or my daughter's. They're stubborn, opinionated, but also smart, savvy, and I wouldn't have it any other way."

"Not to mention beautiful," Jason said.

Randal chuckled. "So beautiful they can make a man lose their minds. I know, I've been there."

Jason could believe that. Randi got her beauty from her mother, and he'd lost his mind over her years ago. Never really got it back, either.

Randal folded his arm across his chest. "There was a time when I wanted to buy a small airplane company, knew it had the potential to be much more, but I needed something in order to buy it."

"Money?" Jason had always figured the man had been well-off, but the stories he'd heard could be wrong.

"No, I had that. I needed a wife."

Jason's head snapped up.

Randal nodded. "Neither Randi nor Joey know this story. Jolie's father had died a few years before we married, leaving the family somewhat destitute. She married me in exchange for me paying the taxes on her mother's home."

Jason grasped a hold of the handlebars on his motorcycle to keep the shock from knocking him off his feet.

"You've met Amelia," Randal said. "Randi's grandmother. She still lives in that house."

Still reeling at the information, Jason nodded. He had to believe the story, because Randal Osterlund was an honest man. He was proof of that. As soon as he'd learned the truth, Randal had gone to the judge to have him released from reform school.

"It didn't take long before I was head over heels in love, but I was too stubborn to admit it. There had never been a lot of love in my family. My mother died when I was young, and my father was bitter. He'd put his focus on making money, like his father had, and I followed in their footsteps. Thinking money, success, was all that mattered."

Jason shifted his stance, not sure he was ready to hear more. His mother wasn't dead, but she'd been gone, his father had been bitter and he'd been focused on making money since he'd left reform school. Because he'd never had any. That was a major difference between his past and Randal's.

"Coming from a man who has been very fortunate makes it sound vain, but the truth is, I would give up every dollar I ever earned, everything I own, for my wife. She is the root of my happiness, of my life, and I know she feels the same. That we could lose everything, but as long as we have each other, we won't have lost anything that matters."

Jason looked down at his shoes. A woman also had to be proud of her husband, and there was nothing in his past for Randi to be proud of. He'd gained a lot of respect for his father-in-law, and knew he could be honest with him. "You know my past. Randi and I are from two different worlds."

"As far as I know, there is only one world," Randal said. "I do know your past, and I'm proud of how you've faced challenges, overcome them. You should be, too."

"I am, but that's not enough."

"For what?"

"For Randi. She deserves the best."

"The fact you believe that, says she already has it."

Jason glanced toward the door that led out of the garage and scratched the back of his neck where it was tingling. That couldn't be true. She deserved love. The kind Randal spoke of. He shook his head.

"The airplane company that I wanted to buy was owned by Jolie's godfather, and when he told me that it wasn't for sale, I didn't know what I was going to do. There were other companies to buy, but I wanted the airplane company and he wasn't selling it because he was giving the company to Jolie. That knocked the wind right out of my sails. She'd married me because her family needed money. Once she inherited that company, she wouldn't. Therefore, she wouldn't need me."

Stunned, Jason didn't know what to say.

"Thank God it wasn't material things she needed, because they wear out. But the best of a person, that part of us that's brought out when we love someone deeply, it gets better. And when two people in love share the same goals, there's no stopping them."

The weight in Jason grew. He'd done nothing but stand

in the way of Randi's goal. Furthermore, they weren't in love.

Randal slapped his shoulder. "Tell me what I need to know about this motorcycle before I go get Jolie and take her for a spin."

Chapter Nineteen

All four of them ended up on the motorcycles. Randi was behind him and Jolie was behind Randal. Jason took it slow, just drove around a few blocks in his neighborhood. Long ago he'd fallen in love with the freedom associated with riding a motorcycle, and more than once had lived up to the reputation he'd built of being a daredevil. Right now, with Randi's arms around his waist, her body pressed up against his back, being a daredevil was the furthest thing from his mind. He was carrying the most precious cargo on earth. His wife, with his child growing inside her.

Pulling up beside them at a stop sign, Randal asked, "Could we go farther? Faster?"

Jason chuckled. "Sure. Any place particular?"

"We should find a café and have lunch," Jolie said. "We haven't eaten."

"Neither have we." Randi's arms around his waist tightened. "We know the perfect place. Mama's."

"You told me about that place," Jolie said. "Let's go there."

"It's half an hour away, in Downers Grove," Jason warned.

"Sounds perfect," Randal said, twisting the throttle to rev the engine of his motorcycle. "Let's ride!"

Randi's laughter echoed in his ear as Jason took off, leading the way to the highway and to Downers Grove.

The sun was out, the roads were dry and the company made it the best ride he'd ever taken.

"That was so fun!" Randi said, hugging him hard as he shut off the motorcycle in Mama's parking lot.

"Yes, it was," her mother agreed. "We are going to have to do this more often."

"We'd need our own motorcycle," Randal said. "We can't expect Jason to let us use his all the time."

Laughing, Jolie climbed off the motorcycle. "You've wanted one for years."

Jason waited until Randi was off the bike before he set the kickstand and climbed off. He took a hold of her hand and threaded his fingers between hers. "Your father might be hooked."

She leaned against him. "Might be?" Giggling, she watched her father climb off the motorcycle. "He is hooked, and so is my mother." She then looked up at him. "So am I. I've always wanted to ride on a motorcycle."

He searched her glowing face, her twinkling eyes, looking for a sign that she was faking it, saying that only because others were nearby.

She squeezed his hand. "I've also always wanted to ride in a red hot rod with a ball of fire painted on the hood."

Most days she looked like she'd just stepped out of a fashion magazine, so refined and beautiful that she took his breath away. Today, dressed in jeans, with her hair windblown, she still looked picture-perfect, and still took his breath away. So did the honesty in her eyes. "Why?" he asked, still skeptical.

"Because I like cars." She placed a quick kiss on his cheek. "And because it's yours."

"This place is adorable," Jolie said.

"It is," Randi replied, tugging him in her wake as she hurried toward the door. "And they have the best milk-shakes."

A moment later, as they walked through the door, Jason wasn't surprised to see several of his family members, including Rachelle.

She was still wearing her braces and using the crutches, but the speed at which she could move had increased substantially. Besides him and Randi, Rachelle included Randal and Jolie in her round of hugs.

"Sorry," Jason said after they'd managed to eat while visiting with several family members. "Everyone gathers at Mama's on Sundays as if it's Aunt Marla's private home."

"I think it's wonderful," Jolie said. "And the food was delicious."

"Yes, it was." Randal laid his napkin on the table. "If you will excuse me, I need to get some change for the jukebox because a little girl promised me a dance as soon as I was done eating."

Jolie slid out of the booth as well. "Excuse me, I'm the cheering section."

As they walked away, Jason asked Randi, "Do you want to dance?"

She set her napkin on the top of her plate, but said, "We don't have to."

He knew how much she enjoyed dancing, and how they were on shaky ground after the last month of barely speaking and then their amazing lovemaking. "I know we don't have to, but I want to."

She looked at him and tried hard to hide a smile. "You do?"

He took her hand and slid out of the booth. "Yes, I do."

A fast song was playing as they arrived on the dance floor. He twirled her under his arm, but just as her spin ended, so did the music. Pulling her toward him, he placed a hand on her waist and held their clasped hands close to his chest. It was complicated and he might be opening himself up for the worst hurt of his life, but if he didn't take the risk, he'd never know. He brushed his lips over her temple, whispered, "I've missed dancing with you in the kitchen."

She stiffened slightly. Looked up at him with a hint of insecurity in her eyes.

He touched the tip of his nose to hers. "And cooking with you, doing dishes, watching TV, folding clothes."

The music started, a slow, soft melody. She leaned against him as they started to dance. "I've missed all of that, too. Very much."

The ache in his chest that had become a part of him the past month, slipped away as they danced. Something took its place. Something light and bright. He didn't ever want to dance with anyone else. Just her, for the rest of his life, but what did that mean, exactly?

Pure happiness had filled Randi on the dance floor in Jason's arms, and that happiness remained until they arrived home and her parents left. Then a sense of panic slithered in to take its place. Her mother had told her where to start, but what if she discovered Jason's goals, the future he wanted, didn't include her? Could she live the rest of her life knowing that?

His fingers wrapped around hers, and his thumb rubbed the back of her hand. "I went to the courthouse a while ago, put your name on the land. You can build your washing bay wherever you want."

Her heart sank. "I don't want your land, Jason. That's why I went to California, to investigate building one out there. My father told me to put it off until next year, but I haven't. I asked Gus to recommend contractors he's worked with to bid the project without anyone else knowing." The frustration inside her doubled. "But the truth is, I don't care if it gets built or not. I don't care if Wayne Klein takes over for my father. Sam can, for all I care."

"That can't be true. Air America, taking over for your father, is all you've ever wanted. I'll help you. Whether it's here or in California, I'll help you build a washing bay."

She was touched by the sincerity in his voice, on his face, but would never expect him to do that. "You're already working night and day. I wish there was something I could do to help you. I'd rather do that than build a washing bay."

"I don't need help, and I know how much Air America means to you. It's the reason you went to college here instead of out east like your brother and cousins."

She blinked at the tears in her eyes, not sure which hurt worse. That he didn't want her help, or that he believed Air America was all she cared about. "Air America isn't the reason I stayed here." A full admission that he was the reason she'd never left town would leave her vulnerable, open for more heartache, and she was afraid of that. "It wasn't my dream. It's what was expected."

A frown had formed between his brows. "By your parents?"

"I was expected to have goals, to work toward them, so did Joe, but the expectations came from others. I was continuously asked which company I was going to take over.

Most assumed it would be JO's Dream Wear, and were surprised when they'd learned I worked at Air America. It became assumed that I wanted to take over the helm."

"You don't want to?"

"Yes and no. I'd be honored to continue what my parents started, but I'd also like to have something of my own. I've never had that. Whatever I've done, whatever I've had, is because of who I am, not my abilities." She hadn't meant to sound so selfish, so ungrateful. She wasn't. She was just being truthful.

"That's why you want to build the washing bay."

"I thought it would prove I could do something on my own. Instead, all I managed to do was trap you in a marriage you never wanted." She hadn't meant to say that. To point out the obvious. It was impossible to hold back her guilt. "I didn't set out to, but that's what happened."

Jason shook his head. "I never said I didn't want marriage, I said I'd never thought I'd get married."

She opened her mouth to say that was the same thing, but he spoke first.

"Let's grab some jackets and ride out to the land." He tugged on her hand, pulling her toward the bedroom.

"Why?"

"So you can see the land, see if it will work, and jackets because the ride home could be chilly."

She already knew the land wouldn't work because she wouldn't build a washing bay on it, but the excitement of riding on the motorcycle again had her walking into the bedroom beside him. "We're taking the motorcycle?"

"Yes."

She hurried to the closet. "I don't have a short jacket. They are all knee length." Scanning her wardrobe, she searched for something that might work. "Would a sweater be okay?"

He reached around her, to his side of the closet. "I have an extra leather jacket. It might be a bit big."

Her heart skipped a beat as he pulled out a leather jacket identical to the one he always wore. Being jacketed by him back in high school had also been a dream of hers. "That'll be perfect." She slid her arms into the jacket as he held it up for her, and the scent of leather filled her nose, as well as the spicy aftershave he always wore. Hugging the jacket to her, she spun around. "It's absolutely perfect!"

"It looks good on you." He gently flicked the end of her nose and grabbed his coat off the chair, hooked it on a finger and flung it over his shoulder. "Let's go."

With the wind whipping her ponytailed hair and leaning with him as he skillfully guided the motorcycle around corners, the ride to the property was wonderful. She couldn't help but hope that there was a difference between never thinking about getting married and not wanting to get married. It was a little thing in the overall scope of things, but perhaps it was a start. Her mother was right. Everything had happened so fast she and Jason hadn't had a chance to get to know each other. Not really. Maybe she needed to quit worrying about what they didn't have and focus on what they did have.

Chapter Twenty

Jason balanced the motorcycle on its kickstand and climbed off, took a hold of Randi's hand. The last thing he wanted her to see was the shack where he'd grown up, but he could relate to her wanting to create something on her own. He'd never considered how difficult things had been for her. All the expectations put on her, and truly wanted to help her with her washing bay. "The cars are in the barn. We'll take one of them out to the back forty."

"How many do you have besides the red one?"

He'd worked Ted Nash's gas station, changing oil and tires from the time he'd been twelve until he'd moved out of his father's house. Other than food for him and his father and other necessities, nearly every penny he'd made had gone back to Ted. First to buy the Chevy, then for the paint job. "There are two others in the barn."

She laughed. "Besides the one in town and two motorcycles, and several pickup trucks."

Three pickup trucks. Stu drove one, as did his cousin Steve, who was the foreman of another one of his crews. "Yes."

She was staring at the house and squeezed his hand. "Could we go look at the house first?"

"There's nothing in there but a few pieces of old furniture and other junk."

"I still want to see it."

"There's mice, and dust, cobwebs, spiders."

She started walking that way and tugged him along. "I don't care."

He was the one to bring her out here, so he complied. Found the key over the door, opened it. The sun was still out, but lowering in the western sky, casting shadows inside. That might hide how bad it was. "I had the power to the house shut off. Still have it in the barn."

She walked farther inside, peeking into the bedrooms. "Did you always live here?"

"Yes, my father built the house and barn before I was born. He farmed the land then, mainly corn. But the Depression hit, and the drought. Without money for fuel and water for crops, everything dried up." He hadn't repeated one of his father's stories, ever, not to anyone, but felt as if he had to justify the plight his parents had faced. "He'd never mortgaged the land, so didn't lose it like a lot of other people, but couldn't borrow against it, either. I was too little to remember any of it, not even him joining the army when the war broke out." He wasn't sure why he didn't remember that, because he did remember other things. Like how his mother had worked at Air America. She used to walk him all the way out to the highway to catch the school bus, and then cut across the field to go to work.

"How long was your father gone, in the army?"

"A few months, but most of that was spent in the hospital. The boiler on the troopship taking him overseas blew up and he was injured. The ship returned to New York. He never made it overseas." Which is why he'd never received any combat pay. That was what his father used to say.

"That's awful. How badly was he injured?"

"I don't know." His father never spoke about it unless he was drunk, hurting. "He had headaches, and would drink, said it was the only thing that helped the pain." That was often and when he'd complain about everything else in life, too.

"I'm sorry he was in such pain," she said softly.

A sense of guilt for never realizing what his father had been through washed over Jason. He'd blamed their being poor on his father's drinking, but never gave the reason his father drank any credence.

He hadn't come out here to walk down memory lane. The letter from his mother was still in the back of his mind; he hadn't had time to process that yet.

Randi was standing near the table, he held out his hand for her to take. "This place is full of mice droppings, let's get out of here."

"Mice droppings or not, I'm not done looking."

"There's nothing else to see."

She walked around the table, to the sink. "Yes, there is." Looking out the window, she asked, "Are the old ropes in that tree from a swing?"

"Yes, there used to be a swing in that tree."

"A big one?"

"Yes, like a porch swing. My father built it for my mother. She used to sit in it—" his throat locked up for a moment "—a lot." For a flash of a second, he'd seen his father and mother sitting in the swing, happy. Laughing. Hugging.

"I can believe she did. I would, too. It would be a lovely place to sit and watch the sunset." She turned around. Smiled. "It had to have been nice, living out here. It's so quiet. So peaceful."

"Quiet and peaceful can drive some people crazy."

She walked around the table, took a hold of his hand. "Show me your cars now. Are they all red?"

"No. Red, white and blue."

She giggled. "All American."

He locked the house after they'd walked out the door, as always, to keep the memories inside the walls. This time, though, while holding her hand as they walked to the barn, he couldn't help but think that he'd come a long way since living in that house. Maybe, with hard work and luck, he'd someday become enough for her. Become someone she could be proud of.

After unlocking and removing the padlock on the barn, he opened the double doors and clicked on the overhead lights.

"Shh," she whispered. "The cars are sleeping."

He laughed at her joke. "I cover them to keep from getting too dusty."

Taking in the toolboxes, metal workbenches and shelves of miscellaneous parts and tools, she said, "You must spend a lot of time out here."

"I do in the summer." He pulled the silk covering off the Chevy.

"It's exactly like I remember it." Walking along the side of the car, she looked in the driver's window. "Four on the floor."

He chuckled. "Yes."

"Do you still drag race?"

He was going to miss that, but her happiness would be worth giving it up. "Once in a while I run her on the track I built. Wally and his friends use it the most. I'd rather they were out here racing than in town where they'll get in trouble."

"Out here? You have a track?"

"I built it a few years ago." He pulled the covering off

the next car, a white two-seat convertible Ford Thunderbird.

"Cherry! I almost bought a bird," she said. "But the Bel Air's six cylinders get better gas mileage than the bird's V-8 would."

He was impressed with her knowledge.

She sighed. "And my father didn't think I needed a car with that much power."

Eyeing her, he asked, "Do I need to worry about your driving?"

"No." She laughed and pointed to the third car. "What's that one?"

He pulled the cover off that car, a blue Buick with a wraparound windshield and tail fins. The aircraft design of that one had reminded him of her. That was the only reason he'd purchased it.

"Man! You own all the best machines!" She roamed around the car. "I love the aerodynamics of this model. Joey and Gus would be drooling right now."

"Is that how you know so much about cars?"

"Maybe," she said, walking back toward the Chevy. She opened the passenger door. "Maybe not."

Chuckling, he walked to the driver's door. "It's loud," he warned once seated.

Her smile showed her pearly whites, and her excitement. "I remember that."

He turned the key and laughed at her glee as the powerful engine made the seat rumble. She looked adorable in his coat that was too large and her hair tied back in a ponytail. For a second it felt as if he was seventeen, taking her out on a date.

The car had get-up-and-go, but he took it slow, drove out to the strip.

"Is this where you're going to punch it?" she asked.

"You want to go fast?"

"Very!"

He knew the car like the back of his hand, and gave her a good run, but not nearly as fast as he would have if he'd been alone.

"Can we do it again?" she asked.

"Are you a speed demon?"

"I've always wanted to be, but never had the chance."

He put the car in Neutral and let it idle. "Do you want to drive?"

Her mouth dropped open and she shook her head. "No one lets someone else drive their hot rod."

That was the cardinal rule, but he was willing to break it, for her. "They do when it's their wife."

She squealed. "Do you mean it? I'll be careful. I promise."

He opened his door. "I trust you. Scoot over here." As he climbed out, he said, "But wait until I get in the passenger seat before you shift it into gear."

She was already in the driver's seat, holding on to the steering wheel and grinning like she'd just opened a gift that she loved. "I will!"

He ran around the car, climbed in.

"Ready?" she asked.

"Whenever you are," he replied.

She shifted into First and took off like a pro.

"Tight clutch!" she shouted above the engine. "I like it!" She advanced through the gears with skill and precision that impressed him, and brought the car to a smooth stop at the end of the track.

"Take her back to the other end," he said.

She bit her bottom lip and looked at him.

"You don't have to if you don't want to," he offered.

"I want to, but um—"

"What?"

"Could I do a moonshiner's turn when we reach the other end?"

There was nothing in the way, so he nodded. "Sure."

"Yes!" She revved the engine, dropped the clutch and spewed dust and dirt in their wake, grinning the entire time.

At the other end she performed a moonshiner's turn that would rival his. "I'm impressed," he said as the car came to a stop.

Laughing, she said, "I used to practice those in the parking lot at Air America, until I almost hit the building. Then my dad made me stop." She grimaced. "I probably shouldn't have mentioned the part about almost hitting the building."

He laughed. "Now I know why he didn't want you to have a V-8."

"I've never driven a car with this much power, it's addictive." She was glancing around the area. "And this is the perfect place for a track." Leaning back in her seat, she looked at him. "Is this why you said you had plans for this property? This track?"

"I have other property I could build a track on."

"It's already built here, why would you move it?"

"So you could build a washing bay."

She turned off the car so they didn't have to shout over the engine. "A washing bay will never work here. It's too cold. Would cost too much to keep it heated for the planes to dry during the winter. I understand all that now. California would work better."

He could see her point. "Is that why your father gave up trying to buy this land?"

"I think Dad just wanted it for expansion. I was the one who came up with the washing bay idea."

"From what you said, it's a good idea."

She scanned the area again. "Not as good of an idea as a drag strip." She gestured with one hand. "You could build a real one. Open it to the public. Have bleachers at the start and finish lines. An announcer's booth in the center. A pit area over there, and concession stands back behind the bleachers."

The hair on his arms stood at the way she'd described the exact plans he'd drawn up. He'd never shown them to her. "Have you been to a strip?"

"A couple of times in California, with Gus. There's not one near us. This would be a real draw." She opened her door, swung her legs out. "We'd have to bring in power, gotta have an electric scoreboard, and lights for night racing."

He climbed out, met her near the front of the car.

Rubbing her chin, she said, "Dirt track would work, but paved would be better."

Astonished, he was tongue-tied.

She turned, looked at him for a long moment. "Is this your dream? To build a drag strip out here?"

"I've thought about that," he admitted.

"And?"

He shrugged, grinned. "And, I have plans drawn up for one. Pretty much identical to what you just described."

She squealed and clapped her hands. "Can I see them? Can I help? Please? I know we both have our other jobs, but we could do this. We could really do this!"

"You'd like that?"

"I'd love it! Wouldn't you?"

Her excitement was rubbing off on him. "Yes, I would."

She squealed again and looped her arms around him, hugged him. "When can we start?"

They spent so long walking around, sharing ideas and

making plans that it was almost dark when they closed the barn doors after returning the Chevy to it.

The few lingering rays of sun were shining on the house, making the glass windows sparkle. Like the shadows inside, the sunset made the house look not so decrepit.

"Would you ever consider living out here again?" she asked while climbing on to the motorcycle behind him.

"No." A drag track out here was one thing, living here again was different. That would never happen again. There were too many memories.

After arriving home and making soup and sandwiches for supper, they settled in the living room to watch television. Randi wondered if he would sleep in the other room again tonight, and couldn't think of a good way to ask him to sleep in their bed instead.

Their bed. That was how she thought of it, just as she thought about the drag strip as theirs. The idea of creating something with him thrilled her beyond belief. She couldn't describe how it made her feel, but she didn't want to lose that feeling.

Lifting her head off his shoulder, she kissed his cheek. "I'm going to get ready for bed."

"Tired?" he asked.

"No." Her heart nearly beat its way out of her chest as she waited for him to respond. Then welled with happiness when he stood and held out his hand.

Much later, after a spectacular bout of lovemaking, she got out of bed to use the bathroom, and on her way back, noticed the envelope beneath the chair near the closet when she stopped at the vanity to remove her ponytail and brush her hair. "A letter fell out of your coat earlier, when my parents arrived. It's under the chair."

"I saw that."

He was lying on the bed, naked, hands behind his head and legs crossed at the ankles. The reflection of that in the mirror made her grin.

"It's from my mother."

The brush stalled in her hand. She turned around. "Your mother?"

"You can read it if you want."

She considered saying no, but couldn't deny that she wanted to read it. Setting down the brush, she walked to the foot of the bed.

"I found it this morning," he said. "At the house, my father's house. It's a sympathy card she'd sent when he died. It had been stuck in a magazine. I never saw it until the magazine fell on the floor this morning."

Being here for him, through the good and the bad, was what she'd promised, and would fulfill. She walked over, picked up the envelope. "What does it say?" She couldn't judge a woman she'd never known, but she knew his mother's leaving had affected him greatly.

"Not much. There's a check in there, too. For the funeral, or whatever was needed, or to go to Texas and see her."

Randi climbed on the bed, sat back on her knees, holding the envelope. "Texas? Not Florida?"

"That's what it says."

"Are you going?"

"No."

"Why not?"

He rolled onto his side, laid a hand on her thigh. "She wrote it four years ago, and I never responded."

"Because you just found it."

"She probably believes I don't want anything to do with her."

Her heart ached, for both him and his mother. "She probably does."

He took the envelope, opened it, handed her the letter. "It's short. Just says she's sorry, that my father was a good man and that she never stopped loving me or him."

She glanced at the letter, but didn't read it. Her heart was too busy breaking for him. "You could call her," she said, giving him back the letter.

He put it in the envelope, dropped it on the table and pulled her down beside him. "Or I could kiss you."

"Yes, you could," she whispered. He might not love her, but right now he needed her, and that was enough.

Chapter Twenty-One

Two weeks later Randi was sitting at her desk when her father walked into her office. "Hey, Dad, what are you doing here?"

Holding his arms out at his sides, he frowned. "That's the greeting I get? No, *It's good to see you*? Or, *I've missed you*?"

She laughed and met him in the center of the room for a hug. "It's very good to see you, and I've missed you." After kissing his cheeks, she added, "And Mom. How many cities did you hit this time?"

"I think it was twenty-three, in six days. Your mother is relentless."

She laughed, knowing that her parents were in this run together. As they'd been in everything. Lately, she and Jason had been, too. Not just in conversations about the drag strip, but in everything. They talked about all sorts of things. Childhood events, dreams, fears and life. They'd formed a connection like she'd never had with anyone.

But there was still something missing, and despite everything else, that weighed her down.

Rather than the chairs by her desk, she led her father

toward the leather sofa that sat along one wall. "Sit down and relax. Do you want some coffee?"

"No, I'm fine, but I do want to talk to you."

She knew why. "Okay." They sat side by side on the sofa.

"I came into the office for a meeting with Wayne this morning, and he told me you've met with him several times, have been instrumental in assisting him with the entire transition."

"I've just given him a few heads-up and some pointers."

"And told him that he can count on you for whatever he needs." He patted her knee. "You have no idea how proud that makes me."

She didn't need praise. In fact, she didn't deserve it. "It was something I should have done when you announced he was taking over." There was more she needed to admit. "You were right, Dad, as usual. I'm not ready to take over for you. I might be, someday, if it works in all aspects." Here and at home. She'd learned things about herself, about life, lately. Jason, the way he forged ahead despite things that had happened, made her want to do that, too. It was hard to explain, but she no longer felt trapped. No longer felt being her father's daughter was a burden. It was a privilege.

Her father grinned, touched the tip of her nose with one finger, before pulling up a more serious expression. "I just had a meeting with Sam, too."

Here it was. She drew in a deep breath and repeated the gist of what she'd told Sam. "I may be your daughter, but I'm also an employee here, and deserve the same amount of respect as everyone else. I'm willing to work on our differences, but he has to, too, otherwise one of us will be looking for a new job." Sitting a bit straighter, she added, "And it won't be me."

His serious expression remained. For a moment. Then it broke into a smile. "I told him I agree with you one hundred percent."

"You did?"

"Yes, I did. He's a great accountant, but I've considered firing him more than once, because of his attitude toward you, and Joe at times. I didn't because I knew if you took control of the situation, that you'd really have what it takes. Not only to run Air America, but to manage whatever life throws at you. Facing fear isn't always easy, but it has to be done."

He was right, in a sense. "I wasn't afraid of him."

"I know you weren't afraid of him. I would have gotten rid of him if that was the case, but you were afraid of what his reaction would be."

She nodded. "I was. I knew he'd tell you, and I was afraid that you'd think I couldn't handle things on my own."

"I've always known you could handle anything." He squeezed her hand. "It was you who needed to figure that out."

She could handle things, and it was time she took care of a couple more. Two significant things that were focused on Jason. She wanted a marriage where she and Jason not only desired each other passionately, but also loved each other openly, honestly, and had figured out how to make that happen. She just hadn't acted on it yet, because she was afraid of how he might respond.

"How is everything else going?" her father asked. "Anything new?"

"The washing bay project is on hold, but Jason and I will be flying out to California this summer to go to a drag race, and I might have discussions about it while there."

He chuckled. "I'd expect no less. Anything else?"

"Will you and Mom be home two weeks from Sunday?"

"We can make sure we are, why?"

The wheels were still turning inside her head. "I'll let you know as soon as I have it all confirmed with Jason."

"Fair enough." He patted the leather seat before standing up. "I have a luncheon, so have to get going, but keep up the good work, and stay happy, it looks good on you."

She gave him a hug goodbye, and walked to her desk, stared out the window. Jason had the ability to love and be loved. There was one hurdle that kept him from seeing that. It was a risk, but one she had to take. She sat down, picked up the phone and dialed the Texas number she'd gotten off the letter from his mother.

Keeping secrets had never been one of her best assets, but this one she would keep. At least part of it. A major part of it.

Jason was already home when she arrived, in the kitchen putting something into the oven. She dropped her purse on the table and walked over, hugged him from behind.

After closing the oven door, he turned, engulfed her in a hug. "How was your day?"

"Good. How was yours?"

"Good, even better now that you're home." He ran his hands down her back, cupped her butt cheeks and brought them closer, so their bodies pressed against each other.

He kissed her, an openmouthed kiss that had her insides swirling.

"If you keep kissing me like that," she said in between

breaths when the kiss ended, "I'm going to forget what I have to tell you."

He wiggled a brow. "Oh, what's that?"

Giving his chest a playful slap, she stepped away, otherwise she might take him up on his teasing. "Are you busy two weeks from Sunday?"

"I don't know, am I?"

She planted her hands on her hips.

He laughed. "What are we doing two weeks from Sunday?"

Dressed, her growing stomach wasn't overly noticeable because she wore loose-fitted dresses or positioned the waistbands of her skirts higher on her torso and didn't tuck in her blouses, but naked, the expansion was very noticeable. What she'd thought had been butterflies, because Jason set those off with nothing more than a look, had been confirmed by the doctor as movement. Baby movement, which was utterly fascinating. "Having a party. I think it's time we tell others."

Two steps brought him directly in front of her, and he laid a hand on her stomach. "People are noticing?"

She placed her hands atop his. "No one has said anything, but I want them to know."

"You want them to know?"

She nodded. "Yes, I want everyone in the world to know I'm having your baby."

"What about your father's campaign? We could put it off—"

"My father's campaign doesn't have anything to do with this. I want everyone to know that we are going to have a baby." She willed her heart to not pound out of her chest. "And that we are happy about it."

He stared at her for a stilled moment, then grinned. "All right. Where are we having this party?"

"At Mama's."

"Okay. Mama's it is." He cast her a hooded look that said his mind was turning to something else. "I have an idea for tonight."

"I'm listening."

"Let's go to the drive-in."

Taken aback because that had not been what she'd expected him to say, she asked, "The drive-in?"

"Yes." He kissed the side of her neck. "You know. Where we sit in the car and watch a movie."

"Yes, I know." She also knew they were called passion pits because there was often very little movie watching taking place. "What movie is playing?"

"I have no idea."

"Okay," she agreed.

The storm broke out halfway through the drive-in movie, making it impossible to see the screen, and a bolt of lightning struck so close the sky lit up at practically the same time the crack of thunder echoed through the air.

Startled, Randi let out a squeal and pressed closer to his side. "Goodness, that was a close one."

"It was." Jason rubbed her upper arm. The speaker hanging inside his window had gone silent and though they hadn't been able to see the movie, the screen that had been lit up was now dark. "Looks like it struck something. The electricity quit."

Horns started honking and car lights came on around them.

She lifted her head off his shoulder. "Aren't you going to start the car so we can leave?"

"No. The wipers can't keep up with this rain. Even if they could, it's too dangerous to drive when it's raining like this." He kissed her temple. When it came to her safety, he was the opposite of the daredevil he used to portray. "We'll just wait it out."

"Maybe you'll get to second base while we wait," she whispered while kissing the side of his neck.

There was no more pretending between them, not in public or private. It was all natural. He was even beginning to believe that he could learn to love. She was loveable, completely. He just had to forget all he'd ever known about it and start over. It was scary, because he didn't want to fail. Not in that. Not with her.

He rubbed her stomach, then slid his hand up to cup a breast. "I got to second base before the movie started. Remember?"

Putting her hand over his, she held it in place. "That's second base?"

"Yes."

"Then what's third base?"

Jason explained aloud, while showing her, and a few other things as they waited for the rain to let up. As soon as that happened, he rolled down his window and attached the speaker to the metal pole before starting the car. "We'll finish this at home."

"Where we don't have to worry about someone peeking in the window," she said while double-checking that her blouse was buttoned straight.

"Yes." He respected her too much to ever want to embarrass her.

She snuggled against his side. "Okay."

By the time they entered their neighborhood, the rain was little more than a drizzle and he eased his foot off the gas pedal at the plethora of red lights flashing.

Randi stiffened beside him, seeing what he did at the exact same time. "A house is on fire! It's not our house, is it? Tanner's home!"

He couldn't tell for sure, but the sinking in his stomach said it was their house. "It's all right," he said, trying to stay calm, yet hit the gas pedal. "He has the doggy door."

A police barricade stopped him before he could turn into the alley, before he could see exactly which house was on fire.

He threw the car in Park. Her hands were cupped over her mouth. He grasped her wrist. "You stay here. Don't get out. I'll be right back."

She nodded and frantically said, "Find Tanner. Please find Tanner. He can't get out of the backyard! The fence is too high!"

He shot out of the car and ran up to the closest officer. "My house is on this block."

The officer held his arms wide at his sides. "Three houses are on fire, sir, I can't let anyone past."

"What—"

"Lightning strike," the officer said. "Hit the electrical pole."

"My dog is in the backyard, it's fenced in, and—"

"I'm sorry, sir. The firemen…"

Jason heard barking and shouted Tanner's name.

As the officer spun around, Jason shot past him, ran. Firetrucks lined the street, pumping water onto his house and the two on the left of his place, but flames were still shooting high in the air. It stunned him for a moment, but another bark sent him forward again.

He ran through the neighbor's backyard, to the alley and to his garage. Throwing open a door, he ran through the garage, to the service door and wrenched it open.

Soaking wet, Tanner shot inside the garage.

Relief filled Jason as he slammed the door shut. Smoke filled the air, burned his nose, and the heat from the fire consuming the houses was intense. For a moment he thought about all the things in the garage. Not only the vehicles, but all of his tools. This is where he stored most everything for his company. There was time to get some out, but then he thought of Randi, waiting in the car. "Come, boy, we gotta go."

She wasn't in the car, she was on the street, arguing with the police officer when Jason ran around the side of the neighbor's house.

Tanner bolted forward, barking and running toward her.

Her squeal had other officers and bystanders looking and moving toward her, until they saw her and the dog united.

Jason wasn't sure if it was raining again or if the moisture in the air was from the water being pumped onto the flames—either way, he had to get her out of here. She was kneeling on the ground, hugging Tanner. Jason grasped her waist. "Come on, sweetheart, we have to go."

She stood, but shook her head. "Go? We can't go! That's our house!"

"There's nothing we can do. The fire departments are here."

"But—"

"Tanner's safe," he reminded, and knowing the only way he was going to get her out of here, save her from watching their home be completely destroyed, was for her to think she was saving someone else. "Let's take him to your parents."

"That's clear across town, our house…"

"I know, but we have to get him cleaned up, make sure he doesn't need to see a vet."

"A vet!" She ran to the car, with Tanner at her side. "Hurry! We have to hurry!"

Her parents had been in bed, but came running down

the stairs practically the moment he, Randi and Tanner walked in the door.

"What's happened? What's wrong?" they asked simultaneously.

"Tanner was home alone and our house is on fire!" Randi answered, dropping down to inspect the dog. "Jason had to rescue him from the backyard, and there were flames everywhere!"

Jason explained the situation, trying to remain as calm as possible, he ended by telling Randal quietly, "She needs to stay here. I need to go back." Everything he'd had to offer her was going up in smoke. If he didn't hurry, he'd have nothing left. Nothing.

"Of course," Randal said. "Give me a second to get dressed. I'm going with you."

Jolie seemed to comprehend how Randi might protest, and said, "Come. Let's get Tanner upstairs and into a bathtub. Get this ash washed off him so we can see if he needs medical attention."

Tanner was black with ash, but walking and acting fine, which gave Jason hope to believe he was uninjured.

The two women and dog were on their way up the stairs when Randal raced back down them. "Let's go, son."

Chapter Twenty-Two

It was odd to feel out of place in the home where she'd lived her entire life until marrying Jason, but Randi did.

Because they'd been constructed of brick, their house, as well as the other two, were still standing, but due to smoke and water damage, the interiors would need to be rebuilt and most of their belongings were beyond salvageable.

"Things can be replaced," her mother said. "People can't."

"I know." Randi drew in a deep breath. "I'm so thankful Tanner got out safely, that's really all that matters, I just… I don't know, feel sort of lost. Homeless."

"You aren't homeless. The three of you can stay here as long as needed. Forever would be fine."

She smiled, because she knew that was true. The forever part. Her mother and father had mentioned more than once that their big house was too empty now. She appreciated their love and their offer, but she and Jason had been making headway and she didn't want that to stop.

The fire had happened Thursday night, and it was only Sunday, but it felt like months had passed.

She lifted her glass of lemonade off the table between her chair and her mother's as they sat on the back porch.

Tanner was lying at her feet, completely fine now. All he'd needed was a bath, thankfully. Jason, along with her father, had left earlier this morning to see what they could salvage out of the basement and empty the garage before vandals realized the burned-out homes might be easy pickings. They'd said it was too dangerous for her and her mother to go over there again until they'd fully inspected everything.

A hopelessness filled her, and she didn't like that feeling.

"Don't fret so," her mother said. "Jason will be able to rebuild your house as good as new in no time."

"I know he can rebuild it," Randi replied. "But he has so many other jobs. People are buying his houses faster than he can build them, and he's looking at buying another apartment complex. The other one is full and has a waiting list."

"There is definitely a housing shortage right now. It's in all the papers and one of the main concerns that comes up at every town hall your father has spoken at."

Randi set her glass down. "I love you and Dad, but I don't want to live with you."

With one of her light, on-a-song-sounding giggles, her mother patted her hand. "I can appreciate that, dear. And your honesty."

"Jason and I cooked together, did laundry together, cleaned together and we can't do those things while we are living here. It might sound silly, but it felt as if we were building something together, the two of us, and I don't want that to stop."

"It's not silly, honey. I totally understand. You were building your lives together. We'll find a place for you to live, don't worry."

She couldn't help but worry, and couldn't get one possible solution out of her head, either. "Will you take a drive with me? There's something I'd like to show you."

"Of course."

Her car had been in the garage, and unharmed other than a thick coating of ash that Jason had already washed off. "We'll take my car so Tanner can come with us."

"All right." Her mother stood. "But Tanner is more than welcome to ride in any of our vehicles just as much as he's welcome to live in our house. He's family."

Tanner barked, as if in total agreement.

A short time later Randi turned off the highway onto the gravel road leading to Jason's land. "Now, don't judge it on first sight. Look at the potential."

"I won't, and I will," her mother replied. "I have a feeling your mind is already set."

"When we pull in, I want to hear your first impression before we get out of the car."

"Okay."

Within minutes she pulled up next to the house, with its sagging porch roof, and turned off her car. To her, the little porch looked cute, sagging roof and all. "Well?"

"First impression?"

"Yes. An honest one."

"I wouldn't give you any other kind. It reminds me of Dad Jansen's cabin. The one we used to stay in when you were little. His sons sold it, and your father has always regretted not being the one to buy it."

A chill rippled up Randi's arm, a wonderful sort of chill. "That's it. I knew I had happy memories of a place just like this, but I didn't know exactly what they were."

"You were only six the last time we were there."

Randi opened her door. "Let me show you the inside." Not tall enough to reach, she had to use a stick to knock the key off the top of the door frame. Once unlocked, she pushed open the door, stepped inside.

Her mother was right behind her, and the first thing she did was gasp.

Randi spun around, looked at her mother, who had a hand over her mouth, giving her no idea if her mother was surprised, or appalled.

There was a full-blown smile on her mother's lips when her hand fell away. "Darling, we could have this place cleaned up and you living in it within a couple of days."

Excitement filled her. "That's what I was thinking!"

Her mother started tossing out ideas of wallpaper, rugs and curtains, and Randi could see every image in her mind. A hint of concern, though, of how Jason might react to the idea, had her suggesting, "Let's not say anything to Jason."

"Why not?"

"Because I want to surprise him. He has enough on his mind with salvaging everything at the other place. He feels like the fire was his fault, and it wasn't."

"No, it wasn't," her mother said. "I see a broom. Let's roll up our sleeves and get busy."

As they worked, her plan grew. She would have the entire place sparkling clean and filled with furniture, curtains, rugs, and the cupboards full of dishes before telling Jason a word about it.

That, however, wasn't to be. She and her mother were still cleaning when Tanner barked, and a moment later Jason's pickup, with the back of it heaped full, pulled into the yard.

"Looks like our secret is out," her mother said.

Randi held her smile in place as she set aside her broom and walked outside. Jason had already climbed out of his truck and was walking toward her.

"What are you doing here?" he asked.

She hurried to him and tilted her face upward, for a kiss. He glanced at her, at the house, and then—as if he didn't want to, but felt he had to, to make her happy—he brushed his lips over hers.

He also grasped her arm as he repeated, "What are you doing here?"

"It's going to take months to rebuild our house, and with the housing shortage, we aren't going to find a house to rent or buy, so we'll either have to stay with my parents, or—" she planted on a big smile "—move out here."

"We'll stay with your parents."

"But this house is plenty big enough for us."

"No, it's not."

"Yes, it is." She gestured toward the barn. "And there's room to store all your work tools."

He shook his head. "You shouldn't even be inside there. It's dirty."

"We've already swept and dusted. We need to have the electricity turned on for the water—"

"Go back to your parents' house."

She drew in a deep breath, mainly to calm herself, to keep from telling him how stubborn he was acting. "No." Walking away, she said to her father, "Doesn't it remind you of Dad Jansen's cabin?"

"It does," her father said.

She hooked her arm through her father's. "And wait until you see the cars in the barn. Red, white and blue. A Chevy, Ford and Buick."

Jason barely looked at her as she and her mother helped him and her father unload the truck of things they'd salvaged from the basement. They put everything in the barn, where he also showed them his cars. Her insides were sinking deeper and deeper. He was pleasant, acting normal, but he was faking. She knew. She'd seen him do it before.

He faked his way through dinner later that day, too. Especially when her mother mentioned that the little house was well built and that it wouldn't take much to make it fully livable.

When her father mentioned that she could practically walk to work if she lived at the cabin, she saw Jason's jaw turn hard.

As soon as they entered her old bedroom back at her parents' house, he said, "We are not living in that house."

They were both wearing borrowed clothes, from her mother and father. Without saying a word, she turned her back to him, silently asking him to unzip her dress.

He unzipped it and walked into the bathroom attached to her room.

She looked at Tanner. He lay down and put his paws over his ears and eyes. "Thanks for the support," she said drily.

When Jason left the bathroom, she entered it. After completing her nightly routine, she clicked off the light on her way out, and climbed into bed, naked as always. Whether they made love or not, she loved curling up next to him, sleeping with their bare flesh pressed together. Tonight was no different, even if he was mad at her.

He was lying on his side, wearing a T-shirt and underwear. She curled up against his back, hooked a leg over his and an arm around his waist. "This has all been so upsetting. The fire, the damage, staying here, but let's not be upset with each other."

Jason held his breath, feeling the irritation that he'd been harboring slipping away. Randi challenged him in ways no one ever had. He rolled onto his back, slid an arm underneath her neck and held her close. Other than a few things in the basement and garage, everything was gone. Everything he'd had to offer her was gone. He didn't even have a home for them to live in. It was so infuriating. Life had been good. So good. Then, out of the blue, disaster. It was like life itself thwarted him at every turn when it came to her. "I'm not upset with you. I'm just frustrated that you lost so much in the fire."

"*We*, and we didn't lose anything in the fire that can't be replaced. We have each other and Tanner. I will live anywhere you want, as long as we are together."

He knew the *anywhere* she was referring to. "I don't want you living in that old, worn-down house, and I don't want you walking to work." He'd worked too hard to get out of that life. He wasn't going to go back, and wasn't going to take her with him. Wasn't going to watch her walk across the field to go to work like he had his mother. "I'll rebuild our house. It won't take that long."

She inched her hand under his T-shirt, ran it across his stomach. "I know you will rebuild it, and I'll help, but that little house would only take a couple of days and we could move in. I could do most of the work myself."

There was no way he'd let her clean that place up by herself, nor could he understand why she would want to live there. "This room is almost as big as that entire house."

"I know. That's why it won't take long to fix."

That hadn't been his point.

"You already have everything stored in the barn." She kissed his shoulder.

Jason could feel things inside him shifting. He wanted to give her whatever she wanted, but that house was a shack, especially compared to the mansion they were in right now.

She scooted closer, was partially lying on his chest, looking at him eye to eye. "I understand that you might have some bad memories of living there. But that's all they are. Memories. We could make new ones. Good ones." She shrugged. "I have bad memories of this house. It's where I got my first spanking. Where my great-grandfather died. This is the room I locked myself in when my father wouldn't buy me a pony."

He brushed the hair away from her face. "How long did you stay locked in?"

"A couple hours. Until I got hungry."

He loved her honesty. "When did you get the pony?"

"Never. I got riding lessons instead, and that's when I started working at Air America in order to pay for them. A portion of them." She ran a finger along his jaw. "This is also the room I spent hours, weeks, months, crying in because I'd laughed when you asked me to go out with you."

His heart tumbled in his chest. He felt bad for assuming what he had back then. She had a heart of gold, was the sweetest, kindest woman on earth.

"I don't blame this house for any of that, and we can stay here for as long as we need, but it'll be so different from what we've gotten used to. No cooking together, no dancing in the kitchen." She kissed his chin. "No home runs while watching *I Love Lucy*."

Certain things would be hampered while living here, he'd already thought about that, and had wondered if he'd ever get used to sitting down at the table and having the food served to him. He also knew she was working her magic on him. "It would take more than a couple of days to get that house livable."

Her eyes lit up. "I'll help. My mom will help. My dad will help."

"You really want to live there?"

"Yes."

"Why?"

She bit down on her bottom lip, a sure sign that she didn't want to answer.

He ran a finger over her lip. "Tell me."

"Because I don't want you to feel trapped, and you might, living here."

Once again, he wished he'd never said that. "I won't feel trapped."

"You might, the dinner parties alone can do that to a person."

Thinking of her sneaking into her mother's office, and hoping he wasn't making the biggest mistake of his life, he said, "I'll have a crew start working on the house tomorrow."

"You will?"

"Yes, but we'll need furniture and—"

She planted a kiss on his lips, then several across his face while saying, "I'll start shopping tomorrow."

He rolled, flipping her onto her back so he could explore her bare skin, inch by inch. "Right now let's give this room some new memories."

"I like that idea."

So did he, and they made memories deep into the night.

By Thursday Jason had to admit that the little house he remembered was hardly recognizable. He'd pulled men off every job site to work on the place. The front porch was now twice as large, and there was a back porch off the laundry room he'd also added to the back of the house. That door was where he installed a doggie door for Tanner. He'd also installed a new-fangled automatic dishwasher where the old clothes washing machine had been in the kitchen. The addition also provided for the bathroom to be expanded. The entire place had been painted, inside and out, and a new swing hung in the tree where the old one had been.

All in all, the place looked good, but he still wasn't seeing it through Randi's eyes. She was in love with this place. That was written all over her face, and reason enough that he'd live here. Bad memories and all.

He pounded in the last nail on the hook she'd asked him to install on one of the porch pillars so she could hang a pot of flowers, and dropped the hammer into the loop of his carpentry belt as a car pulled in the yard.

"Place looks great," Randal shouted as he climbed out of his Cadillac.

"It'll do," Jason replied, walking down the steps of the porch as Randal opened the back door on his car and Tanner leaped out.

"The women are grocery shopping now," Randal said. "Tanner and I were given the job of bringing out the items they bought this morning."

A silent chuckle rumbled in Jason's throat. The house was full of furniture, the cupboards were full of dishes, pots and pans. The bed was made, curtains hung on every window, even the closet and dressers were full of new clothes.

"I was told to put it all in the bathroom," Randal said, opening the trunk.

Jason lifted out a couple of bags. "That's the only room not full yet."

"I have a feeling you are never going to get Randi to move back into town." Randal closed the trunk after lifting out two other bags. "Can't say I blame her."

"I think you're right," Jason admitted. "Once I get

caught up on other jobs, I'm going to start building a house on the other side of the barn, near that grove of trees. A brick one. Modern style."

"Well, when the time comes, and if you decide you want to sell this one, I'm first in line."

"Why?" Jason asked as he opened the door to the house.

"I've always regretted not buying Carl Jansen's cabin. Jolie and I loved going there, both before and after the kids were born. It was small and we liked that. Sometimes I spend what seems like hours searching our big old house for Jolie. I considered buying Carl's place, but it was too far away. We could never have gotten there often enough, but we could drive out here whenever we wanted, and when the baby is older, you and Randi can just open the door, and tell him or her to go see Grandma and Grandpa."

"I guess we could." Jason set his bags on the floor in the bathroom, and took the ones from Randal, set them down as well. Once again, he was surprised that all he'd once assumed about the Osterlunds hadn't been close to the truth. They had money, but they were good, honest people. People he liked.

He also was amazed by how he could tell Randal things, and not be judged. "I just want Randi to have the best of things."

"I appreciate that." Arms crossed, leaning against a wall, Randal looked around, then back at him. "And I think she does. She has you. I could never have asked for someone to love my daughter more than you do. I see that every time you look at her."

Chapter Twenty-Three

Everything was backfiring on her.

They'd been living in their little house for over a week, and Randi feared she'd made a huge mistake. The biggest mistake she could have made.

Jason was faking it again.

He was kind. Considerate. Caring. And distant. More distant than he'd ever been.

The house didn't leave much room for actual physical distance. It was more like he'd built a wall around himself.

She'd thought living here might open his heart to love, but the opposite had happened and she was to blame.

They were sitting at the table, eating lunch, after he'd spent most of the morning clearing the last of the items out of the basement and garage of the old house. "Do you want to cancel the party tomorrow?" It was more than the party she was worried about canceling. That had seemed like the perfect place for him to see his mother again, but now it didn't.

He looked at her, frowned. "No. Why? Do you?"

"No, but—"

Tanner barked, several times, and trotted to the front door.

Jason pushed away from the table. "But what?" he asked on his way toward the living room to see who was pulling in the yard.

Without answering, she stood, followed. The curtains were open, showing the car that had parked in the driveway.

"What is a taxi doing here?" he mumbled.

Her heart crawled into her throat as the driver got out, opened the back door for a woman to exit.

The sound of his intake of breath told her what she feared was true. It was his mother.

He turned, looked at her.

"I called her," Randi admitted. "Invited her to the party tomorrow."

"Why the hell would you do that?"

Her fears hit a high she'd never known, and all she could do was tell the truth. "Because I was afraid."

"Of what?"

She couldn't tell him. Not with his mother walking toward the door. She gestured at the door and turned, walked back into the kitchen.

The opening of the front door was quiet, but echoed in her ears like thunder. Thunder from the storm she'd seen on Jason's face. She wanted to run into the bedroom and cry, but that wouldn't relieve the pain in her chest. He'd never forgive her for this. Never.

How could she have been so wrong?

Because she'd been desperate.

Desperate for his love.

Forcing herself to move, she cleared the table, rinsed the dishes and put them in the dishwasher, all the while wishing she didn't need love. But she did. She'd known it her entire life and couldn't bring a baby into a home where there wasn't that kind of love shared with everyone.

She was wiping the table when footsteps on the front porch had her looking up, watching Jason walk through the door. Alone.

"Where's your mother?" she asked, barely sounding like herself.

"Outside."

It was hard to look at him. He was everything she ever wanted, yet he couldn't give her what she needed the most. Love was a need. Stronger than desire. Stronger than passion. And she couldn't live without it.

She turned, carried the dishcloth to the sink. "Aren't you going to invite her in?"

"No."

"I'll go to the bedroom, stay there, or leave. Go to town."

"No, you won't."

She closed her eyes. Her heart felt open at both ends, raw. To the point, when he touched her arm, she flinched.

His hold tightened and he forced her to turn around, to look at him. "You aren't going anywhere until you tell me what you're afraid of." He was frowning. Deeply. "Is it me?"

Her first instinct was to say, "No." But then she had to correct it. "Yes."

"Which is it?" He released her arm, stepped back. "Why?"

Instinct again had her stepping forward, closer to him, but she stopped herself after one step. "It's not your fault. It's mine. I tried to convince myself that for the baby's sake, it would be enough. Whatever you were willing to give would be enough, but—" She had to stop in order to swallow.

He cursed.

She pressed a hand to her lips, knowing he didn't want

to hear it, but she had to say it. Explain it. Fast, while she could. "But then we'd pretend. Act like we were so in love. It hurt, knowing it wasn't real. It hurt more when we stopped pretending, because then I had hope. And I shouldn't have. I know that. I know it's not what you want. But I couldn't help it. Every day I fell deeper and deeper in love with you. I couldn't stop it from happening. I told you I didn't expect you to love me, and I honestly thought I could live like that. But I can't. I was afraid that it was going to slip out, that I was going to say it and I was afraid of how you'd respond. I thought, if you saw your mother again, found out that she still loved you, then maybe you wouldn't mind so much if I love you, too."

He ran a hand through his hair, shook his head.

Her entire body was trembling, and her heart pounded so hard it was echoing in her ears. "I understand why you can't love me in return. I do. Truly. My entire life I've had people expect things from me, but you never did. I had to try so hard to make you notice me in high school. Then, when you did, I behaved foolishly, and then my brother let you take the blame and my father sent you to reform school, and then, years later, I show up on your doorstep and end up pregnant. I haven't done anything to make you love me, ever. But you, you've given me so many reasons to love you that—"

He moved so quickly, silencing her with his lips, she was stunned at first, couldn't respond. But that didn't last. Her passion for him was too great. Her entire being responded to his slightest touch. And did so now. She melted against him even though she knew she shouldn't because passion wasn't enough.

Still, she drank it in, because their passionate times were when she could let her true emotions reveal themselves. She'd slept with him the first time because she'd loved him then, too. Just like she had for years before then.

When his lips left hers, she was more afraid than ever. What if that had been a goodbye kiss? She couldn't bear the thought and a sob escaped.

He cupped her face, forced her to look up at him. "I love you. I've loved you for years."

Her vision was blurred, her hearing muffled. Her mind momentarily blank. She could barely get out the word, "What?"

"The reason I said that I'd never thought I'd get married, was because you were the only woman I'd ever want to marry. The only woman I'd ever love."

"Love? Me?" Stunned, shaken, she shook her head. "You can't."

Jason had never been shot so close to death and back again as the roller-coaster ride his emotions had just gone through while Randi had been speaking. From fear to ecstasy and everything in between. Biting back a grin, he asked, "Are you trying to talk me out of loving you?" He caressed her cheeks with his thumbs. "Because it won't work. I already tried that."

"When?"

He'd made an unspoken pledge to himself as a child to never be vulnerable again, but it was time to break that pledge. Actually, he'd already broken it. "Since the first day I saw you. You were walking into the school building, wearing a pink skirt, white blouse, red sweater and black-and-white shoes. I didn't know your name, but knew you were the one." He huffed out a breath. "As soon as I did learn your name, I tried to fall out of love with you. But couldn't. Everything I've done, from motorcycles to hot rods, to building houses, I've done because I wanted you to notice me. Including trying to stop Joe and his friends from breaking into the Air America building."

"You have?"

"Yes, but I was convinced that you could never love someone like me. Someone with a shady past and bad reputation. When you became pregnant, I knew I couldn't live without you, without our child, and decided that I'd do everything within my power to make sure you had everything you wanted. Then I met your parents and was afraid that I'd never be able to love you the way you'd always been loved. I'd never known that kind of love, never seen it." He shook his head. Shrugged. "Never believed it was inside me. But you found it, forced it to come out, and when I realized that, I was even more afraid, because I knew I needed it. Love. Had needed it for years."

Randal had made him face the fact that he loved Randi every time he looked at her. Every time he thought about her. Day in and day out. Up until this moment he'd been in hell trying to figure out how to tell her that he loved her, but that he also needed her love. People had been expecting things from her for years, and he didn't want her to feel obligated to give him anything. Especially not her love.

Tears were trickling from her eyes, and he wiped them away. "The harder I fought it, denied it, the deeper my love for you grew. I was pretending, but it wasn't what you think. I wasn't pretending to love you. I was pretending that I didn't love you, and it was the hardest thing I've ever done."

"It was so hard for me, too."

It was ludicrous that they'd both been fighting the exact same thing. He pulled her close, held her tight. "I didn't want to hurt you, to disappoint you, but that's what I've done, and I'm so sorry. So very sorry."

She lifted her face, looked at him with those amazing blue eyes. "No, you haven't. You've made me the happiest person on earth. Given me everything I've ever wanted."

"I thought I had to give you material things." Her living in this tiny, old house had eaten away at him the past week. "The best of things."

"I've had the best of things my entire life. My parents loved me for myself. Somehow, years ago, deep inside, I knew you could give me that, too. Love me for myself. That was confirmed when I saw how you loved Rachelle at her birthday party. I fell in love with you again that night, and have loved you more every day since, but I didn't know how to show you that was all I wanted. Not your land. Not a big house. Not a big diamond. Just you. Your love. I love you, so much. So very much."

He now understood how precious love was, and how fragile it could be, and why people would give up everything for it. "You have it. I love you. Always have, always will."

Capturing her lips with his, the rush that filled him was like none other. All the love he'd kept locked inside him was now free to flow without any barriers or limits. It was incredible, freeing, and a happiness he'd never experienced filled him. Laughter bubbled inside him.

Their combined laughter parted their lips and he picked her up, twirled her around as their happiness filled the room. Filled the house.

Her laughter stopped abruptly. "Your mother! Where is she?"

He set her down, kissed her forehead. "Tanner is showing them the barn."

"Tanner is a dog!" Her eyes grew wide. "What if she left?"

"She hasn't. I sent away the taxi." With his mind fully on Randi, not greeting his mother and her husband affably, he'd excused himself. "I told them we were in the middle of something."

"I'm sorry."

The grimace on her face made him smile and kiss her. "It's fine. Everything is fine. Better than fine."

"Go get her. I'll put coffee on. I made cookies this morning, and—"

He stopped her from saying more with another kiss. One that left her breathless. Him, too. "I love you." Later he'd show her how much he loved her. Right now he needed to show his mother his greatest accomplishment—his wife.

Hours later Jason wrapped his arms around Randi from behind, and relished in how easy it was to love her. It had always been easy. He just hadn't wanted to accept that he deserved love. Everyone did.

Including his mother.

She and Scott, her husband, had left moments ago, borrowing a car to use during the time they would be in town. If he hadn't married Randi, the visit may have gone differently. He may still have been too full of himself to listen, to believe that things hadn't been exactly as he remembered.

"You didn't know, did you?" Randi asked quietly. "About the shrapnel embedded in your father's skull."

"No, I didn't." There had been a lot of things he hadn't known, including how that shrapnel had changed his father. How kind and loving he'd been before his injury. How, when his father had told his mother to leave or she'd regret it, she'd believed him. She'd left him behind, with his father, because she'd feared that alone, his father would never have survived. Jason believed that, too. Without him, his father would never have eaten, never had food to eat or fuel to heat the house. Even after he'd moved out, he'd continue to bring groceries to his father, pay the utility bills.

"He didn't want to be injured, didn't want to be in pain, and she didn't want to leave," Randi said.

Jason now had empathy where loathing and embarrassment had once lived. The knot that had lived for years inside him was gone, but it hadn't left all on its own. Randi was the reason it had disappeared. Her love, her actions, had dissolved it piece by piece, without him even knowing it. "I know." He kissed the side of her neck. "Thank you for inviting her here." He was glad he knew the truth and had the opportunity to know his mother again.

"You're welcome." She twisted in his arms, looked up at him. "I love you."

He'd been so foolish. He'd had all he'd ever wanted and had still been so blindsided by his past that he could have lost it all. "I love you, so much, and I swear I'll be here every day, building a life, building a family, with you, every step of the way."

"That's all I want." She poked him in the ribs. "Along with a racetrack." Giggling, she said, "I guess I do want your land, after all."

He laughed. "Our land." Touching her hair, he said, "There is one thing I'd like to know."

She frowned slightly. "What?"

He wasn't sure if she even remembered, but he'd always been curious. "When I got out of reform school, there was a letter waiting for me. From you."

She nodded.

"What was in it? I wanted to open it, but thought it was probably telling me to never ask you out again, so I wrote return to sender on it and put it back in the mailbox."

She ran a finger along his jawline. "It was the opposite. I apologized and asked you to please ask me out again and said that I thought you were a very special guy. I still do."

He picked her up and realized there was something to be said about a small house, because within a few steps they were in the bedroom.

The old pride he'd held on to so tightly transformed into one he'd become honored to carry. That of being married to *the* Randi Osterlund-Heim.

Their love grew with each passing day, and Jason could hardly believe how fast summer passed and fall descended upon them. What he could believe was that he was the luckiest man on earth. His favorite thing to do was lie in bed beside her, with his hand on her stomach, feeling the baby move and talking about if it would be a boy or a girl. He didn't care, as long as they—the baby and Randi—made it through the delivery with no problems.

Dr. Spencer said there was nothing to worry about, that Randi's pregnancy had been perfect right from the start. He had to agree with that, but he was still worried.

The crib and cradle he'd made were set up in the second bedroom, along with a rocking chair he'd made, and there were so many toys, clothes, blankets and bottles from her baby shower that he'd had to build a set of shelves along one wall to hold everything.

Her due date was only a week away, and there were a large number of people who hoped they'd still be in town when the baby was born. Others, as well as her cousin and brother, had arrived yesterday, because today was Election Day.

He reached over and laid his hand on Randi's stomach. They were on their way home after standing in line to cast their votes, in the Thunderbird because it was a warm, sunny day for the first part of November. She looked adorable, wearing a pair of big sunglasses and her hair held back by a blue-and-white polka-dotted scarf that matched her dress. "How are you feeling?"

"Wonderful." She laid both of her hands atop his. "I'm going to make oatmeal cookies as soon as we get home. There's time before we have to be at the hotel."

Everyone who had worked on Randal's campaign was meeting at the hotel downtown to watch the votes being announced. Then, to celebrate the win.

"We can stop and eat if you're hungry," he said.

"No, I just want oatmeal cookies."

He chuckled. "I love you."

She let out a big sigh. "I never get tired of hearing that."

"You never get tired of oatmeal, either." Giving her a wink, he added, "I'll help you make the cookies as soon as we get home."

At the house, once the first batch of cookies was in the oven, he went out and pulled the Thunderbird into the barn. While he was at it, he pulled the Chevy out. Joe and Gus were on their way over to take it out to the track. They always did that when they were in town, and normally, he and Randi would go with them, but not with her due date being so close now.

He was walking back to the house when Joe and Gus pulled in. "Keys are in her," he told them. "Total her and she's yours."

"Don't tell him that," Joe said, pointing at Gus as they climbed out of their car. "He'll total her on purpose."

"Not if he knows what's good for him." Jason leaped up the steps and entered the house, which smelled like cinnamon.

Randi met him at the door. "You can go with them."

"I'd rather stay here with you."

"Baking cookies instead of racing?"

"Yes."

She rubbed her stomach. "If my belly still fit beneath the steering wheel, I'd be out racing with them."

He steered her toward the kitchen. "I know you would be." She loved racing as much as he did. "But then you wouldn't have oatmeal cookies."

The cookies won out, and when they brought the Chevy back, Joe and Gus enjoyed them almost as much as she had.

"By the way," Joe said, taking another cookie off the plate on the coffee table. "You are now looking at the director of the art department for JO's Dream Wear."

"Art department?" Gus asked. "Man. Leave it to you to get a job doing what you've been doing your entire life."

Jason looked at Randi, but she shrugged. "What's he been doing his entire life?"

"Drawing pictures of naked women," Gus answered.

Randi threw a pillow at him. "Will you ever grow up?"

"Why?" Gus asked. Having caught the pillow, he acted like he was going to throw it back at her.

Jason gave him a warning by simply shaking his head.

Gus dropped the pillow in his lap.

"Brat," Randi said to Gus as she scooted to the edge of the sofa.

"What's wrong?" Jason asked.

"I have to go to the bathroom."

Jason helped her up, walked her to the bathroom.

"I gotta get back to town," Gus said. "Put on a monkey suit for the party."

"I told him that I'd catch a ride with you and Randi," Joe said. "Mom's bringing my suit to the hotel."

"That's fine," Jason answered, noting he'd have to change clothes soon, too.

"Catch you on the flip side," Gus said, heading out the door.

Jason stood in the kitchen, talking to Joe and glancing at the bathroom door, wondering what was taking Randi so long until he couldn't wait any longer. He knocked on the door. "Are you okay in there?"

The sound was muffled, but he heard enough to throw open the door. She was crouched down, holding on to the bathroom sink with both hands. Hands that were so white, they looked as if no blood was flowing into them.

He shot into the room.

She was huffing, panting. "My. Water. Broke." She let out a low growl while squeezing her eyes shut. "The. Contract—"

He heard no more, picked her up and ran out of the room. "Her water broke!" he shouted at Joe while running for the door.

She let out a groan and laid her head on his shoulder. "I think it stopped. I think the contraction stopped. It wouldn't in the bathroom. I couldn't even shout for you."

His heart was pounding. He'd read about labor and delivery, accompanied her to every doctor with lists of questions, and this was not how early labor had been described.

"What car?" Joe asked, running beside him. "I'll get the door."

"The hot rod," he answered. It was the fastest, and

from what he'd read, she needed to be at the hospital already.

Joe opened the door and Jason slid her in.

While running around to the driver's door, he told Joe, "Take whatever car you want." Jumping into the car he added, "And grab her suitcase out of the bedroom."

"My parents, Dad's party!" She let out another moan and arched her back, grabbed a hold of her stomach. "Oh, no, it's another contraction!"

"And call your parents!" Jason shouted, hitting the ignition, shifting and stomping on the gas in swift order. The hot rod held the record of zero to sixty in less than eight seconds on the strip, and he was trusting her to beat that record now.

After they hit the highway, Randi swiped the sweat on her forehead. "I don't think it's supposed to be this hard, this soon."

He knew it wasn't, but said, "Dr. Spencer said every baby is different. It's all going to be fine. We'll be at the hospital in no time."

"I hope so, because, oh, no, here it comes again!"

His foot couldn't press on the gas pedal any harder, and he was trying just as hard to remember everything he'd read. "It's going to fine, honey, just keep breathing. Don't hold your breath!"

They'd no sooner hit the city limits when a siren sounded. Usually, red lights in the rearview mirror had people stomping on the brakes. Not him. Not today.

"We can't stop!" Randi shouted. "Unless that cop knows how to deliver a baby, because this one is coming out soon!"

"We aren't stopping and that baby's not coming out until we get to the hospital!" Jason hoped by saying it, it would be true. "The hospital is only a few blocks away. Just keep breathing."

"I am breathing! You just keep driving!"

"I am driving!"

"Go faster! Or let me drive!" She doubled over, holding her stomach again. "Oh, here we go again." Between groans, she added, "There's another cop!"

Jason saw them, and the third one.

Minutes later he slid to a stop so fast in front of the hospital, the tires were smoking. He jumped out, ran around and lifted her out of the car. "We're having a baby!" he shouted at the man near the door as he ran. "Open the door! Now!"

Randi's face was red, and she was letting out growls of pain.

Jason shot through the open door. "Get a doctor! Get a doctor!"

A nurse rushed forward. "Calm down, sir."

"She's having a baby!"

"I know. I know," the nurse said, walking down a hallway. "This way, we'll get her on a gurney."

"Jason, Jason, don't leave me. Please don't leave me alone."

He kissed Randi's forehead. "I'm not going anywhere, honey."

"Right here," the nurse said, entering a room. "Put her right here and we'll wheel her down to maternity."

Jason slowly lowered Randi onto the sheet-covered cot on wheels, and held her head because there was no pillow. "She needs a pillow."

"We'll get one. You can leave now, go check her in at the front."

Randi was doubling up in pain again, groaning and clutching his arm.

"I'm not leaving," he told the nurse.

"Sir, you can't—"

"It's coming!" Randi shouted. "It's coming!"

"It just feels that way," the nurse said.

"She said it's coming!" Jason shouted. "Check!"

The nurse lifted Randi's skirt and immediately started shouting, "Doctor! We need a doctor!"

The room filled up and though several people told him to leave, they were too busy to make him, because within minutes his son was born.

Randi was sore in places but was too happy to focus on that. She had a son. A beautiful little boy, who, just like his father, was already setting records in racing to the finish line. It seemed as if it had been hours since they'd made Jason leave the room so they could clean her and the baby up and transfer her to an actual room rather than an examination station.

Dr. Spencer walked into the room shortly after the nurse who had wheeled her into the room left. "I believe that was the fastest delivery this hospital has ever had. You don't mess around, do you?"

"Only with my husband," Randi answered. "Where is he? And our son?"

"Your son is in the nursery. I just checked him, and he's perfect. Jason will be up here in a little bit, and I've made some special arrangements considering the circumstances."

"What special arrangements?"

"Adjustments to visitors and visitation hours. This is a private room—Jason's orders—so don't worry about that bed on the other side." Dr. Spencer folded back the sheet. "I need to give you the once-over, make sure all's well."

After some poking and prodding, Dr. Spencer assured her that all was fine. "I'll find Jason and send him in."

"Thank you, and our son?"

"I'll let the nurse know that he can be brought in, too." The doctor left, closing the door behind her.

Within minutes it opened again, and like always, her heart skipped a beat at the sight of her husband. He had flowers in one hand and a huge stuffed bear in the other. Setting them both on the table, he arrived at the bed and engulfed her in a hug.

"I love you so much," he whispered. "So, so much."

"I know you do." She knew that sounded conceited, but she was conceited when it came to him. "And I love you."

He kissed her forehead.

"John Jason Heim," she said. Jason's middle name was John, and she was set on flipping them around for their son.

"J.J. Heim," he said.

"Yes." Happiness filled her all over again. "That's a good name for a drag racer, don't you think?"

Jason kissed her again. "Cars and airplanes, you are a special woman."

A knock sounded and the door opened. A nurse entered, wheeling a bassinet. "I have a precious little bundle for you."

Jason lifted J.J. out of the bassinet and laid him in her arms while sitting down on the bed beside her. They spent several quiet moments just holding their son, before the nurse entered again.

"I have a few people waiting to come in. Dr. Spencer approved it."

"Yes, please, let them in," Randi answered.

Her mother and father entered first, and after a few

minutes Joe joined them. Next came Stu, Lottie and Rachelle, and following them came others, until the room was practically bursting.

"You should all be at the hotel." Randi looked at her father. "Especially you."

"This is more important than election results," her father said, kneeling next to the chair where her mother was holding J.J. "My first grandchild."

"What time is it?" Randi asked Jason, having long ago lost track.

"After nine. The results should be coming in soon."

Now that her mind wasn't fully occupied with their son, she asked, "What about the police?"

Jason glanced at her father.

Catching a look between them, she asked, "What happened?"

"When Joe called and said Jason was taking you to the hospital in the Chevy, I called the police station and told the chief that you needed an escort to the hospital," her father said. "They had an officer waiting at the edge of town, but he couldn't keep up. Neither could the other two."

The room erupted in laughter that only stopped because the phone rang.

Her mother handed her J.J. and then wrapped her arms around Randi's father's arm. "It's the election results."

Cradling J.J., Randi looked at Jason. "You answer it. Please."

He picked up the phone, and the smile that appeared said it all, even before he told her father, "You won! You won!"

Cheers were still filling the room when the door opened again and—carrying a child's pedal car, red, with a ball of fire painted on the hood—Gus entered the room. "Never fear, Uncle Gus is here!"

Jason leaned closer, whispered, "He's from your side of the family."

She giggled. "I know, but you love me, anyway." Then, not caring that the room was full, she kissed him, let him know she loved him, too.

Epilogue

"Look, J.J., there's Daddy," Randi said, pointing to the starting line where Jason was lined up on the asphalt quarter-mile strip.

Twenty months old, and completely enthralled with his father, J.J. jumped up and down in her arms, clapping. "Da-da. Da-da!"

Family members surrounding them laughed and clapped with him, and Tanner, never far away from J.J., let out a bark.

The flag dropped and the cars took off, speeding to the finish line. It was over within seconds, with Jason winning. As she knew he would. Yet, it still thrilled her every time. He loved racing that car, and she loved watching him. She also loved driving the car, and did so regularly.

The racetrack was as much of a success as his construction company. People had come from surrounding states, and sometimes farther away, to race during the months since they'd opened it.

"We'll keep J.J.," her mother said. "Go join Jason."

Randi kissed her son's forehead. "Mommy will be back." She hurried down the bleachers and ran over to where Jason was turning his car around to drive back past the bleachers.

He stopped the car, pulled off his helmet. "Hello, beautiful. Want a ride?"

She opened the door. "Are you picking up chicks?"

He winked. "Only one."

With a laugh, she climbed in. "Congratulations!"

"Thanks. I'll expect a kiss as soon as I park this old girl."

"Only one?"

The announcer came through the loudspeakers. "There he is, ladies and gentlemen, Chicago's own Jason Heim. He's not only the winner, he and his wife Randi are the owners of this fine new racetrack. How about a round of applause for them?"

She and Jason both waved out their windows as they drove past the bleachers full of cheering race fans.

The announcer continued, explaining the races that would happen throughout the day, and where concessions could be purchased, as Jason drove the car off the strip and around a fence into the pit area.

She scooted across the seat, hugged his arm. He had built them another house, a bigger one on the other side of the barn, and tonight she was going to tell him that in several months one more bedroom would have an occupant. Baby number two.

He'd be thrilled. As thrilled as she was.

"My parents have to be back in Washington next week, so they are staying at the cabin all weekend. And your mother is arriving on Tuesday to stay for two weeks."

"When do we fly back out to California?" he asked.

He'd helped her with the washing bay by overseeing the construction. "Three weeks. Sam's out there, counting nails to make sure we don't pay for any extras before the washing bay can be officially opened."

Jason grinned. "He is good at what he does."

"I know." She and Sam had worked out their differences, and she agreed that his accounting skills were a real asset. The washing bay was only one of her projects that had come to fruition. Someday she'd completely take over for her father, but not until she was ready.

Who knows, maybe someday she'd even run for office. Or maybe Jason would. He'd be a shoo-in.

Or maybe they'd create a division for female drag racing at the Heim track.

Whatever they did, they'd do it together.

Jason stopped the car and shut off the engine. "I'm ready for that kiss."

She looped her arms around his neck. "Me, too."

He was everything she'd always wanted and that would never change, but what made her even happier was knowing he felt the same way about her.

* * * * *